The Knight's Last Stand

Bear Pardun

Copyright

Published by Defiance Press & Publishing, LLC

Bulk orders of this book may be obtained by contacting Defiance Press & Publishing, LLC. www.defiancepress.com.

Defiance Press & Publishing, LLC

281-581-9300

publishing@defiancepress.com

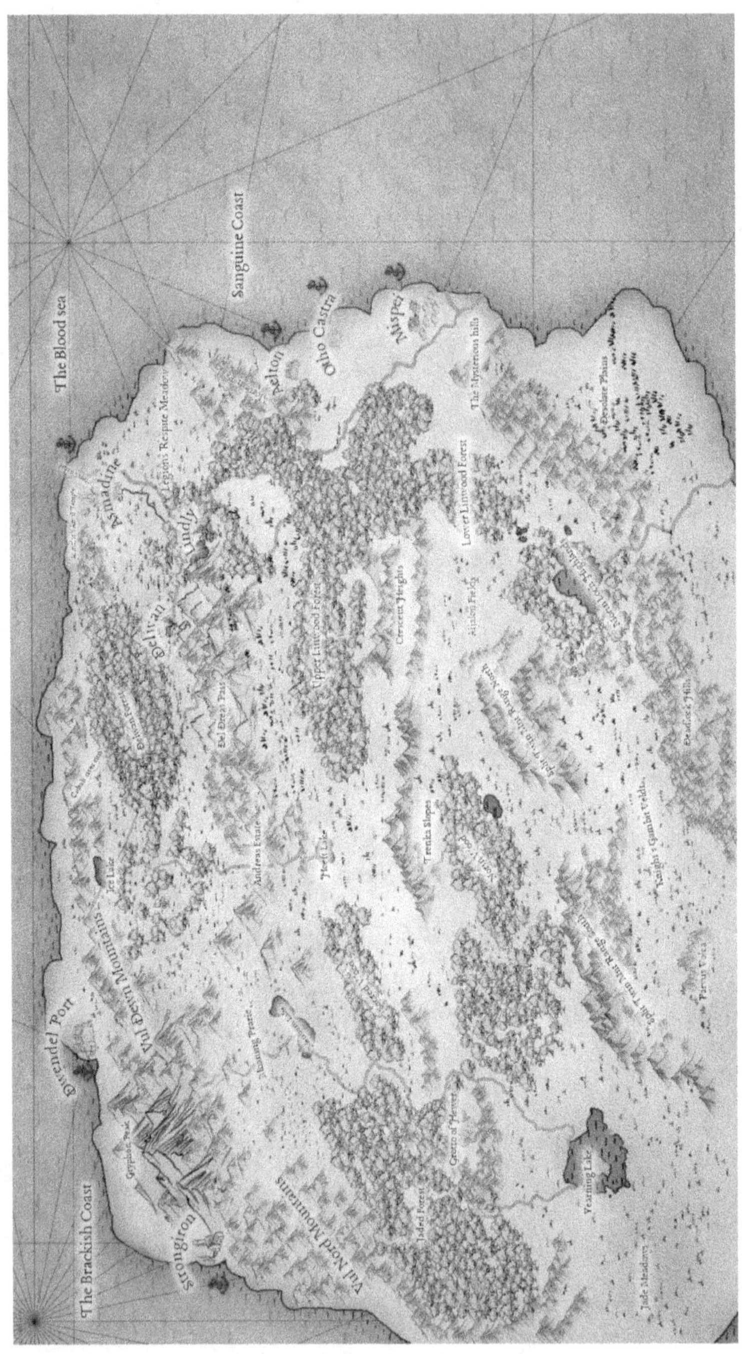
The Blood sea
Sanguine Coast
Otho Castra
Relton
Asmadine
Legions Respite Meadow
Lindly
Delwan
Upper Linwood Forest
Lower Linwood Forest
The Mysterious hills
Desolate Plains
Crescent Heights
Bel Drear Pass
Andreas Estate
Trenka Slopes
Deadlock Hills
Ice Lake
Val Dern Mountains
Direndel Port
Strongiron
The Brackish Coast
Vul Nord Mountains
Jaded Forest
Yearning Lake
Jade Meadows

Scribe Note

I, the humble scribe of the Order of Requirement, do willingly and wholly attest to the truth of these historical archives.

This is a telling of our forgotten antiquity.

Many generations have passed since the events described in this tome. Some of you reading this for the first time never lived through the tyrannical rule of the self-righteous Asmolor, the defiler Eu'rok, and their ambivalent sister Malakas.

When I was asked to keep a record of all that has transpired, I was overwhelmed. I wondered where to begin. So, after a long deliberation with the council, we concluded that a lesson in the Pantheon and how it related to the mortal races was the best place to start. In this forgotten era, the gods were in our daily lives. Each of the god siblings had created four prime-archs, also known as avatars or demi-gods. Within these prime-archs was the template to create all the mortal races. They wielded immense power—demi-gods to the primary three: Eu'rok, Asmolor, and Malakas. The prime-archs subjugated their creations and children, the mortals. They even garnered worshipers for themselves, all under the watchful eye of the three sibling gods.

The prime-archs created a small path for mortals to obtain a form of immortality by proving themselves loyal and having supreme skill. In this way, a mortal could be given the right and honor of being an arch. This was rare, but the chance spurred many to redouble their devotion to whomever they wished to achieve an archdom under.

As we understood it, the Pantheon was split between the three siblings. Malakas was the mother of all creatures, the guardian of the wild and its secrets. Asmolor the Righteous, with a sense of honor, revealed himself as the savior of the world with an air of grandeur. He commanded his faithful with a firm hand, and anyone who strayed from his teachings was met with stern consequences. Last is Eu'rok the Firstborn. He believed it to be his duty to challenge his siblings to be greater, though he did this by using his prime-archs and creations to attack the others, causing war for generations. We can find few reprieves from this ongoing war in our history, but one of the longest stretches started four hundred and forty-four years before Aris Tin's birth, at the conclusion of the second great war.

For a more thorough breakdown of the gods and demi-gods, I have drawn out a hierarchy below. I have also included a copy of the old world map, which will help in locating and relating the provinces to modern cities.

Now let us begin the unadulterated tale of Aris Tin. A man all the world knows of now, but then, he was just one of many countless others under the yoke of the gods' whim. And this, as I can attest to, was a heavy yoke indeed.

Prelude: 20 years before

Aris Tin's birth

The cavern was dimly lit with oil lanterns. A small voice quietly sobbed as the robed figures muttered amongst themselves. Her name was Desa, a young woman who had only recently reached adulthood. Looking around in an attempt to discern who had stolen her from home, she saw eight figures dressed in dark, purplish-red robes. Desa pulled her wrists apart to loosen the bindings. Muttering a small curse, she cried louder. One of the robed figures walked over to her, shushing her. "Shh, all is well, child." However, his eyes showed wickedness and hunger.

Desa, crossing her legs and pulling them close, did not meet his gaze. "Why have you taken me?" she asked, hoping it was all just a mistake.

The man began gently stroking her back as he bent down. "We have chosen you to be a part of something magnificent. Be patient, and you will see." Desa, watching him closely, saw him pull out a dagger. She gave a little shriek, but he quickly reassured her. "Hush now, I am just cutting the ropes." Slicing away the rope that held her, he rose to his feet. Desa thought for a moment she could run. But run where? She had never been in this cave. The stalagmites all looked the same, and the only sound she could hear was dripping.

Looking up at the man, who was removing his cowl and stretching his hand to her, she heard him say, "Come with me." His face was no longer animalistic but soft, warm, and inviting. She felt as if she were being lifted, weightless, as she grasped his hand. "You are home. The baby in your belly is healthy. Your husband is still talking with his grandfather in the other room. Rest now."

She was standing upright, though she could not feel the cold stone beneath her feet. "But I need to…" she began but trailed off, hearing, "Hush, child. Rest. Feel the warmth of love for you." She did, and it beckoned her to obey. "Yes. Yes, you are right." Her voice trailed off as she embraced the warmth and gentle movement of her body.

The man was twisting his right hand as he hummed hypnotically to her. Each movement of his hand slowly twisted her until she was lying four feet off the ground on her back. He motioned now to the others to get into position. Desa, dreaming, thought how beautiful and soft the clouds were. A soft, harmonious voice was singing to her, and it was so pleasant to hear. She never wanted to leave.

Other cloaked figures started to come together in a crescent moon pattern near a hewn slab. The craftsmanship was remarkable on this black stone. The strange demonic glyphs seemed to swirl as if rocked by an unseen sea. It had depressions carved into it that led like a river to nine scarlet jeweled cups at the bottom.

Everyone quickly made their way to their appropriate spots. A silhouette appeared from beyond the shadows near the slab. His robe was a combination of purple and red, similar to the rest, but it was bordered in silver. The man watched as the cultist slowly brought the woman to him, tightening the grip on his ceremonial blade. The intensity of his adrenaline and excitement was clearly visible. This was an occasion to acquire power and authority. As a testament to his firm devotion, his willingness to do whatever task was asked of him was inspiring, and he encouraged the same eagerness in those who followed him. Lestar, the dark elf goddess and mate of Eu'rok, would surely appreciate this offering. This sacrifice was the last commission that would solidify Lestar's trust in him by displaying his willingness to do whatever she required. "Perhaps," the cult leader mulled, "even I can ascend to archdom in time and prove my worth to the goddess. Maybe even share a bed with the deceptively beautiful creature," Nibarn mused, smiling.

Desa's dreamy state persisted even as she was locked in icy iron manacles—first her feet and then her arms. Two large leather straps were fastened down against her chest and thighs. With her head being last, they placed a frame around it, giving her a crown-like look. The cultist slowly turned a lever, allowing the headpiece to fit snugly onto the woman's cranium. The cultists then interlaced straps into the fastened helmet and snugly attached it to the slab.

Desa smiled as the incantation wore off, attempting to rise from what she believed to be a deep sleep in her own bed. She quickly realized something was wrong. She shrieked and called out for her husband. "Erik! ERIK, HELP!" Unable to move, she struggled and shook on top of the slab. Her rage won out against her fear. She was pregnant, and it was her belief that this baby was a gift from Asmolor. A terrible accident in childhood had caused many medicine men to claim she would be barren. "Release me now!" she yelled. "I am with child. My firstborn." Her anger flushed away as she spoke the words, morphing into sobs, tears welling in her eyes. "P… Ple… Please let us go. Please let me go home to my family, my husband."

The silver-trimmed, robed figure was standing over her right shoulder. "No. You have been carefully selected. And you are opening a gateway to something far greater than yourself." Her cries continued as Nibarn watched coldly. "Nevertheless, I understand your fear. And do you want to know a secret?" Leaning his head next to hers, all she could do was tilt her eyes in his direction. "We orchestrated your marriage to Erik. We made sure that you would have this child." His smile was broad, and his voice was but a whisper. "And we did all of this to have the purest sacrifice." Desa shook her tight shackles in fear as she sobbed uncontrollably. Nibarn laughed, grinning, “No… no, stop your crying. It will be over quickly, and your husband will be waiting for you in the afterlife.” The cruel man paused as if in thought. “Wait... no… no, he won’t. Neither of you will be in Asmolor’s paradise. No, Lestar already claimed his soul for Eu’rok. Apologies, sweet Desa. I guess torment awaits you and your family.” Shrugging as if it were nothing, he ripped at her dress, tearing a piece off and stuffing it in her mouth. “I need you to be quiet,” he scolded. The young woman felt the cloth slipping down her throat, soaking up the moisture. Desa struggled to breathe, her sobs muffled as she forced herself to focus on breathing.

Desa’s lips moved silently as she whispered her prayer, attempting to quell the fear in her heart. Her prayers were to Asmolor himself and then to the patron god of humans, Kalisdel. Asmolorian was her upbringing, and the humans had Kalisdel as their patron god through that faith. Never in the holy texts had the gods failed to help their people. She believed and clung to that hope. The man who had taunted and mocked her began speaking to the other cloaked figures. But she still prayed, begging for salvation. Desa’s thoughts continued even as she mouthed the words. “Asmolor protects. Asmolor delivers. Asmolor, the salvation of man.” The Asmolorian paladins and knights would eliminate this contamination from the universe, and thus, she would be rescued. She tried to nod in affirmation of this belief, but the device on her head and the straps kept her pinned. She put all her trust in her prayers and visualized her own liberation in hopes that it would become a reality.

Nibarn moved as he began speaking to those gathered. “We are ready to begin.” He turned his gaze behind himself as he moved to the front. “And it seems our goat has accepted its fate,” he said, waving his hands over the docile female form. Hushed chuckles rose from the crowd. Nibarn smiled wickedly as he pulled up the cowl concealing his face. “Begin!”

In unison, the figures began a low chant. Turning his back to them, Nibarn began his own prayer, one that would initiate the magic that would bind all participants to Lestar. The lanterns hanging shifted in color and began sprouting black flames to illuminate the cavern. The chanting continued as Nibarn spoke loudly over the chorus. "With this sacrifice, we willingly, wholly, and completely bind our bodies, minds, and souls to the Mistress of Shadows, Lestar. We become her instruments. Her strength is our strength. Her power is our power. This woman is the last descendant of the great cleric, Bryce Anvil—the first human marked by our mistress. Today we end the lineage and bring glory to Lestar. She will find us worthy."

The others did not break their chant as he spoke. This desecration of a prayer offered altered the atmosphere around the crescent circle and the altar itself. As the lanterns oozed out, their black flames filled the area, and the warmth of their glow enveloped the space without burning anything. Few knew the consequences of this type of dark clerical binding. Nibarn had dismissed the fears as paranoia and a children's tale to frighten peasants into paying homage to Asmolor. The overpowering desire for power caused them to overlook the warnings. They welcomed the darkness like children playing with a match in a mountain of hay.

The moment the sacrifice was complete, all of their fates would be tethered to the will of Lestar. Her beauty was captivating, but it was only a disguise masking her true darkness. Nothing in the world mattered to her, save for her beloved creator, Eu'rok. She gave out power and favor one day and stripped it away the next. She enjoyed using and toying with mortals and particularly loved turning Asmolor's children against each other. Whether those serving her failed or succeeded, in the end, they would become slaves. Their souls would be fuel for Eu'rok or put to use as anti-paladins, Dread Reavers.

Passing the dagger from hand to hand, waiting for the magic to do its part, Nibarn envisioned his future: kingdoms bending to his will, wealth beyond belief, and actual power to remake the world with his new queen, Lestar—perhaps even unite and turn all humans into servants of Lestar. The dark flames passed around the altar, captivating his gaze. A vibrating hum emanated from the hand that held the dagger. When he cast his gaze downward, he saw a spectral hand, exquisite and beautiful, extending out of a flame at his feet. It touched the dagger; the shape remained the same, but it was a foaming, pulsating cloud of darkness. Moving it again to his more dominant hand, it trailed ash. A voice spoke into his mind, or what he thought was a voice. "Well done, Nibarn. Now… do it."

He shivered in excitement at the sensual voice. "Yes," he whispered.

Desa, still praying, struggled against the restraints. The panic showing in her eyes seemed to spur the man on with glee. His dagger had transformed into a phantom blade, and he was moving closer to her. Placing the blade on her wrist, Nibarn looked right into her eyes. It horrified her to see a whirlwind of black flame with what seemed to be tiny people floating, trapped all around her. He smiled down at her as she felt the flesh tearing open on her wrist. She felt the warmth of blood rolling down from her wrist to her body. The sound of liquid dripping into glasses resonated in her ears, and she knew that it was her blood pumping out of her body that was making the sound in the cups. The man repeated the cut on the other wrist. More blood pooled on the slab and began draining toward her body and down, filling the cups. Nibarn took one step over, his hands raised high. Desa tried to yell. With what little life she had left, she tried to plead for her child. The dagger swooped down and pierced her belly. Her mind raced and began to slow, the shock of it all seeping into her core being. The hope of her happy life was gone. Her gods, the promises she lived her life upon, stripped bare. "Where are you?" was the last question she ever asked, the last thought she would ever have.

None in the room dared move. The blade had been thrust to the hilt into the mother's womb. However, before Nibarn could remove it, the blade vanished into ashen smoke that hovered above the punctured belly. A vivid blue hue was slowly being infused into the gray cloud. The wails of a baby filled the room with an icy chill. Those watching cringed for the briefest moment before quickly returning to awe, lest someone accuse them of being unworthy. They watched, complacent, as the baby's soul cried out in horror, receiving a torment it had never earned. Even Nibarn was taken aback by the sound of the cry. In a joint wave of terror, the mother and the child's soul screamed out, a sinister melody that filled the air with an oppressive feeling, enjoyed only by the most wicked of beings. Then, in an instant, the cloud was gone, and the dagger re-materialized in the woman's dead body. The blade was no longer humming or calling for death; it was just the ordinary dagger once more.

Looking away from the blade as he pulled it from Desa's body, he turned toward his cultists. He moved down and around, reaching to grab the most ornate cup filled with blood. "We honor our matron. We honor our mistress. Forever hers!" Tipping his head back, he forced the warm blood down his throat. In an attempt not to throw up, he let some pour onto his face. Tossing the glass down, he motioned for the others to partake.

Only slightly hesitant, they moved forward to embrace the promised reward of their deed. All drank; a few gagged, but all drank. It was one of the most profane acts Nibarn had ever done or even thought about. It was just the beginning, he thought. He reveled in the darkness.

The eerie silence following the drinking, combined with the black fire, was enough to keep everyone on edge. They had completed the initiation ritual as instructed by the dark elf priestess who had guided them. Nibarn pondered that perhaps they had miscalculated and grabbed the wrong woman. He quickly reminded himself that the months of preparation would not have been in vain.

Laughter rose from nowhere and everywhere. As the flames flashed wildly, they increased, causing everyone to stammer away. "Well done, my faithful humans. My faithful children. Today you have killed that bastard cleric's bloodline." Everyone looked around, trying to steal a glance at this unseen woman. "From this murder and a willingness to accept my patronage, all of you are now mine." Her laughter began again as dark tendrils reached from the flames, pulling all the faithful cultists to their knees. Heads bowed in terror, most missed seeing the long silver-haired woman rising among them. They all realized that they were being compelled to kneel. The tentacles that reached from the flames were also glowing as if they too were on fire, though none burned. Looking up, Nibarn saw the female. His voice croaked, "Wow."

The others took notice of her, their eyes wide with wonder. Both male and female among them found her beauty irresistible yet unattainable. This delicate, slim elf continued to rise far above them all. Her form was crisp, and the colors were vibrant, though she seemed almost ghostly. She wore clothing that was crafted to perfectly accentuate her curves, the fabric brushing against her skin with every movement. Her eyes were painted blackish purple, and her hair lay over her shoulders onto her appealing breasts. Every part of Lestar's visage was lustrous and stunning.

Nibarn took a lot of effort to work up the courage to address her, stammering slightly as he said, "We have pleased you, mistress? This… this has been our sole goal: to find a way to be worthy. May we…"

She gestured with her hand to stop him from speaking. Contemplating her next move, she then spoke in her duplicitous, sultry tone. "You have pleased me. And yet, much more must be given and done before you will be worthy. Now come, child, and take a piece of me and be mine."

The flamed tendrils released Nibarn. Shocked and shaking, he rose to his feet and stepped forward, his head held low in deference to her. "No… no… no, look into my eyes." Her voice dripped, teasingly inviting him. His eyes lifted. Her form leaned closer, almost into him. Excited, he licked his lips and then quickly tried to hide the instinctual action beneath a cough. His thoughts were on being kissed by her, and yet Lestar did not. She instead opened her mouth, and a small violet orb floated from her to him.

He quickly adjusted his mouth to receive this little orb. Swallowing hard, he panicked briefly as it felt lodged in his throat, coughing slightly and then swallowing again. Every part of his body felt empowered; euphoria brought him back to his knees. The feeling was beyond any pleasure or experience he had ever felt before. "I feel… I feel you. I feel the power."

Lestar's lips curled up in a smirk, and she gave a subtle nod of approval, understanding that all she had provided him was merely a momentary feeling—a magic that would create an ever-unquenchable desire for her, to be whatever she needed him to be. This spell created an addiction to her, making those tricked into becoming willing slaves for the rest of their lifespans and thereafter. Not only would they have a miserable corporeal existence, but their life force would know a horror beyond comprehension. Her gift brought about a common destiny, leaving no one with a choice in the matter.

Lestar bestowed her power on each cultist, a feeling of warmth washing over them as they imbibed her tiny orbs. She gave them all instructions, her voice ringing out in the cave's stillness. The dark goddess readied them for the dispiriting sensation of having duties delegated to them by her agents. "I will not be delivering what I decree you to do in person. You must wait and heed my priestesses and priests. From this point on, only those who continue to garner my approval will have the honor of being in my presence. But today you have done wonderfully and earned the right to become my children. I will be keeping an eye on all of you."

She spoke her last words, which echoed eerily throughout the cave, before she vanished. The flickering yellowish flames of the lanterns filled the room with a warm and comforting light, the tranquility of the cave only broken by the occasional crackle of the flames and the soft, steady drip of water filling the space between heavy breaths from all those gathered.

1

36 Years Later…

Victus stood outside the doorframe of the adolescent Aris's room. He rose extra early so he and his adopted son would make good time. Today was a special start to a yearly two-week trip, a pilgrimage they made every year to the ceremonies in Delwan honoring their dead loved ones.

During their trip, they would hunt, fish, spar, laugh, and enjoy the reprieve from the city. Being the highest-ranking knight of the city, he had many responsibilities, some of which took away from the time he wanted to spend with his son. The city of Lindly was the last land-based city before the capital, Asmadine—Asmolor, god of holiness's most glorious creation, in his own disillusioned mind. For his vanity had become so substantial that he could only see greatness in structures, having forgotten the joy of his mortal, living creations. His design took centuries to build and centuries to rebuild after Eu'rok, his brother, razed it.

Victus's nickname was the half-pal or half-paladin. This title, filled with fondness, was given to him when he finished his official training to become a paladin. Despite having finished his training, Victus departed from the order, hence the nickname *half-pal*. He had unquestionably proven himself worthy of joining the Caedes. It was whispered among the people that he was the chosen one to ascend to archdom. His mentor, Johnathan Skylighter, known simply as Sky, had achieved archdom centuries ago during the first great war of the brothers. By completing the gods' trials, Sky achieved a feat no other human had ever accomplished, earning personal recognition and a promotion from Asmolor himself.

It was widely known that Asmolor held humans in contempt. They served as instruments to toil in the fields, maintain the roads, and perform all the duties the greater races deemed unworthy of themselves. Asmolor needed more warriors for the first war, so he had to resort to conscripting humans into battle. Skylighter had worked tirelessly in those first few years and proved himself to be invaluable.

Skylighter had known a few others like himself, but none of them impacted his conviction like Victus. This man had surprised him. Victus had surpassed all the other trainees and had been the rising star of House Andreas. It seemed to be understood that Victus would face the trials of Asmolor's children. But he stepped down and decided he would rather be a father. After rescuing the baby, Aris, he never looked back, forging an alternative path for himself.

Victus pulled down the latch and entered his young son's room. As he entered, Aris slept soundly, and Victus's mind traveled back. He remembered the chaos of war as if it were yesterday: the shouts and screams of terror, some crying out for aid, others shell-shocked into mental infancy. But the smell—the smell he would never forget. He swayed slightly as the scent seemed to slip up his nostrils. Shaking it away, he looked down upon his sleeping son. Sixteen years ago, Skylighter's Gryphon Shock Troopers arrived at Delwan, a mining city's aid. Though they could cover leagues much faster than their horse-bound comrades, the gryphon-borne knights, their metal breastplates glinting in the sun, were too late to save the day. Something had set ablaze the city of Delwan, the small stream nearby saturated with blood. Tagar's calling card was unmistakable, the red river a winding ribbon of color, creating a vivid trail. Above them, the paladins could smell the acrid smoke and hear the crackling of the fire that showed the extent of his destruction. But it was the river of blood that was the most disheartening sight. Tagar had a formidable ability to instill fear in the hearts of the mortal races. The constant terror that Tagar and his followers had instilled in the descendants of Asmolor was unrelenting. The feeling appeared to be entrenched in their very bones, fortified by the sight of the scarlet rivers flowing through their territories.

Tagar was the prime arch to the orcs, ogres, and trolls. He was disgustingly grotesque in his behavior towards Asmolor's children, demanding his minions retrieve any survivors from every battle and slit their throats in the nearest river. If no river was nearby, he flayed the surrendered civilians and soldiers, women and children borne naked, staked to crossed posts and tortured. The devastation wrought by the depraved orcs and trolls was evident on all the riders' faces. Skylighter gestured to his men, commanding them to search for survivors, though he was sure none would be found.

An hour into the salvage, Sky heard Victus yell, "I have found a child." Before the words were fully processed, Sky was blistering towards the sound. Not registering the word "child," he believed the enemy remained.

"Some stragglers, perhaps wanting some loot," Skylighter thought. Sky arrived to see Victus's helm clattered against the ground, its metal echoing in the silence. His sandy brown hair was cut short, and his beard was trimmed close to his face. The pale metal bracers gently cradled a sleeping child. Sky, relieved that no attack was underway, asked hesitantly, "Does the babe live?" He expected the answer to be no.

Victus lifted his gaze to Skylighter, his eyes a captivating greenish-gray. His mouth tensed as he inched his hand up to his mouth, barely making a sound. "Shh," and Victus nodded yes.

~~~

Aris slept, looking almost completely as he did that evil, wonderful day—sleeping soundly and in peace. Though, of course, he had grown. The young boy was studious and took his training profoundly seriously. His father's men would
~~~

often call him the ‘old man.’ Aris was tactical and wise for his age, but Victus had made certain that his son remained humble in this. For all the military training, for all the knowledge that one could learn, humility was to be the shroud of an authentic hero of the light.

Young Aris rolled over, facing his father, his eyes popping wide as he looked groggily into his father’s face. “Oh no, I slept in?” his voice croaked.

Victus smiled down at him, reaching down to pat his son’s shoulder reassuringly. “Not even by a minute. I am early. Just started making our meal before we leave. And I have a gift for you.” Pausing, his voice changed tones, taking on that of a female maid. “Make yourself ready, Master Aris Tin of the noble House Andreas.” Victus gave his son a curtsy as the boy laughed. His father continued in the maiden’s voice, “Breakfast will be ready when you are.” Aris was one of the few who got to see this silly side of Victus, and something about it always made Aris laugh.

“Ya know, Dad, that voice is truly awful. Not to mention you are one ugly maiden.”

Heading for the door so Aris could dress, he turned on his heels towards his son, squealing out one last time, “Oh... Oh… my lord… how could you say such a thing? I am the finest maid you will ever know!” Both laughing, Victus quipped, “Don’t dawdle. And pack appropriately.” His voice was warm and fatherly as he shut the door.

Aris heard his father’s footsteps as they departed, echoing throughout the quiet, ranch-style hall of the house. It was a timber-framed and stone-encased home with the hearth in the middle. The noise of dishes and pots being displaced could be heard muffled outside. Aris could smell the food, and his stomach growled in anticipation. Springing from his bed, he ripped his evening shirt up and over his shoulders. He grabbed his boots and folded pants from under the bed. One leg and then the other, hopping as he stuffed his feet into the boots. He opened the shutters on his window to peer out and feel the air of the weather. Sniffing as he spoke, "Cool morning. No clouds." Watching the sky above doubtfully, he said, "It's going to rain," grabbing his brown padded shirt as he moved toward the wafting smell of his breakfast feast. He turned and ran over to the end of his bed, grabbing his rucksack, which he had packed the night before. Now he was ready. He loved the two-week adventures with his father every year, and he was filled with the hum of anticipation. Reaching the door, his shirt and bag in each hand, he quickly thought over what he had with him. He grabbed his steel blue cloak off the hook. Holding the cloak, shirt, and bag, he bounded down the hallway to the hearth.

Upon reaching the kitchen, his father was ladling gravy over toasted biscuits and sausage. Victus looked up as he placed a knife and fork out for his son. "Young squire, you are not dressed for duty!" Instantly, Aris dropped his gear—his cloak and shirt—and stood at attention as if he were in the drilling auditorium. He offered a confused look to his father. Victus looked him over and repeated, "You are not dressed for duty, young squire!" His father's eyes stared right into the boy's bare chest.

Aris dipped his gaze down, looking at his gear. "What have I forgotten… Oh?" Snatching up the leather-padded tunic, he wiggled it over his head. Then he stood at attention once more. His father smiled, his eyes twinkling, and beckoned him closer with a wave of his hand. "Come sit and let's eat." Aris did not notice his father use the word *squire*, and this amused Victus. The young lad had been working very hard to become a squire but had not yet been given the rank until this morning. Victus's lips spread into a satisfied smile as he glided toward his seat.

Both father and son sat across from each other at the small table, laughing as they ate and talked about what lay ahead of them. Every year, they celebrated Aris's life day with a trip. This journey took them two weeks there and back on horseback, and they would always come across some interesting characters. Their destination was the tragic desecration of Delwan. Now sixteen years rebuilt, it hosted a remembrance ceremony—a place where those who lost loved ones or friends could go to honor the dead. Respect for the customs and traditions was important to Victus, and he instilled in Aris this legacy of recognition for those who paid the ultimate price, dying in this never-ending fight against the tide of Eu'rok's vile subjugation.

In addition to celebrating Aris, it was a special time for him to recognize his parents, who died on the day of the Delwan massacre. Holding this space for their memory was important to him.

The journey also offered them a break from the hustle and bustle of their day-to-day life in the city. It was full of lessons, both planned and unplanned. Victus capitalized on this with his young son. The Academy of Soldiering, the Temple of Kalisdel, and the Scientific Mysticism Library were where all the young students learned. But Aris's father was an unconventional and creative thinker and teacher. Aris received instruction from him every day. The most essential thing to Victus, however, was becoming a righteous, duty-bound man—not only from what his father said but from his own actions. His father's words echoed what was in Aris's heart, which was seen in his actions.

After the third helping of food was finished, the two cleaned up the kitchen together. Aris was washing the dishes in the basin, craning his neck to watch his father pick up a crate and place it on his work table. It was a decent-sized box with an inscription burned into the side. Aris tried to squint and read it, but the words were too small. He moved to dry off the pots and plates, then set his bag on the kitchen table, pretending to double-check his things. His father smiled as he faced away from his son. "Would you like to come see what I have for you in the crate?"

Aris hurried over, nearly sprinting into his father's table as he tried to hide his eagerness. "It's a pretty nice crate. Solid wood. Is it walnut?"

"Yes, now open it."

Aris first read the words on the side. "Aris Tin of the House Andreas." He smiled widely at his father, excitement building, and lifted the lid.

The inside of the box was layered with fur pelts. Aris thought it looked like rabbit. He removed the first layer. His jaw dropped. He looked from his father to the pristine leather. Victus, a hand on his chin, grinned proudly. "Take it out."

Aris lifted the torso-formed leather piece out of the box. It was very sturdy but not stiff. The brown was so dark it looked black. In the center of the chest piece was a Peregrine insignia. The color matched his steel-blue cloak. "This is amazing, da! Can I put it on?"

Victus nodded and helped Aris with the straps, tightening them. "Snug. Comfortable?"

Aris twisted side to side and placed his feet in a fighting stance, moving his arms in a simulated attack. "Perfect!"

His father smiled. "Back to the box, son. There is more."

Aris reached in and removed the next layer of white pelts. He saw interlocking shoulder guards made of the same leather. The pauldrons were crafted with small falcons on each. Reaching in again, he saw the greaves and bracers, with two falcons centered on each piece. "A FULL SET!" Aris yelled in excitement. Offering the pauldrons to his father to help him attach them to the torso, he quickly reached down to fasten the belt loops to his calves.

Patting Aris in confirmation that he had finished, his father added, "It will take some time to get used to wearing it. Your movements may be sluggish at first."

Aris twisted and moved his hands up and down to test the weight. "Yes, but it is not as heavy as I thought," Aris said, smiling at his father stupidly. "I want to fight." Leaning his dominant foot forward, he crouched into a pounce and kicked back, rolling as if to disengage from an enemy. “I see what you mean, Da.”

Nodding, his father quipped, “Wear it every day and practice.”

Victus tapped his finger on the box. “More.” This time, Aris rolled back toward the box. He missed his mark and rose underneath the table, smacking his head. His father laughed heartily. “Practice and patience.” He pulled Aris up.

Aris, ecstatic, didn’t really feel the knot he had just given his head. He reached in again, tossing the pelts aside. The leather belt, sheathed dagger, and gladius were yanked from the box so quickly that Victus had to duck to avoid being hit on the head. Aris had the belt on in seconds. “You’ll have to be quick at putting the armor on yourself someday.” Chuckling as he watched his son, Aris pulled the dagger out first. It was unblemished, save for some nicks. It was sharp and had the initials VA etched in the handle.

“It was my first dagger when I became a squire,” his father explained. “The pommel can be replaced from a bear to a falcon, like the sword and armor.” His father’s face was slightly sheepish, as if waiting to hear disappointment from his son at the sight of his own insignia still on the weapon's pommel. But all he heard was, “It’s perfect.”

Aris placed the dagger back on his belt and reached to hug his father. Victus embraced him and kissed the top of his head. The excited young man said, “Da, it’s perfect.” Aris stepped back from the hug and looked down at the ivory pommel of the dagger. “Besides, keeping the bear means I will always be fighting with you nearby.”

Victus hoped the day would never come—the day when he would not be able to stand with his son. But the sentiment was understood. Pleased, Victus said, “Now the sword; look it over and test the weight.”

Aris pulled the small sword out. Looking it over, he saw it was made in the traditional fashion of the knighted legions of Kalisdel: sharp and balanced. The pommel was the only significant difference; it was crafted from obsidian into a falcon’s talons, clutching a small sapphire stone. The grip was wrapped in dark leather with the initials ATA. “Aris Tin of House Andreas,” he whispered to himself.

Victus, hearing this, nodded in agreement and said, “You are a fully fledged squire under our house name.” His hand gripped young Aris's shoulder. “You are to be my personal attaché. The parchment and your insignia pin are all that remain in the box.”

Aris's eyes went wide in disbelief. “Officially? I am not yet 17.”

His father reached in and pulled the falcon pin out, walking over to Aris's cloak as he spoke. “You have received the highest marks in all your training outside of my work with you. The council here has found you worthy.” He draped the cloak over his son, allowing him to tie the leather strings. Then, leaning in, he fastened the pin to him. “Aris Tin, first squire of the new order of the Peregrine under the House of Andreas. Do you accept to be a defender of truth, righteousness, and a protector of the defenseless?”

Aris straightened his shoulders and puffed out his chest, his chin raised high in pride. He looked up into his father’s eyes. “I do swear, Da.” His face was bright red as he blurted, “I mean, I do swear, sir.” His right hand balled into a fist pressed against the falcon emblem on his new armor in salute. His father returned the salute and grinned as Aris hugged him again.

“Thank you, Da! Thank you for all that you have done for me. I love you.”

Victus held back the wave of tears welling in his eyes. “And I love you, son. I always will. Now, ready the horses. We leave within the hour.”

2

Nibarn paced in his personal chambers. He had inherited the stewardship of the city of Lindly from his father thirty-five years ago. He had made many sacrifices during these thirty-five years, and yet this was another sacrifice he was willing to make in his reach for the dark power Lestar offered. His tremors were terrible these days. Feeling anxious and worn thin, he tried to stop the shakes with stiff drinks, though this would only temporarily ease the tension. He was, he thought, "dreadfully ill." He muttered to himself, "I need more, I need more," and he could not put his thoughts together beyond that utterance, but his body knew the routine. So he moved closer to the cabinets. Upon reaching one, his hands hastily pulled it open. Fumbling and knocking over a few glasses, he finally grabbed hold of one. Frantically, he poured the bottle of River Wine into the small glass. However, his hands were shaking so badly that he missed the glass completely. He threw the glass down to the ground, and with impatience, he just lifted the bottle, chugging until it too dropped to the floor, breaking. He felt the tension ease quickly. He gazed at the broken glass and pooling liquid as he heard a soft patting on his door. Nibarn straightened and began kicking the broken glass underneath the cabinet. He tossed a lambskin cloth down on the spilled wine.

The guard knocked softly again and added, "Milord, the Inquisition's Ambassador is here to see you."

Nibarn hurriedly cleaned up his mess and tried to keep his voice calm and dignified. "Quite right. Please enter and escort the esteemed emissary of Asmolor."

The door slowly opened, and the female high elf stormed past the guards. She turned and pushed the nearest one back, slamming the door shut. The guard just stood dumbstruck, looking at the others. One spoke up, “Milord?” he called through the door.

Nibarn kept his voice calm and answered, “I am fine. Our guest is in a hurry. Nothing to fret about. Back to your stations.” Scurrying mixed with the clanking of armored men echoed through the hall to his room.

He turned his attention solely to the female elf and kept his voice low, though clearly vexed. “I summoned you six months ago. How am I supposed to complete our mistress’s will if you don’t even show me what and how you want the work done?” Nibarn demanded, feeling that he had the upper hand. He turned back to open more wine and pour a glass for the emissary and himself. The female high elf was blonde, slender, and of small stature, and had the distinct bearing of a queen. Her clothing represented a station of Asmolor’s favored elvish house, Elivi. It was a facade. She removed the ring that disguised her appearance. Her hair turned black as night, and her skin shifted to a raven gray, retaining only her beauty. She walked behind the insolent human as he poured, but it was in the way a green viper would slither after its prey. She listened to the pathetic steward berate her further. “What, no response? So you fear my power, eh, elf?”

Before he could utter another word, his knees buckled from two quick kicks, and his head slammed down to the floor, the glasses shattering next to his face. Dazed, he tried to crawl away. Coughing on the blood now streaming from his mouth, he gasped for air. In his fear, he reached inside his cloak for his wand or something he could use to defend himself. The dark elf bore down upon him, her dagger ready to slice open his neck.

Her voice was soothing, not reflecting the contempt on her face. “Tsk… tsk… tsk,” she flicked the words out mockingly. “Are you not a servant?” She meant slave, but "servant" sounded so much better. "Are you not blessed by our matron herself?" The blade in her hand pressed harder into his throat. He didn't dare speak, so he just gave a small wiggle of affirmation. "Ah, that's a good boy." Hopping off him, she holstered the dagger and said, "Get up and clean yourself off," waving him away as she sardonically spun to pour herself a glass of wine.

She drank the wine as she watched the dazed man, his face streaked with blood trickling from the many cuts caused by the glass. His head was ringing. He grabbed some cloth from his desk and began frantically wiping the wine off his hand-embroidered tunic. Droplets fell softly onto his silver and red clothing. He instinctively reached for the cuts on his face with the cloth and began soaking up the blood. The dark elf finished the last bit of the wine, placing the glass down delicately. He watched her turn and walk back toward him, and he thought about how eloquently her body seemed to sway. Her movements were purposeful yet effortless, as if she were the wind. This female elf was the definition of grace, a subtle movement of sensuality. *So attractive. So beautiful.* he thought, quickly adding to himself—*and deadly.* She was inches from him, close and intoxicating. She raised her arm, touching his wounded face with the tip of her index finger. Speaking in a foreign tongue, his wounds healed. His aching head subsided, and he bowed in reverence to her. Weakly, he apologized. "Forgive the outburst. I was beside myself in frustration. My fits are growing worse."

She nodded in understanding as she spoke. "You are in disfavor, Nibarn. Our spies indicate your cult is being unraveled by the city's commander, Victus. You have become sloppy, and your murders are too frequent. If you are discovered, our invasion, our subterfuge, will be halted before it fully sets in."

Nibarn straightened, nodding in acknowledgment. "We have perhaps gotten a little careless." He rubbed his neck as if willing his voice to continue. "But we have replaced all members of the council who were not on board with us, save for Victus." Speaking with more confidence, he continued, "He has the garrison, and the people adore him. We cannot threaten or bribe him. Even your own scouts, who have watched him, say that the risk of exposure is high, especially if we attempted to kill him."

The priestess thought as she listened. After a moment's consideration, she suggested, "Perhaps you should turn his investigation back onto him. Set up evidence, make him the villain. Of course, the peasants will take some convincing. However, disclosing to them his covert leadership of the cult for years, along with irrefutable evidence, will likely influence them. Based on that evidence, you can charge all his subordinates, including the lieutenants and sergeants, as accomplices. After which, you will already have my personal guard here, disguised and ready to take on the role of guardians of the city. The rank and file will snap to attention at being led by high elves." She spat on the ground as if the words *high elves* tasted terrible. "We will be your shadow enforcers until the city is turned into the staging ground for our other plans."

Nibarn was grinning wickedly at the thought of finally getting rid of this thorn, Victus. "I will see that it is done. I have two weeks while he is on a journey away from the city to prepare, and my son—the fool—will be in charge of the guard until he returns…" Nibarn hesitated but added, "Priestess, do you have anything else for me?" The question was twofold: a hope that she had an orb of power for him to swallow, something to help with the ever-unquenchable thirst he had for his mistress, Lestar. But it was also to be certain that she had nothing else to share with him. He shifted his gaze from her to the desk. "I mean not to rush you. It's just that many things are awaiting my attention, and I will have to summon the others so we can prepare."

The priestess, with a coy grin, said, "I may have something for you." Her hand raised, and she pointed directly at him as she continued, "But I want to hear every detail of your plan." Nibarn placed the documents he was holding down. He attempted to show that he was not really all that interested in what she may or may not have. But his insides were screaming, begging him to attack her and take what she had. It sounded as if another person was in his head urging him. The gnawing, overwhelming compulsion of a man trapped in an addiction he did not know he had. *Go to her, kill her, and take what is rightfully yours. Lestar craves chaos and death. She would approve.* Shaking the thoughts far from his head, he felt the fear and undeniable understanding of these dark elves. How many others like her were actually in the guard? In the city? Enough that it would mean absolute oblivion and death if he tried to kill the priestess; he knew that. He quickly collected his scattered thoughts and motioned for another glass of wine. Surprisingly, she walked over and poured him one. Though she gave no visible sign, she knew what he had thought. Passing him the glass, she turned from him, grabbed a chair, and sat down, looking directly at him. "You know, Nibarn, if you were able to kill me, this meeting would never have happened in the first place. Now drink your wine and tell me how you plan to set Victus up."

3

Aris beamed as he strutted around the horses, securing the travel packs. After affirming that the saddles were set properly, he led the two auburn horses to the trough for some food and water. After Aris prepared the oats and chopped apples, he looked for the bucket to fill with water. He spun around, but he couldn't see it. *Where is it?* he thought, looking at every corner and surface a second time. Frustrated, he walked back to the stables to see if it had been left behind.

A small voice giggled, and Aris's head snapped back toward the horses. He laughed as he saw the strawberry-blonde girl laughing hysterically on top of Victus's mount. In her lap sat the bucket he was looking for. "I have been looking all morning for that bucket, Serin."

She dropped the bucket down to him, giggling again. "I thought you were getting presents from your dad this morning? And… and I know you were not looking for it all morning. I was watching you through the window." Her hands twisted as she explained how she snuck down onto the horse. Aris put his arms up as he listened and lifted her down from the horse. "I was just trying to be sneaky, and I did it." She gave Aris a big hug, her arms grasping him tightly. "Happy birthday, Aris." She leaned in and placed a kiss on his cheek.

Aris blushed. The words he spoke seemed stuck in his mouth. "Th… Thank... Eh hm." Clearing his throat, he tried again, turning from her as he grabbed the bucket. "Thank you, Serin. I really appreciate that. Umm…" Having never been kissed, his head was swimming. She was a princess. She was the daughter of Nibarn. *Did anyone see her do it?* the young squire thought. He wondered if someone had seen it and if it would get her into trouble.

Serin was tapping her foot with her arms folded across her chest. "Aris Tin, Mr. Knight! I have not finished talking with you."

Her stubborn and playfully irritated look made Aris smile. "Yes, my lady, what else do you need?" Aris placed the bucket down in the dirt and gave her a small salute.

She warmed, smiling, but kept her voice nobly stern. "I have a present for you too." It was her turn to blush. Her face expressed shy terror at the idea that he might not like it. She was so red in the face that Aris thought she was going to really let him have it. Her voice cracked. "See? I have a present for you." Her hands reached into a pocket sewn into her ocean-green dress. "I had to make it. My father wouldn't let me pay someone to make it. So I asked for help from the blacksmith and fletcher. It took me a while, but I got it." Smiling at him as he approached, her hand held a little tinderbox. Aris took the box, which had a small silvery-blue ribbon tied neatly. Unraveling and clicking her gift open, he saw a circular wooden token strung through the top. "It is me and you. A necklace," she spoke much louder than intended. Wincing, she whispered, "Just in case you couldn't tell." Her eyes dropped down as a new flush of red flooded her face. Aris looked down at her. He saw, engraved on the small token, a fox on a hill, while a falcon flew above. The initial "A" was near the bird, and an "S" was near the fox.

"I think it's excellent," he said, smiling at her. He stretched out the string and pulled it over his head, tucking it beneath his new armor. "I will keep it next to my heart." The young squire leaned into her, his arms wrapping around her. She embraced his heartwarming hug as she smiled.

Aris returned to his bucket, talking to Serin as he moved. "We are leaving soon. Da is getting his letter of parchments ready to give to Calder and to hand over the garrison command to your brother, Brandan."

Not caring about all that, she interrupted him. "So, Aris, how long will you guys be gone this time?"

He continued looking over the horses as he responded to her. "Looks like two weeks. It may take a few extra if the weather turns sour on us." He craned his neck back toward her. "But either way, it's always an interesting trip."

She returned his gaze with a smile. "I am going to miss you. And since no one else trains with me, I am going to be so bored."

Aris looked around to make sure no one was near them. "Keep that to yourself, Serin. I would be reprimanded if they found out I was training you. Your father has strictly forbidden it."

She shrugged, not caring too much. Though she quickly responded by hushing herself. "I don't care. I deserve to try too and to serve Asmolor, however I see fit. My father is dreadfully dull. He barely speaks to me." She paused, thinking something over. Aris watched her curiously. "Come to think of it, the last time my father spoke to me was over a year ago. Your father is more of a father than mine is."

Aris nodded, agreeing. "What about your brother? Does he not have an interest in spending time with you?"

She laughed. "He invests his time drinking, partying, and spending money on new tunics. I do not think he even knows how to hold a proper sword."

Aris chuckled. "He has trained with a rapier."

Serin laughed. "Trained and competed. I bet he paid the trainers and those he fought so that he could win. Either way, the rapier is a girl's weapon and not a proper sword." She giggled.

Aris squinted his eyes, grinning as he responded. "Yes, but you most definitely know how to use a sword. You knocked mine away and then from my hand." He smirked at her because he knew she had cheated. "Even if it was an unorthodox attack," he added, letting loose his laughter.

She laughed with him. "Well, you did not expect a tomato to the face. Just remember, Sir Aris, that not all your enemies will fight fair." She pointed at him as if she were his commander. "Lose focus for a moment, and you're dead."

Aris bowed. "A hard lesson to learn, my princess." His gaze lifted from his bow. "I will never falter to a tomato again." She playfully kicked toward his shin to see if he would react, and he did. His leg had already made the movement before he even thought of it. He crouched with his hands out as if to catch the flurry that soon would be upon him.

Serin's tenacious, womanly storm kicked high, then low, sweeping behind him with a half cartwheel cut short by a kick toward his head. Aris just played defensively, putting up blocks where her feet attempted to break through. Her foot nearly clipped his head; ducking, he rolled to disengage. The new armor caused his miscalculation. He rolled over and into a freshly mucked pile of horse dung. He heard a giggle and her padded feet scurrying toward him.

Great, was all that he could think as he rose. A tiny foot was planted firmly into his chest, knocking him back down into the dung.

"Did I win? Do you yield?" she demanded, laughing uncontrollably.

"Yield," Aris said, standing and shaking off the muck.

"Sorry about getting you dirty," she said, realizing how fresh the pile was and how dirty he had gotten.

"It's nothing. I will run down to the stream real quick."

They moved down together; Serin took Aris's arm and wrapped it around her.

"Oooh, you stinky," she said, immediately removing the arm.

He laughed and sprinted into the stream. He dove headlong into the deceptively deep water. Cool and refreshing, he loved the water, especially when the rains would come. He would often sneak out in storms to swim in the rain. He continued to swim deep, holding his breath and making certain he kept himself low and unseen below the waterline. A few moments passed, and Serin watched. Worry slowly crept into her mind, so she moved closer to the brim of the river. “Aris?” Her eyes scanned the water. “Aris! Come on!” She stepped in a bit, looking for him as she hiked up her dress, which doubled as pants. It appeared to be a dress when she walked normally but split into pants. This made it easier for her to be a lady of the city, but it also gave her the ability to be the carefree spirit of an adventurer. She had them specially made for herself. As she tiptoed further in, her fear set in completely. “Aris Tin, you come out right now!” The water current moved, and she saw something deep swimming fast toward her. Too late did she understand that Aris was tricking her and that she was trapped. She let out a little shriek as she fled back to shore. Aris popped up from behind and dragged her down. Under the water, she squirmed, and he held her tight. She couldn’t escape, so she went limp. He leaned into her, kissing her underneath the water. Her eyes were closed as she embraced the kiss. The moment they emerged from the water, Aris's blue eyes opened; she opened hers. They stared for a few heartbeats, each taking a moment to look into the other’s beautiful eyes, but more clearly, they saw each other’s souls. In that moment, they knew that no one would ever come between them. He smiled, she smiled, and he hoisted her up and toward the shore. They sat there for a long moment at the edge of the stream, watching the water move. His hand lay on top of hers this time. This friendship between the two was something neither would ever forget. No matter how far, no matter how long the time would be, both knew it was forever. They dared not speak the words "marriage" or "family" someday, though both thought about it. They were young and had their lives ahead of them. However, how much better would it be together? It was the most normal life children could have in a world that forced everyone to grow up fast or be crushed. The two were interrupted by the sound of her brother approaching. His personal guard yelled to make way as they headed to Victus's home.

"Well, I will see you when you get back, Aris Tin, squire of House Andreas." She beamed, giving him a quick hug and another peck on the lips. "Be safe. I have to hurry back. I have embroidery with Vela." Her face contorted in disgust and boredom, thinking about how tedious it was. She leaped up, very soaked. "I will have to change, too." Running off, she yelled back to him, "Have fun and be safe!"

The only words he knew she heard were "Bye. Thank you for the necklace." Though he had said more to her, it was rather quiet. He mulled over the words he had uttered and shook his head, speaking to himself and to her, though she was gone. "I love you, Serin. Now and forever." Staring in the direction she had gone, he stood watching until he could see her no longer. "Now and forever."

4

Brandan paraded himself through the streets as if he were the emperor of the universe, but he was the son of Lindly's steward, Nibarn. He had his personal guard shout as he passed every street, "Make way for Lord Counsel Brandan of House Neske." Outside of Victus, he was the most well-known citizen of rank, or at the very least, the most visible. He was lengthy, like his father, with his hair pulled back in a ponytail. His angular jaw, combined with his smile, made most female humans swoon. Even the elves would give him a second look when they saw him, often wondering how his features could be so elf-like yet still be human.

The young man had grown up in wealth, and he knew how to spend it. However, his management of the city's treasury five years ago almost caused the city to fall into bankruptcy. Victus had taken on a tutor-like role with the twenty-five-year-old man, but Brandan never wanted more out of life than fun. He did, more so in the past year, understand the responsibilities laid upon him. Even if he was not enthusiastic about the work for the city, nor successful, he did care for the city and its people.

Brandan paraded around town with his advisers, guards, and litter bearers for his lady of the week. The city knew he was all pomp and bark, but they played along with it. Regular citizens often gathered near the area he was traveling through, and they did this because at least once a week, he would invite a family to a dinner party. He chose them on a whim and hosted a splendid little gathering for them. They even left with gifts, well beyond their means. Overall, this clod was their clod, and he was kind to them. As far as the town was secure and businesses ran efficiently, the townspeople had no major complaints.

The intermittent town murders were a blight upon both houses, Neske and Andreas. The citizens of Lindly were aware of a cult operating within the city walls. However, most of the public's knowledge was hearsay and rumors. What they understood was that the murders were cultish in nature, devoted to one of the vilest demi-gods, Lestar. The murders appeared to be random folk sacrificed, and bodies were never discovered until the rituals were far concluded. The unwilling participants were reported missing, which would lead to a gruesome body being found—sometimes strung from a tree, other times in a well, light posts, and even in the forum. It had become common practice to just carry on after the murders, as this had been happening since the time Desa and her husband were murdered. Every year, there were only a few deaths, mostly overlooked. It was something Victus had not let slip from his view and was actively pursuing, with the aid of his trusted soldiers.

The council under Nibarn had no interest in the investigations, nor did any member of House Neske. But for Victus, unraveling this enigma of a cult was a personal vendetta. Other than this, the town's other endeavors yielded positive returns, even to the extent of being one of the most profitable cities in Asmolor's kingdom.

~~~

Aris heard another shout from the House Neske guard, closer this time. He knew Brandan was near his house, and he hurried back to the horses. Watching and waiting from the path, stopping the horses, he saw his father open the door, waiting to greet Brandan and his entourage. He knew his father did not care for the fanfare but would respectfully play along, especially considering Brandan technically outranked him. Victus smiled over at Aris briefly, his gaze quickly returning to the sound of Brandan's approach. Young Aris followed his father's gaze. He saw the flowing banners of House Neske. The golden fringes and ocean blue backdrop,
~~~

made from the finest linen and embroidered in maroon upon the cloth, displayed a sand-glass and a fore-staff precursor to a sextant. Aris began thinking about House Neske, remembering it was once a mighty seafaring family and that they were the first humans to survey all the seas. House Neske was a proud clan in its heyday, as were most of the older human houses. Most of the noble houses of humankind suffered loss of life in the wars and mistreatment from the other races. Humans, being versatile and resilient, still had many houses remaining, but they were far from the glory they had once achieved. It was admirable that Neske, and through that, Nibarn, Brandan, and Serin had clung to their roots so deeply. Many of the old houses had either collapsed or reinvented themselves into new houses. For the few that still adhered to their heritage, it became an achievement of longevity—something all humans respected, considering their relatively brief lifespan compared to the other races. It also made it easier for such a house to garner followers to support their leadership in a town.

Aris snapped from his rumination as the guard shouted outside the gate.

"I present, Lord Counselor Brandan of House Neske, seeking an audience with Commander of Chevaliers Victus Tiber Andreas." The house guards moved from their square formation, parting into two columned lines alongside the cobblestone path. The herald stepped aside, moving behind the tall man, Brandan.

Victus was moving down the path toward him. Upon reaching Brandan, the young man reached out to embrace him. Victus, however, stopped and saluted. Brandan never remembered all the protocol that he tried to imbue. Quickly, his hands went down and then to his chest as he spoke, embarrassed. "Yes, thank you, Commander." He stepped toward Victus and offered a hand instead. Victus squeezed the young man's hand. "You leave today, no?" Brandan inquired, motioning toward the home.

"Yes, we do. As soon as we are finished here," Victus replied.

Brandan turned back toward his guards, his eyes drifting to see the young boy staring and holding horses. He turned back to Victus as he spoke. "Was your son pleased about the council's decision?"

Victus chuckled. "Of course. It is an honor."

Brandan smiled, touching his chin. "Sometimes, agreeing with you—over my father," he rolled his eyes, "and his sycophantic politicians is the right thing to do. I never understood why they were all so opposed to the lad becoming a squire. It is clear by the testimony of all three directors of mysteries, war, and theology that he was well beyond his current placement. I have never understood my father." The young man's anger flared for a moment. "But at least I was able to get it approved. Happy day for the Andreas House, nay?" He smacked Victus's shoulder and awkwardly laughed, not knowing if he had displeased the commander with his commentary.

Victus looked firmly over to Aris. "No, it is a great day, as you say." Commander Victus slid to the side of his door, opening it and gesturing for Brandan to walk through first. Smiling, the noble walked in.

The door closed, and Aris continued to watch the guards left outside the house. He observed the commotion as a few of his father's own guards arrived. They spoke with the House Neske guards and then moved down the pathway, awaiting their commander, mostly chatting amongst themselves. One short, stout man moved towards the stable, and Aris pretended to check the packs on the horses. He knew this man. His name was Calder. The renowned human was a hero of the siege of Geoar when the city shut its gates to prevent the onslaught of Malakas's enraged forest folk. Calder had knocked out his commander and opened the gate to the fleeing people, saving many of Asmolor's children and gaining respect among all races. He was a fun man and loved to make Aris laugh. He also had an enormous family—thirteen children and another on the way.

Aris continued pretending he did not see the man but turned when he heard a voice. "Hey you, old man! What man did you steal those weapons and armor from?"

Aris turned, grinning. "Must not have been much of a man if I took his weapon, let alone his armor. Mind your business, human." Aris added a high elven inflection to his voice, mixing in the natural distaste they used when saying *human*.

Calder looked him over and burst into a roar of laughter. "Oh… your tongue is quick, ol' man. Get over here and shake my hand, squire!" He congratulated the young boy with a punch into his armor and a sturdy shake of his hand. "You have earned your place. We stand together as one."

Aris nodded, repeating, "As one."

~~~

Brandan had walked into the house, glancing around the frugal home. His face shifted uneasily. "You live a very plain life, Commander."

Victus closed the door and turned to face the man. "It suits my son and me," he replied. "Can I offer you a drink?"

Brandan, fascinated by some of the older tapestries, responded with a nod. Then he stopped himself and said, "No, no. I am afraid my stomach is unsettled. I drank a bit too much last evening."

Victus expressed understanding. "Yes, well, you do throw splendid parties." Victus had never stayed long at a dinner invitation from Brandan. Too much pomp, pageantry, and lick-spittles about to actually have a pleasant time. He had always preferred the company of soldiers and dwarves. Continuing, he suggested an old remedy for hangovers. "You should have your cooks boil wine with lamprey. Have them remove the less desirable parts of the fish and boil its blood in the wine. That little trick has saved a lot of us from puking our guts out. The dwarves in the south know how to throw a party. They swear by the remedy, and it has always worked,"
~~~

he said, smirking. "You know, if you threw a party or ball in the dwarven fashion, I bet you would draw quite the crowd."

Brandan found a suitable chair, dusted it briefly with his hand, and sat as he mumbled, "Yes, the dwarves…" He was feeling queasy, and the thought of the eel-like fish and how disgusting it looked made Brandan question internally, *Was it a snake, fish, or eel? Who would eat such a thing?* Swallowing hard, Brandan answered Victus, "No… I think lemon water will suffice."

Victus grinned as he moved to get him the honeyed water he and Aris had with breakfast. Victus handed the wooden mug over to him and sat next to the young noble. Victus sipped from his own mug. "Sorry, we have only honey, no lemon."

Brandan nodded as he drank deeply. "It's fine."

Victus placed his glass down. "To business then?" Brandan put on a face of curtness and focus. Victus unclipped the city's keys from his leather belt. The keys were ceremonial rather than functional. The actual power to run the city guard and whatever else needed doing in the day-to-day was the ornate rod of Lindly. It was the symbol of the steward's authority; thus, whoever wielded it acted on behalf of the steward and the city. Victus never carried it around like his predecessors, but he expected and knew that Brandan would. On the table near them, encased in a medium-sized oak box, was the rod. Victus took it and placed it into Brandan's eager, open hands. "The city is yours. The guards are yours. It is your solemn duty to safeguard all that reside in this city."

Brandan nodded eagerly as he took up the box and flipped it open. He clenched the rod as if he were a starving man reaching for bread. He became uncomfortable as he noticed Victus staring directly into his eyes unflinchingly. "Uh... yes, I have the city. I have the guard. And all those who live in the city are under my protection."

Satisfied, Victus rose from the chair. "I will be gone for a fortnight. If you have any problems, reach out to the capital. All trade is to continue, and our gates are open to travelers.

There is a contingent of high elves who will stop through next week. Nothing major, just some nobles. Other than that, you should be fine. Oh, and make sure you keep the dwarven smiths and gnome tinkerers from altering the set prices. They continue to be a nuisance, though I believe it is less about the gold and more about getting free drinks—all under the pretense of peaceful price negotiation. You will have to loosen your purse strings and get them well-oiled. Or perhaps host them in your palace." He quirked an eyebrow and began moving toward the door. "Any questions?"

Brandan sat up from his chair, rod in hand. "No, I am ready. We will have nothing like the last time." He self-consciously looked away from the inexorable knight as he spoke, "It will be as if you never left."

Victus opened the door but paused. He looked back at the young noble, watching him straighten out his outfit and take another swig of his honey water. "Brandan," Victus said softly.

"Hmm? Yes?" the young noble responded, pouring another drink.

"Look at me," Victus said with a fatherly tone.

Brandan looked up in confusion, his face conveying a fear of the upcoming reprimand stemming from past mistakes. He swallowed as his eyes met Victus's. Instead, the commander smirked as he understood the man's expression and thus his thoughts. "Your past failures are not a reflection of who you are today. Yes, you have much to learn and work on. But the efforts you are making will someday yield a superb noble and leader. Stay on the path and work on yourself each day so that you can become what you truly desire: a man to be respected and loved, a leader who is wise and compassionate. Be encouraged, not discouraged. Hold to your duties, and I thank you for your visit, even if it is just a formality."

Brandan sighed in relief. "Thank you for saying that. I am trying."

Victus nodded. “I know.” He pushed the door open for the young noble.

~~~

Outside, Aris listened to Calder as he spoke of his squiring years. “It was a tough lot for me. I squired for two knights, and both were buffoons. They had me cleaning armor and fetching food and drinks. It wasn’t the best way to learn about soldiering.”

Aris laughed, still watching the front door. “Sounds like you were more maid than squire.”

Calder’s face crinkled in posed rage. “I was a damn excellent maid, too. Our first battle proved that I was more maid than soldier. I stood next to those knights as they shouted commands. I felt more in the way than an actual participant. But you learn quickly, or you’re dead.”

The conversation ended abruptly as the front door opened and Brandan walked through, holding the small staff of Lindly. Sighing, Calder watched the young lord. “Oh, he is going to parade around, showing everyone how in charge he is. Pompous ass.”

Aris did not say a word, just watched. But he thought it was interesting to be a part of his father’s crew, at least officially now. Being one of them was something valuable, like being a part of an exclusive club. Of all the world’s opportunities, this was his purpose.

Brandan continued to move toward his guards, who promptly began the march back through the city, with shouts now accompanied by the blowing of a large kingly horn.

“I guess he waited to blow the horns until he officially became garrison commander,” Calder said in jest. “Come, Aris, your father is motioning for us to go over with the others.”

Aris stared again as the parade marched off. “Make way for the Lord Counselor of the City and Garrison!” A loud horn
~~~

echoed after the shout. Shaking his head, Aris hastened to catch up with Calder. As he did, though, he saw an elvish woman riding a horse. She was clearly noble, and she was moving with purpose towards Brandon's guard. Though Aris was curious, he focused on getting to his commander, his father. Victus wanted to speak with Calder and his trusted soldiers before his departure. But the female elf lingered in his mind until his additional responsibilities as squire forced their way forward and made themselves known as far more important. Moving behind and to the left of his father, he listened to the greetings, waiting patiently for any command that might be given to him.

"Half-pally, how are ya?" Calder, in his jolly but gruff voice, asked over the others. Victus smiled at all of them. "I am well, but pressed for time. Aris and I should have left a half-hour ago."

Straightening, Calder looked over his shoulder. "Ye lot heard him! Attention! We have work to be doing."

The guardsmen snapped straight up, making sure pikes were high and shields ready. In unison, they slammed their pike-encased gauntlets into their shields, chanting as they did so.

Crack! The gauntlets collided into their chests. "Victus!" Crack! "Victus!"

Victus responded with a curt salute to his chest. Aris mused that the unusual chant of his father's name was done out of respect and adulation for their commander, not as intentionally sacrilegious. Though he was certain that if Asmolor's Inquisition found out, there would be a serious investigation into why the men seemed to revere the human. Most armies would chant a deity, not a mortal. Most humans got away with it because their demi-god was a bit of an outcast herself. Kalisdel was actively helping her people, the humans, unlike any of the other gods.

Kalisdel, or Kali, as most called her, was adored for her love of her creation. She encouraged them to find loyalty and bonds that were beyond even the gods' understanding. "In this, they make better soldiers. They rally to each other, not just at the thought or sight of the gods." This was the argument she used long ago in the first war of the brothers, Asmolor and E'urok. "She was right," Aris thought. His father was speaking now, pulling him away from his thoughts.

"I have work for you. But it involves travel, and I cannot make the trip. First, I know I am being followed and watched. More than likely, even now." His eyes scanned across the faces watching him intently, taking in the importance of the moment. "Second, my son and I have our yearly pilgrimage to Delwan." His men nodded as they listened, clearly aware by Victus' tone that this meant danger for all of them. Victus continued, turning to his ranking officer, "Calder, once we leave the city and night sets in, you and the rest of the men will need to come to my house. Under my bed is a magically sealed box. The only people able to open it will be myself and Arch Commander Skylighter. This crate has to be delivered to him and him alone."

The men nodded, and Calder stepped forward. "It will be done."

Victus saluted his men a second time. And again, the shields were smashed by their gauntlets. Crack! "Victus!" Crack! "Victus!" Calder dismissed the men and turned to speak to Aris. "Squire well, lad." Calder nodded at Victus in respect before turning to follow the men from the house.

~~~

The dark priestess, disguised as a high elf, moved swiftly on her white horse to catch up with the oaf, Brandan. When she caught up to him, she greeted him sardonically, though the young noble could not pick up on it. "Greetings, Noble Counselor—Commander Brandan, son of House Neske."

The man puffed out his chest as he held the rod in his hands. "Yes, noble elf," he said, dipping his head low in respect for the higher race.
~~~

When he looked up from his bow, she was motioning for him to come closer. "Prying ears," she explained seductively.

He nodded, hurrying over to hear what he thought was gossip or a juicy exclusive party for elves and nobles. Maybe he would be invited to one of their evening cabals! "Oh, that would be fun," he said aloud, not realizing the words had been uttered.

The priestess looked him over, puzzled. "What would be fun?" Her lips pursed as she grinned wickedly, preying on the man's ego and guessing that, like most males, he would be thinking about something done behind closed doors.

Brandan's face bloomed rose, and he coughed, saying, "Ahem, excuse me, I was thinking of a possible theme for our next joust. Continue, please."

Holding her grin in place, she whispered, "The men who are currently being dismissed by Victus need to be followed. Discreetly. No doubt Victus enlightened you that more of my kind would be coming?"

Nodding, the man's eyes grew wide as he listened.

"Well, it is not a coincidence. We are coming because the taint of the cult in Lindly has greater implications." Brandan, clearly concerned, almost yelled to urge her to explain further —implications of what? She glanced side to side and leaned next to his ear. "Implications of war. That this city is being groomed for takeover. And if the dark elves are the ones behind it, you know that everyone in this town will be subjugated or killed. Then, from this city, hopefully unnoticed, they would strike at the capital, Asmadine."

The man looked dreadfully ill as the blood, recently surfaced, rushed from his face. "But... but… subjugated how? Like slaves or soul slaves?"

She looked slightly angry that this man was truly this daft. "Do you not know the dark elves? Do you not know of their evil?" The word *evil* cut slightly as she reveled in the reverence of her goddess. She self-corrected her thoughts before continuing, *divinely evil.* After a brief pause, she softened her tone. “Do you not know of their evil mistress, Lestar?” Spitting on the ground for emphasis, she continued, “She will consume their souls, and they will be husks enslaved. Do you understand, handsome Brandan?”

He nodded stupidly, asking, “What is it you need me to do?”

She realized that she would have to spell it out for him. “From this moment on, you have all those men followed. The ones closest to Victus. The ones that he is speaking to right now. If they leave the city, capture them and bring them back. If they try to hide anything of note from you, have it brought to your father.”

Understanding, he nodded confidently. “Yes, it will be done. Does Victus know his men have gone traitor?”

She mulled over her response. She thought of how sweet the taste of treachery was, how much fun it would be to watch these humans turning on each other. Her thoughts consumed her in complete bliss, imagining Lestar draining all the souls of everyone in this pathetic town. Her horse turned away from Brandan as she trotted it slowly away, and she raised her voice so he could clearly hear her. The man stood waiting for a response. “He is the leader of the cult, fool.”

5

As Calder and his men rounded the corner, Victus looked behind his left shoulder in the direction of his son. “Are we ready, squire?”

Aris clicked his boots together and saluted as he answered, “Yes, commander. All is ready.”

Victus nodded. “Good.” The right side of his face showed the hint of a grin. His voice was direct and steady, as if issuing commands to men on ramparts. “Stay at this spot. But beat me to the horses. Do not disobey me. If you do, the horse will have no rider for the trip. She will just be happily carrying supplies. Understood?”

Aris's brow furrowed in alarm and confusion as he responded, “Uh, yes, sir.”

Victus began his walk to his mount while Aris pondered his father’s puzzling directions, not moving an inch. All kinds of ideas were jumping through his head. As he watched his father, he could feel each step pounding heavily in his heart. The squire puzzled over the thought, “Was this a lesson in not disobeying orders? Could it be this is a lesson about how sometimes you *should* disobey commands so you could win?” He shook his head, muttering, “No… No. That can’t be right.” Aris was now positively panicking that he had not figured it out, and he was running out of time. The idea of walking on foot all the way to Delwan was awful. His father was getting closer. Aris could feel the sweat dripping down his forehead, trickling down his nose. It itched, and as he reached to scratch, his fingers grazed his lips. “That’s it!” he yelled. Placing two fingers in his mouth, he blew, gathering a large push of air from his lungs. His whistle rose high and lingered, then dropped quickly and sharply. At the sound of the whistle, his horse started heading in his direction. As trained war horses, they responded to specific sign language and sounds. Aris had been working with this specific mare since she had been a foal. Although he had only been eight, they had developed a strong connection right away.

His horse had run up close to him, keenly positioned for Aris to hop on. Aris did not, though. Instead, he raised his hand to the front and then quickly down to his left. His horse understood that this meant she was to be on his left flank. Once she was in place, Aris grabbed the reins and stood in the spot he was told not to move from.

His father, just now reaching his horse, turned, smiling, and said, “Smart lad. Come on, let’s get going.”

Aris, with his horse in tow, drew closer to his father. Victus spoke before his son could ask. “Sometimes a difficult problem can be solved with the simplest of solutions, especially when we are put under time constraints. People tend to think that if the problem is huge, the solution must be even more so. The most efficient solution is often the simplest.” He smiled again, and the sound of the leather saddle creaked as his son mounted his horse. Victus breathed out heavily, the aroma of sweat and leather increasing with the heat, and then he continued speaking to his son, “Maybe we can make some headway.”

Victus tapped the sides of his mount, giving an authoritative “Hiyah!” His father’s horse swiftly increased the distance between the young squire and himself, as if he were a cockroach running from a candled lamp. Pursuing after his father, Aris tried to keep up as his horse galloped farther away.

~~~

Nibarn heard the first knock upon the council room door but ignored it. He and many high-ranked citizens of Lindly, who were also members of the cult, were in a sequestered
~~~

meeting, where they were discussing plans regarding Victus and the town. The knock came again, louder this time, and the others in the room heard it too. A hush grew over the table as they waited for Nibarn to respond. Highly irritated, he motioned for the door to be opened. One member wearing regal attire, her green and yellow robes flowing, opened the door.

Nibarn began yelling at the unseen disruptor. "I said we were not to be interrupted..." Trailing off, he rolled his eyes as he recognized his son Brandan moving past everyone, heading directly to him.

Nibarn looked back down at his parchments and let out a sigh. "What do you want, boy?"

Upon reaching his father, he kept his voice in a low whisper. "I spoke with the high elven emissary. Did you know about this?"

Nibarn lifted his head, leveling his eyes toward Brandan. Cocking his brow, he asked, "Know what?"

His son's face burned with anger, his voice rising. "About Victus! His men. Following and arresting them all? Highly irregular, and to me, this is a miscalculation. Victus is not the —the—…" He trailed off into silence as the crowd murmured among themselves.

Nibarn's voice rose to match his son's. "You dare defy me? You dare defy the emissaries of Asmolor's chosen children? We do not act rashly or without purpose, boy. Now I expect you to do what you were commanded. And…" Nibarn paused, walking over to a large slab where his cultist council was congregating. The woman who had opened the door passed him a sealed parchment scroll. Nibarn then handed the writ of dismissal to his son. "This is to be given to all of our cohorts in the city. They are to be formally discharged from service. They will have their wages paid for the next year. Our elven friends will be relieving them. We need the very best, and according to the priestess—" He corrected himself quickly as he continued, "Er—The emissary of Asmolor and the Inquisition believes if an invasion starts here, it will and should be the elves defending. Not our pathetic *human* men and women. Make certain they are disbanded and turn in all weapons to the armory."

Brandan felt the confusion like a heavy weight inside him, making it hard to think. His face shifted from red to purple in boiling fury, vexed by his perplexity. Through gritted teeth, he growled at Nibarn. "This is highly irregular. And for me to be kept out of the loop is—"

His father slammed his fist down on the table, cutting him off, his own face reddening in anger. "This is far bigger than you or me. Do as you're told! This is what is best for the city."

Brandan shook his head no but quietly responded, defeated. "As you wish, my lord." Turning without being dismissed, he gripped the rod of Lindly tightly, wanting nothing more than to beat his arrogant father with it. He thought to himself, *What a terrible end it would be for me if I did. Plus, how would I explain that one to Victus? Everything is wonderful in the town. One minor detail: I murdered my father in a fit of rage*. The young lord smirked, but he maintained a steady gait, demonstrating that his pride was still intact. He was about to close the door behind him when he heard his father's words ringing through the air.

"You know, boy, if you hadn't nearly ruined the city and weren't such a pathetic excuse for a man, you would be privy to all this and to all that is to come." The crowd in the room roared with laughter, mocking and jesting. Brandan sighed, looked away from the room, and closed the door without a word.

Brandan stood outside the door for a moment, listening to the laughter from within. His gaze finally connected with his personal guards, and he felt a shiver of anticipation course through his body. They stood waiting at attention, not even a hint of a snicker or laughter. They stood poised, professional, and ready for their next command. He was relieved but shrewd when he spoke. "I need all the city watches at the grand assembly. I am going to dismiss all of them. No longer will they be defending the city. They are to be replaced with the high elves."

His men were silent, but their helmed faces portrayed the confusion, fear, and anger that lurked beneath them. Brandan placed his hands up as if telling them to hear him out. "I will not be dismissing my personal guard." They were relieved to hear that at least they would not be out of work. Most of them had grown up as soldiers, not as farmers or seafaring folk. They trained from their youth to be defenders of humanity, specializing in marshaled combat of a disciplined legion. With this training, they would serve the kingdoms of Asmolor and humanity.

Brandan was calm, stoic even, as he continued, "And we will pay all those who are being dismissed for a term of one year. It seems Asmolor's chosen are attempting to put us back into the seas and fields. We are in disfavor. Have the word spread to all officers and knights that tomorrow morning, every single soldier will need to be in attendance. We will make exceptions for those in the infirmary."

All the guards hastily left, save one. She stayed behind and removed her helm to reveal blonde hair tucked in a tight bun on the top of her head. Brandan noticed the scar first as he looked her over. It stretched down from the left side of her forehead to her nose, where it went jagged to her right cheek. The roughness of battle had weathered her, adding a few extra lines to her otherwise externally beautiful figure. But war had also honed wisdom into her short twenty-seven years.

Her beauty, blended with her rugged appearance, stunned Brandan so that he missed her first two sentences, wherein she began to express her displeasure unflinchingly. His brain finally refocused on the woman speaking. "I, Jess, daughter of Cato, the armorer of no house, formally resign my post on your personal guard. All of this is rushed and out of place. Elves are deliberate but slow. This is chaotic and hurried."

Brandan nodded as he believed every word she spoke. He knew it was all terribly wrong. But he was the son of the Lindly's steward. His first duty was to the steward, his father. "I understand," he said as he watched her toss her halberd down and cling her gladius in its scabbard. His eyes willed her to just surrender the sword and leave. Then, when she did not, he spoke. "All weapons of those dismissed, or in your case resigned, are to be yielded over to the city."

She shook her head fervently. Lifting her voice coldly to him, she said, "I have resigned my post to you. But I am sworn to a knight, which means I am not dismissed and am not required to turn in my shield or sword. What kind of cavalier would I be without my sword and shield? My duty to Knight Commander Chevaliers Victus of House Andreas bids me to not tarry. Good day to you, noble citizen."

The term "citizen" was an insult, to be sure, Brandon thought. People with no aristocratic background were labeled as citizens, and it was a customary way to greet people. He comprehended that her intent was to emphasize the word "citizen" to denigrate him as lowborn. He said nothing as she spun sharply and strolled out confidently.

A great weight lifted from her as she walked further out of the Councilor building, only to be replaced with an even heavier burden. At that moment, her new mission sank in. Jess's pace unintentionally picked up as she made her way straight to the garrison stables. Muttering to herself, she began to run. She could feel her heart pounding and knew it was not because of the run. Jess was in far better shape than most. The words Victus had commanded her consumed her thoughts. Flowing like a fountain in her mind, she recalled his every word: "If anything out of the normal circumstances within the city occurs, you must surrender your post and seek Arch Johnathan Skylighter in Asmadine. He will be expecting people from me, so you will find him readily available. Tell him all that you see, and from there, serve him until I can reconnect with you." In her heart, she knew something was terribly wrong, and she knew it all had to do with Victus's investigation into House Nibarn.

The duty officer guarding the stables tried to stop her with a "Halt!" But she ran past him, yelling, "On orders for Victus!"

The guard shrugged and did not pursue her. She saddled a horse and rode through the city gates as quickly as she could manage, thinking only of her destination: Skylighter.

~~~

Aris finally caught up with his far superior riding companion. When he did, he kept quiet and maintained his position directly behind his father. They continued to ride hard, breaking off the main road in favor of a shortcut through the woods. It would lead them back to the main road, but much farther ahead, allowing them to make up time. The elk trail they used was well-trodden, making it a much easier ride for them and the horses. By the time they cleared the forest and were back on the road, it was well past the afternoon, and the sun had begun its descent.

When Victus hopped off his horse, Aris followed suit, and they led the horses to an old caravan camping spot. It was about a quarter-mile from the main road, next to a stream.

"We will make camp here. I will get the tent started. Unsaddle the horses and take them towards the water."

Aris nodded towards Victus in acknowledgment but had already begun to do exactly that. He knew the routine and wanted to make sure he was working, thinking, and living in sync with his father's will. This was not necessarily a dangerous area, but bandits or highwaymen could strike and devastate travelers in seconds. The horses snorted in relief when he removed the saddles. Leading the two mounts over to the stream, Aris began gazing into the woods opposite him. He thought over what he would do if some unknown enemy came barreling towards him and his father, wondering if they would stand and fight or flee to a more defensible position.
~~~

"I guess it would depend on how many, who they were, or what it was." He spoke low to himself, puzzling out different scenarios. Aris went and grabbed a water canteen from their supplies. The water in his canteen had become stagnant and warm. He dumped the contents on the ground and made his way back towards the horses. He wondered about a dragon before speaking out loud. "A dragon flying low above the trees. What would I do?" He laughed to himself, reaching the stream and filling the canteen. He began pouring cool water on the horses' heads. It was all the invitation the horses needed. They both slowly moved to wade in the water. Aris answered his own question, still laughing. "I would run like a fat goblin chasing a sweet cake."

Victus was nearly done with the tent. It could hold up to five people comfortably, and the canvas was magically enchanted, allowing it to blend into the surroundings. The concealment worked better when looking from above. Ding, ding. Victus paused his hammering. "Dragon? Goblin? What are you doing over there?"

Startled, Aris spoke, "I was just planning. Well, I was just thinking about if we were attacked. Depending on the invaders, I imagine we would respond differently. And I thought, what would we do if a dragon attacked? And I laughed because that's an easy one to answer: flee or hide."

Victus cocked his brow. "Flee? Where would we flee? We would be consumed before we got a hundred feet." The man chuckled, continuing, "But if you ever face a dragon, aim for the eyes. Unless you have a mage or some sort of war machine to bring it down, that would be the only actual option. You'd better start practicing a bit more with a bow if you intend on battling dragons."

Aris moved back towards his father, grabbing a hammer to help with the pegs. "What about the..." His lips formed the words, but he trailed off as he just mouthed words while they both stopped to listen. Both of them heard a roar from above and searched the skies. A melodious cackling echoed in the valley up the stream. It was high-pitched, a constant laugh or maybe a cry. Neither Aris nor Victus could figure it out at first. But they quickly realized in confusion that it sounded like an insane giant child laughing.

"Wheeee!" They searched the sky above them.

Aris caught sight of a ball of flames in the sky, his face pale in disbelief. He reached over and grabbed his dad's shoulder. "Da! Dra… dra... dragon!" The terror in his voice was real and sobering.

Victus turned to look at where Aris had been pointing. A giant flame wyvern was bouncing in the air. Victus scrutinized the sky imperiously. "Not a dragon, a wyvern. But I have never seen one engulfed in flames."

Aris's hand loosened on his father's arm. "Are you sure?" His voice was calming, though clearly still scared. The wyvern flew closer, distant and still bouncing merrily towards them. Victus thought and squinted, noting a tiny, insignificant figure on its back. "See how it's flying? It's bouncing. The wyvern is trying to get something off of its back. That is why it is flying so haphazardly."

Aris watched with curiosity as the high-pitched voice rang louder.

"Weehheeeee hahaha... fly, beastie! Weeeeehheeeee! Hehehehehe!"

Aris looked at his father. "I think it's getting closer."

Victus rose, dropping his hammer to the ground. Aris immediately stood, holding his hammer like an axe, unsheathing his gladius and holding it up as well.

"Sheathe your sword, son." Victus shook his head. "He's not an enemy."

Aris hesitantly put his blade away, but he held the hammer just in case, and they both watched the spectacle a bit longer. Suddenly, as the wyvern was nearly over the camp, it snuffed out in a blink.

The flame wyvern had vanished without a trace, leaving only the sight of a smoky matchstick rising from the spot. The diminutive creature atop was now plummeting hundreds of feet downward right toward them. A high-pitched voice was screaming in terror and excitement. “Weeeehhhhheeeee! Oh... Ahhhh!!! Contingency! Contingency! Ahhhh!” the figure shouted as he persisted in shrieking and plummeting. His giggles were making Aris a little uncomfortable. Did this creature realize it was about to go splat? Aris held his watch, and at a separation of nearly twenty feet, the miniature entity was upright, gazing directly at the two, levitating, and now slowly descending. Brushing off his red fire-like robes as he hovered down to them, he exclaimed with a final, “CONTINGENCY!”

He pounded his tiny hands together, not taking into account just how close Aris and his father were. The small man peeled off his giant goggles and tossed them, where they thudded to the ground a few feet away. His hair was frazzled, creating a spiky texture when he ran his hands through it. Soot and ash largely obscured his face, with only the whites of his brown eyes visible. His voice was high-pitched and more of a squeak now that he was not yelling or screaming, and he began cordially, “Greetings, Half-pally! Greetings to you, little Aris.”

Victus stepped closer to the little gnome-mage. “Good to see you, Biddy. Still playing with fire, I see.”

The gnome nodded emphatically as he spoke. “It’s the only magic worth doing.” His attention turned to Aris. “I have not had the privilege to meet you, and I am honored to meet the son of Victus.”

Aris looked down at the gnome, barely reaching his knees in height. “Pleased to meet you, Master Mage.”

Biddy giggled. “No need for that. Just call me Biddy.”

Aris knelt back down to help his father finish pegging the tent down.

"Biddy, would you mind setting up our cooking pit?" Victus asked casually, but as Biddy's soot-covered face lit up with glee, he added, "A normal fire pit. Nothing crazy."

The face of the gnome drooped sadly. "I could really make..." His voice was soft and high-pitched, as if a child had been denied the chance to play with his toys.

"No, I think for now a normal one will suffice. Besides, Biddy, you understand, we must not draw attention to ourselves."

Huffing into a sigh, the gnome caved. "Okay… okay," he whispered as he moved from the pair. "Just a little flair."

Victus heard and sternly said, "No flair!"

Biddy giggled, "Whoopsie!" It was too late. He had cast a spell that had summoned or created—Victus did not know—hundreds of little fire ants. They were quite literally ants on fire. They scurried about building a little fire pit and then began gathering little sticks and twigs. Biddy was directing them as if it were an assembly line. "No. We need more here. Carry them carefully. You don't want to burn the forest down."

Victus shook his head, and Aris just watched, amazed and utterly confused. The ants continued to build, and when the pit was complete, the twig pyramid stood taller than the gnome. All the ants congregated at the base of the unlit pit and burst into tiny balls of flame. The flames ignited the wood. Biddy cackled, "Little flair, little fire. Who's hungry?"

6

Darkness was soon to set over the city of Lindly. The hurried dismissal of the garrison by Nibarn, carried out by his son Brandan, went without issue, especially in light of everyone being given a year's salary in advance. That day, a multitude of formerly serving soldiers, taking their families with them, set off for Asmadine or to a location nearby, hoping the money upfront would help them start new lives. Those without families went to taverns for drinks, gambling, and companionship. Overall, the city was overjoyed to have the high elves guarding the gates and towers. A few, including Calder and his men, refused to hand over their weapons and armor, using the oath they all took as their reason for refusing dismissal. This stirred Brandan to believe that perhaps what the female high elf priestess had said regarding their allegiance was true. Calder and his men were all that remained after all the sorting and coin exchanging had transpired. Calder made sure all present in the parade yard could hear his voice.

"We are lifers. Sworn to this city but first sworn to our commander, Victus. We can only be disbanded through death, or from him in person."

Nibarn said nothing but waved his hand, turning from them and from his son. "Deal with this."

Brandan watched his father and the ever-elusive priestess murmuring in hushed tones. The young noble supposed they were speaking about the new additions to the towers. He turned his focus back to Calder and the soldiers in the yard. His voice calmed into a facade, pretending to understand their plight. “You are correct in this. Can we come to terms, perhaps?”

Calder stepped from his platoon and towards Brandan. “You cannot bribe us! We have sworn an oath. We are loyal.”

Brandan raised his hands, waving and shaking his head. “No. No. No. Not a bribe. A gift. For the fulfillment of services rendered to the city.”

Calder took off his blue-plumed helm, staring directly into Brandan’s eyes and speaking sternly. “Do we still breathe?”

Brandan nodded flippantly.

“Then we will still serve.” Calder placed his helm back on, still staring at the young noble through his battle-worn helmet. Brandan started to speak but was cut off by Calder, who shouted, “Legionnaires right face! March!”

Brandan did not try to stop them. He just stood stupidly, trying to puzzle everything together. *Unquestionably,* he thought to himself, *the high elves were right. All signs point to Victus having a hidden agenda. My father has been able to discover a way to uncover and disclose all of Victus's most loyal followers. Yes. Brilliant.* Turning around to his house guard, he said, “I need refreshment. Lead me to the palace. And let me know everything Calder and his men do. If they attempt to leave the city, have them all arrested.”

~~~

The centurion and his legionaries marched in a single-file line from the parade yard to the barracks, their boots echoing on the cobblestone.

Night was in full swing now as Calder spoke to them all. “We have our orders from Victus before his departure. Undoubtedly, we will be watched. Titus, you will put on my armor and lead everyone out of the city. March to Delwan and find Victus. Tell him everything. The high elves, the dismissal of our legion here. All of it.”
~~~

His stern-faced men acknowledged with nods. Everyone could already feel the tension, the quiet eeriness that sets in before combat. Titus watched as Calder started to unbuckle his armor, and he followed suit, the leather straps creaking as he released them. "Sir, where will you be?"

Calder glanced at him briefly, keeping his focus on his breastplate straps. His gruff voice was determined. "I have my orders. But my destination is Asmadine."

The sergeant, Titus, did not pry; he just continued removing his armor. He knew that Calder was convinced the only path to accomplishing Victus's original instructions was to separate.

One of the legionaries, Marcella, sang a hymn to all the others. "O' dah roa' we on is perilous. We are servants of Kalisdel. Her holy light makes us weariless. O' dah roa' we on is known and death is our companion. We walk prepared to join our ancestors in the glory of Kalisdel. Prepare us to be a living sanctuary for those in need. O' dah roa' we on is calling. We walk together to our fate. Holiness and righteousness holding us afloat."

An interminable silence ensued when she concluded. But all present could feel their spirits lifted and their courage renewed. Everyone was already determined and prepared, but her voice had a way of elevating their resolve. The music reverberated in their minds, a gentle reminder of their responsibility for the greater good. They were prepared and at peace.

Calder was now wearing a normal citizen's tunic and hat, with an unassuming dagger hidden in his boot and a gladius strapped to his belt. "From this point on, everyone is to address you," he pointed directly at Titus, "as Calder. Lead your men out of the city." He saluted the man who assumed his command, his identity.

Titus looked at the sturdy, proud few. "Legionaries, we are off to find Commander of the Chevaliers, Victus Tiber Andreas. We march!" Spears tapped the barracks floor.

Clank, clank, clank. In unison, the soldiers marched two by two with Titus, while Calder led them from the barracks to the city gates.

~~~

Jess had been riding hard, and her horse was already weary when night fell. She kept pressing on, still focusing on the words, "Find Skylighter." She knew that the route she had chosen would take her twice as long to get to Asmadine; however, it provided a more camouflaged approach. When the night was half past, she slowed her horse. Resting by a nearby pond, Jess dismounted and fed the horse an apple from her satchel saddlebag. Then, allowing it to mosey on over to the water, she stripped off her heavy armor, hoping that by doing so, it would lighten the load for the horse, further allowing her to make up for the time she was losing.

She gave herself a few hours' rest, sleeping on the mount's back, using the muscular neck of the beast as her pillow. The horse jolted her awake, its front legs lifted high off the ground as it neighed in anger, its back hooves kicked back, hitting and making a twisted metallic crushing sound. Jess was fully awake. Unable to see in the dark, she just told the horse to run.

"We need to go. Ride… RIDE!" she shouted.

The horse was in motion, darting through the woods. It wove in and out of trees in an attempt to flee this unknown threat. Jess could hear pursuers but could not see them. "RIDE! Come on! We need to go!" Her head whipped from side to side as she heard small clicks, quickly followed by the sound of thuds into the trees she was passing. She knew the sound; they were darts shot from a hand crossbow, and she knew they were missing but nearing their marks. All she could do was ride and hope to elude the enemy. More clicks, and the horse groaned in protest. Jess reached back, feeling the horse's rump and then her neck, looking for the darts. Jess knew at least one had found its target. She found a line of them underneath the horse's mane and plucked them out. The
~~~

noxious smell told Jess all she needed to know. "Dark elves," she whispered as she felt her stomach churning in disgust and fear. Her soft voice spoke to the horse, encouraging it to press on. "Fight the toxin. We can make it! RIDE! Come on!" She heard more clicks. This time, all of them found the beast, and it moaned in defeat. The head of the beast drooped down as the legs kept running at full speed. Its head collapsed further, and the horse tripped head over hooves, sending Jess flying through the air. She had no clue where she was flying to but desperately hoped she would not lose consciousness when she landed.

When she inevitably hit, she landed at the base of a tree, back first, her shield absorbing most of the blow. Though she stayed crumpled on the ground, the shock and trauma had knocked the air from her lungs.

Her body ached in pain as she gasped for air. She heard footsteps in the distance and tried to look for her assailants. Jess inhaled deep, labored breaths as she struggled to regain her breath and her footing. She noticed the pink and orange hues of the horizon and the whisper of the wind through the trees. The sky was beginning to lighten in the distance, coloring the horizon with a brilliant pink and orange. Maybe it would be enough for her to see. Maybe she could make it, she thought.

~~~

Brandan partook in dinner in the parlor, savoring all sorts of delicacies. The caviar was imported from the seas under Eu'rok's control. The toasted crackers were brought in from the high elves' district in Asmadine. His wine of choice, 'Manoir of the Phoenix,' cost more than a human soldier would make in three years of service. It swirled around in his glass, magically enchanted to keep the spices spread evenly. Brandan took another sip, reaching for his marbled caviar spoon. The day had been busy, far busier than he would have preferred. But at least now it was over. The nocturnal hours had begun, and he could drink, eat, purge, and begin again. In about an hour, a few of his hand-picked companions would
~~~

arrive. Ultimately, he would choose one to share his bed for the evening. "Everything is as it should be," he thought. A soft rapping on the door disrupted his leisure. "You are early. I am just having a snack before heading to my natatio." Brandan's words were tinged with a level of frustration that was hard to ignore. His open-air swimming pool, his natatio, was among the most luxurious in the world. He had spent nearly all the city's coffers on its design and construction years ago. No one but him ever used the monstrosity until Victus made him open it to the public a few weeks a month. It was the city's money, and they deserved to enjoy it. In an effort to recoup the monetary loss incurred by the structure, Victus held a series of water games. The plan introduced and anchored floating platforms that would be positioned on the surface of the water. The contestants would engage in a form of Bedlam Ball, based on the popular Asmadine city game. Each team would battle for the leather ball in the middle, attempting to accumulate a point by making it to the foe's goal. It was merciless, and cheating was permitted. Victus' inaugural tournament garnered more revenue than all the other cities' events combined for the calendar year.

The knocking came again. Brandan wrapped his robe tight around his exposed body. "What is it? Just come in!" When the door opened, he saw his house colors on chainmail armor. "What do you need? I am having my time. My time! MY TIME! And I am not to be interrupted." His voice was infuriated, sounding more like a mewling child.

"Of course. Yes… Of course. Apologies, your lordship." He was bowing repeatedly in deference.

Brandan's eyes rolled, tipping his head back to drink his wine. "Well?"

The guard moved towards him and gave him a small parchment. Brandan snatched it aggressively and read. "Ah… I see they are marching to leave the city. Good, the elves will kill them—" He stopped to shape his words in order to adhere to the accepted protocol. "No, I mean… they will be arrested in the woods and tried for treason. Then executed.

We do not want any of the populace intervening or stirring up my father's work in unraveling the cult."

The guard bowed. "Of course, sir. Is there anything I need to do or you would like me to pass on?"

Brandan looked back at the parchment, sighed, and said, "Umm… no. Not directly. Please continue to have them followed once they leave the city. Send only one to track them out of the city. Have them confirm exactly what happens when the elves attempt to arrest them. But the follower is not to interfere. Observe and report only. Now leave me. Please ensure that my guests are escorted to the pool instead of the parlor, where they can feel the refreshing cool of the water." He turned and poured another glass of wine as the guard bowed and left him.

~~~

Calder sat in the barracks, the dim light of the lanterns barely illuminating his surroundings. He waited until he heard the last drunken cries of the night, making sure the city taverns had closed, before he made his move. His order from Victus was simply to get the small, magically sealed crate. It was in Victus's house underneath his bed. Calder believed all of Victus's evidence of the cult activities was inside. And from what he saw today within the city, something much bigger was going on.

When he looked out from the door entryway, all he could see was the eerie emptiness of the abandoned garrison encampment. Exhaling a sigh of relief, he stepped out of the barracks through the side door, feeling the cool night air on his skin. He paused, deep in thought. The lack of sentries was completely absurd. Normally, even this late at night, guards would be at their posts and walking the perimeter of the parade yard and barracks. He noticed a purplish-black glow coming from every sentry tower in the city. "What is that?" he said aloud, speaking to himself. Tilting his ear to focus more, he heard a symphony of hammers striking and the clatter of construction.
~~~

"At night? Under the cover of darkness. This…" His heart beat faster as the realization seemed to move from his heart to his lips. "This is an infiltration!"

Calder, cloaked, walked silently out of the vacant tents and barracks, the sound of his boots barely audible. His mission changed slightly, as he felt like an outsider in his own city. As he made his way to Victus' house, he used the darkness to hide his approach. Inwardly, he hoped his men would make it to Victus safely, but he would have no way of knowing if they were successful. He used the stables, where he had spoken to Aris earlier that day, as his last cover point before moving to enter the house. His eyes scanned the roof and sides of the building. Not seeing anyone, he moved gingerly over to the front door.

Once in the house, he made his way to Victus' room. Searching under the bed, he found the small crate. He stuffed the box into a small satchel and headed for the door. He noted the towers again as he moved back toward the main street. The glow was brighter and yet somehow darker. They pulsed but did not flicker like a flame. Perhaps the high elves are using some sort of magical lanterns. But if the high elves were hiding things from the humans, it would be nothing new. "What if it is not high elves? What if it is *dark* elves?" He whispered the thoughts to himself as he stayed in the shadows.

Continuing, he retraced some of his movements down the quiet streets. All the main gates to the city would have their portcullis down by now, so his plan was to use one stair to an archer's walkway and climb down the other side. He paused near enough to see, but not close enough for the elves walking the walls to see him. Calder could hear them talking but could not make out the words. Though it sounded like Elvish, it did not sound like any Elvish he had heard before. The elven guards continued to walk along the wall towards one of the smaller towers, and once they went inside, Calder began his sprint as fast as he could up the stairs. He made it to the archer's walkway and unraveled the rope in his satchel, tying it off onto a part of the wall. He hopped up and over and began to lower himself down. Pushing off the wall and sliding a little at a time, he used his grip to slow his descent. As soon as his feet touched the ground, he tugged three times and then two. The rope untied itself and fell down in a small coil at his feet. Grabbing up his rope, he moved to the woods and in the direction of Asmadine. His pace was quick and his determination unwavering. He knew that he had to present the evidence to Skylighter so that he could convince the council of paladins to bring the Inquisition of Asmolor with Skylighter's knights against whatever vileness had taken root in the city of Lindly. Calder understood that Victus would not even attempt to bring in the Inquisition unless he had irrefutable evidence to bear. So he kept pace, relaxing only slightly when he was out of sight of the city walls.

~~~

Biddy had summoned a few fire imps, to Victus' displeasure, to help cook. Biddy was not accustomed to living in the woods. Though in Biddy's mind, he believed he was really roughing it, especially considering he was only using a little bit of magic to help. His silly, high-pitched voice chirped, "Okay, so I am roasting… hehehe, or my little friends here are roasting some nice boar. And I have wine ready—"

Victus cut him off, "No wine. Water only. We will remain sober."

Biddy nodded and continued, "I have pastries in the stone oven. And some nice toasted buttered bread."

The small fire pit had turned into more of a small kitchen. Once the food was prepared, the waiters, or rather imps, ran the food over to each person and then disappeared. Aris was watching all of this in awe. Never in his life had he seen someone using magic so easily. Never had he seen someone like this little gnome. From Aris's understanding, magic was useful, but it was to be used as a tool, not as an escape from the hardships of life. It was to be treasured and saved for moments when you needed to call upon it—not squandered
~~~

on petty things. But Biddy did not seem overcome with exhaustion. He did not even break a sweat. It was curious to Aris, and he wanted to ask; however, the moan of his belly got the better of him, and he devoured the food instead of finding words to ask his questions.

Finally, after the hungry men had finished their food, Biddy brought them each an icing pastry. At first, Aris believed it to be a cupcake and then realized it was actually a miniature cake. But Aris accepted it gleefully. “Where were you cooking these?” Aris asked, somewhat confused.

“They, my dear boy, were in the oven. Hehehe.”

Aris turned to his father, who answered Aris's unasked question. “Biddy is using dimensional doors that we cannot see. He is able to have and do multiple things in these little pockets of time outside of our vision. They are there, but we cannot perceive them as we are not as in-tuned to magic.”

Biddy nodded, laughing. “Many projects. Many plans. Many contingencies. Heeheehehe.”

Aris was stuffing the cake in his mouth, muffling the words to them all. “So... so how come everything you do with magic has fire?” Coughing, he continued, “What I mean is, Master Mage Biddy, sir, is there are tons of magical schools and veins to study. But you seem to be obsessed... err—focusing on fire.”

Biddy grinned wickedly and waddled over to Aris, his stubby finger pointed in his face. Aris leaned back and away from the wiggling finger. Biddy burst into another giggle and then placed his hands on his hips. “I have studied at many schools of magic. I have been kicked out of three schools of wizardry and sorcery.”

Aris interrupted him with a laugh of his own, “Not very good if you get kicked out.”

Biddy paused, taking in the boy’s words, and then laughed again. “From their perspective, I guess I wasn’t. Hehehe! And I may have blown up a few too many things. Hehehe!

Nevertheless, Aris, fire is the only magic that has spoken to me. The flames talk to me, and I talk to them. They are beautiful. They are living creatures, flames. They need air to breathe, food to eat, and space to grow." Biddy's eyes were wide, and he talked faster in his excitement. "We gnomes are an industrial people. Many of us die young because our tinkering and inquisitiveness get the better of us. But I have survived many failed experiments. Riding the goblin rocket was one such thing. I am digressing, excuse me. Anyway, I love fire because it is so useful. For example, many of the machines we have been working on start with combustion. Which is?" Biddy looked expectantly at Aris.

Aris was getting more of an answer than he really cared for. "Fire."

Biddy clapped excitedly. "Yes! I have been working—" He stopped and looked around the camp. As if he were making sure no one could hear him, even though it was just the three of them, his voice dropped to an excited whisper. "I have been building a mechanical suit that can harness broken bodies. That is to say, a body that is beyond healing. And all of this is because of *fire.*"

Aris looked at the gnome incredulously. "A suit that keeps your body alive even after death?"

Biddy inclined his head. "Well, yes, that is the plan, at least. But for now, I have created successful body parts or limbs mechanically infused with magic to function and operate mostly as a lost appendage. Still testing it, though. I could give you a sample if you need a replacement leg or arm. Maybe just a finger?" Biddy turned to Victus. "What say you, half-pal? Can I take a leg or two for science?"

Victus smiled and then chuckled. "I think he will use the ones he has. Give him some mechanized appendage, and he might become some type of god." They all laughed together, and Aris was relieved to realize that the gnome was joking.

Victus stood and stretched. "Best time we lay down and rest. Another day of riding tomorrow."

Aris thanked the gnome for dinner and went to the tent to find his small bed. Victus did likewise. Biddy excitedly said, “I will take the first watch. I have contingencies to work on anyway.”

Victus called from inside the tent, “Biddy, you always take the first watch, but you do know that is the easiest watch to take?”

Biddy snorted. “Hehehe, yes! But I do not require as much sleep. So it is best that you two rest up first.”

As father and son lay in their respective beds, talking low but comfortably, the sound of Biddy ‘working’ was a tad loud to fall asleep to easily.

“Da... he is a goofy one.”

Smiling in the darkness, Victus said, “He is. But he is a truer friend than most. Good in a fight, and I can ask him for anything. Not to mention, he is the one who enchanted the armor I crafted for you.”

Aris looked and felt his armor on his body, as his father suggested. “What do you mean, enchanted?”

Victus rolled over towards him. “It grows with you. You will never need to have it resized or mended.”

Aris grinned wildly in the darkness. “That is amazing.” The young squire beamed.

Victus continued with satisfaction, “I am sure between Biddy and Thorm they did quite a lot to that armor. But only time will tell.” The way Victus said that to Aris had him crawling out of his skin with excitement. He wanted nothing more than to run back out of the tent and ask Biddy. But his father’s voice brought him back to where he was. “You can talk to Biddy tomorrow. And you will meet Thorm in Delwan. Now let’s pray together and get some sleep.”

They both began to recite their holy prayer to Kali. “We serve the light. We are the protectors of the innocent. Bring favor and peace upon us, Kali. May we be instruments of destruction to our enemies and beacons of hope to those who despair. Amen.” They concluded, and Aris rose from his bed. Victus sat up and watched him as he walked over, leaned down, reached over his shoulders, and embraced his father. “Sleep well, Da. I love you.”

His father held him tightly and said, “You too, my boy.”

7

The horse whinnied in pain and let out a scream that chilled Jess's bones. She knew, though her sight was limited by the darkness, that her enemy had just slaughtered her horse. Her breath had nearly returned, and she stood up, hastily pulling on the strap to adjust her shield. It whipped around to her left arm, in place and ready. She drew her sword and slammed it into her shield.

"Come and get me, you bastard cowards! I am the light Kalisdel!" she yelled.

The shout was met with laughter from the unseen horde surrounding her. The sound of the voices gave her an estimate of how many enemies she faced. Jess used the tree as a buffer to guard her back but knew this would not hold for long. Her mind raced as she fumbled through a prayer of aid and protection. She had no option but to use a knight's flare, a magnificent invention from the dwarves and gnomes. She thanked Kalisdel that she had one. It was built into the shields of officers, knights, and nobles and was even known to be crafted into certain weapons. It would shoot high above and illuminate an area, revealing hidden or shadowed units. But it also shot into the sky a signal that a unit was under attack. If any legionaries saw the flare, duty compelled them to investigate and send aid. Her heart pounded as she reached her sword arm behind the shield. Her hands were shaking, knowing she had seconds before her unknown enemy would attack. She unscrewed the tube and pulled the leather string hard. A brilliant gold light sprang forth and upward to the sky above the trees.

Her enemy, who was mere steps from her, daggers poised to strike, fell back, blinded. *Dark elves*, she concluded, while some even dropped to the ground to hide their eyes. Their night vision was sensitive to light, and the brilliance of the knight's flare was too much for them to endure.

Enraged when they regained their composure and sight, they all charged in, attacking Jess like rabid beasts, with all cohesion appearing to be gone. She planted her shield firmly into the face of the first dark elf on her left. The sudden movement cracked his nose and knocked him out cold. She began a countdown of sorts in her head, recalling her training with Victus. *"Dark elves attack in patterns. The first will come from the left or right flank. Then two opposite the first attack. The next will be directed to your center, either from above or behind. They want you unsteady and panicked. Keep your footing. Focus and stay disciplined. Do not chase the kill."*

Two more arrived on her right side, her gladius clanking against their synced thrust and pushing them back with a swing from her shield. She put her feet back into her defensive posture and re-centered herself against the tree. A shrieking female elf ran toward Jess head-on, her spear poised to skewer the knight. Jess knew that the metal-tipped point of a dark elf's spear would be poisoned, pulsating with venom. The spear aimed at Jess's chest spun back and away as the elf ducked low and twisted. Jess groaned as it nicked her calf. Her shield dropped too late to stop the cut. Anger welled up within her as she saw the dark elf grinning darkly. Both women knew that it was only a matter of time before the poison moved through her veins and she, like her horse, would be dead. Jess watched as the elves backed off, egging her to move forward and fight. They taunted her, calling her pathetic and weak.

"Sleep now, little knight!"

Laughing, another added, "Quite feeble, human."

Jess could feel the poison now; its effects were slowing everything around her. She held her shield up as high as she could, though she knew it was too low. In an instant, amid laughter, one of the elves charged in, striking toward her neck. Another went for the opposite side, but low. She barely blocked the first with her shield. Simultaneously, she swung her sword down, blocking the other attack. Her arms were becoming heavy, and she could feel the poison clouding her mind. Jess stumbled forward from the tree, briefly losing her footing. She used the tree to help hold herself up as she continued to defensively fend off the attacks. The dark elves were getting irritated that she had not collapsed. Their style of fighting was mostly based on quick, debilitating engagements. They preferred to strike without even being noticed, or at the very least, to be the last thing someone saw before they died. But this knight, this beautiful woman with the scarred face, was holding them off, and the female dark elf had had enough. She spun her staff high over her head, then around her back, and back in place to charge. She charged and yelled, "Durikl Fa!" One of the others ran and knelt so that the female could use his hands to spring high into the air, still fending off the prods with her shield and sword. Jess was vulnerable to the spear from above and let out a growl of frustration. She was enraged—not because she was about to die, but because she felt as if she had failed Victus. She screamed, "VICTUS!"

A single horn blew loudly, the sound reverberating through the forest nearby. The female elf flying through the air glanced left toward the concussive sound, her face scrunched in confusion as a pilum pierced through her chest. Swiping her from the air like a fly from someone's face, she fell impaled and, in seconds, lay dead on the ground.

More horns blew, or rather, Jess thought she heard more as she faded to darkness; the poison causing her to crash down to the earth. Her eyes were fuzzy and unable to see or even perceive what was happening. The dirt she was lying on felt moist from the cool midnight air. She closed her eyes, accepting death.

~~~

Biddy walked into the tent. His night watch was over, and his body urged him to rest. Swaying as he stumbled over towards Aris, he chuckled to himself, seeing the young man laying on his stomach, rump high in the air. Looking for the young man's face, Biddy thought the lad may have used dimensional magic; his face was nowhere to be found. Getting closer, he noted that the boy's head was buried nose-first into the pillow, which swallowed his head whole, snorting quietly. He whispered to the young lad, "Aris… Aris... it's time for your watch."

Slowly, the head unburied itself and looked over. Aris's hair was a mess, and the prints from the pillow were embedded into his face. "Already?" he croaked.

Biddy smiled, his eyes slack and weary. "Yes... Yes. It is time for me to sleep."

Aris rolled over, sliding down from the bed. He walked over and strapped on his sword belt and his little medicus kit. Crouching, he reached for his boots and put them on as well. Yawning and stretching his arms wide, he heard a thud. It sounded like someone had tossed a bag of potatoes to the floor next to his bed. Startled, he twisted quickly to see Biddy on the floor. From Aris's estimation, the gnome had flopped down onto the bed, and the pillow had sprung him off and down onto the floor. Aris snickered and shook his head, bending low to pick Biddy up. Gingerly wrapping the gnome in his arms, he placed him on the bed. Leaning down, he thought he heard Biddy whispering, but it was little snores sounding curiously like "con-tin-gen-cy." Rubbing his eyes, he smiled and left the tent. He glanced back through the tent's flaps to see both his father and Biddy sound asleep.

The first hour of Aris' watch, he just tried to keep himself awake as he marched in a circle around the camp. In the second hour, he practiced rolling forward and backward in
~~~

his new armor. Eventually, he felt that his body had become accustomed to the movements and weight. He pulled out his dagger and gladius, rolling with them. He began to test it with both weapons sheathed and then again unsheathed. Aris could feel, from his feet to his hands, an energy—something he knew his father called "Knights Harmonization." It was when your feet, hands, head, and body moved so fluidly that your movements were not even being registered. You tapped into the physical and mental clarity that made you an instrument of destruction or protection.

He began running and bouncing off trees, pretending he was engaged in a fight for his life. Sweat pooled on his face, but he kept his dagger and sword dancing in the moonlight: up, down, slash, spin, duck. Constantly imagining that after he vanquished one imaginary foe, another sprang up behind him, and then another from above. Not having a shield, he needed to be nimble and quick. He knew his first job as a squire was to protect his lord. If he was to be in the fray, it would be behind a shield wall, and he would be guarding flanks or scouting. His training was focused and tailored to that of all squires—melee combat, fast and effective. Speed, strike, regroup.

Aris continued well past the second hour, persisting in his training. He took a break as the third hour neared, sitting by the small fire and drinking water. Panting, he noticed his father's outline by the tent.

"How goes the watch?" Victus asked as he moved toward his son. He had been watching Aris over the last hour and was impressed and proud of his son's willingness to always be better, to train like he trained. A better son a man could not have asked for.

Aris smiled. "The watch was quiet, sir."

"Good." Reaching the fire, Victus crossed his legs and sat down. "Aris, I noticed something when you were training." The boy's eyes widened as his face flushed in the firelight. He had been unaware that his father had been watching him.

"It's nothing major, but something you need to note. When you are pressing your attack, especially if you are not using a shield to absorb assaults, you need to pull your arms back faster. Do not let them linger away from your body too long. The enemy could use that to their advantage, and you will lose a limb. Quick, decisive strikes. Think of it like this: if you are fighting with only your fists." His father rose and put his fists up towards his face to show Aris as he spoke. He punched in the air once and then twice from his other side, arms extending and retreating back to their defensive positions around his face. Aris could not believe how fast his father could move. It was inspiring. "See what I mean? Your extension will work fine against most single targets. But when you are fighting multiple opponents, you have to expect the enemy's allies to capitalize and move against you while you're moving against them."

Aris nodded, got up, and passed behind his father. He saw the scars from whipping on his back from long ago. Aris had heard rumors about what happened, but never from his father's own mouth. He had wanted to ask his father many times about them, but he had never done so. He resolved that he was going to ask him after he practiced what his father had shown him. His father stepped to face him and motioned as he spoke, "Try to hit me." Aris did not even hesitate; he just let his fists fly out towards his father's stomach and then his jaw. His father blocked both and slapped down hard on the arm that went for his jaw. "You are overextending. If you can't reach your opponent's head, pick another part." Aris nodded and tried again. This time, though, he went for the side of his father's stomach, punching as hard as he could. His arm was caught by his father, but Aris reversed his arm backwards and spun from his father's grasp. He was now behind his father. Hitting him twice in each kidney, Aris then attempted to get some distance by flipping backwards into a cartwheel. However, his father had already twisted his torso and kicked the squire square in the chest, knocking him into the dirt.

Aris coughed and heard his father’s voice, “Being too clever can get you killed.” His father’s arm reached down and lifted him up to his feet easily. “You had the advantage when you rolled out of my block but lost it when you began your counterattack. What should you have done instead?”

Aris grimaced, frustrated. “I should have disabled your ability to move. By taking out a leg or both, I could have claimed the fight.”

Victus smiled approvingly. “I know that you are athletic and love to be clever and creative, but in an actual fight, when your friends and comrades need help, they don’t care how fancy you look killing the enemy. All that matters is keeping your men and women alive and dispatching the enemy as quickly as possible. A battle can change in seconds, and you, as a squire now, can be integral to the outcome of a battle.” Aris's frustration passed away as he heard his father’s words. Victus stepped back to the fire and sat down.

“Da?” Aris slid down next to his father.

“What is it?” the half-pal asked.

Taking a deep breath, Aris first thanked his father for the advice. Then he asked, “Can you tell me how you got the scars on your back? I am a squire now, even if I am not of age. I can know now, right?”

Victus looked into his son’s eyes, gave a brief nod, then placed his elbows on his knees and leaned his head onto them, staring into the fire as he spoke. “I had been recently knighted into Arch Skylighter’s GST—the gryphon shock troopers, that is. We were on leave in Asmadine, enjoying the city before our one-year tour. A few of my buddies and I were at the market. In the center of the market, a few of the religious zealots with their heads shaved and golden chains wrapped around their sackcloth tunics were shouting about Asmolor’s justice. As we listened to the rantings of how all were sullied and fallen from his grace, we noticed that his sermon was more of a justification for their own corruption and intentions. The leader had brought out a sickly older woman and thrown her onto a stockade platform. He began explaining how this woman was a thief and had not been paying her tithe to the clergy. She was caught with no money for the temple, and the zealots assumed she had stolen all the goods she had on her, which she did." He turned to his son briefly, his eyes connecting with the young squire's. "She was a thief, but not in the conventional, steal-to-better-myself type of way. When I saw the zealots ripping off her clothes, Sempronius, I and a few others intervened. We confronted the zealots, and I asked her, as I covered her naked body with my cloak, 'What is it you have done?' She explained to me she was stealing to feed her family; that her son and daughter-in-law had been killed serving in the fifth legion and that they had not been paid the honorary tribute for the loss. I then turned to the zealots and asked them, 'Is it not a greater crime to not feed the families of our fallen soldiers? While you preach and persecute the weak, our enemy kills actual soldiers. How dare you desecrate this woman for trying to provide for her family!' The only response the zealots gave was, *'Law is the law. We serve Asmolor's will.'* I tried to reason with the fools, but to no avail. So I asked my brethren to escort and see to the elderly woman. Then I offered my own back for the punishment."

Aris was mesmerized as he listened and tried to imagine it all in his head. "You took the injustice and upheld the purity of our code. Not just our knight's code, but our personal code. Loyalty above all else, save for honor. You defied them. The zealots of Asmolor?"

Victus tossed a log onto the fire. "I did defy the zealots. And I would defy the gods themselves if they stood against righteousness and justice."

Aris winced and looked around quickly. "Da, you cannot say that."

Victus smiled and patted him, continuing, "If anyone, no matter who, asks you to dishonor yourself or those around you, then they are not worthy of your loyalty."

Aris began to anxiously chew on his thumb as he continued to listen. "This is why you will never see me praying to any god but Kalisdel. She is an outcast from Asmolor's court, and she serves those created, not the other way around. The House Andreas creed is 'Loyalty above all else, save honor.' We hold true to that. Our honor is found in doing what is right, doing what is good, upholding truth."

Aris thought he understood what his father was saying. It was not that he was suggesting actively rebelling against the gods; he was saying that standing up and doing what was right was more important. He had stood against those who used the name of the gods as an excuse to impose their own will. A few minutes passed in silence, father and son enjoying the fire. Aris looked over at his father and asked another question. "Da, would it be possible for me to become both knight and mage? To use magic as a knight, I mean."

His father grinned. "Of course it is. But you would have to wait until you complete your training as a knight first. Then from there, you could spend some time training in Asmadine in one of the schools of magic."

Aris raised his voice slightly in his excitement. "Well, really, I want to be a paladin and then become a mage."

Victus chuckled. "If anyone can do it, I believe you could do both."

Aris imagined himself wearing half-plate armor and casting magic as he fought. He noticed his father beginning to meditate, his breath becoming slow and deliberate. His legs were again folded across himself as he rose inches from the ground. Eyes still closed, he rose another foot, and the surrounding rocks began to float, orbiting around Aris and his father. Aris was dumbfounded. "Da, what are you doing?" His face sprawled with a stupid grin. "Da, are you doing this?"

Victus said nothing but lowered himself back down and turned to his son. "Psionics. Mind magic. The only real magic I have studied. More of a hobby, but something I have always been fascinated with. As I said, you can become whatever you wish."

The young man just sat, amazed that this had been by far the best year of his life. Serin and he had a blossoming relationship that was bordering on courtship. He had surpassed all of his training and was given his squire-ship early. His father had given him his first personalized armor and weapons. Most of all, his father was looking more and more to him like a brother-in-arms and less like just his son. He was treating him as a friend, soldier, and son. Beaming with pride, he asked if he could head back to bed. Victus smiled, "Go on and rest; I will finish out your watch and start mine."

Aris, glad to be able to head back to sleep, went in and lay on his father's bed. Sleep snuck up on him before he even knew that it had come.

Victus meditated for most of the time he was on watch. The air was cooling, and he could feel the morning moisture creeping in. When he knew the sun would be up soon, he decided to get breakfast started for everyone. Placing a good portion of wood on the fire, he waited for the temperature to peak before he would start cooking. In the distance, a few miles back, high in the sky, he saw, in disbelief, a knight's flare. It sprung up and forth to the top of the trees, visible but not completely. Enough of the emblem showed that Victus was able to recognize it as one of his own officers. He moved to the tent, grabbed his chain shirt, shield, longsword, and two pilums.

His voice was measured and firmly snapped the two awake. "Legionaries are under attack. Let's go."

Biddy hopped out of bed, wide awake. Pulling a tincture from his pouch, he tossed it to Victus and the slower-waking Aris. "Refreshes the body; drink it," his voice squeaked as he drank one himself. Without hesitation, Victus drank and felt the effects immediately. He felt in peak physical condition. Aris, seeing his father drink, gulped his down.

“WOW!” Aris said as he felt his body awaken and refresh itself, cleansing all tiredness and soreness away. The gnome and Victus moved from the tent.

“Biddy, I need a knight’s threshold opened.” This was a way for the legions to move troops rapidly. A knight’s threshold created a dimensional portal near or on top of the location a flare had been released.

Biddy nodded fervently. “Yes… Yes… working on it.”

Aris ran out of the tent straight to his father. Looking past him in the distance, he saw the sigil flare. Keeping his comments to himself, he couldn’t believe he was seeing a real one being used.

“Biddy, we are losing time. I need the threshold now.”

The gnome was running around frantically, placing stones and drawing in the sand, muttering to himself, “Contingency!”

Victus looked down at his son, more serious than Aris had ever seen. “This is not training. We are going to the aid of our knights. Keep calm and follow my lead.”

Aris could feel his adrenaline flowing, and he was nervous. He was scared. Biddy was casting with his tiny hands, flashing as he waved them over and over in circles. “Nearly there,” he cried. Aris pulled out his sword, and Victus handed him a pilum. Though Aris had trained with javelins, he was not quite strong enough to do any actual damage, but he was determined to do his best.

“After I throw the first, pass me the second,” Victus said. Aris was relieved that he did not have to throw it and nodded, “Yes, sir.”

The knight’s threshold could be seen now. It was a rather large circular doorway or arch. The color resembled the surroundings as it was translucent, but a clear golden line defined the outline. “The threshold is ready, Commander Victus.” The gnome’s voice sounded less like a silly creature and more like that of a trained and battle-tested mage-legionnaire. “It will hold for as long as you require. And if anyone gets through, I will have a contingency for them here! Hehehe!”

Victus smiled at him in thanks before peering in and seeing dark elves attacking a lone knight. Not just any knight; it was Jess. “Biddy, have it drop us here.” The mage was already adjusting the position, making certain they would step out where Victus requested.

“Good to go! Go! Go! Go!” Biddy yelled. Victus stepped through, his arm already cocking the javelin. With his other hand, he pulled up a small horn from his belt. He blew it hard, and it boomed, sounding like thunder. He released the pilum as soon as he was through the threshold. It soared right into the female dark elf’s chest. Aris followed his father and glanced back to see Biddy summoning something made of fire while laughing maniacally and pulling down his goggles. The squire turned back just in time to see the exceptional throw from his father. The dead female elf was impaled into the dirt. Aris passed the other pilum to his father when Victus reached over for it. Aris's hands were trembling as he reached down and pulled out his dagger to accompany his sword. He moved himself closer to his father, standing opposite Victus's shield arm. “I am with you, Commander,” he said confidently.

8

Calder was determined and on his way, thinking that he had secured his escape. He ran hard for a man of his age. He was resolute in reaching Skylighter and alerting him to all that had transpired. Delivering the evidence box to him would almost certainly result in the dispatch of the Inquisition to root out any malevolence that had established itself in Lindly.

After all, this was not just his post; it was his home. It was where he met his wife and raised his children. Everything he treasured—duty and family—was at stake, and his mission was paramount.

Taking care to follow the road to Asmadine in the shadows, he noted when he could have taken the road in the opposite direction towards Victus in Delwan. He thought of Titus and his men, wishing them again the luck to achieve their goal.

After a few miles closer to Asmadine, he felt a presence. Someone was trailing him. He continued for yet another mile and then found himself surrounded by what he believed were high elven knights from Asmadine.

Spears appeared from behind the trees and pressed Calder into the center of a small circle. “Halt, citizen,” said the high elf commander.

Smirking with a sigh, Calder put his hands up. “As if I’ve got anywhere to go.”

The high elf looked him over and nodded. “It is him.” A few of the guards pulled up their spears and approached with shackles.

As the high elf spoke to Calder, his head swiveled casually around in search of a way out.

“You are citizen Calder. The Steward of Lindly discharged you earlier this day, and you are now under arrest for the crimes of subterfuge against the town of Lindly, willingly aiding and taking part in heinous cult activities. This includes the charges of indecency, murder, and sacrilege.”

Calder laughed at him, the mocking tone carrying out like a whirlwind among the elves. “Charging me with all that? All lies! No one is going to believe you. What’s your name, elfling?”

The high elf, disgusted, spat out his words, “I am Lieutenant Commander Ilunar.”

Calder’s arms were held out as they shackled them together. “Well, listen here, Loony-lanar. None of what you are doing is orthodox. The dismissal, this arrest. What are you playing at?”

Ilunar condescendingly retorted, “It is not for you, a mere human, to dictate to us, the high elves. We are the firstborn of the gods. We alone know the will of Asmolor, and this is sanctioned under the watchful eye of Elivindel.” The high elves frequently employed this strategy when communicating with other races. Their patron deity, Elivindel, served as a reminder that they were the original offspring of Asmolor—his beloved elder children.

Calder spat, “Asmolor’s firstborn. Aye, you are. But between those pointy ears, you ain’t got a lick of sense–” Before he could continue, one guard searching his body punched him in the stomach. He let out a large gasp, buckling down with his hands on his knees.

All surrounding him laughed as their lieutenant spoke. “Did you find anything on him?” The elf who punched Calder removed a dagger and Victus' box. “Just this, sir. Is this what the inquisitor was looking for?”

Ilunar reached for the box, and upon looking it over, he could see it was magically locked. "It is. But more importantly, we need this man. The priestess has something special for him. An opportunity." His eyes trailed from the box to the man. "Gag him and let us make our way back to the city."

Ilunar motioned for one of the guards to come over. "Send word to our priestess and Nibarn. We have Victus' man and the box." The guard saluted, spinning away from his commander and jogging ahead of the now-marching elves. The elven knights surrounded Calder and kept him centered in their ranks, prodding him when he dawdled, regulating his pace with theirs.

~~~

Marcella was singing as she strummed her harp. Her fellow legionnaires had always appreciated her music while marching, and right now, it was particularly encouraging. Having formerly been dismissed by the city of Lindly's stewards, they had remained loyal to Victus. Every lyric Marcella uttered reinvigorated the men and reminded them of their duty to the light. She was a legionnaire, but her heart lay in magic. Her proficiency in music enhanced her practice of magic. Some called her the bard of Victus, but to herself, she was just a soldier doing her best. If inspiration, healing, or combat were required, she would be there for her men. She watched the soldiers surrounding her with proud satisfaction. They had refused to be dismissed, believing that it was not right and that something terrible was coming to Lindly, or that something was already there, moving in the shadows.

Titus had been told that he was to take charge of the unit and lead them as if he were Calder. Thus far, it had been going relatively smoothly. Night had crept upon them, and they maintained the march. Calder's orders were for Titus and the rest of the legionnaires to seek out Victus and explain what had transpired earlier in the day. Titus had led the soldiers from the city's main gate onto the main road toward
~~~

Asmadine, and they had branched off in the direction of Delwan, the destination of their commander, Victus.

Titus spoke back toward the men and women, "We will not be making camp. Stay alert; we will cut through the woods. Hopefully, we will reach Victus's camp by morning, if not sooner."

All responded with quiet nods of acknowledgment. Marcella's melodic voice softly sang, "Knights of light. We never waver. We move as one, holding our haggard heads high." She had not stopped her singing even when Titus spoke back to them; she simply lowered her beautiful voice and allowed her magic to speak through Titus, ensuring steady and ready hearts. Some of the other legionnaires hummed along with her, while others silently scanned the woods for enemies.

Dark elves, who had been following the Lindly legionnaires, were now poised to strike. They were given instructions similar to those who had apprehended Calder: capture and arrest under the guise of being high elves. If they resist, kill them all. Before the leading elf could signal the ambush, a flare flew into the night sky a few miles from where the legionnaires were marching. The commander held up a hand to the poised and ready elves. The predators' eyes gleamed with anticipation as they waited for the perfect moment to attack the humans. The soldiers stopped in their tracks, their attention drawn to their commander's hand raised in the air and the direction of his gaze.

The elves all knew the telltale signs of a knight's flare—it meant that any lumbering Asmolorian soldier nearby would come to it, which would decrease their odds of success. The commander motioned with his hands to break off the attack and to fall back. Vexed and annoyed, they turned from their prey and headed back to the city of Lindly, not wishing to run into any *actual* high elves who would inevitably see through the subterfuge and possibly unravel their goddess Lestar's plans.

The soldier spy who had been tracking the elves as they tracked the legionnaires, as per Brandon’s and, more crucially, Nibarn’s instructions, kept an eye on the elves as they retreated. After considering his options, he concluded that he would be more secure and at ease by withdrawing with the elves. So he also turned away, preparing his explanation for Brandon and then, of course, for Brandon’s father.

Marcella noticed the flare first, her harp striking the wrong chord as she gasped aloud, “Knight's Flare! Our legions’ mark! It’s Victus' emblem!”

Everyone halted for the briefest of moments, looking up. Titus spoke loudly and assuredly to his men. “We have found our quarry, and they need us. If this is not Victus, it is still our people. Double time.”

Not having a powerful enough mage or cleric, the ‘knight’s threshold’ was unavailable to them. Though they were given a boost to their stamina and speed by Marcella, who was no longer singing. She was muttering and playing her harp, imbuing them all with whatever benefits she could offer.

~~~

Nibarn leaned over his veranda balcony, watching the work on the towers. He was accompanied by the impostor dark elf priestess, posing as a member of the noble high elf house of Elivi. They were drinking fae wine, both marveling at the successful unfolding of Lestar’s plan. Nibarn had not felt this healthy and whole in a long time. Serving Lestar’s will was rewarded with the little orbs of ‘power’ from the priestess, and things were progressing far better than he had imagined. Only an hour ago, a scout had returned, informing them both that Calder was arrested and the small crate with evidence against the cultists had been recovered. Nibarn had been pondering why his deity had not just killed those who stood in her way but reasoned that she thrived on chaos and deception. She wanted to watch the humans betray one another, wanted to watch them turn on their holy guardians
~~~

and then be consumed. Turning from the tower work and looking lecherously towards the priestess, Nibarn noted that her eyes were fixed in the distance, watching the towers, and the small seductive grin on her face.

“More wine?” Nibarn slurred slightly as he finished pouring into his own glass.

She did not turn her eyes from the towers. “No. It is not time to celebrate. This has only just begun.” Her voice longingly pressed for the storm of war—for all of her god’s wrath to be poured down upon Lindly.

Nibarn poured his glass and another, downing the latter in one big swig. Mockingly muttering, “One for me…now two for me. You dark elves need to live a little.”

The priestess’s head snapped back to the man. “What did you say?”

Nibarn’s mouth clenched shut, and his lips went limp in a frown. “Oh…nothing. Nearly spilled the wine. So how does the next phase of our matron’s plan unfold again? I want to be certain that I am prepared for no mistakes.” He bowed low, thinking to himself he was very pious.

She looked at his pathetic intoxicated state and shook her head in disgust. “You’re spilling wine.”

In his attempt to show her his veneration, the wineglass had tipped over, pooling onto the mosaic-tiled floor. “Apologies, mistress.” He straightened as he moved himself back to the balcony and steadied himself against the beam.

The disguised elf was staring again at the purple lights in the towers. Nibarn was spellbound by her, much like a moth drawn to a flame. Sublimely, she spoke, her voice barely above a whisper. “The evidence captured from Victus' man, Calder, will be altered by one of our mages, thus giving proof that Victus and all loyal to him have been the treacherous cultists. Calder will be given the choice to testify against his commander for clemency. If he accepts, his family and he will be rewarded. If not, well, you know what we will do to him. What we will do to his family." Her neck twisted briefly, and he could see the depraved smile on her face. "We will put Victus on trial for all the town to see. It will be mandatory for residents of Lindly to attend. When they, the mob of useful fools, demand justice be meted out against Victus and his men, we will begin the release of Lestar's vengeance."

Nibarn stopped her there, asking, "And what exactly is this vengeance? I imagine it has to do with the crystals brought to the towers?"

The priestess laughed. "Oh, it does, and it will be the most beautiful raking of souls ever. The crystals, when unleashed, will release a noxious gas into the city, chasing after any and all life. It will envelop all that it contacts, tearing their souls from their bodies into Eu'rok's bosom. Not one man, woman, or child will be able to escape. Once the souls of everyone are siphoned, the bodies will remain husks, with no will of their own. The madness created from a soulless body will make them all easily manipulated by Lestar. She will have them all tear down everything in this town, razing it and, in turn, having them kill each other."

Nibarn swallowed hard on his next sip of wine. "What of your soldiers? What of those loyal to Lestar? Do we become consumed?" His first thoughts were for his own safety, not even considering the personal devastation he was helping facilitate on the innocents.

The mistress of Lestar sardonically smiled as she saw the fear in the man's eyes. "You have been touched by Lestar and will be safe. Though you do not have our bloodline, so I cannot be certain. Best that you not fail Lestar in this, nay?"

His head nodded slightly and then more empathetically. "Oh yes, of course. No, I will not." Nibarn forced a small yawn as the two stood watching in silence. "I think I will go away to bed, mistress."

She dipped her head once in acknowledgment, knowing the man was drunk, tired, and scared. Nibarn left the veranda, sobering a little as he walked down the hallways of his castle.

He felt the intoxication fighting against his adrenaline. For the briefest of moments, he was concerned. Not just for himself, but for what he was doing. A small voice he had suppressed since the day he stepped into this all-consuming darkness spoke inside his head. “What have you become? What are you doing? You have time. Stop it all. This is too much, too far.” He wrestled against himself, grabbing his head and screaming aloud. “NOOOOOO!!!! No…no...no! Too late. I…am…hers...I serve willingly!”

His personal guards trailing him stopped and looked at each other in confusion. One whispered, “He’s just drunk.”

His hurried, faltering steps echoed in the corridors as his guards trailed behind him. Again his head pounded with a loud voice, “If you do this, you seal your fate! End it now!” This time the intrusion was too much, and he collapsed. His guards watched, afraid to approach. Nibarn began to sob as he spoke to counter the voice. “What do you know? I am Nibarn of House Neske. The greatest of my house, and I will be ever greater. The power she will yield to me will make me the most powerful human that has ever existed!”

His men stood utterly dumbfounded, waiting for him to recover. A few moments passed, and Nibarn was standing again. Wiping himself off and completely oblivious that his men were still following him, he continued down to an unassuming plain wooden door and unlatched it.

Pushing his way in, he yelled, “Mage, get up!”

The mage was sleeping on a tome, with candles that had been burning all night nearly extinguished. “Hmm, what?” Elias, the steward’s personal mage, said groggily.

Nibarn hurriedly pushed through the mage's messy room and got right up to his face. “Do you have the portal stones created for me?” Adding after a moment, “The portal stones you created for me and the council?”

Elias pinched his chin as he thought, attempting to wake himself up. “I have them, my lord. They are over there on the table. In the box. Untraceable, as you requested, and single use only. All you need to do is hold the stone and say the command word."

Rushing over, Nibarn grabbed one from the plain box. "What is the command word?"

The mage thought for a moment, trying to remember what it was. "Umm…I believe it is 'pigeon flight.'"

Nibarn mouthed the words but did not say them. "Thank you, master mage. As ever, your services are undeniable. This will remove me from the palace to the secured outpost far from these lands."

Nodding, the wizard rose from his seat, happy to explain. "It will. I traveled to the specific location you requested and made certain that they will work, testing them multiple times. But be certain to use it only once. I have used the spares to double-check if they were enchanted properly, and with a hundred percent confirmation, they do indeed work."

Nibarn smiled. "Thank you, Elias."

The mage, pleased to serve, bowed. When he rose back to his full height, he saw Nibarn grabbing his head. The voice had returned stronger—his conscience, or what he thought was his conscience, spoke again. "You still have a chance. Stop this. Save your people!"

Nibarn shook his head. "No…no…no! Deception and lies. I am *hers*!"

Again the voice said, "If you do this, your fate is sealed—turn away now!"

Nibarn, feeling that he was losing control, grabbed his jeweled dagger from his belt. He looked at Elias, his dead eyes being consumed in darkness. "I AM HERS!" he screamed.

Elias stepped back, frightened. "My lord? Are you okay?"

Nibarn walked a few steps closer. The mage stepped closer to his table, where he reached toward his black walnut wand. "My lord, I believe you need the medicus!" He made a grab for the wand. He did not wish to harm the lord, but if he could put the steward to sleep, then he would be able to get help. It was too late, though; Nibarn was in a frenzy. He slammed Elias into the desk, stabbing wildly.

“No…my lord…NO!!!” The mage tried to cast, but the punctures were happening so rapidly that his body was going into shock. Elias cried, “My lord, please…please.” He began to slide from the desk to the ground. “No…”

Nibarn did not let him go down alone. He was straddling the mage, hand raised high above his head. “I AM HERS! MY FATE IS SEALED! I HAVE FOUND POWER! YOU WILL NOT TAKE IT!” He let loose his hands, pressing them hard into the mage’s chest. The blood gurgled in the man's throat and mouth. Elias mouthed unintelligible words and went slack, eyes wide, staring horridly at Nibarn. The steward rose and grabbed the stones from the box to be given to his most loyal followers. He walked from the room and passed the horrified guards, who did not say a word.

Nibarn, now realizing that it had all unfolded in front of his men, said coolly, “He was a traitor. Throw him into the river or feed him to the dogs. I do not care. Find me another mage.” Storming off into the corridors, he called back, “And I don’t need an escort to my room.”

9

Victus' grip was tight around the second pilum. Not wishing to waste his next throw, he blew the horn again. He wanted the dark elves to hear and feel the might of his wrath. His countenance of sheer valor caused the dark elves to pause in fear. The sound of the horn challenged and compelled them to come and take him.

The elf who had been knocked out stumbled to his hands and knees. He looked around the scene unfolding around him and tried to determine what had happened that caused the odds to turn so drastically. As he glanced about, the elf realized there was a knight's threshold. He saw the intimidating figure standing outside the portal with a smaller knight next to him. Grabbing his dagger, he crawled behind the tree Jess had been using to hold herself up.

Victus watched but held his throw, knowing that it was too close to Jess. Then, outside the light from the flare, a group of dark elves made enough noise to be noticed; they were still hiding in the darkness. It sounded to Victus like the crunching of leaves.

He spoke calmly, keeping his eyes fixed on the two near the dead female elf. "More outside the light. Stay in the light. We are going to move slowly. Half-steps to Jess." As soon as the elf who had knelt to boost the female elf into the air moved, Victus released his javelin. The dark elf was attempting to grab the pilum from his now deceased leader, but it was in vain as the second javelin pierced its mark, driving the male down to the ground next to his commander.

Victus took small steps as he pulled his shield around to his front, dropping the horn to the ground as he unsheathed his longsword. Aris stepped in sync, watching the left flank where the dark elf was hiding behind the tree. His eyes bounced between the last standing elf he could see and the tree, uncertain who would attack first. Victus, with half his body facing the unseen enemies in the woods, left his flank open but knew his son was there. He hoped it would draw the two nearest enemies into an over-eager offensive. Aris could feel his hands shaking, the combination of the tincture from Biddy and his own fear. This was his first actual combat. His first chance to prove to himself and his father that he was ready. At that moment, it was as if time had frozen. Nothing was happening, and it was making him anxious.

Victus yelled, "Shield!"

Aris reacted instinctively, not actually hearing his father, and ducked behind his father and shield. He heard the tinks hit the shield and knew they were arrows or bolts. Aris kept his eyes on the tree and the other elf. As soon as the second round of tinks hit the shield, the dark elf sprang toward Aris and his father. The young squire stayed low behind his father and the shield. Taking a deep breath, he tried to calm his nerves. The dark elf behind the tree, in a full sprint, now charged confidently toward the young man. Now there were two engaging—one toward Aris and the other toward Victus. Aris had seen the elf by the tree slip farther to the left in a charge. The elves believed they had the advantage, especially when they realized it was just a young squire. *What kind of knight charges into a nest of dark elves with a child?* The two inside the dawn of the flare had been thinking this before they ran to engage the young human and his father. The elves outside the flare line charged, understanding that they were not getting through with their hand crossbows. Victus, peering from the side of his shield, saw the first four enter the flare's light and held his ground. "Four more incoming—" He stopped as he saw at least half a dozen more running into the light. "It's a full squad!"

Biddy, who had positioned himself on the opposite side of the portal as a preventive measure against potential intruders, successfully completed the summoning ritual of a colossal lava creature. Speaking to it as if it were a child of his, he said, "Now I need you to go through this doorway and help my friends. Kill the nasty dark elves."

The deep, stupid-sounding voice of the lava creature responded, "P R O T E C T BIDDY'S FRIENDS! KILL DARK ELVES!" The lumbering eight-foot-tall creature squeezed its way through the portal. Upon reaching the other side, it saw the charging dark elves. Biddy's lava creature yelled in its deep voice, "KILL! PROTECT BIDDY'S FRIENDS!" It slammed its dripping magma arms down on the ground, and a ring of fire sprang around the inner edge of the flare's light. The creature metamorphosed into a fiery ring, devouring everything except for the initial quartet of shadowy elves and the duo charging Aris and Victus. Aris estimated that the fire rose twenty feet high into the air. Despite the haunting screams that filled his ears, Aris remained resolute and pushed aside his fear. Biddy was laughing hysterically on the other side of the portal, his voice distorted. Dark elves and Aris were all enchanted by the magnificence and power of this newly unleashed creature. Victus, however, was not. Taking advantage of the moment, he turned away from the four, who halted to look back at their friends being burned alive.

Nudging Aris, he said quickly, "Take the left. I will take the one closest." The squire snapped himself back into the present and charged the unsuspecting dark elf. Victus was upon his elf first. His shield moved to counter the first thrust to his side, cutting back to block the second swipe from the other hand. He held his sword arm in place, waiting for the moment when the elf would go to strike his center. Victus was not attacking, just parrying with his shield. The elf, overzealous, thought he saw an opening. Victus blocked a thrust with his shield, holding it out in the hope of goading the elf. This left his center open, which the elf believed was a fatal error, but it was by design. When the elf thrust back in, Victus spun his body away from the blow towards his shield arm, hitting the elf from behind. His sword swung low, slicing into the elf's leather boots, cutting deep into arteries. The dark elf shrieked in protest as his legs gave way. On his knees, he spun around and swung at Victus with reckless abandon. His ankles spurted blood from his body as he desperately tried to kill the human who had doomed him. Victus simply swiped the daggers from the elf's hand and finished him with a clean press into the elf's chest. Aris, having the briefest of advantages, used his father's dagger first as a feint, hoping to pressure the elf into a defensive posture. The elf surprised Aris with a backward roll away. Aris followed him and quickly realized he had over-pursued. The elf was now pressing his attacks, first with the dagger and then a sword materialized in the dark elf's hand. It was black, and it swooshed down fast. Aris, using his own dagger to counter the other, lifted his gladius to block the black sword. It hit, and Aris' knees gave way under the ferocity of the attack. The young squire pushed himself up, the sword moving out and to the side to slice him while he was down. Missing, the dark elf again began the blade dance. Spinning the dagger to reverse the grip, Aris understood this meant he was going to be attacked down with the dagger, which also meant the dark elf was going to get close. Aris kept his dagger and gladius close to his body as the attacks began again. Striking high, then low, it was a flurry, and Aris was barely keeping up. This elf wanted him dead, and Aris had never experienced such hate from someone or anything. Aris was fighting harder than he had ever fought before; the advantage had gone completely into the dark elf's favor, keeping Aris unbalanced and defensive. Aris, to his credit, stayed defensive purposefully, realizing that if he could hold out, the elf would make a mistake. Each attack was getting closer and harder to hold back. One cut came so close he felt the tip of the blade cut into his neck. Aris kicked back his head; his feet stomped hard, pushing him into the air and backward, tumbling and landing on his feet. The elf was already on him again. Aris felt like the elf was getting faster and more unpredictable. The elf would not let him get away. He could not gain any ground to make a counter press against this onslaught. Time was running out. He needed to turn the fight soon, or he would be dead.

Victus, having vanquished his elf, was coming to take the pressure off Aris. He saw his son fighting in a furious blur. Overmatched in strength, age, and speed, his son was holding his ground but was losing. Many brave knights had stood against the dark elves in the past and never put up half the defense his son was. His son's dagger and gladius were parrying and deflecting assault after assault. Victus knew this was a black-blade sword master, and Aris would need his help. A black-blade sword master was a fanatic and very skilled in one-on-one combat. They were masters of assassination, and Victus's boy was holding his own against this evil. But the knight knew it would only be a matter of time before the dark elf master would get past his son's defenses. The dark elf fighting Aris saw Victus's approach and yelled to his fellows, who were just now returning to their senses. One of the four dark elves let loose his whip and cracked it. Victus felt the tight grip on his foot, the tug pulling his right leg. He slammed his sword down, cutting the whip, and continued to his son. Aris was dripping with sweat. It was impossible to distinguish the individual blades as they spun by in a blur. Victus could not tell where Aris's arms ended and the dark elves began. All he saw were the two taking steps as their elbows and upper bodies moved. They both were in this duel to the end. Both had accepted the challenge, and both knew only one would survive. The snap of another whip cracked, and Victus was wrapped, feeling both his legs being tugged. He lost his balance and toppled to the ground as his legs were forcefully brought together. He let out a yell as soon as he hit the ground.

"Aris, move to me!" Victus was already cutting the whip, lying halfway on the ground when the four elves sprinted to him. Aris kept his defenses up, the clanging of the blades sounding as if two masters were perpetually locked in a loop of combat. On instinct of hearing his father's voice, he disengaged quickly and completely. He sprang forward like a coiled spring, sprinting towards his father with the dark elf pursuing closely behind. In an instant, Aris stopped, ducked, and rolled towards the elf. The dark elf sprinted past the now rolling Aris. The young squire jumped up mid-roll behind the dark elf and plunged his father's dagger into the dark elf's backside toward the heart. His sword followed suit into the opposite lung. The surprised elf's face dropped in disbelief as Aris ripped the weapons from the elf's body. Not stopping to think about what he had done, not realizing that he had just taken his first life—he sprinted back towards his father.

Victus had released himself, but his shield was lying near him on the ground. The elves surrounded him and closed in, striking from the left and right flanks in twos. The attacks were difficult to block, but Victus's son flew past him, a little blaze of fury. His young face unleashed rancor that his father knew to be righteous indignation and adrenaline. He took on the two from the left, pressing his dagger against one and sword against another. Pushing them back on the defensive, Victus used this to clear his right and hurriedly grabbed his shield. Aris, having pushed the two back, held his ground, backing tentatively to his father's side. The dark elves to the right of Victus were the first to engage again. Aris stepped behind his father, out of their field of view, and used the moment they met Victus's shield and sword to pop out from the right side and stab one cleanly in the side. Victus brought his longsword down fast and hard as the dark elf bent over to grab his side, swiping the head from the body. Aris hopped back behind his father and again used his father's shield and physical build to once more obscure himself from the adversary.

The dark elves, losing confidence and hesitant to keep the fight going, looked for somewhere to flee. But they found no escape from the two determined humans, as a towering inferno blocked the path. Victus took a step towards the two on the left, and they turned to attack him again. Charging in, the first hit hard against the shield, attempting to wrench it from Victus. But this was a fatal mistake, as Aris was already on his flank, slamming his dagger hard into the side of the elf. Seeing the same move he had just witnessed used on his friend, the other dark elf from the right attacked Aris. But Aris had already pulled his dagger out and faced his assailant. Victus wrenched his shield arm back from the injured elf and pushed it hard, knocking him down. The second attacker from the left tried to stab into the knight’s thigh but overextended. Victus relieved the elf of both of his arms in a swift motion. The elf began bleeding and screaming as he crumpled to the ground.

The final elf on the left was holding his side and weakly trying to hold on to his dagger. Victus turned quickly, the sword pushing past the feeble block into the elf’s chest. Aris had his elf already pressed against the wall of flame. The beleaguered elf had nowhere to go but towards the young squire or into the fire. As the trapped elf stepped a bit too close to the flame, a magma arm reached for him, with a loud voice thundering, “PROTECT BIDDY’S FRIENDS. NO ESCAPE, NAUGHTY ELVES!”

Victus turned from his targets to go to Aris's aid. But this time, Aris did not need it. The dark elf jumped from the voice towards Aris, who simply sidestepped the hurried blow. Aris sidled in close, pressing his gladius up through the elf’s armored stomach. Pulling out and back from the dead elf, Aris disarmed him as he also crumbled to the ground. Aris ran back to his position next to his father. Standing back to back, they surveyed the carnage, assuring themselves that no other threats remained. Victus was the first to speak of the two of them, panting. “Clear!” Victus said firmly.

Aris responded with a gasp. “Clear!” Victus strapped and swung the shield back around to his hind side while he ran over to Jess, still slumped against the tree. Aris suddenly saw the elf with no hands crawling away. The elf would not make it. Aris knew it, and the elf knew it. Aris walked over to the elf, who rolled over to face the young man. He spoke pleadingly in a foreign tongue. Aris could see the fear in the elf's dark red eyes. Aris felt pity for the severely injured dark elf. Victus, who was now searching for wounds on Jess, looked over his shoulder at Aris and said, “End it.”

Aris hesitated only for the briefest of moments before he took his gladius and pressed it quickly into the elf’s chest. Gasping and cursing, the dark elf glared at the young lad before expiring. Before Aris could start to think about the fight that was now over, he heard his father calling for what he needed next.

“Aris, bring your med kit. Biddy, we are clear. Come through and help me,” Victus spoke directly, giving orders. Aris ran over, tossing his kit down to his father but turning away from Jess and Victus to vomit. He sat crumpled on his hands and knees, retching. The adrenaline, the fear, the disgust he felt for the dark elves was evacuated in the only way the young man’s body knew how—retching over and over. Victus sympathetically reached over to pat the boy. “It will pass. You did good. Let it out.” Tears formed in Aris's eyes as the comprehension of what he had done and what had happened came to his awareness. Still vomiting, he tried to ask, “Is she going to be okay?”

Victus, using Aris's medicus, began cleaning the only wound he found on her motionless body. “I believe so,” he said. “The poison has her body locked in paralysis. But she should live.”

Biddy walked through the threshold and clapped his hands. The circular fire extinguished, and the lava beast stood before him. “I PROTECT BIDDY’S FRIENDS?”

Biddy giggled, “Oh yes, you did marvelous, my friend. Now go rest.”

“I DID GOOD!” The magma monster’s voice boomed, singing and then becoming almost a whisper. “I… DID... G O O D! I…did good. I…did…” It continued as it shrank and shrank until it disappeared.

Biddy walked past Aris, who was puking, and looked over the limp Jess studiously. “Hmm, poisoned?” Victus nodded at Biddy, reached into his little belt, and said, “Pour this over the wound and wrap it. It should stem the poison’s longevity, but she will still need a proper healer. Dark elf poisons are nasty little beasties.” Victus poured the little vial over the wound as Biddy had instructed, and the woman groaned. Having done all he could for the woman, Victus turned his attention fully to his son. Aris was still dry heaving repeatedly, his empty stomach lurching painfully.

“Aris, look at me.” Aris's bloodshot eyes looked into his father’s. “You did well today, squire. You did good. Come here.” His arms outstretched to his son, and they embraced.

“I was so scared, da!” Victus nodded as he patted his son’s back.

“I know. And the first battle is always the hardest.”

Biddy chimed in from his place next to Jess, “Yes, little Aris, you did well. Very impressive, to be sure.”

10

By the time Calder, now under arrest, made it back to Lindly, the sun was well risen. The cool morning air filled his lungs as they marched him through the main gate. The commander of the elves moved farther down the road, seemingly headed straight to the palace. Calder hoped he would be taken to the prison, which was near the barracks, because he knew a way to escape from the prison, being a commander of the city. However, his hopes were quickly quashed as they escorted him past the barracks and, subsequently, past the prison.

Next, he wondered if they would take him to the center of the city. This was where particularly dangerous prisoners would be taken—often the main city square was used for trials by combat. Either that or prisoners were put on display in the stockades for public humiliation. For the serious violators of the law, this was where the executions took place.

Calder waited for the turn to the heart of the city, but again, the guards kept their slow, steady pace. Now Calder was feeling bewildered and slightly confused as he continued to follow. Finally, Calder decided to just ask and raised his voice, "Oy! Captors! Where are we going?" His shackled hands reached around his chest to gesture as he slowed to a stop. "I mean, you missed the prison by a good half-mile." He chuckled before continuing, "Right, I forgot. You lot are all new to the city. Don't have everything figured out yet. Well, if we make a right at the next street, that would put you on the path back around to the prison. Then I could use my keys here in my pocket to lock myself in." He clinked the keys hanging on the left side of his pants with his chained hands.

One of the guards passed his spear to another and walked right up to Calder. Staring into the man's eyes, he looked him over, spat on the ground, and then punched him square in the nose. Calder laughed, his nose crunched, as he reached up towards his bloody face. As he spoke, he sprayed the blood that dripped onto his lips. "First, you forget to check all my pockets. Then you punch a prisoner for simply trying to help. Greenhorn?" He cocked his brow questioningly at the now seething elf, who was wiping droplets of blood from his own face. The elf punched him again, this time in the stomach, causing Calder to double over. A few other elven guards came over and began searching him again, finding no keys. Calder, bloody-faced and beaming, smiled when they found nothing. "Oh, must have been in my other pants. Apologies, good elf."

Cursing and turning from the human, the elves continued leading him down the city streets. Eventually, after taking the longest route possible, they made it to the palace. They led him up the steps and into the palace garden, where the high elf commander was standing in the center. He began speaking in Elvish to his soldiers as they neared, and all Calder could understand was something about being dismissed. "Dismissing all charges?" he chimed in after he heard the word he knew in Elvish and saw the guards leaving.

The high elf commander smiled, but it was not warm. "No. The charges stand, but the Priestess of House Elivi would like a word. I suggest you listen to her. Your life and your family's lives depend upon it."

Calder's amusement over this entire process vanished at the mention of his family. "What does my family have to do with my *supposed* crimes?"

The elf smirked, pointing towards a covered section of the garden with an arbored entrance enveloped in the most colorful flowers in all the realms. "She is in there waiting for you."

Calder moved cautiously, his chains clanking over the sounds of birds playing in water and singing. His thoughts drifted to his grandfather's words from when he was young: "Never let your prey know fear; it'll spoil the meat. Make certain they are comfortable and relaxed." Hearing the words as if he were six again warmed his heart and felt like a stern warning in his mind. He looked back at the commander of the guards, offering him a grim smirk as he spoke. "I understand and accept the path before me. Death or life, I go willingly." The armored elf said nothing; he didn't even acknowledge Calder with a glance. Under his breath, Calder added, "Doesn't mean I have to be quick about it." He continued walking, dignified, soldierly, and brave, at a slightly slower pace than his normal trot. Entering the hanging garden, the canopied path was more vibrant than he remembered. Having such a busy life with his soldiering and family, he did not have the luxury of visiting some of the finer places in Lindly. The last time he could remember actually being there was well over two years ago. Barely a beam of light passed through the thick and layered canopy, casting an eerie greenish glow on the path. The few rays of sunlight that wiggled past the lush flowers and plants gave the path before him an otherworldly appearance—a place beyond his mortal body. Somewhere divine. Moving further down and following the bend, he could feel eyes watching him. It was as if someone was following so closely he could actually feel the breath on his neck. "Obviously," he thought. "They wouldn't let me have this much freedom." His mind drifted from those watching him to his family, wondering how he would explain all of this to them. He worried about how his family would survive if they executed him. Pushing the thoughts far from his mind, he trudged on. Neither walking fast nor slow, he strolled purposefully but casually. Along the path, he couldn't resist stopping to run his fingers over the silky petals of a vibrant violet flower protruding from the carefully manicured flora. Intrigued by the flowers, he scrutinized them and discovered that their hues varied based on the angle of view. Calder swore he heard a groan of annoyance from one of the hidden figures. He smirked a little at the thought of annoying the elves.

The path led him into a clearing that formed a perfect circle. The white sand from the path had transitioned into a hard-packed surface, covered in small stones. The cobblestone clearing was a work of art, with every stone meticulously cut by hand. Each stone was carefully placed, with green moss peeking out from in between. The fae-like forest was manufactured in appearance, and the low canopy only added to its breathtaking beauty.

Calder, adding a clink from his chains to the peaceful sounds, walked in, twisting a hundred and eighty degrees, craning his neck to look above and around the perfect clearing. A voice interrupted his wonderment. "Citizen Calder." He came to a sudden stop mid-spin, and his eyes landed on the woman who had spoken with a voice that was both firm and melodic. He saw a female high elf, her hair borne of light, slender in figure and prepossessing. She was small in stature, sitting at a granite table in the center of this open area. Looking past the beautiful female, he saw two small chests on the granite table. One he knew was Victus's, and it was unopened. From Calder's conversation with Victus, he knew it was magically sealed, unable to be opened by anyone outside of Victus or Skylighter. Calder hid his relief that it appeared to have worked thus far. The other box Calder did not recognize. But next to the box he did not recognize were parchment, quill, and ink.

Her voice resonated in his body and drew his attention back to her. "Citizen Calder, come sit with me. We have much to discuss." Her eyes glossed over briefly to a darker hue of silver and then back to normal. And then Calder understood why he could feel her voice—she had been casting. His chains snapped apart and dropped to the ground. "I see no reason to keep you in chains," she explained. "Now come have a conversation with me."

He felt his body moving while his mind was still trying to figure out what was happening. Taking a deep breath, he focused on keeping himself in check, muttering softly, "Be polite. This could all be a mistake. Nothing rash. Calm, ol' boy."

As he made his way over, she poured two glasses of fae wine. He took the seat opposite her, accepting the glass as he did. Before he spoke, Calder watched the female drink some of the wine. Then he took a sip of his own, knowing this to be a formal yet informal discussion. The elf wished to make him feel as if he were an equal—to make certain she believed they were actually old friends from long ago. However, Calder knew this was all a ruse. He knew that most high elves despised humans as an incompetent and weaker race. But he would play along.

"What possible business do we have to discuss? I mean this arrest? The warrant placed against Victus? This invasion by you *noble* high elves is unwarranted, unwanted, and absolutely unforgivable." His anger was rising as he spoke, so to curb this, he paused and drank from his glass. "I mean no disrespect," he continued as she sat silently. "However, I believe you all have been guided here under false pretenses."

The slender elf smiled politely as she nodded, understanding the man's frustration. Before her response, she reached down into a small pouch and pulled out a tiny metallic shield that fit nicely into her hand. Emblazoned upon it was the gold phoenix of Asmolor on a dark red backdrop, trimmed in gold. Calder's eyes widened, and his mouth fell open. Stunned into silence, the female used this time to place the miniature shield gingerly on the table next to the parchment. "I trust citizen Calder, formerly knighturion, hero of all Asmolor's children in the city of Geoar, father to some thirteen children with another babe in your wife's belly." The mention of his family made Calder queasy. "You see the signet before you?" Still reeling, he simply nodded. "This is the seal of Asmolor's Inquisition, as you well know. And this gives me and my soldiers the authority to do whatever we deem necessary in assuring the purity of our faith in Asmolor. Our fight against the scourge that is Eu'rok's misguided followers is a treacherous one and often hidden. Alas, the events that have brought us here are quite valid and have deadly consequences." Calder was not thirsty but drank again from his cup as she continued. "So let us start with the facts. You were entrusted with this box." She slid Victus' box closer to herself. "A box that was to be given to Arch Commander Skylighter?" Calder's eyes bore into the wine glass in his hands. She asked again, "Is this not the truth, citizen Calder?"

He shook his head no, but in truth, he was shaking away the thoughts of his family. "Yes, this is true," he stated. Her smile broadened at the affirmation of what she had already known.

"Excellent. Continue with the truth, and all charges against you will be dropped. You may even be rewarded for your duty to the city and the Inquisition."

Calder perked up at the thought of being released and rewarded, reassuring himself that he was right—that all of this was a miscalculation on someone's part and he could possibly put things right again. "Yes, ma'am."

The high elf impersonator pursed her lips as she smiled warmly in appreciation of his cooperation. "To the best of your knowledge, this box was to contain evidence of some cultist activities? Links to certain citizens' deaths and possibly proof of an invasion in the fair city of Lindly?"

He sipped again on his wine, offering it over to her to refill. "May I have some more, please?"

She reached to refill the glass and waved her other hand, where a platter of cheeses shimmered into existence upon the table. "Perhaps something to snack on with the wine?"

The man raised his hands in protest. "Oh, no thank you. I haven't been right in my stomach for a day now. Just the wine."

The female touched her chin with her index finger. "I believe that your stomach senses the troubling of your soul... Now, what is your understanding of the materials in Victus' crate?"

Calder drew in a deep breath and spoke as truthfully as he could. "My understanding is as you say. The items in the box were to be given to Skylighter. Excuse me, Arch Commander Skylighter. Upon giving the box to him, I believe that Victus expected the arch to summon his Gryphon's Shock Troopers and the members of the Inquisition to come to hold a trial against House Neske, or more directly—Nibarn."

The female elf leaned forward and pushed Victus' crate towards the man. "Shall we open it together and see what is held inside?"

Calder caught the box but nearly spilled his wine glass as it slid across the table. "I do not have the means to open this—it has no key and I am not magically gifted."

The female elf wiggled her finger disapprovingly at the man. "Indulge me and open it."

Sighing slightly, Calder grabbed the box firmly in his hands. Gripping it tightly, he was going to use all of his strength to pry the crate open, but when he began, it just unfastened itself and opened. "Oh… how'd I do that?"

The female elf let out a small chuckle. "The box's magic is unable to function in the presence of a priestess of the Inquisition, especially if the magic within it is of our own design."

Calder nodded as the female elf rose and approached him and the box. "I would like to see it for myself, with you."

Calder lifted the lid higher and looked inside. The dark elf peered from behind him, breathing close to his ear. "That is quite a bit of parchment. Carefully pull the first scroll out," she instructed.

Calder inclined his head toward the voice and reached to grab one of the scrolls. But the high elf stopped him—as a gyre swirled up and out of the box. In the brief second that Calder saw it, he knew a magical trap had been sprung. She pushed Calder from his seat and yelled, "Cover! Vortex bomb!"

The man dropped into a ball as he fell to the ground, his eyes closed as he expected to be sucked into the maelstrom and devoured. But when he dared a peek, he saw the female elf swirling in its midst. She was levitating and holding the spiral from spreading and becoming larger. Eventually, the winds passed into nothingness, and all was calm again. Dropping down from above the table, she leaned down to help the man up. “Do you see what that was? Do you understand now why we are after Victus? This was not evidence; this was a trap. This gyre bomb would have swirled and consumed all within a hundred meters, including the great Arch Skylighter. Your commander has misled you. He is leading a cult, and you have been duped into his service—as we at the Inquisition expected.”

Calder shook his head, disagreeing with her. “No! That is a mistake. It’s because I opened the box. I told you I was not able to open it!”

She reached over and grabbed a scroll from the box. “Let’s see the evidence.”

The moment her fingers brushed against one of the scrolls, the words started to morph and transform, moving around on the parchment, disguising what was truly written. It happened faster than Calder’s eyes could track. She handed him one of the scrolls. Calder began to unroll the parchment and attempted to read it. “It’s gibberish,” he said as she thought. “The letters are all garbled and unreadable. Perhaps a code?”

She shook her head as she paced around the table, away from him. “No. It is the slow descent into madness by a man who has been corrupted by the followers of Eu’rok. I have seen it many times.” Her tone dropped and sounded regretful, even sorrowful. “Once the seed of corruption takes root in one’s heart, they are nearly always doomed.”

Calder slammed his hand on the table. “No, this is not true. It cannot be true. The murders started before Victus even began his post over Lindly. He could not be…” He trailed off, stopping as he saw the knowing look on the elf’s face; she was already aware of this.

“He was not in charge of the city. True. But when he served with the Arch Skylighter, they often took respite in the city of Lindly. According to the records of service, they and Victus were on furlough here on the night of the poor lady Desa’s murder. Which means they were also in the city when her husband was murdered.”

This was all true. Victus had been in the city. But the murders had bothered Victus from the start. The investigation, or rather the hastily brought-about charade of an investigation with the quick hanging of some beggar thief, did little to dissuade the itch of curiosity in Lindly or with Victus. Victus had left the city to continue on with his regiment; Calder knew this, and he knew that Victus, deep in his soul, knew that something terrible happened that week, long ago in Lindly. When Victus had taken over the city garrison, it had become a personal mission to root out the culprits. Calder was in a state of dismay, not believing any of it. But the cold hard facts were forcing him to consider it as a possibility.

The elf completed her circle of the table, stopping next to the quill, parchment, and inkwell. “Now what we need from you is a signed confession of your complacency in Victus's crimes. Accepting that you helped him and facilitated his every need while under his service. This does not mean you will be tried for his crimes, but it will require you to admit your negligence, thus preventing you from being able to provide for your family as a soldier.”

Calder had already placed his elbows on the table and his hands on his face. He could not believe this was happening. He waited a moment before speaking, and when he did, his words were firm. “I will not admit to doing anything I did not do. This cannot be right about Victus.”

The elf paused and allowed the man to vent his frustration before continuing. “Since you will not be able to provide for your family because of your aid to the Inquisition, we will provide for you." She tapped a small rune on the unopened box, and the lid raised to open.

Calder's eyes narrowed on the box as he saw gold—more gold than he had ever seen in his entire life. "This is a down payment for your future in the city of Asmadine. We will move you and your entire family. You and your large family will have every creature comfort you can imagine. All you need to do is sign the parchment and condemn the man who deserves this. Think of all the pain he has caused. How he has cleverly used and abused his power. Think about all the pain and suffering of what has been done. And what could have been done with the gyre bomb?"

Calder weighed the options in his mind. On the one hand, the evidence was pretty damning. But on the other, Victus was a truer knight than any he had ever met. Sure, he did not like the hierarchy of the religious elite, but then no one did, unless, of course, you were part of the tyranny. All of that, though, did not make him a traitor.

"No, I will not sign your parchment. Nor do I accept this bribe," he said confidently as he stared at the gold and looked into the elf's eyes.

A veil of darkness shadowed the female elf's face briefly as she gritted her teeth. "Then I will have no choice. You, therefore, accept all charges against you and willingly accept the judgment of the Inquisition?"

Calder sat straight, puffing out his chest. "I do."

The high elf sat down, pushing the confession paper to the side, and began writing on a blank sheet, reading aloud as she wrote. "Citizen Calder, formerly knighturion under Commander of Chevaliers Victus Tiber Andreas, is found guilty on all charges. He will be hereby dragged to the city center to be executed on this day. His wife and children forfeit all rights to citizenship in all kingdoms of Asmolor and will be branded traitors—"

Calder stood up, enraged, and smashed his wine glass. "They have nothing to do with this. None of them are soldiers. None of them have anything to do with this!" His voice rose and began to shake with his anger.

She held up a hand to quiet him as she continued writing. "No, but as you know, we cannot allow the spread of this vile taint of Eu'rok to exist. So by your own hand, you have condemned your family." She glanced up at the man and saw his face purplish and fuming. "Of course, we at the Inquisition are not without mercy. I will allow you to choose one of your children, and they will be absorbed into the Inquisition. A new life."

Calder's anger was pressed with grief over the idea of choosing just one of his children. Tears welled in his eyes. "But you said branded as traitors, not *killed* as traitors."

She nodded curtly, her eyes fixed on the parchment again. "Yes, I did. Branded publicly and left to starve. Caged and hanging from the city walls as a warning to all those who dare to delve into Eu'rok's refuge."

The picture formed inside Calder's mind as though he could see it all transpiring before his eyes. His children were marched into the square. The crowd was roaring, tossing trash at the disgraced family. He saw the hot iron as it branded each one of his children and his wife. He smelled the flesh of their bodies as they decayed on the city walls. All of this was brought to his mind like a vision of things to come. It was real, but he knew it was an illusion projected into his mind as a way to emphasize that this female inquisitor was not exaggerating. She was showing him exactly what would happen. This proved too much for the man. Calder spun from the table, cursing. Pacing away from the table, he tried to reason his way out of his *situation— I could charge her and try to take her hostage. No, that won't do. Perhaps make a run for it? No, they are surrounding me. If I kill her, I can at least attempt to fight my way out. I more than likely won't get out, but if I could just warn my family to flee the city, they would have a chance...*

He worked himself up into a fury and stood stewing. The female just watched her trapped prey as he tried to puzzle out his options. She knew what he was considering; the question was whether Calder would attempt it.

At the end of a moment, Calder made his decision—he turned and charged, determined to tackle her to the ground and bash her head over and over until nothing remained of her beautiful face.

The elf's brow cocked coyly, and she smirked, rising from her seat. "Perhaps you misunderstand." Her hands reached out towards the man as if to catch him. The burst of speed put out by this human caught her slightly off guard, and she was not certain if her spell missed—until she knew it had missed. Calder was inches away from her now, and then she was being thrown to the ground hard on her back. That is where the assault stopped. He hurriedly jumped off of her as if on fire and began screaming—but not at her. He held his head, attempting to flee this invisible onslaught—he could see and feel his family's pain. The voices of his children were swirling around, yelling, "Papa, why did you let us die? How could you, Papa?" Over and over, the voices just rotated between all of the children. "Papa? Why?" Then it switched to his beloved wife. "How could you, Calder?" The man's resolve was crushed—he could do nothing. "NO!" he shouted, "Stop it! NO! NO! I will sign the damned confession. Don't hurt my family—please."

The dark priestess rose to her feet, irritated at herself that she, in her arrogance, had been surprised. It had delayed her ability to cast and react. She composed herself, placed the quill in the inkwell, and pushed them over to the opposite side of the table, then rose and walked the parchment over to him. The man was on his knees, pleading and sobbing.

"All you did, citizen Calder, is what any man would have done under these difficult circumstances. Thus, I forgive the outburst. Now, here. Sign."

Calder began reading over it. 'I do confess to the below crimes in which I was complicit in cultist activities, though I never actively participated in any of the carnage.' He stopped reading as tears flowed from his eyes down onto the table. He grabbed the quill and signed, unable to read any more of the lies. Never in his life had he felt so helpless. Never had he felt this cold. He just signed over the best commander and best friend he had ever had. Collapsing completely to the ground, he sobbed, "Don't hurt my family, please. Please, noble Inquisitor. Please have mercy."

The high elf grinned wickedly and said to him, "You have done honorably today. No harm will come to you or your family. The arrangements will be made, and you will leave the city with your family—wealthy and unmolested."

11

Victus and Biddy finished tending to Jess, even going as far as creating a portable bed for her. Victus used the trees to create the frame and added a handle so that it could be pushed like a sled. Biddy used magic to enchant the wood to hover just above the ground, making it light as a feather. Biddy and Victus carefully moved Jess over to the newly created bed. For comfort, instead of leaves or grass, Biddy created tiny clouds, which they used to stuff in and on the bed. This gave her body the most comfort possible.

Biddy looked over at Victus and saw the man's concern for Jess. "I think she will be okay, half-pal. We have a few days before the poison moves to the next phase."

Victus grunted, "Yes, but the sooner we can help her, the less likely she will have lingering consequences."

Biddy nodded his little head and whispered, "Contingency."

He watched the human knight pat the young woman's hair and then lean over and kiss her forehead. "We are here. You are not alone." His eyes closed to hold back the formation of tears lingering near the bridge of his nose. "You hang in there—that is an order."

Aris, still recovering, just sat on the ground. He touched his neck where the dark elf assassin's blade had nicked him and thought to himself, *That was nearly the end of squire Aris Tin. I need to be better.* He wondered if anyone had seen how close the blade had gotten. The wound was covered in dried blood, which Aris easily cleaned off using the reflection of his father's dagger. *Next time I need to bring my arms in closer. If I can keep my attacks smaller and faster, I think I could have had him sooner.* He rose from his seat, pulled out his sword, and began cleaning both blades thoroughly. The fight replayed in his head—every step, every sword thrust, every dagger slash—every counter of his and the assassin's. His mind rewound everything from the moment they stepped through the portal. He gave each weapon another once-over with his mithril-fiber cloth, a dwarven invention to both clean and sharpen the blades. He stood up and rolled the weapons in his hands. He closed his eyes, reenacting the whole fight again. His movements were slow and deliberate, retracing and retracing. His father looked from Jess and watched his son, proud to see the level of commitment to his craft—to be better than he already was. His smirk and nod of affection at Aris's closed eyes brought about a feeling of dread in the man. He was both proud of his beloved son but also regretful that he lived in a world where war was inevitable. Looking over to Biddy, he spoke quietly, "Have I been a good father to the young man? I often wonder if I have failed him. No—not failed him but rather, doomed him."

Biddy took the liberty to add a bit of levity to the question. "Where would he be if you had not raised him? Dead? A slave?"

Victus chuckled quietly. "Yes, true enough. But you know the question was not referring to the nature of his body. I mean the heart and soul of the young man. Have I made him an instrument of destruction or a tool to be used by the gods? Or did I create a free, liberated soul bound in honor, love, and discipline?"

Biddy took off his goggles and pondered for a moment. As he contemplated, he reached down into his small satchel and pulled out a long pipe. Placing some dried leaves in the pipe, he tamped it down into the open top. Snapping his stubby fingers, the perfect fiery cherry formed in the middle, allowing the gnome to puff an enormous ring of smoke. "The way I see it, half-pal, you gave this man a heart—based on who you are as a human. Charismatic, kind-hearted, heroic, loyal—you are a good man. I would dare say a great man. A testament to your race. Yes, you have trained and disciplined your son to be a warrior. He will bring destruction and doom to those who stand against righteousness. You taught him when and how to fight. It is actually remarkable to see such a young human so beyond his years. Some of your kin live to their twilight years without even a quarter of what that boy has in his head. You have done right by him and by me, personally." He took a long drag on his pipe, once again allowing a giant ring to puff out high into the air. "I think his life will be filled with adventure. Challenges and trials, but in the end, he will live a goodly life. And even out-rival your station and potential," Biddy grinned at the thought.

Victus smiled in agreement. "I do hope so. Promise me, Biddy, that if something happens to me, you will offer any aid you can to my son."

Biddy leaned over Jess's body, having placed his pipe down. His little hand was outstretched to Victus. "I swear that squire Aris, eventually knight Aris or even master mage Aris —" He winked and giggled as he said the words 'master mage,' "will be a friend of Biddy Baslalorais. You have my word that I will be there for him as I am here for you."

As Aris finished his replay, he saw that his father was leaving Jess's side. He watched his father move over to the two pilum-impaled bodies. "What are you looking for, da?"

Victus glanced over as he turned out the pouches and pockets they carried. "I am looking for anything useful. If I can find a signet or intel on the bodies, we can use it to our advantage."

Aris sheathed his blades and moved toward his father's side. "I see."

Biddy, still sitting next to Jess, repositioned to face the son and father. "Check the black-blade assassin's body. The rest were all of a lower station and will unlikely have anything of use."

Victus agreed with a nod but added to Aris, "Biddy is correct. However, after the battle, we search all the bodies.

Oftentimes, you can find a personal journal or a letter between lovers, or a note to the family. In these seemingly innocent pastimes, your enemy could divulge information unwittingly."

Aris was maneuvering the impaled male elf's body so he could unfasten his belt, which Aris thought would be filled with all kinds of dark elf treasures because of the large pack attached to the back of the belt. The body was stubborn, though, and not easily moved, so Aris pushed on top of the body, sliding it farther down the javelin. The angle of the body now gave Aris an easy reach to the pack. He flipped it open and found miscellaneous items, dried meat, and fruit, but nothing like he believed he would. Sighing, he walked away from his father, who was still working on the female elf's body.

"Aris, check his boots and pockets too. Look for necklaces, rings under gloved hands, earrings—anything that can distinguish what house the elves belong to. If you find jewelry, do not put it on or take it off," Victus warned. "Often these things are cursed to those outside of the dark elves. Have Biddy or me come to look it over."

Aris hustled back to the dead elf he had previously checked, wishing to finish this one up and move to the one he had killed first. The most dangerous of all the elves was the one he was certain would have something unique. Part of him wanted to collect a token of his first victory but was uncertain how his father would take the proposed idea. So he decided to wait and perhaps ask later. As he searched the elf, he found no jewelry, and when he took the boots off, all he found was stinky feet and dirty socks. "Nothing, da!"

Biddy had noted the boy's curiosity about the dark elf assassin and picked himself up from beside Jess, making his way over to the body. He was poking a stick into the corpse when Aris arrived again. "This elf could have contingencies. Just checking."

Aris began with the elf's feet, removing the boots, shaking them out, and tossing them to Biddy. The gnome had not asked for the boots, but Aris saw his eyes and knew Biddy wanted to investigate. "Thank you, Master Aris. You see, many of these nasties get every piece of garment and weapon enchanted. I would like to take every piece of his clothing and gear to examine it thoroughly. No need to remove the shirt or pants. My goggles will help me find what I am looking for."

The young squire was listening but was looking over the body. His curiosity peaked when he noticed the missing black blade around the fallen elf. "Where did his sword go? He used magic to pull it out of the air... But—" Aris lost his train of thought. He was caught off guard and laughed at seeing Biddy wearing goggles that had at least ten different lenses, making his eyes bulge.

"What seems to be causing you discomfort, Master Aris?" Of course, Biddy already knew the reason but was being droll.

Shaking his head, Aris replied, "You know how silly all those different lenses attached to your goggles look? Your eyes look like they are going to burst out of your face."

Biddy laughed, "They are quite useful. Each lens helps with different things. In particular, this larger one actually allows me to see the magic woven into things like clothing. Thus far, the only thing of note that I can see is the necklace on the elf's neck and his arms. The rest is as mundane as a rock. Or so I believe. I still need the rest of his clothing."

Aris stopped fiddling with the belt attached to the dark elf and switched his attention to the elf's arms. He unfastened the bracers and then rolled up the sleeves of both arms. On the dark gray skin, he saw single lines tattooed from the wrist to the bend of the elbow, each grouping a different color: dark greens, blues, reds, black, gold, white, silver, and purple. A smaller, fainter tattoo was underneath the ones nearest the wrist—the shape of a sword, with what looked like a faded bird on the hilt. "What are these?" he asked aloud, believing they could be the magic Biddy could feel and see.

His father, now standing behind the two, answered, "The small lines on the body denote kills. Each color signifies a particular race or rank in the race he has killed in combat. Check the other arm, and you will see small black stars. They are for successful assassinations."

Aris reached over the body and rolled up the sleeve, not even caring to remove the bracer. His face dropped in utter disbelief. "He has killed hundreds, if not thousands!" The tattoos on both arms looked more like an undershirt or sleeve than actual skin. All three of them stared for a moment, realizing even more the grave danger that Aris, his father, and Biddy had been in.

Victus continued the conversation as Biddy smacked Aris on the back encouragingly and whispered to Aris under Victus's voice, "Well done indeed."

"Good job, squire. Got yourself one of the best I have ever seen," Biddy declared aloud.

Victus, smiling, continued, "What of the necklace you mentioned, Biddy?"

Biddy leaned over, examining the leather armor and then carefully removed the necklace. Aris saw it briefly as it passed from the gnome to his father. It was an insignia of a Kraken with different weapons gripped in its eight palpi. His father pursed his lips and cocked his brow. "A weapon's master too. And of the highest dark elf house Weratar, reporting directly and only to Lestar herself."

Aris was looking supremely confused, doubting and even reasoning to himself that he could not have actually beaten such a foe.

"House Weratar," Biddy repeated, the 'W' sounding more like an 'R' when Biddy said it. The words came out in reverence from the little gnome.

Victus pocketed the insignia and looked down at the two. "This is far more dangerous and far darker than even I expected. Something is terribly…" He stopped when he heard muttering from Jess. "Continue searching the bodies," he said as he ran over to her side. Lowering his voice as he hurried to kneel beside her, he said, "I am here. Hush. Shh... Shh. It is me, Victus. Be at peace as you are amongst friends." He sat next to her, brushing her hair with his hand. "Shh... rest."

Aris and Biddy did not need the order to continue searching the bodies; they were far too excited about what they could possibly find. Biddy was searching the elf's different pouches and pockets. Aris was still thinking about the sword, and it dawned on him that the sword had to have been magical. Tapping Biddy on the shoulder, he asked, "What of this tattoo?"

Biddy looked at the young man's hand, which was pointing right at the sword markings on the elf's arm. He flipped a few lenses down and then hastily flipped them off again. "Hmm... it is—" The gnome placed his head down so low that his nose touched the elf's skin as his little eyes ogled the fascinating marking. "Hmm... I believe it is a rune tattoo. Whereby the magical weapon, in this case, a sword, is imbued into a user's appendage, using a motion or command word to summon the object whenever required."

Aris immediately said, "I want one."

Biddy leaned back up and said, "Oh... no... no. You cannot use this. Who knows what kind of darkness could be unleashed within you if I tried to transcribe the rune to you."

Aris's whole body slumped a bit as he looked dishearteningly at the gnome. "Well, it would be pretty advantageous to have a rune blade," the young man said with regret. "What of the rings he wore? Can I have one of them?"

Biddy looked over and waved his stubby hands. "They are not magical, just trifles given for rank and reward." Aris reached down and began pulling off the small violet gem-encrusted one first. “No, not that one. You do not want that one. It shows that you are a consort of Lestar. Perhaps this one.” He pointed to the other hand, seeing a silver-banded ring with small prongs holding a tiny Kraken figure with hands in its tentacles.

Aris smiled, “Yes. I know it is odd, but I feel a certain bond with this dark elf and would like a small token to honor the dead and remember how close I came to my own.”

Biddy grinned, “No need to explain yourself to me. You have earned the right to the spoils. And as I see it, that is a rather equitable choice, considering some of the things warriors collect or display after fights.” Aris tried to fit the ring on his pinky as the dark elf had worn it, though the size proved too large, so he opted to place it on his thumb. Biddy jumped up, “Ohhh! Contingency!”

Aris took the look of the gnome to mean he had an idea since he used the word “contingency” to mean so many things. The gnome stood up and hurried over to open a small dimensional doorway, only large enough for a hand to fit through. First, he stuffed his hand inside, and Aris could hear things being knocked over inside the portal. The gnome squinted as he reached for something but could not quite reach it. The gnome removed his arm, moved the portal down a bit, and stuck his head in. The headless gnome’s body looked rather ridiculous standing bent over without a head. Biddy squished a hand through next to his head and began pulling himself up off the ground, his little legs dangling. He was now up to his waist in the dimensional hole; the portal seemed to be stretching to allow him in further. “Don’t let me fall in!” his muffled voice said to Aris. The squire grabbed the little gnome’s feet and held on. “Almost… almost… got it!” The gnome’s voice squeaked with excitement, “Pull me out! Tug, tug, tug!” Aris leaned back and pulled hard until both he and the gnome were on the ground.

Aris, curious as ever, looked at the gnome waiting for him to explain what he was doing. Finally, when the gnome did not give an answer, Aris asked, “What did you get?”

Biddy spoke but did not look up from the small book he now held. “It’s a book, can’t you see? You warriors do know what books are, don’t you?” he replied with sarcasm, as if it were a good enough answer for Aris's curiosity.

Aris's head dropped to his chest. “Yes, I can see that it’s a book, but what kind of book?”

Biddy’s eyes glanced over to Victus and then back to Aris with a large, wicked grin on his face. “It is about how to turn things into body runes. For example… hmm, let’s say turning your sword or dagger into something like that of the foe you defeated… Interested?” Biddy knew the answer before he even asked.

“YES! Will it hurt?”

Biddy shrugged. “Probably. Maybe. I dunno?” He thought for a second and then nodded. “Okay, okay, yes, it will hurt. When we get back to our camp, I will study it, and when I am ready, I will call on you.”

After stripping and going through all the corpses, they finally stacked them all up and burned them. “Do you understand why we burn them, Aris?” Victus asked as they watched Biddy set the bodies ablaze so fast and so hot that they turned to ash in seconds.

“Because the warlocks and necromancers of Eu’rok would use the bodies to fuel their undead armies.”

Victus nodded. “Necromancers, in particular, prefer to use the dead soldiers of Eu’rok’s armies as their tools or instruments of devastation. Being creations of Eu’rok, they have a desire to harm and hurt the other races, which makes them much easier to dominate and control. Compared to us, whose souls and bodies would fight the dominance of the darkness found in Eu’rok’s creations, making us unreliable and downright worthless to them.” His father made a mental note of the ring on Aris’s thumb before he turned from the pile of ash towards Jess. “We will stay here until the last of the knights’ flare vanishes—which should be by the time the sun reaches its apex."

Biddy waddled over behind Victus as he moved closer to Jess. "Just so you are aware, I am going to be working on creating a rune tattoo for Aris. Is that okay?"

Victus turned and looked past the gnome to his son, smiling. "He is a man, a soldier, and my son. If he believes it will help him in the battles and eventual wars to come, then by all means, help him. That is a decision he will make for himself."

The gnome clapped his hands together. "Excellent! After the flare fades, meet me back at our camp. For now, I am going to head through the threshold and keep watch."

Victus acknowledged him with a worried smile. "Be safe and be ready in case the flare has drawn the attention of more enemies." His thoughts passed from his son to Jess, lying motionless, save for her breathing.

Aris walked over to his father. "I am going to scout the woods a bit since we are holding up here for a bit longer."

Victus's eyes traced his son's newly acquired ring. "Something to commemorate your first victory?"

The young man blushed, reaching to cover the hand with the ring attached. "It's so I never forget this day. It will keep me grounded and remind me that no matter how good I think I am, a squire could someday end my life."

Victus grinned. "There is no shame in your spoils and even less in your reasoning for keeping it." Aris relaxed as his father seemed to understand his explanation and did not disapprove. Victus leaned toward Aris and patted his leg. "Off with ya, squire. Make your range a quarter-mile, no more."

Aris snapped his heels together and saluted. "Will do, sir."

As Aris left the area and Victus lost sight of his son in the trees, his attention returned to Jess. He leaned close to her ear. "I am here with you, love. Hang in there." He kissed her cheek, and she moaned out, "Victus! Skylighter!" sounding more like a warning than her recognition that he was present —but for Victus, where there was life, there was hope.

12

It was under the cover of darkness, where the towers glowed violet and black, that Serin made her escape from the city. After her goodbye to Aris, she went for a stroll in the city, eventually making it back to the palace. Despite all the commotion, no one seemed to notice the strawberry-blond-haired girl returning. She decided to climb up to her desired spot amongst the rafters in the main hall, which led to the council chambers. She listened and watched all that came and went. She had been quite bored and was already scheming a justification to follow Aris and Victus. She understood it was supposed to be their time together, but she wanted to be with them both and share in their adventures. Her young heart longed for a father who was truly noble, not just in title. Her fondness for Aris grew every time she was with him. Often, she would show up at the door of their house to share dinner, and on occasion, Victus would allow her to sleep over. She felt safe with them. She felt like a family with them and wanted nothing more than to be with them wherever they went. As the next hour passed, she decided that she would pack up her belongings and take her brother's shire mount without his knowledge or permission.

It was such an enormous horse that it stood twenty hands high, or six feet off the ground to its withers. Her brother would not even notice it was gone, as he never rode anymore unless he was forced to. It was fast—extremely fast; it had been bred as a racing horse. The only reason Brandan had purchased the beast was that he fancied being a racing pundit that week.

As she contemplated the direction of Delwan from the city and her route, she saw something interesting below her perch in the rafters. Two of the replacement guards were escorting a beautiful elven noble into the palace's arched hallway. They were moving with purpose but speaking casually. She could hear that it was Elvish, but some words were not of any Elvish she had ever heard before. Because of her highborn status, it was expected that she would serve as an emissary when she reached the age of maturity, until such a time that she would be handed over in a marriage alliance agreement. Because of this, she was forced to learn all the variations of High Elven. It was the noblest language, a language of the gods—so she knew this was some slang version of the language. But as she watched the female elf disappear behind the large doors into the council chambers, the guards continued speaking. Slowly but steadily, she crawled down from the rafters, and as she neared the ground, she nearly slipped and caused the guards to glance up. She froze, clinging tightly to the side of a pillar; she dared not move. One of the guards shrugged and dismissed the sound, and the guards continued to speak. Serin took a deep breath and slid herself the rest of the way down the column. Now she was a few feet away and could hear what the guards were saying much better. But as she tilted her head to listen, she could not understand them. The more she listened, the more her mind wandered about the particular dialect of Elvish that was being used. It was not High Elven, nor was it the more common variation. Serin grew bored with deciphering the elves' language and resorted to using the pillars as cover. Bounding from one to another, she cautiously started to sneak away, her mind focused on her goals outside of the palace. Suddenly, a phrase spoken by one of the elves caught her attention: "Eu'rok Vitan." A phrase uttered by those devoted to Eu'rok, meaning "Eu'rok victor." She froze like a statue and listened carefully. She was unable to pull herself away, wanting to know more. Comprehension dawned in her young *mind—the reason I cannot understand—it's Dark Elvish!* She listened again, the voices continuing quietly. The name "Lestar" stood out, and then the two guards, obviously believing they were alone, laughed at whatever they had said with her name. If these guards were discussing and laughing about Lestar, then they were most certainly dark elves.

Serin was mortified. *Dark elves in the city. I have to get out of here and tell Victus.* Her mind reeled—what if she was wrong? What if she was just sticking her nose in where it didn't belong? Something her father, Nibarn, had always cruelly and repeatedly reminded her. She could hear his voice repeating the scolding: "Serin, must you always be in others' business? Must you always be underfoot? Leave us!" Thinking over his words, they dug deep into her little heart like tiny daggers. She felt rejected by both her father and her brother, Brandan. Although Brandan was never intentionally cruel, he was ambivalent. Her present situation pushed the thoughts of her family away, and she focused on the dark elven impostors. She understood one thing for certain: if she was correct, they would likely kill her if they thought she was onto them. Noble or not, she would be seen as a threat.

She listened for a few more minutes before concluding that it most definitely had to be dark elves. Using the pillars and the miscellaneous statues to conceal herself, she made her escape from the palace. She awaited dusk to approach the stables, and by sunset, she had stolen her brother's horse. In her disguise, she looked like a tiny gnome on an oversized horse.

The towers began glowing as she made her way to the city gate, where she hoped that she could sneak in behind the last caravan that left the city for the day. Watching the wagons lining up, she went to the tail end and approached the burly, long, reddish-gray-bearded dwarf and spoke up bravely, "Can I please tie my horse to one of your wagons and leave with you?" She held up a pouch of gold into the air, waiting for him to respond.

"What are you about, lass?" he asked, turning to face her as he continued issuing orders to the rest of his people.

Serin cleared her throat. “I would like to buy passage with your caravan, please. I can pay.” She dangled the gold above the dwarf.

He squinted, looking her over. “You sure? We are heading down through Eu’rok’s lands, lass. The fastest route back to our kin.”

She nodded, hopping down from the horse. “Yes, I am sure. Just get me out of the city, please.”

He chuckled, “Aye, and what kind of trouble have you gotten yourself into?”

She held out the gold to him, pleadingly staring at the dwarf through the cowl of her brown cloak. The guard at the gate was motioning for the next group to move up. “Please. Take it. I need to find some friends of mine.”

The dwarf seemed to think for a moment, made up his mind, and grabbed the gold. Before he could ask anything further, a dwarf from the front yelled back to him, “Dundin, they be needing our papers!”

He gave Serin a reassuring nod in affirmation that she could tag along. “Aye, coming! Hold your hammers!” he yelled towards the front dwarf. He looked back at Serin, pointing. “Attach your horse to this wagon and sit on the top bench here. Just lead them on out; I will be back.”

Relieved, she added her horse to the wagon and climbed up to the top as instructed. Keeping her head low, she waited nervously. The towers were glowing with heightened brilliance, and she couldn’t resist looking at them. Despite being stunning, they provoked fear in the young girl.

In her heart, she knew something was wrong and that her stupid brother and father were too blind to see it. Dundin made his way to the front and tossed the parchment to the elf captain. “All in order, pointy ears?”

The elf clicked his tongue in disgust and motioned for them to carry on. Dundin yelled back over to his people, “Right, let's get a-going; move out!" He stood there waiting until the last wagon passed out of the gate while Serin was staring down, tapping and then easing the reins gently to keep the horses and ponies moving.

The elven guard grabbed Dundin's arm, speaking sharply, "Your papers did not have a shire horse on them."

The dwarf turned bright red in anger, smacking the elf's hand off him. "First off, pointy ears, don't be touching me. Second off, I just purchased it and didn't have time to get the papers adjusted. You going to halt my whole caravan because of one lousy horse?"

The elf looked down at him, rolling his eyes. "Careful, dwarf, I could have all the stores you carry audited."

Dundin stared up at the elf as if to dare him to do it.

"Aye, Da. Just be givin' him a little taste of the gold. He can have drinks on the Dundin clan tonight." Dundin turned his head to Serin, who had adopted a dwarvish accent, trying to diffuse the situation.

The male dwarf grinned. "Ah yes, you and yer boys be needing some coin for a drink later?" he asked, but he was already passing some gold from the pouch to the elf. "That be enough to get ya through the night."

The elf pocketed the gold, said nothing, but added, "Let them through—my mistake."

Dundin climbed up next to Serin, grinning broadly. "Dutiful daughter of mine, being good at keeping her da from a fight." He placed his calloused hands over hers and took the reins, and they left the city.

A few miles from the city, Serin offered the dwarf a small hug and kiss on his cheek, which caused Dundin to blush. "Thank you for your help. I best be going to find my friends."

The dwarf helped her down from the wagon. "Aye. Lass, you be traveling alone, and it is dangerous out here."

She smiled as she untied her brother's horse and climbed the tall beast. "I won't be alone for long. My friends are only a few hours ahead of me. Half a day, maybe a little more."

Dundin let out a little sigh. "I won't stand in your way, young one. Be safe. And in a few months, we'll be back in Lindly. When ya hear of us returning, you look me up. That way I be knowing you are okay."

She sat atop her horse and smiled. "I will make sure I do, Da—Dundin. Thank you again." When she teasingly referred to him as Da, he blushed, and she responded with a playful wink. Tugging the reins, she shifted in the direction she wished to go.

The dwarf turned to head to the back of the wagon. "Wait for just a second, lass."

Serin looked over curiously. "I really need to be on my way."

From behind the canvas of the wagon, she heard him bellow, "Don't you be riding off yet. It's bad luck not to accept a gift from a dwarf." She scrunched up her nose, slightly confused. He slid out holding saddlebags. "You may only be a few hours behind, but you did not pack enough supplies. You will be needing water and food, just in case you cannot find your friends."

Serin nearly smacked her head. "Oh, I guess I forgot my bags." The truth was, she hadn't really packed anything but a few personal items. How could she have forgotten food and water? "Thank you again, sweet and noble Dundin."

He threw the saddlebags atop her horse and fastened them securely. He was using the wagon as a makeshift ladder to ensure it was secure. "Got one more thing for ya." He again hopped in the back of the wagon.

Serin waited patiently, relieved that this dwarf was caring enough to look after her. "I really do appreciate all the help. You have been more than kind."

The response she heard was nothing but cursing as the dwarf fumbled about, looking for whatever it was he was searching for. "AH! Here we are!" he shouted with a groan, indicating he had found what he was searching for. He walked over from the wagon and reached up, holding a small war hammer. "It's not much, but it's the lightest weapon I have. You don't have to be trained; just smash 'em with the flat end and they will be a-hurtin'."

She leaned down and grabbed the leather-bound handle. It was light. She used the loop and attached it to her saddle. She looked at the dwarf inquisitively. "How is it so light?"

The dwarf touched the tip of his nose and winked. "Been fashioned for a youngling or woman. Dwarven secrets, lass."

She smiled, warmed by his generosity, slid down from the horse, and gave him another enormous hug and kiss on the cheek. Again, the dwarf went bright red. "Well, off with ya. Can't be getting farther behind than you already are." He helped her up, giving her a toss when he thought she wasn't going to make it.

"Truly, Dundin, you are a credit to your kin."

He let out a "Bah" as he returned to his seat on the wagon. Serin turned the horse and strode off the main road. Before she cut through the woods toward the city of Delwan, she turned back, giving one more glance and wave to the dwarf, who pretended not to see her but did say loudly, "I best be getting that hammer back when I get back to Lindly."

A few hours into her ride, she began to worry. She thought that she would have caught them by now; it had seemed an easy task in her mind in the rafters of the palace. But the darkness of the woods seemed endless. Slowing the horse, she peered as far as she could and then checked the sky and the stars. "I am going the right way… Where are they?" She continued on, growing tired as she rested her head on the neck of the horse. Before she knew it, she was asleep.

When she awoke, she found that the horse had remained on course, following the direction she had set. The sun was rising, and when she looked up at the quickly disappearing stars, she saw an insignia in the sky. “Is that knight’s flare?” she asked more audibly than she had meant. She surveyed the vicinity and then stretched her neck to catch any noise of fighting.

Not hearing any sounds that would prelude combat, she altered her horse’s direction toward the flare. She gave the horse a gentle push with her boot, and it sped up much faster than she expected, nearly knocking her off the horse. The shire horse was at full tilt through the trees. Everything beside her was a blur. At one point, she thought she saw—in the distance off to her right—a party marching through the woods. She dismissed it as she focused on the insignia, which was slowly disappearing in the morning sky. The speed of the horse was more apparent when she noted the insignia was nearly above her, and she pulled back on the reins, deciding that it would be best to approach the area slowly and stealthily.

When she deemed it a suitable distance to investigate the flare without being noticed, she discreetly removed the hammer from the saddle and gracefully dismounted the horse. She took the reins and wrapped them around a dead tree trunk. Her eyes darted around the forest, an uneasiness causing her to grip the small hammer with both hands as she continued toward the flare. She could feel eyes on her, but she could not tell if it was just her imagination or if the small animals had stopped their daily business to watch her. Keeping her head low and using the bushes and trees as cover, she moved slowly toward the knight’s flare.

~~~

Aris’s patrol of the surrounding area had yielded nothing. As he finished the circle—he had gone a quarter mile out from his father—when a rider approached on a huge horse. He ducked and hid, watching silently. The rider dismounted with
~~~

a hammer and tied the mount. He couldn't make out who or what it was, but his adrenaline began to pump blood into his ears.

His body readied for a fight, and he began to stalk his prey. Whether friend or foe, he wanted the surprise to be his. Whomever this was, they were not stupid, using the bushes and trees cleverly to mask their approach. Aris pressed his toes into the ground softly, his heels following suit as he was ten feet away from this trespasser. He heard a whispered curse from the figure as Aris continued his approach, now five feet away. He knew that voice. He stood up, dropping all pretense, and said, "Serin?"

The young lady swung her body around, hammer cutting through the air in fear. "Who's there?" she shrieked.

Aris bounced back defensively, hands out to his side. "It's me—Aris."

She lunged toward him, embracing him as he wrapped his arms around her. "I found you. Oh, I was worried…I was so scared I could feel someone watching me."

Aris smiled, leaning back from her. "Just me… But—what are you doing here?" sounding more incredulous than he intended. "I mean, you shouldn't be out here. We just had a fight with dark elves."

She bounced her head up and down. "Yes! I know. Well—I mean—I didn't know that you fought. But I am here because dark elves are in the city. I have to tell your father."

Aris scrutinized her, then grabbed her shoulder and pressed her down to a crouch. "Shh." Aris could hear the sounds of armored men in the distance. His voice was a whisper. "Follow me."

Serin pointed back to her horse, a question in her expression. "Leave it. On me," Aris said, motioning for her to follow closely. Keeping low, they moved back in the direction of Victus.

Now Serin could hear the armored party too and asked, "Can you hear them? Sounds like someone is singing?"

Aris turned back to her. "Shh, keep your voice down." It was at that moment that horns bellowed from the direction of the moving, unseen enemy. It was similar to his father's horn, but there were many more of them. He thought perhaps it was possibly another attack, but his mind told him it was friendlies. "Time to go." Aris tugged Serin and began sprinting back to his father. Upon reaching the camp, Victus was already standing and looking in the opposite direction of Aris and Serin. "Commander, someone's coming," Aris reported quickly.

Victus glanced sidelong, smiling. "Indeed—friends." Aris let out a sigh of relief as his thoughts were confirmed by his father. Victus turned fully to face Aris, startled to see Serin. "Serin? What in the—" He was cut off as the first spears pierced the clearing in the woods, followed by the shining shields.

The voice of Titus poured out through the synchronized steps of the legionnaires. "Fan out!" The back second line of soldiers split into two groups and spread to the flanks, while the main group of five kept marching. Now fully visible, all parties saw each other. Victus turned from Serin and Aris to the legionaries. Titus moved from behind his men, and Marcella put down her harp and followed. Both offered salutes to Victus. Titus spoke first. "Commander Victus, are you injured? How can we assist?"

Victus returned the salute. "We have a wounded knight. Marcella, please tend to her and use whatever magic you can to mend her."

Biddy's voice carried out through the threshold, heard by everyone as he yelped, "CONTINGENCY!"

Sprinting through the threshold, he was in mid-summon of his fiery beast from the previous battle. He stopped abruptly when he saw that it was some of Victus' soldiers. Biddy's half-formed lava giant said, "Biddy forget to finish spell? I come to kill baddies!"

Biddy shook his head. "No, no, Biddy did not forget. I do not need you right now."

The lava beast moaned in disagreement. "B U T! I am a friend to Biddy's friends! But—" the lava giant stuttered, "you have too many friends. I kill just a few of them for you?"

Biddy began to scold the giant beast as it was shrinking away. "We do not kill unless we have to. And these are Biddy's friends. And I can have as many as I want."

The creature spoke sorrowfully before it disappeared. "F I N E. Bye, friends of Biddy."

Serin smiled at the beast and said, "Bye."

13

Marcella focused on the female knight before her. The lifeless expression on Jess's face meant that the poison had taken over completely. The danger, though not currently lethal, was still very real. Given enough time, it would rot her from the inside out. Marcella reached into her kit and pulled out some small salves and a tonic. Lifting Jess's head, she gently tipped the tonic into her throat. Marcella kept the portions of each offered sip small, not wishing to drown her patient. Within a few minutes, the knight's body began showing signs of life. Her legs bent slightly, and her feet twitched a few times. Soon, the movement spread to her arms and neck. Like a wave crashing over a seawall, her body groaned as if waking from a deep sleep. Marcella softly soothed the knight, hushing with her voice, and watched as the effects of the assuaging tonic made from gryphon's tears took hold. Above all other creatures, gryphons and hippogryphs were the favored beasts in the Asmolorian armies because of their unmatched loyalty, inherent healing properties, and exceptional combat skills.

Jess's face began contracting faintly until her eyes began fluttering open. "Good, Jess. You're safe."

Everyone, save for Marcella and Jess, had formed a broken circle surrounding Victus. Resting all weapons easily, they intermingled, hugging and congratulating one another. All present felt a remarkable sense of appreciation in the midst of uncertainty. Humans and gnomes alike enjoyed the grateful reprieve from combat and loss. Separate parties honored their duty by coming to the aid of a fellow brother or sister, which represented something remarkable to all humans. No matter where you lay as a citizen or within the ranks, noble or lowborn, soldier or farmhand, you were human and part of a larger family.

Beset with both pride and respect, Victus looked around at all those present. For him, this moment was the culmination of a lifetime of living out the principles of chivalry, duty, loyalty, and love. He might not have had the opportunity to work with each and every soldier he came across or that served under him, but his charisma and love for his people had a way of seeping into the hearts of others. Regardless of his own imperfections and missteps, all those who stood there did so voluntarily, motivated by affection and obligation to a man who had encouraged them to become better versions of themselves. Victus spun as he embraced yet another legionnaire in thanks.

"Why have you come? Surely you could not have seen the flare from the city?" Victus asked finally, looking from one face to another.

Titus moved closer to his commander as the surrounding conversations died down and answered, "Sir— We were commanded to find you by Knighturion Calder after we were formally dismissed by the steward of the city and his elven companions."

Victus' elation about the unexpected events drained away. A powerful feeling of righteous indignation instantly substituted the initial emotions of joy and pride. His smile waned, and he adopted an indomitable, focused face, his jawline set firm and high in the air, his arms relaxed but enclosed together behind his back—he listened to every word. He had known something would happen soon. His investigation had led him to believe that the murders were attached to something much larger.

Young Serin chimed in, "Yes, they dismissed all the soldiers. The city is now controlled by the elves. I overheard some of them talking while I was hiding, and they were definitely talking about Lestar… in what I believe was dark elvish." Murmurs hummed through the group.

Titus let the young girl finish before continuing, "Calder set off for Asmadine with the mission you gave him before you left. We were being followed. At least I believed we were, but they left us once the flare appeared. Or lost us because of the speed—Marcella had us traveling faster. As for the elves the young princess speaks of, they say they are from the Inquisition."

Victus said nothing; the heartbeats passing between them felt like an eternity. Everyone bore into their commander, and he could feel the weight in his heart. He knew what he had to do; he knew what they had to do. He understood the price they would all pay. It was something he had asked of his men and women before, but he never relished it.

One of the veteran legionnaires, with a cord of gold and black attached to his spear, broke Victus' quiet contemplation. "We are with you, sir. To whatever end. Say the word; we are yours to command." He ended his sentiment with a low mantra of, "Huh! Huh! Huh!" which led all gathered to chant, "Huh! Huh! Victus! Huh! Huh! VICTUS!"

The commander's right hand offered them a salute, and they quieted. He walked over to the legionnaire, twenty years his senior. Victus had been the only senior officer who would accept the man's reenlistment five years ago. He knew this man was born to be a soldier. He lived and breathed the life of a soldier, and Victus was glad to have him—not just because the man was an experienced, battle-hardened veteran, but because he also inspired others, and Victus himself learned from him. Merely a week into active duty under Victus, the man had shown his worth ten times over. He was of average height, and Victus looked down at him, peering underneath the man's helm. Victus saw scars too numerous to count and turned down to look at the embroidered black and golden cord wound tightly around the spear, a serpent on a branch.

When Victus spoke next, his adoration was visible. “Twenty years, legionnaire Janus had served. Then, after his retirement, though well earned, he reenlisted to continue his service to humanity.” Victus spoke loud enough for the group to hear, a tone he used for larger crowds. “After another twenty years, this man again earned his retirement. But again, he volunteered for service. Forty-five years this hero has been in the legions. Thank you for all that you have done and sacrificed, legionnaire Janus. Your dedication and that of your fellow soldiers ease the weight of leadership from my shoulders. Legionnaires such as you are the inspiration that encourages me to carry on. Your courage and selflessness are the personification of what it means to be a knight legionnaire.” He saluted the soldier as everyone around roared. Aris cheered as he put his arm around Serin, who was whistling and hooting.

As everyone calmed, Victus turned and looked each of them in the eye before speaking again. “We have lost the city of Lindly. The dark elves have infested our homes. Cowardly! Hiding behind mirages and cloaks of darkness. But my aim is to stop them. Tomorrow we will march back, feigning ignorance of their designs. Let them believe they have won. Then we strike.” He stopped and looked down towards Biddy beside him. “I have to ask you for a favor.”

Biddy giggled, “Anything!”

“I need you to get to Skylighter in Asmadine.” Biddy squeaked as if to protest—after all, he was on an elven kill-on-sight list. Biddy had embarrassed one of the Apexa, a group of high elven mages, who set the rules for magic use. The gnome was also responsible for some structural destruction from some of his experiments. Most of the other races chalked it up to exploration and intellectual curiosity; however, the elves responded by banishing the gnome from all of their lands and from the capital, unto death. When they realized the gnome honored that punishment, and that they wouldn’t get to kill him, they decided that it was time to just officially make it a kill-on-sight warrant.

The gnome closed his eyes, taking a breath to acknowledge facing this peril as well as the magic required to travel to Asmadine. He would have to enter the slipstream in order to reach Skylighter's paladin's inner sanctum. "I will leave tomorrow when you break camp."

Victus nodded, gratitude displayed across his face as he grinned down at his friend. He knew the risk, but he also knew that Biddy would be the fastest way to get to Skylighter. Again speaking to everyone, Victus smiled, "Let us make way through the threshold. Set up a perimeter around the campsite. No one is to be alone—four guards will march in pairs. Tonight, we will have Biddy host a feast and plan further."

Titus responded with a salute, "Right you are, sir." Spinning, he moved to the portal and yelled, "You lot heard him! Let's go." Hustling, they each began stepping through the threshold. Biddy watched, his goggles resting on his forehead, smiling as he thought about what to conjure for dinner, his ideas getting more and more grand as he waited.

As everyone was making their way through the portal, Jess's eyes were wide, and she tried to speak. All that Marcella could hear was the breath from her lungs blowing against her cheek. Jess reached, rather, tried to reach up to Marcella and use her to pull herself up. Understanding what Jess wanted, Marcella wrapped her arms around her and pulled. Jess tried to stand; her feet were somewhat under her control, but she could not stand by her own strength.

Jess stared at Victus. From the back, she saw his broad shoulders, the subtle sway and movements of his arms as he spoke, his demeanor penetrating. Tears formed in her eyes, streaming down her face. She mouthed his name. Faster and faster, she pushed the words from her lungs. Her vocal cords were softly vibrating as she said, "Victus." The name she had called out seemed to dissipate into the air, carried away by a gentle breeze. Continuing, she pushed harder, while Marcella stabilized the young knight and heard the whisper, "Victus.

Victus." After a few moments of trying over and over, her voice returned forcefully—"VICTUS!"

The commander snapped his head back towards the cry. Seeing Jess on her feet, he sprinted up to her, nearly knocking Marcella over as he enveloped Jess. "You're alive! How do you feel?"

Jess smiled, but it didn't reach her eyes as she said, "Like I have just been reborn; just gotta wake everything up is all." Her eyes looked down to her feet, and Victus pulled her arm over his shoulder. Using his body against hers, he carried her, helping her walk.

After a moment of silence, she let out a small sob. "I thought I had failed you. I thought I would never see you again."

He craned his neck to look down at her, speaking gently, "Never could you fail me. As for seeing me again, our paths will always cross. Whether in this world or the next, we will never be separated for long."

Her tears streamed silently but lightened a bit as she was gaining more control of her body and emotions. Clearing her mind, she focused on what she needed to tell him. "I was not dismissed, Victus. I gave up my command under Brandan after seeing the garrison disbanded. Everything was happening behind the scenes. Everything was rushed and disorderly. But…it was with purpose and deliberate. Messy."

He nodded. "I have heard."

It was then she saw some familiar faces marching into the knight's threshold. Since she had been undercover in the personal house guard of House Neske, it made it more difficult to remember names. She looked into Victus' eyes. "They were the soldiers that refused dismissal. Calder's men!"

Marcella, who had been following behind, interrupted, "Are you feeling any ill symptoms? And I don't mean muscle numbness or loss of motor functions. That will be sorted in about an hour." Jess turned and shook her head no. Marcella smiled. "Good." She saluted Victus. "Sir, I am heading with the others."

Slightly tilting his head down, he smiled. "Thank you and well done."

Serin and Aris watched Jess and Victus's interaction in merriment. Both of them had believed for a long time that they would be well suited as mates, though duty had prevented any formal recognition of affection. Aris broke the silence in a whisper, "My father loves her. Jess has come by our house many times late at night. She was placed in House Neske's personal guard to gather intel."

Serin grabbed Aris's arm and tugged gently. "She loves him." Her dark jade eyes bore into him until he turned and met hers. For a heartbeat, with only their eyes, they could feel one another's love as they stood staring. Serin whispered to Aris, "I am scared about tomorrow. Does your father realize the elves outnumber us?"

Aris smirked. "He knows. We all know now. And Serin, I am scared too. But we must use that fear as fuel to do what is right. What happens to all those innocents if we do nothing? The dark elves do not have anything pleasant in store for our city, nor for the people in it. We have no choice."

She tugged his arm, pulling him close, and wrapped her arms around him. He could smell her hair as he leaned his head down on hers. His heart was beating so fast, and he flushed with something he had only felt with her. The love he felt was intoxicating. Her voice muffled, she said, "No matter what happens, Aris." She leaned out of his embrace to meet his eyes. "No matter what happens when we go back, know that I love you. I know it sounds silly. But I do. No princess has ever had better or nobler knights. Your father and you are my family. I love you."

Aris's stomach was in his throat, his face warm as it reddened. "I…I love you. We go together, united as one, to whatever end." His tone reflected the confidence and assuredness he felt in their duty.

Her lips turned upward. “If we fight, I want to be near you.”

Aris reached down and grabbed her hand. “Come, let’s go back to the main camp. As for tomorrow, if we do fight, I imagine we will—follow my lead.” He looked over at her as they moved past Victus and Jess.

Biddy trailed behind the two younglings, interrupting their privacy. “Aris, when we get back, I intend to start the preparations for dinner. But once that is done, we have the ‘contingency’ to work on.”

Aris, only a few steps away from the threshold, turned and smiled. “I am ready when you are.” Serin looked between the two, confused. “What contingency? What are you doing?”

Aris grinned. “I am getting my weapons made into rune magic. It will give me the ability to recall my dagger and sword from within my body. The dark elf assassin I killed was marked with rune magic. He pulled his black blade from nothing. Hard to explain, but you can come with us and watch if you want. Biddy still has to work out some of the details.”

She scrunched her face and squinted questioningly at him. “Sounds... interesting. And painful.” They continued through the threshold.

Biddy was giddy and remarked, “Oh, it’s gonna hurt. Never done this before.”

~~~

Jess and Victus were the last ones at the flare site and took the moment for themselves. They hugged, and Victus leaned in and kissed her lips. His hands traced over her scarred face as he spoke. “I have loved you since I met you. I will love you long after I die. You have done more than required, and yet I must ask more of you. Tomorrow, if combat is on the path set before us, stay close to me and Aris. He still has much to learn, and if there is a choice to be made between his life or mine—save his. This is a personal request, not an order.”
~~~

He could see her hesitation briefly before she nodded. "I will do as you ask, Victus."

He hugged her in thanks. "After all of this is settled, I am going to request that we are given the proper disposition to be married—if you will have me? I think we have earned the right to be both soldier and couple. You would be taken from my command, but under the circumstances, I think it would be allowed."

Her conservative smile covered the welling in her heart to hear these words from the man she adored the most. "Of course, Victus. But if you are given the choice between your career as a soldier, as a leader, or being a husband, promise me that you will honor that commitment and not choose me. You are too valuable to our people. You must choose to serve them over me. We need more leaders like you, and I will not be the one to steal that away from them." She knew Victus, and she understood that this man would not be able to live with walking away from his work, his career, his soldiers. It was his whole life. He loved her; that she knew. But she never wanted him to make a choice between her and soldiering, nor would she ever ask him to give it up.

He smiled, hugging her again. "I promise." He heard a hoot and instinctively looked up, his eyes scanning the treetops for any sign of movement. On top of a branch nearby, an owl hooted again. He looked at the bird curiously. Letting go of Jess, he said, "Can you manage through the threshold? I have one more thing to do before I go."

She tried to cock her brow, but the words had to convey what her face could not. "What's going on? What are you looking at?"

He chuckled. "I believe an old friend is here and wishes to speak with me."

She turned to look around and saw nothing. "Who?"

Victus pointed to the barn owl sitting on the branch, hooting once again. "Thorm-Hammer of Clan Hewer."

She turned on him as if he was crazy. “You call *him* friend? He serves and plays both sides. He is a mercenary under Malakas. No loyalty and no honor.” She nearly spat the words out, disgusted.

Victus knew Thorm was an arch of Malakas, that his people sought her embrace back before the first wars, and he knew that though Malakasians preferred balance and neutrality, they often helped Eu’rok’s side and Asmolor’s, hoping to maintain a balance between the two brother gods. Thorm was as honorable as they come, at least in his own personal fashion. “I trust him,” he said simply. Victus smiled reassuringly at Jess as the female knight tilted her head, half looking back toward the owl.

“I trust you, Victus. Be safe, and I will see you on the other side,” she said, kissing him swiftly, her voice a whisper, “I love you, Victus Andreas.” She stepped out on her own two feet, holding her balance, but before she stepped through the portal, Jess paused and indiscriminately raised her voice for all near to hear, though she only really saw Victus. “If you hurt him, I will hunt your people down in the Netherwood, Grotto of Hewer, and anywhere else until I have killed you and all your clan, Thorm-Hammer.” She stepped through, and as she did, she noticed Victus's grin widen in response to her threat.

And then it was just Victus who stood there, staring up at the owl, feeling a sense of reverence.

14

Nibarn was standing in the council chambers inside the palace with his advisers and the elf priestess. They had gathered this early afternoon to see a demonstration of Lestar's plans for the city. Lestar wanted them all to see and understand the nature of what they were going to do. She wanted them to witness her will being fulfilled. She wanted them to grovel in deference to her power, her corruption, her darkness. Though she personally had yet to arrive at the city, as far as everyone was concerned, the priestess had her orders and would die to see them through. Nibarn motioned for his peers to find their seats as the priestess stepped into the middle of the circular chamber. She spun her hands out wide, as if embracing the room. "Though we all have different pasts and we have been separated by our race, by our birthright—we are all one in our goddess, Lestar. Our love and devotion to her is boundless." All present nodded and affirmed her statement with soft claps. "In this, we willingly give up our lives to serve. We sacrifice all that we hold dear to embrace her. Today we test her new creation, the siphon." The priestess turned to one of the elven guards near the entrance. "Bring them in."

The guard opened the door and ushered the children in. Nibarn watched the street rats, some no older than five, enter the chamber. They were all of a singular mind—terrified and uncertain. The first in, being the eldest, must have been around thirteen, Nibarn mused. The young man puffed up his chest, mustering all his courage, and made his way to the priestess. She smiled at him and the others. "Come. You are receiving a gift. You are no longer going to have to toil in the streets to survive. Today, I will bestow power to you that can only be offered by the gods themselves." At this, all the children smiled and relaxed. "Please come stand here and wait to be called by name. This is a formal ceremony in which you all will be given a chance at a new life. New beginnings."

The children formed a close-knit circle in the center of the room. "Perfect," the priestess said as she turned and moved from the center. Lifting her hand, she flicked it toward someone unseen in the shadows. A small barrier of silver and red formed, surrounding the children. The oldest of them saw the danger first and tried to run past the magical wall, which was arching into a dome over them. He was shocked and knocked back—trapped. Many of the other children began crying. Nibarn was smiling darkly as he licked his lips, as if he were feeding off the fear. His peers were not as inclined to embrace the terror as something cheerful. The priestess strolled around the now-imprisoned children and spoke. "This magical barrier represents the city walls." As she continued, four guards stepped in with toddler-sized purple-black crystals. "These crystals the guards carry are the smaller version of what sits in the towers presently. When activated, they will rise from their cradles and arch toward the center of the town. As they do, they will release the siphon."

The guards moved up to the magical barrier, where four holes opened. They dropped the crystals inside the barrier, which then hovered an inch from the ground. One of the kids attempted to kick a crystal, but instead of making contact, he was knocked out and flung to the other side of the barrier with surprising force. Nibarn chuckled, and the others followed until they were all laughing at the trapped, petrified children. The sound of laughter and screaming echoed through the room as some of the children lost control of their bladders and created puddles underneath their feet.

The eldest of them tried to reassure them. He huddled them close and told them to close their eyes. The priestess continued, "Within the next few moments, the crystals will rise to the peak of this small dome and consume the souls of these pathetic creatures."

Not three heartbeats had passed when the crystals began rising. They each looked like small rain clouds dripping a sparkling violet-black substance. It fell to the ground like rain but left nothing. The children huddled tighter as the crystals rose. "Keep your eyes closed," the eldest boy said. He watched as the crystals formed above them into one crystal and pulsated with darkness as if someone were covering and uncovering a candle. The hue was violet, but it was so dark it appeared black. The sparkling gaseous rain touched all of them and poured down on them. None of them were wet, yet they felt something pulling, or rather weighing them down, as if it were a deluge on a spring morning.

Those watching the display saw the souls of each child being pulled up toward the crystals. All the faces of the tormented children were now pacified, lifeless. Standing in place, husks —unmoving and dead-looking. The souls were all floating above and up toward the crystals. The faces represented the genuine horror of everything. Screaming and crying without a sound being heard, they were sucked into the darkness.

The priestess again flicked her hand, and the crystals detached and became four pieces again. Lowering themselves down to where they were dropped beside the soulless children standing there, unblinking, dead but still alive. Their hearts were beating; they were still breathing. But all that they had once been was gone.

The priestess laughed vilely, "As you can see, we have sent their souls to our father, Eu'rok, in Lestar's name. Nothing does she desire more than to feed him the souls of innocents. And because of our devotion and love, we offer them willingly. As we will with this entire city. All of them will be hers, and in that, his." She walked toward the lifeless drones standing inside the barrier. As she neared, the barrier dissipated. "These soulless bodies are now slaves to our mistress's will. We shall wait to see if she gives them a command."

Nibarn and his cultists watched eagerly, some thinking to themselves that at least they did not suffer. Although the torment was incomprehensible to the children, they were now under Eu'rok's influence. The cultists themselves would eventually pass on and reap their deserved reward. Each one of them held the conviction that their piety towards the dark gods would guarantee their eventual salvation.

Suddenly, the eldest boy sprinted from the center of the circle right towards Nibarn. It happened so fast that Nibarn jolted back and froze in place. The young man had his hands wrapped around Nibarn's throat. Nibarn scrambled to scream and say something, but the boy's grip was tight, and he could barely grasp his breath. The priestess began laughing, "It seems our mistress has full control. And all of our hard work has not been in vain."

The elven guards laughed with her, and Nibarn's friends, if you could call them that, were running to help pry the young man off him. Their attempts were futile—hitting the boy and trying to pull him off did nothing. He had strength beyond them all.

The priestess walked over as Nibarn grew blue. "See, nothing can stand against Lestar. Step aside." Those gathered stopped trying to free Nibarn and bowed to the priestess. Just as quickly as the assault began, it stopped. The young boy stepped down off the chair and away from Nibarn; his eyes were unseeing and empty.

Nibarn coughed roughly, gasping to catch his breath. "Truly… a magnificent power. Praise be to Lestar." He strained the words through broken breaths and coughs.

The priestess reached over to touch Nibarn's chin. "All of this you have helped bring to fruition, and you will be rewarded. Lestar appreciates your loyalty. Have her token, as you have earned it, Nibarn of House Neske."

The man eagerly gobbled down the small orb she offered him. Still coughing, he cravenly forced the small pearl down his throat, allowing the darkness to consume and fill him up.

"Good boy," she said, laughing, and then walked to the middle again, speaking to the guards casually. "Take the children and cut off their heads. We mustn't spoil the surprise for tomorrow."

Without hesitation, the guards stationed around the chambers decapitated the children.

Nibarn felt amazing. He felt as if all that he ever wanted was just a day away. He was euphoric. The priestess spoke to them all once more before leaving the chambers. "Be certain to stay close and near me at the appointed time. Or—be caught up in the siphon." She shrugged and left the chambers.

Nibarn, his lips turned upwards in a magnificent grin, confidently spoke to the elven guards nearest the dead children. "Clean this up. We have a council meeting in an hour, and I will not have blood on my floor."

The elves cursed him with their eyes but obeyed the orders. From behind Nibarn's chair, some of the stones began to crack and slide open—Brandan was using the secret passageways to enter the chamber. He walked in, not realizing that it was in use, and tried to backtrack.

Nibarn yelled, "Idiot boy! What are you doing in here?"

Brandan stopped his backtracking and stepped forward. "I am still a little drunk and took a wrong turn in the passageway. For some reason, I was inside the castle walls. Too much wine." He chuckled nervously, still approaching his father. His head was low as he bowed to his father. But as he got closer and his head rose, he saw the lifeless bodies of the children. He saw the heads lying on the ground, the blood pooled, and high elven guards cleaning and removing them. Horrified, he yelled, "What…? Why are they dead?" His body was erect, facing his father; he stared, enraged and disgusted. “WHAT IS THIS?”

Nibarn snarled and backhanded Brandan so forcefully that the young man recoiled. “This is none of your affair. These were leeches upon a great city, and the Inquisition determined they would better serve Asmolor dead.”

Brandan stepped back from his father even more, his hands raised. “This is madness. They were children.”

Nibarn pointed at his son firmly. “Know your place, or you will end up like them. The Inquisition does not play games. And if they decide to end a life, I will not stand in their way. Not even to save my weak idiot of a son or your stupid sister. Understand me?” Brandan nodded, inwardly hurt by the cruelty of his father’s words. “Now get out of here. I do not want to see you until tomorrow when the Inquisition renders its judgment.”

Brandan said nothing and bowed. He turned back into the secret passageway and attempted to remember how to get back to his room.

He spent the next hour wandering the halls, never making it back to his room. His mind, no longer clouded with alcohol, reasoned through everything that had happened since Victus left. Something was wrong, and those who spoke up against it had left the city. He was alone, and he did not know what was truly going on. Nor did he know what to do. Eventually, he came to the only conclusion that made sense: he would leave the city today and head for Delwan. For Victus. He would try to warn Victus of what he had seen and perhaps repair the damage his father was doing. Upon reaching his chambers, Brandan grabbed the rod of power to the city of Lindly. He changed his clothing into something more comfortable for traveling. It was still ostentatious, but he concluded that anyone would look upon him as a wealthy merchant—not the son of Nibarn.

He made certain that nothing he had on him denoted his rank or his House. He packed some food and wine and made his way out of his room.

Carefully looking around the halls before moving, he made his way to the House Neske guard chambers. Upon reaching them, two guards sat playing dice. "I require your assistance," Brandan said as he pushed into the room.

One of the guards laughed. "Piss off, we are not on duty." Both turned, one sighing in defeat as the dice rolled in the other's favor. Both of the guards laid eyes on the man and immediately hopped from their seats.

"Apologies, my Lord—I didn't know it was you."

Both bowed deeply. The second guard asked, "What do you need of us?" His words dripped with alcohol.

Brandan did not care who they were or what they had said. He was nervous but excited. For the first time, he felt that he had a purpose. He had something meaningful to live for. "I require you both disguised as civilian bodyguards."

The two guards looked at one another. "Of course, sir. Do we need to bring anything?"

Brandan looked back out the door. "Your swords only and food for a few days. Hurry, we leave immediately."

The two men scrambled to dress, placing well-seasoned studded leather on and plain gladii into their belts. One grabbed a backpack and began tossing bread, cheese, and water skins inside. "Where are we headed, my lord?"

Shaking his head, Brandan sighed. "No time to explain. We must be going now."

The two plain-looking guards and the rich merchant left the palace as inconspicuously as possible.

Brandan led them to the stables, where he was instantly puzzled. "What? Where? Never mind—there's no time!

Come take a mule instead. We will travel mostly on foot. That should keep us from being noticed too much."

One of his guards began packing the supplies on the mule. "Sir, someone is coming."

Brandan shushed and shooed them along, and they jogged from one side of the stables to the other, farther away from the approaching stable guard.

When they were clear of the stables and well on their way on the main street of the city, Brandan began to speak to himself but also to the two following him. "We have to leave the city and find Victus. The city is in trouble, and I am at a loss on how to stop it." Both guards stayed a few steps behind Brandan, tugging the mule and listening. "We have to fix this."

They kept a steady pace, and as they reached more crowded areas, Brandan pulled his cloak over his head. The older of the two guards asked, "Fix what, sir?"

Brandan stopped abruptly to face the man. "We have to stop whatever it is that is going on here. I don't know, but it is wrong, and I have been too stupid to see it." This did not satisfy the guard, but he let it go and continued to follow. They continued throughout the city until they reached one of the city's major gateways. "One second," Brandan pulled them off to the side, out of the line of merchants and travelers going about their daily routine. "I need to make a pass out of the city."

He reached into his pack on the mule and pulled out a metallic seal of House Neske. Hastily, he grabbed a piece of parchment, a quill, and dipped it in the small travel-sized inkwell. Scribbling a note that read, "House Neske dressmaker. Allow free passage to and from the city." Glancing up from the note, he made sure no one was watching as his guards pretended to check the packed mule. Brandan whispered to one of the guards, "I need a light." The older guard reached into his pocket, pulling out a small tinderbox, and tossed it over. Brandan grabbed a candle from the pouch as he put the quill and inkwell back. Striking the match, he melted some wax on the parchment and pressed his House seal into it, blowing on it to allow it an extra moment to dry fully. He then folded the parchment and passed it to the elder guard. "When we reach the entrance, pass this to the guard."

The next ten minutes had Brandan sweating out all the alcohol he had drunk the night before. He could smell it on him, and his stomach growled in fear and hunger. When they finally reached the gate, he kept his head low and fiddled with the mule as the elder guard spoke to the elven sentry. The elf simply motioned for them to carry on and let them pass. Once outside the city wall, Brandan bent over and puked. One of the elven sentries turned at the sound. "He alright?"

Brandan collected himself with his head low. "Drank too much last night. I am fine."

Pressing forward, they followed the others who were ahead of them on the main road from the city. After they had made some distance, Brandan slowed and asked, "What is the fastest route to Delwan? That is where Victus and his son are headed, and we will find them on that path."

Moving from the back, the younger guard motioned to follow the main road. "If we follow this and make camp just off the main road tonight, then we can cut through the woods early in the morning. It will shave a few days off our journey. But without mounts, we are still going to be slow going, my lord."

Brandan nodded. "Whatever it takes. We have to get to Victus. No matter the cost, we have to get to him."

The two guards dropped back behind their lord as he walked in front of the mule, one whispering to the other, "What has gotten into him? It's as if he actually gives a damn about something."

The elder shrugged, responding less enthusiastically, “Doubtful. He is still drunk. He probably doesn’t even know what he is saying or doing.”

15

Victus looked up at the barn owl in the tree as Jess said her piece to Thorm, who at that time had fashioned himself as a barn owl. Jess vanished through the threshold, and the owl stepped off the branch and glided down toward Victus. As he closed the gap from the branch to Victus, his wings began turning into feathered arms, and his taloned feet morphed into short, stout legs. Thorm transformed fully from the brown barn owl into an exceptionally tall dwarf who stood at five feet, five inches; he towered over most of his brethren.

Victus looked the dwarf over, noting the distinct patterns of leather he wore. Victus knew that each piece of animal hide concealed what was underneath—the magical half-plate armor the arch dwarf wore. The animal skins were more of an adornment, denoting his station within his clan, but they also displayed a hidden rank or druidic hierarchy that Victus did not completely understand. Only those serving the sister goddess Malakas would know.

The owl feathers represented wisdom, while the wolf pelt represented freedom. Each piece had significance to Thorm and his clan. Thorm had embraced and embodied the spirits of all animals but had his preferred modes of traveling in animal form, such as the barn owl. The two just stood staring at one another in consideration of the other. Thorm touched his auburn beard, strumming the braids and beads. "What're ya about, Victus?" The dwarf's scruffy brow arched high in curiosity, his gruff voice hinting at anger.

Victus smirked knowingly. "I am about my duty, faithful Thorm."

The dwarf's face scrunched in posed anger. Victus intentionally and playfully called him 'faithful.' It was a term used derogatorily against the dwarf and his kin. To most of the other races, they were nothing but mercenaries. They served Malakas, and she switched sides in the wars on a whim, never favoring one brother or the other for long. The relationship between Thorm and his fellow Malakasians and those serving Asmolor or Eu'rok was fraught with tension due to this changing of "faiths."

However, Victus knew that deep inside, the dwarf hated serving under Eu'rok's generals, and his true love was his own clan, his friends, and fighting itself. Victus had come to trust the dwarf, and the dwarf had grown to care more for this human than any other before him. Being an arch of Malakas and having immense power and immortality, he had seen many humans in the thousands of years he had lived. But Victus and his son were his kin in his mind.

The dwarf's face reddened as he held his pretend anger at bay, then he burst into a roar of laughter. "Come here, lad. Ye bastard half-pal!" His arms stretched out to embrace the human.

Victus started laughing as he wrapped his arms around the sturdy dwarf. The dwarf's laugh was a catalyst that led many to either laugh with or hate him. "Been far too long," Victus said as he stepped back. "What brings you here? I figured you would be well on your way to the ceremony in Delwan."

The dwarf shook his head and looked down away from the man. "Nah, lad, I had to come back to get you back on your way."

Victus scoffed. "Back on my way? We had already set out for Delwan. Present circumstances have forced me to recall my pilgrimage to Delwan. Lindly is being overrun or has been. Dark elves have infested it, and House Neske has turned traitor and cultist. I need to stop the injustices that they will surely bring upon my people."

Thorm sighed; the moan came from deep within his soul. He grieved as he spoke, "Lad, I know all about it. Some of my boys were working with the damned darkies years ago, crafting some type of crystalline magic. At first, it was done in concordance with Malakas's commands. When I snooped a bit, I found out that it was a massively devastating weapon being crafted. I brought this to Malakas's attention, and we halted all aid." Victus listened and visibly saw the sunken grief plain on the dwarf's face. "When Malakas found that the project was intended as something other than to heal the land, but rather to destroy and consume souls, aye, she was furious, and it has caused her to become indifferent to the wars after and to come. Now she cares only for herself and her people. We have become complacent and stunted."

Victus nodded as he absorbed all the information. "What does this have to do with me?"

The dwarf reached up to the man's shoulders, grabbing them tightly in his firm grip; his two hammers jingled at his waist as he did. "Because some of my boys kept helping them, and it was completed. And I'm telling you true, it will be tested on a grand scale in your town. I know this. Balaster, the dark elf emissary, informed me after a bit of dwarven persuasion."

Victus shook his head, vexed. "Then I am running out of time. I need to get back as soon as possible."

The dwarf stomped his right foot. "No, lad, you ain't been hearing me. The crystals are primed and running under dark magic in your city. It will consume all souls and leave no one alive—soulless and dominated by the will of Lestar or even Eu'rok. There ain't nothing you can do to stop it. Nothing you can do for the city. You best get your boy and head on to Delwan with me."

Victus was indignant, then calming. He responded, "I will not abandon Lindly. I will not abandon the people. If what you say is so…" He paused as he took a deep breath. "If this is so, then I have more of a responsibility to go back. That is my city, my people. I know we can make a difference by being there for them in their darkest hour. I won't be a bystander as the darkness preys on the innocent."

Thorm squinted, flipping his hands up and waving them at the man. "Stubborn as a daft dwarf. You will be killed, and your boy, too. There ain't no stopping it."

Victus looked high into the heavens above and closed his eyes. "Even if I cannot stop it, if I can save one life, I will. I will not abandon the city."

The dwarf's hands were on his hammers, tapping them in thought. He knew he could defeat Victus in combat. He was aware of the fact that he had the ability to knock him out and take both the boy and him to a secure location. But he would never do it; he could only try to bluff. "Now don't be making me take yer lad. Just come with me, bring your boy." But he saw that his words fell on closed ears, so he tried a different tactic. He let loose his tongue, using all the persuasive magic he could muster. "Think of your boy—Aris. He has a future, with a wife and kids, happy and alive." All of this was plastered into Victus's mind.

Victus saw a much older Aris and a beautiful grown-up Serin. They were happy, laughing, and chasing four children around a modest yard. Then he saw himself much older, walking up to them carrying gifts and wine. Jess was in tow with their own child. Victus's eyes glossed over with tears as he saw what could be and then closed his eyes. "Thorm. It will not work. I am going back to put up a fight. You should come with me. Call your bannered warriors. Call your clan to war. I am not asking you to join Asmolor and his pompous elves. I am asking you to join me. Join the humans and fight as brothers and sisters together. Two people together. A union between races that even the gods cannot *stop—join me.* We can stop them. We can stand against the tyranny together!" Victus imbued every word, not with magic like the dwarf had but with passion and charisma that urged the dwarf and gave him chills.

Thorm felt his people had been abandoned first by Asmolor, then by the dwarven god Dwendel, and now by Malakas. He knew they needed to move past the gods and form a fresh path. But the timing wasn't right. Too many of his own people were infighting and without purpose. Because of the connection Thorm had created between their minds, Victus could hear Thorm's thoughts, due to his meddling in psionics. "This could be what reinvigorates your people. Brings them purpose, brings them the freedom you have always wanted for them. Have the courage to stand with me!"

Thorm shook his head. "I can't do that, lad. I just can't. I cannot doom my people because you feel that we can win together."

Victus clenched his jaw tight and spoke softly, "Thorm, I am not charging in without a plan. We can do this. Skylighter and his gryphon riders will reinforce us, and hopefully more. It is not a lost cause. The battle is not decided; the outcome is not guaranteed. You can be a part of this with us."

Thorm reached under his leather garments into his satchel. He pulled out a bark-skinned mug, closed his eyes, and muttered in prayer. The mug filled with Dunderdee ale, frothy, foamy, and delicious. Victus could smell the aroma. It was harsh but inviting. The dwarf took a large swig, the foam covering his beard and mouth. "Good ale, lad—drink." Victus nodded and took the mug, which was still full. He drank a large amount, if not slightly more than the dwarf. With most dwarves, disagreements or discussions were done over fine ale and food. Thorm used this ritualistic drinking out of tradition but also for the desire to drink away differences.

Victus passed the ale back to the dwarf, knelt down, and began drawing in the sand. A shield caught Thorm's eye, and Victus sketched his coat of arms—a bear—within the shield, using a stick. He then drew two hammers and an anvil. The anvil was placed at the bottom or tip of the shield, and the hammers were on the sides. At the top of the crest, he wrote in Dwarvish: "Broktas ven Blouda," which read in the Common tongue as "Brothers in arms."

Victus rose from the dust and looked intently at the dwarf, who could not help but grin. The inner turmoil Thorm felt tore at his guts. "We can do this together, Thorm. My people, your people, our people." Thorm drank deep from his mug and passed it again to Victus, who also drank.

The froth-covered dwarf pleaded, yielding slightly, "I will join you. We will make this move together, lad. But we won't be doing none of that if you be dead. Now chalk up the city as a loss and come with me to Delwan. We can discuss plans for the future together."

Victus finished his giant gulp of ale, nodding, and the dwarf's eyes widened in what he thought was a deal well struck. He reached for the mug and began guzzling it down his throat in joy. Victus patiently smiled at the dwarf, who was truly imbibing the drink even more. "I have spoken to you for years about where your people could find a home in union with humans. Even your kin would embrace you back. Never once have you truly given it a thought. Now that you see Malakas has failed your people just as the others have, it is time. Time now to choose your own path. Not relying on the whims of gods, but on what is best for you, your clan, and your friends. Choosing to join me in the next few days does not make a damn bit of difference if you will not stand now when it matters. And mind you, it matters now. We need your help, and from your own words, we cannot win. You must stand with us."

The dwarf spat some ale from his mouth and nose. "Damn half-pal, you made me spill the ale."

Victus cocked his brow. "It doesn't empty."

Shaking his head, Thorm chuckled, "Not the point. Ye made me spill the ale."

Victus saw the punch coming and knew it had nothing to do with spilled ale. He took the punch in his gut, though it was half-hearted in its thrust, and his armor absorbed most of it, but he still stumbled back a step. The dwarf was anguished and stepped back from Victus in defeat. "Lad, I cannot be doing what you be asking. Not right now. I have to be tactful, and isn't that what you always be telling me that I need to be doing?"

Victus rubbed his brow in frustration. "You sit on a fence long enough, Thorm, it will impale you."

The dwarf gave him a knowing grin. "My position requires me to dance on the fence, not sit." At that, they both laughed, and the dwarf passed the mug back to Victus. "Ya know, lad, that will make a good crest someday," he gestured at the drawing in the dirt, "House Andreas with clan Hewer."

Victus nodded in affirmation. "It will." The two looked over at each other as they passed the mug back and forth, quietly drinking in thought together.

The dwarf's cheeks flushed with blood from the alcohol as he spoke. "If I can't convince ya not to be doing the dumb thing you plan on doing," he said as he passed the mug over, this time so he could rummage through his satchel again. He pulled a circular disk out of his pouch. "I have had me boys working on something that may help you. If you see the crystals floating and generating the dark magic to consume all, throw this down and smash the gem in the center." He passed the disk over to Victus as he, in turn, took the ale back.

Victus saw a bluish-green gem in the center. "What does it do?"

Thorm swigged again, belched, and replied, "It provides a temporary shield, much like the ones Skylighter's troopers use. It will not hold out magic for long, and it will not prevent the enemy from coming in and dragging your arse out. But it will keep your soul intact."

Victus nodded. "Just one? I can't save myself and watch the rest fall."

Thorm chuckled. "Oh no, no, lad. It will encompass a quarter of your city. And you can bet your shiny arse they will be coming for you when you drop that down. We crafted it off of what was built, the hope being it would be a temporary safety net until you can get the help you need."

Victus was relieved and overwhelmed; he grabbed the dwarf and hugged him. "This is what I am talking about, you stubborn dwarf. Work with us, help us. You already are. You know the differences between our sides. You know what we stand against. I would be honored to have you with me." Victus leaned back from the dwarf, looking him square in the eye, his dwarven accent spot-on as he spoke. "Broktas ven Blouda."

The dwarf smiled and said, "Someday, Victus."

Stepping back from the dwarf, Victus bowed in respect to his friend. "Even so, Thorm, you have come to warn me. You have come as a loyal friend and brother to me and my kin. I thank you. I embrace you as my beloved brother and will always be there for you and yours. This device you have brought me will save many lives, and in this, I accept your aid. I do understand the terrible position you are in, and I do not hold that against you."

Thorm reached his hand out to Victus, and they clasped arms together. "Half-pal, lead your men well. I wish you good fortune in the war to come."

Both smiled, and Victus added, "Thorm, I have never known a more honorable dwarf in all my life."

The dwarf scoffed, "Bah, don't know many of my kin then, do ya?"

The two laughed, and as Victus began to turn for the threshold, Thorm grabbed his arm. His voice was soft as a whisper to hide his excitement and curiosity. "How'd the boy like the armor?"

Victus stopped, inclining his head. "He loves it. Thank you for adding the enchantments with Biddy."

The dwarf beamed. "I do believe it was some of the finest work since before the first war."

Victus pursed his lips in thought, then asked, "Besides the growth rune embedded, can he socket it how he wishes as he ages?"

The dwarf crossed his arms and nodded. "I left it open for him to attune as you requested. It will hold up in combat if he wishes to remain in the army. But he will be able to use it to enhance his magic if he chooses to follow that path. In the end, Victus, whether he chooses to be a warrior or wizard, he will be well guarded."

Victus nodded in appreciation. "Thank you." He reached over to Thorm and patted him on the shoulder. "I will see you when all this is done."

The dwarf began spinning away as his body transformed back into that of an owl. His voice was solemn. "Aye, lad."

Victus watched the owl soar high into the clouds. The disappointment etched on his face made him wince, as if experiencing invisible pain. It was a pain that didn't afflict the body, but rather the heart. "What a difference the fight would be if Clan Hewer fought with us," Victus stated out loud, the resonating sound of his spoken words cutting deep into his heart. He knew the next day would be the test of not just him, but of his soldiers and his son. If he failed, they would all perish. If he succeeded, the victory would be hollow for the loss of life endured, even more so if he lost his beloved son. Whispering a prayer to himself, Victus turned from the sky above and walked to the threshold portal. Looking back for a second, in the hopes of seeing Thorm return, he let go and stepped through.

16

Nibarn watched his son leave, disgust dripping from his face. With a fierce snarl on his lips, he stared at the closed council room door. He shook his head and turned to the councilors, his cultists. “Each of you has your stones prepared? If Lestar turns on us, we will make our escape and pursue our work elsewhere. I have prepared a place.” None answered, but they all nodded in solemn agreement. “Though I do not expect any reason we would actually need them. Best to be safe, though.” He turned from the group, walking to another hidden door that would lead him to his personal chambers. “I will be in my study. Get some rest. Tomorrow will be the pinnacle of our climb to archdom.” His thoughts were on his own ascension and his reward for serving Lestar. He craved her; he desired to be with her. It was not just a lustful impulse, but a psychological and physiological drive. Nothing gave him more joy and pain in his life. As he walked down the stone path inside the castle to his room, the voice returned in his head with a loud and sharp shout. “Stop this now! End it! Turn back!” It sounded like an echo in his head and yet somehow reverberated off the walls.

He shrieked in fright at the words he heard. “Who’s there?” He spun around the darkened hall. The voice again spoke, much more prominently and coherently. “Turn back from this now. You doom yourself.”

Nibarn’s eyes were wide with anger. “Silence! You know nothing of me or my plans!” he shouted, his hand reaching for his wand.

The voice danced on the air as if it were being passed through the cracks in the stone; the voice whirled in and through him. "Turn away. You do not have to do this. Put a stop to it now–" Before the voice could continue, Nibarn flicked his wand in the direction of what he thought was the person or creature talking to him. A lightning bolt struck forth from the tip, and it cracked into the stone. The force from the hit blew out the dim light from the torches magically ensconced on the wall. Nibarn drew back his wand again, ready to strike if the voice returned. His movements ushered new light from the flames, and they flickered on again. Scoffing, he continued down the serpentine hallway. "Nothing," he said to himself. "It's in my head. I need another orb to calm myself." He thought about how many of the delicious orbs he had gained. The dark elven priestess had given him dozens to hold and devour when he so desired. He had been rewarded, and this was just the beginning.

A foot from the secret entrance to his chamber, the voice returned, its words penetrating his mind and settling deep within his soul. "Turn back now. Or be damned."

Nibarn hunched over, gasping as if he had been punched in the stomach. Within him, he felt his soul cry out in protest, fighting against his body as he tried to stand again. It was crying for him to listen. The sliver of light left in the man fought to overcome the darkness. "Nooo! I am a servant of Lestar, and she will make me immortal!"

He composed himself, stood upright, caught his breath, and entered his study. Upon entering, he went straight to the desk and pulled out a drawer. Desperately, he grabbed two orbs and swallowed them whole. Sighing, he whispered, "Ah… now that is better." Instantly revitalized and filled to the brim with confidence, he checked himself in a mirror. Brushing some of his hair back from his face, he smiled as he looked himself over in the small hand-held mirror. "Magnificent." The orbs removed some of the wrinkles and smoothed out his skin, making the man look and feel younger than he was. He glanced at the door and looked from his desk out the window at the sun. He muttered to himself, "They should be here now."

He rose from his desk and moved to the cabinet holding his tonics, tinctures, and wine. Pouring a glass, he raised it in a toast to himself and then quickly refilled it. He twisted his head towards the door where a guard was standing. "Have my guests arrived?"

The guard's voice answered, "Yes, milord. They arrived only a few moments ago."

Nibarn shook his head in frustration. "Usher them in, please."

The guard opened the door, moving aside to allow the substantial bearded dwarf into the room. The human guard realized he needed to move out of the doorway because the dwarf was so large. As the guard moved to close the door behind him, he uneasily watched as the twenty or so companions of the dwarf moved to follow their leader. The guard glanced back at Nibarn and the leader, a gray-skinned dwarf who said, "No boys, ye sit and wait. No harm comin' to me here. But if this one—" He pointed directly at Nibarn's personal guard in the doorway. "Gives ya any grief, kill 'im."

The guard's face went white as he closed the door and watched the others turn back to sit, wide grins on their faces. Inside the study, Nibarn gave a half-hearted bow to the dwarf known only as the Collector. "Wine?" he asked the dwarf.

The dwarf walked over to Nibarn's cabinet. "Ye got something stronger?" His large fingers found a bottle of rut-gut grain rum near the bottom.

Nibarn tried to dissuade him. "I use that for cleaning only."

The dwarf barked a laugh. "I be using it for drinking."

Nibarn gingerly slipped past the dwarf and sat back in his chair. "Please sit, Collector."

The dwarf took a big swig straight from the bottle and sat himself down in one of the guest chairs. The image of the dwarf sinking so low in the chair gave Nibarn amusement, and he cleverly used his wine glass to cover his grin.

"Damned chair is too small." The dwarf looked like a giant potato as he tried to sit up taller. After a few wiggles and grunts, the dwarf sat, obviously uncomfortable.

Nibarn placed his wineglass down, turning his hands up in a gesture of parley. "Have you brought the rest of the retainer?"

The dwarf belched before his response, "I brought that and more—do you have my bride?" Though the dwarf was paying for a bride, he had no interest in her as one. He collected things and people, placing and keeping them in a magical stasis underneath his palace in Asmadine. He wanted Serin because she was of noble birth, but in his mind, she was also the most beautiful human he had ever laid eyes on.

Nibarn nodded gleefully. "I do. She is here in the palace. My personal guard will have my daughter brought here momentarily." He looked past the enormous dwarf, which proved difficult to do. But he was able to remain dignified as he yelled to his guard, "Go and fetch my sweet daughter, Bolo."

The guard's voice bellowed through the door. "Milord, are you certain I should leave you alone?"

Nibarn snapped, "I gave you a command."

The guard quickly apologized, "Sorry, milord. Right away, milord."

Nibarn returned his attention to his guest, who he saw was finishing the cleaning liquor bottle. Belching again, the dwarf asked, "Ye got any sweets?"

Nibarn shook his head no, reclining back in his chair. "May I see a sample of what you have brought me?"

The dwarf reached down to his belt but could not find his waist, so he stood to retrieve the coin purse. The chair rose with him, and with that, so did his anger. The dwarf's face flushed a darker gray as he grabbed the arms of the chair and broke them off. Standing now unencumbered by the chair, he grabbed the purse and tossed it on the desk in front of Nibarn. He looked inside and saw a black, chalky powder and dumped it on the desk. The dwarf smiled broadly. "Beautiful, isn't it?" Nibarn's eyes widened as he gazed upon the exquisite black powder, noticing the way the light caused it to sparkle like a thousand stars.

Nibarn looked up from the desk. "Is this what the ancient dwarves used to craft with? Is this really void powder?"

The dwarf walked over to the cabinet, grabbed a bottle of rice wine, and crunched the top of the bottle clean off. Chewing, he answered, "Aye, that is the stuff Clan Hewer used long… long ago. Then they swore themselves from ever using it again."

Nibarn nodded. "Yes, I have heard the tales. Too powerful, too dangerous. My interests are purely academic. No need to worry."

The dwarf, clearly not worried, swallowed the broken glass and then the cork. Lifting the jagged edges to his lips, he drank the bottle in one large gulp. "I wasn't caring what ye did with it. Honest and fair trade. The rest of it is being stocked at the location you requested."

Nibarn leaned up from his chair and swept the powder back into the bag. As he swept, he noted it left no residue. It reminded him of gunpowder but was dazzling to look upon and much less messy.

The dwarf turned his head as he heard the clinks of mesh armor and the steps of boots running down the hall to the study. Nibarn, too, heard the sounds and took the small pouch, placing it off to the side where it would be less noticeable.

Nibarn rose from his chair as the door opened to the room. "How dare you!" he scolded the uninvited intruder, stopping when the guard interrupted him.

"Your daughter is missing. She is not in the castle. We have our guards and the high elves scouring the city for her."

The dwarf laughed, "Bah ha ha! Timid bride, eh? Never ye worry. Me boys can stay and help locate her. I need to be heading back for the tourney." The Collector, above all things, treasured his master of ceremonies' role in Asmadine. He had been running it for the last two hundred years. His guild was the largest and most powerful in the city. In all the events, games, and duels, his 'Princes of the Rose' were unrivaled, unstoppable, and undefeated. And the dwarf made certain it stayed that way every year. His guild's advantage rose from his own rise to archdom under Eu'rok; after a long and painstaking agreement with Asmolor's own archs, he resided comfortably in Asmolor's capital city, Asmadine. He swore an oath never to join in any of the wars that the two god brothers may have. Though he honored that on the surface, he undermined the authority of Asmolor's hierarchy in the city. Any rivals that would rise, he absorbed into his criminal network, or if that did not work, he would have them killed. Instead of the guilds operating as they were created for —to offer a centralized location for engaging caravan guards, securing loans, or identifying specialists in diverse domains for mentoring or innovation—most were nothing more than criminal organizations now. Now they were nothing but thugs, stealing and killing anyone who stood in their path. Each guild was a petty little kingdom within the realms of the mortal races.

Nibarn thought over the dwarf's words carefully, not wishing to give offense or openly decline his offer of aid. However, he accepted the aid, albeit begrudgingly. "I appreciate any assistance you give us. I do believe, though, if my men cannot find her, the elves certainly will." Smiling behind his gritted teeth, he gave a small bow to the large dwarf.

"Ye may be right, but I be needin' to be certain that they will accompany her to Asmadine," the Collector said as he walked out of the room, squeezing himself through the door and out into the hall. Waiting for him in the hallway was a dark-skinned dwarven magic user, whom Nibarn saw but could not make out their words. He could see the smaller of the two dwarves drawing on the ground. After a few flushes of his hands and inaudible words, an emerald-colored portal opened, and the Collector walked through, leaving his twenty guards behind.

The guild members made their way down and out of the hallway and eventually out of the castle, splitting into small groups and melding into the busy city's populace, looking for the young girl.

Nibarn's guard bowed and began to apologize for the interruption, but Nibarn waved him out of the room. "Who does that dwarf think he is? The fool will rue the day he allowed me to have void powder. Someday soon, I will be powerful and wield unlimited power in service to my mistress…" His words trailed off as he stared down at his desk. The guard overheard some of what he was saying but decided to shut the door and not press his luck.

Nibarn continued his dialogue with himself, "Perhaps when I have ascended under the grace of Lestar, I could take his guild over. Take over the city of Asmadine, in Lestar's name." He rubbed his hands together in thoughtful bliss.

Nibarn contemplated his future, but the voice within his mind interrupted his vocalizations. "The path you are on will leave you with nothing. Turn away!"

He slammed his arms down on the table. "Enough! I have nothing? I rule one of the largest cities in the north. My service to Lestar has been rewarded by Lestar herself." His hands pulled open the drawer with his small pearl orbs. "And someday I will become everything."

While the drawer was open, he grabbed another two orbs and swallowed them. His eyes rolled back into his head as he slipped back into his chair. Intoxicated by the power and lust he felt for Lestar, he nearly nodded off to sleep when the voice again spoke. "In the end, you will be nothing. All that you believe is false. Turn back now."

Drooling slightly, he fumbled the words out, "Nuh-uh…I can feel her power, and it grows in me. Nooow shussshhh." He closed his eyes and fell into a deep sleep.

Upon entering his dreamlike state, he saw himself. However, it was a much younger version of himself standing before his older self. Nibarn watched the older and younger selves interacting from a distance. The younger self was warning him to stand down, to stop all that was going on, to call upon what was left of himself to become the hero he always wanted to be. He observed with amusement until he realized that both versions of himself had turned and made eye contact with him.

A sudden rush of wind hit him, and he felt like he was free-falling. As he plummeted downwards, he strained to make a sound, but his voice failed him. In the darkness, he frantically reached out to grab onto something to slow his descent but felt nothing.

Soon, the blackness turned into blurry visions of his past: his childhood and his loving mother's embrace, the times his father beat him. Still, he fell, swirling in the blurry chaos that was his life. He saw the death of his wife again, and the pain struck him deeply. He saw Desa's soul crying as it was drained with her baby into Lestar's embrace. Tumbling, he tried to close his eyes away from all the pain, but it was compounding inside his body and mind. He could hear screams and pain, and he cried out for someone to help.

In that moment, he froze, suspended, no longer falling and no longer seeing the past and pain he had already caused. He no longer felt the pain of his father's hate for him, and all was calm. He opened his eyes and saw a dark sapphire-robed figure before him. "Turn away from your path, Nibarn of House Neske, or a greater torment than this will be your reward." Nibarn struggled to reach out and grab the man. He screamed and thrashed towards him, but the man did not move. The hooded man shook his head. "I have warned you.

Turn away." The man clapped his hands in front of the suspended Nibarn and vanished.

Nibarn awoke from his brief sleep, gasping for breath and sweating profusely. He felt as if he had been stranded in the desert. The sweat and thirst left him feeling dead. "Guard! GUARDS!" he yelled hoarsely toward the door.

The first guard entered, followed by a second. "Lord?"

Nibarn reached out to them, his voice too weak to continue. They rushed over to him, scanning the room for intruders. Nibarn's raspy voice whispered, "Water. Intruder. Mind."

The guards turned, expecting an attack or to see someone they had missed. Seeing no immediate threat, one of the guards poured Nibarn a glass of water. Clutching the goblet as if someone would steal it away, he sipped from it. The two guards glanced at each other. "Lord, shall we raise the alarm?"

Nibarn shook his head, his voice still a whisper. "No, it was just a dream."

17

Upon stepping through the portal, Victus surveyed the hustle and bustle that was their camp. Biddy had set up his fiery imps to perform tasks such as cooking in a summoned outdoor shack. Biddy's fire ants formed a line from the woods to the fire pit, carrying twigs, sticks, and even a small log. Near the fire pit, which was being expanded by other fire ants, Victus noticed the little fire ants swarming around a wooden structure being built to look like Biddy. Victus grinned. The area was being transformed into a magical wonderland for the evening. Biddy's added efforts to the celebration created a more profound and enjoyable sense of camaraderie. He noted with approval Titus patrolling between two sets of soldiers on opposite sides of the camp. About fifty feet into the woods, he saw a large lava creature walking in circles around the camp. He heard a soft but booming voice say, "Butterfly, butterfly. Come here!" Then he distinctly heard, "Oh nooo—I just wanted to hold you." Shortly after that, the lava creature said again, "Butterfly, butterfly!" Chuckling to himself and marveling at Biddy's creation, he then looked off to the left. Aris and Serin were playing. It seemed Aris was reenacting the details of his fight with the dark elves. To his right, Jess was moving, having grown tired of waiting for his safe arrival through the portal. Her pace slowed when Victus met her gaze, smiling warmly at her.

Behind him, the Knight's Threshold blinked out of existence, and he turned, giving a reassuring nod to Jess. She asked, "So what did the dubious dwarf want?"

Victus looked out toward the other soldiers, who were hoisting a large tent to encompass the entire party. He tilted his gaze to Jess as he moved forward toward his own tent. “He warned me of the dangers we face. Asked me to stand down.”

Jess scoffed, “Of course he did. He is probably worried you will disrupt his work of playing both sides.”

Victus shook his head, his footsteps heavy as he walked toward his tent. “That is not it. He had information regarding the terrible things to come and wanted, for my safety and that of my soldiers, to desist.”

Jess scowled. “He knows you would never stand down from your duty. He knows your honor is above reproach. Why would he even ask? What game is he playing?”

Victus stopped mid-stride and looked her pointedly in the eyes. “Because he is a loyal friend to me and does not wish me to come to harm. I asked him to join us in the fight.”

At this, Jess’s head leaned back in surprise. “Will he join us?”

Victus exhaled a deep breath, morphing into a sigh. “No. He is unable to join us. However—”

Jess raised her hands in frustration, cutting him short. “You see! He is not about to help you because it will interfere with his other dealings. Thorm is a selfish and vile creature. He is a turncoat; his clan is disgraceful.” She spat on the ground in disgust.

Victus had heard enough but kept his anger in check. Jess’s protective nature towards him was endearing, and he separated it from his stance regarding Thorm. As a knight specializing in subterfuge, her suspicious nature was amplified. She was always vigilant for angles. Jess was fiercely loyal, always keeping a watchful eye on everyone to protect their best interests. Victus was aware that Jess shared his heavy burden, perhaps even more so than the rest of them. He raised his hand to pause Jess’s rant. When she quieted, he spoke. “However,” he said purposefully, starting from where she had cut him off, "he offered me something. A device that will help us in the battle to come. We toss it on the ground and stomp the gem within it. Once the mechanism has been crushed, it will provide a temporary shield against Lestar's weapon. But it will not hold for long, and it will only cover a portion of Lindly."

Victus did not wait for her to respond; he just continued on towards his tent. Jess was thinking it all over, her frustration towards the dwarf slightly eased. As they both neared Victus's tent, Marcella stood beaming, clearly happy with the results of Jess's recovery. Her chipper voice rang with joy. "You seem to have made a full recovery, Knighturion Jess."

The knight responded with a polite smile, "I am a little stiff, but Victus is going to help me with that."

Marcella's face blushed dark red, her smile awkward. "Ah well, then you won't be needing anything from me presently. If you do, I will be helping prepare for this evening. Just come find me." She turned to Victus, giving him a fist-to-chest salute, and moved along, allowing Victus and Jess to approach the tent.

Victus gave Jess a coy smile, a question in his eye. "Help you stretch, eh?"

She returned his look playfully. "Yes, Commander, you are the only one that can help me in this regard. I assure you I do need you."

Victus reached out for the tent flap, holding it open for her, and chuckled as he trailed in behind her. Victus watched the woman move some of the cots together, centering around a small box. The box would offer them a makeshift table for a game of 'tum tums,' a dice game favored by human soldiers. The object of the game was to roll the set of colored dice in a cup and toss the cup over, keeping the dice covered. Then each person playing would guess the colors under their cup. For each color guessed right, a point was issued. The first person to reach thirty would win the game. Victus and Jess had been playing for as long as they had known one another, but every time they played, he would lose. Despite possessing psionics, which he refused to employ, he remained unsure of his ability to defeat her. After she had positioned herself in her preferred cot spot, he moved to sit opposite her, a smile on his face. Her particular smile in response led Victus to conclude that the stakes of the game were clothing, not coins. "So what are we waging, my dear? A silver piece or gold for a win? We betting each round or doing a fixed ante round?"

She laughed as she shook her own dice in the cup. "I am betting to share your bed."

Victus nodded but then began shaking his head in amusement. Both of them slammed their cups down on a count of three. Victus allowed her to call hers first. "Three green, one red."

Victus called, "Two green, two red." Both of them lifted their cups to reveal that Victus had missed all of his. They were all blue.

Jess snickered as she got three of the four right. "Points to me then." For the next few hours, they laughed and played games together, having their own personal celebration and reunion. Although they were eager to explore their passion for each other, they allowed it to develop naturally and without any pressure. They had a deep regard and affection for each other that could only have developed over the time in their past, and they each found pleasure in simply being close. Their love was already complete, but the physical expression of it was the exclamation point at the end of the sentence.

~~~

Biddy had been scrutinizing his imps and fire ants like a hovering mother hen. He wanted everything to be perfect. The wooden sculpted visage of himself was a crescendo of sorts in the power of his fire and was good for a laugh. The food would be that of the divine; he checked and tasted everything his little fire imps made and scolded them when
~~~

they made something too spicy, befitting their own palates and not those around. "No. No. No. Chuewpa! That is far too hot. We need savory and sweet. Not just fire and heat! Add more sugar, and for the meat, it should be glazed with a mixture of herbs and oil. You brush it over and allow it to cook into the meat. The taste should be a perfect balance of sweet and savory, exploding on your taste buds," he instructed forcefully but added, "With a hint of heat." The small fiery imp, wearing a little chef hat, made himself flash more red in anger, tossing his little ladle to the ground and began squeaking in its fiery language. Biddy understood the creature was upset because some of the other imps were not listening. Biddy nodded and clapped his small hands together. "Okay, listen up, all of you." The fire ants stopped carrying little twigs, and Biddy pointed a stubby finger at the fire ants building and quickly added, "Not you—you keep building." As all the little imps encircled Biddy, he began, "Everyone. Chuewpa is the master chef, second only to me. We have to do this right, and as a reward for doing such a good job, I will make you a lava bath." Little squeaks of cheers could be heard, and they all began to scramble back to their jobs. However, Biddy stopped them. "BUT!" he shouted, and the fire imps froze. "If you do *not* do a good job and you rush the food? I will turn you all into water imps, and you will never play with fire again." With that, all the imps screeched and began to work methodically and carefully. They hated water and wanted nothing to do with it, and the idea that they could be turned into a water imp made it very clear that their master was serious. Biddy knew this was all nonsense, as he could not turn them into a water imp even if he wanted to, but the result had the desired effect. Confident his imps were preparing everything properly, he moved away from them towards Aris and Serin.

Both were sitting side by side, facing away from everyone with their fingers intertwined. Aris overheard the gnome approaching and stood up quickly, speaking up a bit— "That's when we heard the horns."

Aris theatrically began pretending to tell the story of the fight again, and both children blushed as Biddy unabashedly smiled and said, "Ah, young love!" Biddy looked over at them curiously, as they both seemed uncomfortable, as if guilty. "Do not be ashamed of your feelings for one another. It is natural and healthy." He studiously marched past them both, motioning for them to follow. Serin looked to Aris, and Aris followed Biddy into the woods, outside of prying eyes. Biddy began a small casting spell, which left a door just sitting in the middle of the woods.

Serin looked over at Aris and asked in a whisper, "You are going to do that rune thingy?"

Aris shrugged at the unreadable gnome as he twisted his head to her. "I hope so."

Biddy turned from his spell casting just as the door materialized. "This is a dimensional door that will hide us here in plain sight but allow us privacy for the ritual. Are you certain you wish to do this? I pledge to you that it will not be pleasant. It will be very painful and will require all of your mental faculties and even your heart."

Aris's face was firm, much like his father's, determined and confident as he said, "I am ready, Master Mage."

Serin grabbed Aris's arm, pulled him close, staring at him full of worry. "Are you sure? I don't want you to be hurt. Is it worth it?"

Aris's eyes softened at the concern on her face and the love in her voice. "I am certain, and if you would join me, it would give me the resolve to press on. Will you support me?"

She hugged him and wrapped her arms around him. "Of course I will, Aris." Her voice lowered to a barely audible murmur, "I love you and will stand with you forever."

Aris whispered back, "And I you."

Biddy did not rush the youngsters and gave them the time required for both to turn and face him. "Ah, all set then?"

Holding hands, they both nodded confidently. "Yes, we are."

Biddy opened the door and walked through, leaving it open for them to follow. Upon entering, the surrounding trees shifted to a dull grayish color, and everything seemed the same except there was no wind or swaying of leaves. No birds chirped, and the light was not the same.

Serin spoke, amazed, "This is so cool. Did you freeze time? Are we on another plane?"

Biddy chuckled, "I have not frozen time, but what a delightful idea. I will consider that for later. No, this is another plane within our own plane. Difficult to explain, but simply put, we encompass the same realm but are seeing it through a different lens—much like my goggles do when I am looking for different things." Serin nodded as if she understood. Biddy walked over and shut the door. "Now no one else will be able to enter."

Aris was still looking at the trees and sky as he turned to watch Biddy shut the door. "What now?"

The gnome walked over and gently ushered Aris to the center. "You stand here." Offering a wave to Serin, he summoned a chair off to the side. "Please take a seat and try to remain silent." He pursed his lips and added, "Even if you are fearful of what you see or hear—do not speak. If you break our concentration or Aris's, it could have dire consequences." Her eyes widened as she made her way to the seat. Not daring to say a word, she sat quietly watching. Biddy pulled out the rune book he had gathered previously.

Aris looked at him curiously. "Have you had time to read it?"

The gnome was flipping pages and pulled out a small vial of what looked like sand. Aris could not tell the actual color because everything was gray. "I have read the important parts. Or at least my brain has absorbed what it needed to."

Aris had a brief moment of hesitation at Biddy's words, but he stiffened and began to prepare his mind, dumping first his senses and awareness of his surroundings.

Biddy encircled Aris with the sand from the vial, then said, "Now I need you to place your weapons in your preferred hands."

Aris reached and unsheathed both his dagger and sword, thinking that it did not matter to him which hand he used, as he could use them both equally. He decided that he would prefer to have the gladius in his left hand and the dagger in the right. He looked at Serin on the sidelines, meeting her eyes before he said, "I am ready."

Biddy nodded and stood before Aris, looking up at the young man. "Now, before I begin, you need to understand that the transference of the weapons into runes on your arms requires body, mind, and soul. The weapons will be separate in the sense that you can still keep them holstered in your scabbards. However, they will be etched into your body and, through that, into your mind and your soul. I would offer you something to take the edge off, but it would slow your mind too much, and the endeavor would fail."

Aris stood straight as if he were about to fight. "I am ready. What must I do?"

Biddy smiled, pleased to see the determination and fortitude of this young human. He thought to himself, *certainly this is Victus' son,* and turned the pages of the book, finding the specific passage, the one that would begin the ritual.

Aris watched the gnome and asked again, "What do I do?"

Biddy, who was moments away from casting, stopped and replied, "Oh right, contingency—sorry. You only need to stand firmly in that circle and not move from it. You also must not drop your blades. Keep your mind present on the task and focus your mind on melding with the weapons. Ignore everything around you, and I suggest you keep your eyes closed. That way, my casting does not disrupt your focus."

With that, Aris closed his eyes; he measured his breath, slowly exhaling and inhaling. When Biddy began casting, his voice came from much farther away than before, but Aris' eyes remained shut.

Serin sat watching, concerned but keeping her words stuffed inside. She watched Biddy start his casting and saw gray beams shoot from Biddy's eyes and mouth as he spoke. They danced over Aris and the weapons in his hand, like a small tornado enveloping the young man until she could see nothing but the whirlwind. Biddy's chanting was methodical and terrifying as his voice morphed into a booming, thunderous sound. "Embraka dua gladi ete daga. EMBRAKA DUA GLADI!" His voice continued to chant over and over. Serin saw a lighter-hued, ghost-like version of Aris step from within the storm. It was his soul—his eyes were closed and straining. She could see his face, but it was disfigured in pain, yet he said nothing. She gasped and covered her mouth to hold it shut.

Aris heard Biddy's words in the distance, though he was only a few feet away, and felt his weapons grow warm and then cold—from one extreme to the other, hot enough to scald his flesh and then cold enough to burn it again. He grimaced and nearly fainted from the first wave but held on. His mind raced in chaos and shock, but he reeled it in, repeating his own mantra, whispering it in his mind over and over again —"Family, duty, Serin. Family, duty, Serin. Family, duty, Serin." The waves of fire and ice washed over his whole body now, and he could feel himself shaking and dripping sweat. An icy wind enveloped him and pulsated into heat, reverting back from one to the other. He clenched his jaw shut and focused on his mantra: "Family, duty, Serin." Each wave compounded and weighed him down. He was losing control; he could feel it, the pain was intolerable. He opened his eyes to see a ghostly version of himself pulling from his body. Terrified, he closed his eyes and shouted, "FAMILY, DUTY, SERIN!" He held firm to the blades, but his hands were shaking so badly that he did not think his body could handle it.

Serin watched Aris's soul and heard Aris's scream from within the swirling wind. Then she saw his soul mouthing words over and over, the mantra, but his soul began fading back towards the whirlwind. She clenched her mouth shut with both hands and fought every instinct she had to run over and grab him from the small storm. She reversed his mantra into one of her own in her head: "Family, duty, Aris. Family, duty, Aris." Thinking not of her own family but of the family she found with Victus and Aris, she kept repeating it in her head—as if she was willing Aris to keep going, to hold on.

Aris's eyes remained closed, and then he felt more pain than he had felt thus far. It felt as if both dagger and sword were being plunged into his flesh, into his arms, piercing his hands. He could feel them slipping into his very bones and flesh. He buckled under the pain, dropping to his knees; his eyes flashed open, and he screamed again. "FAMILY, DUTY, SERINNNNNNN!!!!!"
After what seemed like an eternity for Aris, the pain subsided, and he was able to rise. He closed his eyes again and focused on his mantra, no longer feeling the blades in his hands; he felt them within him. He felt them as an extension of who he was—a part of him. Slowly, the whirlwind stopped, and Biddy's chanting ended. Aris opened his eyes, still standing in the circle, looked quickly over at Serin, and smiled, then back to Biddy. "Did I do it?"

Before Biddy could respond, Aris's eyes rolled and slid shut, and he collapsed on the ground.

Biddy giggled. "Contingency! Hehehee, you did it." His own vision returned to normal only after the young man had collapsed.

Serin, however, ran over to Aris, screaming. "Aris! ARIS! You killed him!" she shouted, accusing Biddy.

Biddy was unconcerned and shook his head as he casually walked over to Aris. He knelt down next to Aris and the now-sobbing Serin, placing a hand on the boy's chest. "Not dead. His soul and body are intact. He is exhausted, is all." Serin was crying and tried to wake Aris, but to no avail. Finally, Biddy reached over and grabbed the young girl's hand. "You need to go sit back down."

She shook her head and, through sobs, said, "Nooo, I need to stay here."

Biddy shrugged, rubbed his index finger into his thumb, and produced an acrid smell of burning embers, so pungent that Serin gagged. Aris's eyes flipped open. "Did we do it?"

Biddy helped the boy up, grinning. "Yes."

Serin wrapped her arms around him and hugged him. "You are okay. You did it!"

Aris looked from her to the ground where his weapons lay, then looked back to Serin. "I could feel your thoughts, Serin. I could feel you pressing me on."

She smiled and hugged him again. "You did wonderfully." She sobbed into his shoulder softly.

Both Biddy and Serin helped the young squire to his feet. Biddy added, "Most grown men could not endure what you have done. Be proud of yourself."

Aris responded with a weary tone in his voice, "I could not have done it without the love I have for my family, duty, and Serin."

The young girl blushed brightly, and Biddy acknowledged him with a pat on the back. "You will be a great knight, Aris Tin."

As Biddy led them both to the dimensional door to leave, Aris turned back to his weapons on the ground. "I need my blades before we leave."

Biddy's brow cocked sideways, and he wiggled a finger. "Contingency, Master Aris. You already have them. Call them forth from within."

Aris took a few steps away from them and closed his eyes. He could feel the weapons as if they were already with him.

He knew they were a part of him now, and he willed them to his hands. Serin watched the blades on the ground turn into a grayish cloud and disappear into Aris's hands.

"WOW," she said, confounded and amazed at this type of magic.

Aris's eyes opened, and he smiled wide. "It works perfectly."

Biddy chuckled. "It works as intended. Well done. In time and practice, you will be able to recall them without even having to concentrate."

Aris nodded as he stuffed the blades in their respective scabbards. "Thank you, Biddy."

Biddy opened the door and led them out. Aris hesitated as he looked at his hands, curious if they had actually been burned or frozen. No marks or signs of distress remained; it was as if it had never happened. *But it did happen,* he thought. He continued to look at his hands and wrists, examining the tattoos freshly etched upon his arm, a bear emblem and a falcon, each denoting his father's dagger and his gladius. He thought that Biddy must have chosen to use the pummels as a representation of the weapons so that if someone ever saw them, they would believe it to be a mundane tattoo and nothing more. He whispered to himself as he stepped through the door, smiling, "Biddy's contingencies."

18

Biddy led the way back to camp, Serin trailing behind with Aris. She leaned into him, bumping him playfully. He pretended to ignore it, then unexpectedly bumped into her back, smiling when she gasped in surprise. They both saw the lava giant in the distance, and Aris asked, “Would you like to go see and talk to the lava giant?”

Biddy turned, a stern look on his face. “Contingency? No. Aris, you need to rest.”

Waving his hand dismissively, Aris retorted, “I am tired, but it’s not strenuous work talking to your lava monster.”

Biddy turned back toward the camp. “Yes, yes, you are right. But do be careful and don’t startle him. No... never mind. Ah dang, contingency. I am going to go with you. He is still uncivilized, so I need to be present in case he does something irrational, I suppose.”

Serin jumped up and down in excitement as she skipped off to see the beast who was supposed to be patrolling, but from the booming words he kept shouting, he seemed to be more interested in butterflies. Aris and Biddy chased after the girl, who was almost running, trying to catch up by hastening their own steps.

~~~

A few hours had gone by in the commander’s tent. Victus and Jess lay in bed snuggling. They were staring into one another’s eyes when Jess spoke through the silent intimacy. “Do you still pray?”
~~~

The commander leaned on his elbow, sitting up slightly. "I pray daily."

Jess nodded; she had known the answer, but she was nudging him toward a deeper question that truly interested her. "Whom do you pray to?"

Victus thought for a moment, considering how best to answer her honest probe. "I do not pray to Asmolor nor to any of his children, save for perhaps Kalisdel. Among the three gods—Eu'rok and his progeny, Malakas and her progeny, and Asmolor and his—she is the most worthy of veneration." Realizing no interjection from Jess was forthcoming, he continued, "Yet she does not ask any human to worship her. So to her, I do offer up my prayers."

Jess was curious and attentive, even as she knew his answer would not be brief. Victus paused and took a deep breath. "But I pray more to something beyond them. Two brothers and a sister claim to be the gods over all of creation. What of the other planets we can see? What of the inconsistencies we see among our own side? Asmolor claims to be the light of the universe, righteous and holy. However, his children, in particular Elivindel, the creator of the elves, are closer to his heart and the closest representation of him incarnate. They are cruel, haughty, and not worthy of praise. Something created them and set the laws of nature in motion. So I pray to the deity, whomever or wherever he or she is. I see a more principled God, one of true justice and peace. Not one with petty squabbles and rivalries like Eu'rok and Asmolor and their sister Malakas. Something truly divine, not just powerful."

Jess leaned closer to him, kissing his lips. "This is one of the many reasons I love you, Victus. You look beyond the surface level and see a deeper understanding of the world before us."

The commander shifted from her after he returned her kiss, his thoughts provoked. "Perhaps I am a fool. Someday we will know the truth of it all." Victus sighed, knowing he must bring the conversation to an abrupt end, acknowledging that they had spent more time isolated than they had intended. "We need to dress, my dear, and get ready for the party. The evening is upon us, and we both have our duties. I daresay we have leisured the day away."

He stood to begin dressing, but as he left the bed, she grabbed him and held him in place. "No matter where or what we face in our future, I go with you wholeheartedly, and I love you. I need you. So you keep being that big thinker and keep us on the path, commander."

Her smile warmed Victus to his heart, and he embraced her in his toned arms and chest. "I will, my love. Now dress." This time he added a little more emphasis on *dress* to ensure she understood. She didn't argue or protest, and he took that as a sign of her understanding. Simultaneously, they dressed themselves and left the tent in each other's company.

~~~

Biddy had caught up to Serin, who stood immobile as if turned to stone. She watched as the lava giant pondered yet another dead butterfly. The lava giant looked from his sad, dead butterfly up to see Serin and was startled. "OH! Are you a baddie? I kill you if you are." Then he saw his creator, Biddy, and his focus was easily redirected. "Oh, Biddy and Biddy's friends. Never mind, little baddie, you are safe. Master Biddy, I catch lots of butterflies, but… they die…" His voice trailed off into a small rumble of sobs.

Biddy shook his head. "Yes, yes, you silly giant. You cannot touch things unless you remove the flame from your hands. You are very hot. This is why when you ask to hug me, I tell you no." Shaking his head, he walked right before the colossal beast and extinguished his large hands.

"Ouchie! Biddy, that hurt me!"

Biddy smiled, soothing the giant. "It's only for a moment, and you can do it yourself. Reignite yourself."

The lava monster looked at his extinguished hands, which resembled cooled coals of a fire, white and black, cracked all
~~~

over. Confused as to how to reignite his own hands, he began speaking to his right and then his left hand as if they would listen. "FIRE! HANDS!" He groaned in frustration and tried the reverse. Surely this would work, he thought, as he smiled down at the others with confidence. "HANDS! FIRE!"

Serin was giggling, and Aris stifled his own laugh. Biddy was shaking his head again. "No... No... contingency! You have to use your control over your fire. Like when you cast your spells. Use your thoughts to turn the fire on and off."

The lava giant nodded in complete misunderstanding this time but with full confidence that he now understood. He clasped his hands together and yelled, "FIRE! HANDS!" Immediately, a ring of fire surrounded the four of them and began to leap up the trees. A wall of flames heated them all, climbing first to ten feet, then twenty. Biddy leapt into action, spinning around and began casting, his little mouth muttering and hands flailing about. As fast as the fire began, it sizzled into silence.

The lava giant boomed, "I DID IT!"

Biddy shook his head no but answered, "Yes. Contingency." He sighed, "We will practice this more later. For now, just stick to your patrol. Don't play with butterflies and don't try to extinguish and reignite anymore. I promise we will work on that when everything else is done." The lava giant emitted a brief howl of sadness that he couldn't capture any additional butterflies. He slowly trudged past them, diligently continuing with his patrol.

Serin, happy to have seen the marvelous creature, looked between Biddy and Aris. "Does he have a name?"

Biddy shrugged, "Lava giant."

"Not much of a name," Aris retorted. "He should have a proper name. What is the word for fire in Gnomish?"

Biddy spoke the word at the same time as Serin, "Logi!" they said.

She smiled at him, "That's what you should call him—Logi."

Biddy shrugged again, “Do you know how hard it is to teach that beast anything new? It took me a year just to get him to talk.”

Now Serin shrugged as if it had been decided. “When he is ready, I trust you will give him a proper name. And I think Logi would be perfect.” Her voice implied the dignified station she held, like a princess offering a handmaiden a veiled request that was really a command.

Though Biddy could see she was hiding her grin and even her laughter behind her stoic face. He chuckled and agreed, “Contingency. When he is ready, I will surely give him a name.”

Aris looked at the now-distant lava giant and mentioned, “I think we should head back to camp. We will be celebrating soon and eating.” At the word eating, everyone’s stomachs groaned in hunger.

“Quite right, Aris. Let us head back now.” With Biddy in the lead, they headed back to camp. The voice of the lava giant returned with a booming sound that everyone heard in the distance. “BUTTERFLY!”

Biddy sighed, “Contingency.” He shook his head as the two children trailed behind him, laughing.

~~~

Janus, the old legionnaire, was standing outside Victus's tent. He saluted as his commander exited and asked, “Sir, might I have a moment of your time?”

Victus returned the salute and bade Jess to carry on without him. “Of course, Janus.”

The soldier stood straight, his scarred face revealed as he held his helm under his arm. “Tomorrow when we march back,” he paused, taking a deep breath, gathering his courage before requesting the favor. “When we march back, sir, may I have the honor of being your son’s shield bearer? Not that he needs one, sir. Just that in the disarray of combat, things can
~~~

get a little messy. And you will want someone with your son as you issue commands." The older soldier's face reddened slightly, and he wondered if he had been too forward.

Victus pursed his lips in contemplation and then said flatly, "No, that honor is given to Jess."

The older legionnaire nodded understandingly, placing his helmet back on as if to dismiss himself. "I understand, sir." The disappointment was evident in the man's voice.

Victus cocked his brow and shook his head. "Remove your helm, knight. I have not dismissed you, nor have I finished."

Faster than Victus could visually process, the helmet was back under his arm. The man was now standing even taller as he puffed out his chest. "Yes, sir. Sorry, sir."

Victus lifted his arm to Janus's shoulder. "Tomorrow you will be my shield-bearer. You will cover my flank with my son and Jess. But your duty will be to my person first. Understood?"

The legionnaire beamed with pride as he acknowledged this honor. "I will, sir. I will make sure you are protected from whatever foe stands before us." Saluting, he waited for dismissal this time.

Victus nodded and smiled. "I know you will. Now let us feast as brothers, not soldiers."

~~~

Biddy, Serin, and Aris made their way back to the camp and up to the fire imps' shack. Biddy was testing the food and seemed to be very pleased with Chuewpa's work. "You all have done splendidly. Now set the table for everyone and place all the drinks and food on the table. Once that is complete, you are dismissed. I will make certain that when you return to your home, a warm lava bath will be ready for you all." The imps chirped in excitement, running and scurrying about to get everything done and ready so they could dip into the warm lava bath they all loved. However, the imps all stopped when they realized no table was there for
~~~

them to set. Chuewpa, with his large chef's hat atop his head, held his ladle, which was used more for smacking other imps in line than for actual cooking, and spoke to Biddy in its weird fiery language.

Biddy chuckled, "Contingency. Yes, sorry." He moved from the shack and summoned a magnificent dining table suitable for up to twenty people. "Easy," the gnome said with a smile as he pretended to dust off his hands. The imps worked quickly, setting the table with precision and care.

Jess walked over to the table, followed closely by Victus and Janus. Aris smiled over at them all as he watched their approach, leading Serin by her hand to find them a seat. Jess noted this and looked back to Victus, giving him a nod to look over at his son. With a smile, he comprehended the importance of the moment she wished to share with him—already his son was well on his way to being a man. As far as Victus was concerned, he was already one, and seeing him act as the man Victus had hoped he would become was a treasure that not even a god could take away from him. Marcella made her way to the table with Titus and a few of the other legionnaires. Titus had informed each of the two groups still outside the camp guarding to rotate every sixty minutes after the feast had begun, which would give everyone ample time to enjoy the food and fellowship.

As everyone surrounded their respective seats, Victus sat in the middle of them all. Aris and Serin sat opposite him. Victus was flanked on the left and right by Jess and Janus. As everyone sat and got comfortable, Victus rose from the table to address all present.

"Tomorrow will be one of our greatest tests as soldiers. We go to stand against the tyranny of Eu'rok and his dark elves. We are outnumbered, but we are not outmatched. None is our equal, and none will be able to stand against our righteousness. Even if we all fall, our souls will cry out in defiance, and we will save as many as we can. Our deeds tomorrow will echo through the ages. We will forever be remembered for our refusal to silently witness our people's suffering in the night. We protect our own. We bring justice to those who would defile our cities. We will humble the haughty dark elves and their gods. We stand united in this common cause, for better or worse. Together!"

All present cheered, quickly quieting as Victus raised a hand. "As for tonight, though, we celebrate as a family. We celebrate the life we have and the blessings of our friendships. We do not take any of it for granted. Now let's have some fun."

Everyone burst into a roar of cheers, banging mugs down on the table, and began chanting, "Together! Together!" which morphed into "Victus! Victus!" He allowed them all the moment before again raising his hand to speak. "Now I must pass your attention to the master of ceremonies, Biddy."

Biddy exaggerated his bow to the crowd, waving his little hands out from his sides. "Well, as you can see, we have plenty of food for everyone. I made certain that we had food for every palate. Everything will be savory and delicious, this I assure you. I have enchanted the wine and ale for this celebration. It will not leave you sluggish tomorrow; it will leave you invigorated and encouraged." The crowd cheered, but Biddy continued, "Now the pastries are particularly sweet, and the icing will leave you wanting more…"

Biddy continued speaking, but all Aris could think about was the smell of the roasted boar, which, to him, had never smelled so delicious. Serin and he kept exchanging glances, trying to come up with a plan to sneak a few bread buns, but finally, Serin spoke over Biddy, "Can we eat it now?"

Biddy laughed loudly, "Contingency! Of course. Of course. Eat, drink, and be merry, friends!" That was all the crowd gathered needed to hear, and food was passed around the table. Wine and ale flowed freely as everyone drank and ate their fill.

An hour into the feast, night had fully set in, and Biddy moved to his wooden pyre. Whispering to his little fire ants, he directed them to their respective positions on the pyre.

Once they were all in place, he set fire to the wooden Biddy, which crackled and popped as it burned brightly, illuminating the entire area. Biddy's voice could be heard intermittently from the wooden figure as it burned, sometimes in fits of giggles and other times uttering a "Contingency!"

Aris and Serin had enjoyed much of the roasted vegetables and meat; now they were arguing about which pastry to try first. Victus walked around the table, exchanging seats with others so that he could speak to everyone. He even brought food and drink to the guards on the outskirts of the camp, unaware of Titus's command of an hour's rotation. Shortly after Marcella started singing, soldiers got up and danced together. As Victus watched from the treeline, he felt his heart content; nothing made him happier than a lively party and spending time with his companions. Seeing others happy and enjoying life brought him immense joy. He possessed the captivating quality of being able to focus on the present and disregard his concerns and fears. Those of House Andreas had a reputation for being able to calm those around them, which made them attractive to many followers. This evening was perfect, and he relished it all. He watched his son laughing with Serin and the others as they danced, some stumbling from the sway of the alcohol. A few chuckles escaped him as he watched, taking in the moments. A wave of love and pride washed over him as he headed toward the group, spurring him to start dancing. It had been a considerable amount of time since he last danced. As he crossed the dancing area, he practiced his moves, and when he made his way to his destination, he pulled Jess into his chest to the beat of the music.

19

Victus moved Jess along the crowd of dancing soldiers, switching the sway and movement of his feet to match the song Marcella played and lead Jess. It was upbeat but needed more instruments to get going. Through the ruckus, Victus yelled towards Biddy, “Music, Biddy! We need more than a harp and Marcella’s beautiful voice.” His eyes met Marcella’s briefly, and there was gratitude in her eyes; she had sung the entire way up here to maintain the men’s pace. In actuality, she had never employed such a magnitude of magic, and afterwards, upon doing so with success, she felt exhausted. Despite the invigorating dinner, she couldn’t eat to her heart’s content because of her queasy stomach. She did not wish to disappoint those around her, which is why she had originally started singing this evening. Victus, however, could see she needed rest, and Marcella was grateful for Victus's request of the gnome.

Biddy nodded and yelled, “CONTINGENCY!” He waved his hands and interrupted Marcella and the dancing. His little voice went to a very low octave but still sounded squeaky as he began singing, “Ye dancing in the fireeeee! My soul cries out for thee! O’ great fire! O’ misty waves are not for me! Only FI-RRRRRRR-EEE!” The gnome elicited amusement and utter confusion from everyone’s gaze, standing in frozen dance moves. His eyes were shut, and he appeared to be exerting himself to reach the high notes of his song.

Victus chuckled, walked over, and patted him on the shoulder, interrupting his singing. “I was thinking more along the lines of producing some instruments so others could play.”

Biddy went bright red and nodded seriously, “Contingency, of course.”

Everyone gave Biddy a cheer for his attempt at a song, but Aris added, “Stick to magic, Biddy.”

The gnome’s face scrunched up, and he glared at Aris, pretending to cast towards the young man. Aris, enjoying the little game, pretended to be struck down by this unseen magic and fell dramatically to the ground. Everyone laughed, and Serin helped him back to his feet.

Biddy marched over to the cooking shack and began taking cooking utensils and turning them into instruments, making a fiddle, a set of hand drums, a lute, and a fife. He carried the instruments out and handed them over to the approaching soldiers.

The music started with the drums, and everyone dancing found their stride. Soon, the music was in full swing, and everyone was dancing again. Victus was dancing with Serin, spinning her and exaggerating his movements to make her laugh. She was giggling when she was passed off to Aris. The young squire tried to mimic his father’s movements but was clumsy. He stepped on Serin’s feet and nearly knocked her down to the ground. She laughed, “So elegant with a blade, but you can’t dance?”

He blushed and laughed, “Not much time to learn. I can slow dance, I think.”

She smirked, “This isn’t a slow dance song. Slow dancing is just holding my waist and swaying.”

“It’s still dancing,” he insisted.

She stood next to him and instructed, “Kick, spin, and roll me with your right hand out, and then pull back.” Aris watched and tried to mimic her movements, though at first, it was a struggle. Eventually, Serin mentioned, “Think of it as if you were fighting, Aris. These steps will keep you alive.” Her smirk was all that Aris needed for encouragement, and he began dancing properly with her. “Aris,” she said with a grin,

"You're not actually fighting. Smile. Stop thinking so much." With every movement they made, he felt himself letting go and fully relaxing into the dance, enjoying the moment with her and forgetting about everything else around them.

Jess brought drinks toward Victus, who was taking a break from the dance—her hands held one cup in each hand. Victus reached for one of the drinks from Jess, but she smiled coyly. "Both for me." Downing the two drinks quickly, she pulled Victus away for another dance. Victus laughed and spun her out, and Janus caught her, pushing her back to the commander. Jess spun Victus out from herself, and he laughed. Titus caught him, but before he pushed him back in, he gave him a large swig of ale from a mug filled to the top.

Victus smiled, froth covering his lips. "Send me back, Titus!" Titus pushed him back towards Jess. As soon as she caught him, he winked, bouncing away from her. The commander was dancing and kicking his legs out rapidly, lowering his body and making the kicks faster and faster. Holding the mug to the side, he went lower and lower—dancing a dwarven-style dance that he had learned as a very young man.

Victus winked at Jess and put the mug on his head, starting a simple dwarven dancing game. The objective was to duck and spin a full circle, catching the mug before it hit the ground or spilled. The hand you used to place it on your head was the hand that had to catch it. Though it was a silly game, the dwarves built off of it, adding more variations and rules. They loved drinking games, teaching many humans; however, dwarves have a stronger fortitude and thus need to extend the game's length to match their capacity for drinking. In most taverns, it was still played the simple human way. Victus winked again at Jess in mock challenge as he paused his dancing briefly to place the mug atop his head. He ducked and spun, but his foot got caught on the ground, spinning only halfway around. The mug fell, spilling all over, and everyone who was still dancing gave a playful boo.

Victus laughed, "No, no. Titus, bring me another. I need a second go, please!"

Titus filled a mug but left it only half full. When Victus grabbed the mug, he noticed it was not full. "No... it has to be full." He leaned to the legionnaire's ear, whispering, "But thanks!" Again, he placed the mug on his head. He ducked and spun the full three hundred and sixty degrees. The mug was flying down, a little out and tilted to the right as it soared past his shins. He reached and plucked it by the rim. His tentative grasp had everyone paused and watching—even the music skipped a beat to see. As he crouched down towards the mug, bringing it up towards his mouth, he attempted to readjust his hand to get a firmer grip, but it slipped.

The crowd laughed and let out a collective, "Aww." Victus laughed, shrugged, and quickly accepted another refill from Titus.

"Perhaps you should stick with soldiering," Titus commented with a grin.

Victus shrugged, clapped, and the music started up again. As the night continued, more games were played, and more drinks were imbibed.

Victus had sat back at the table to enjoy some more meat when Aris walked over. "Did you have any of the fried dove?" Aris asked as he sat down next to his father.

Victus's eyes looked at the meat he was holding, wiggling it as he ripped into the small bird. His mouth full, he replied, "I believe I just did."

Aris smiled and watched out into the crowd, reaching for another pastry. "So, da— I did the rune ritual with Biddy."

Victus finished another bite of the bird and asked, "How did it go?" Aris grimaced slightly, and his father thought it fared poorly. "Ah well, sometimes these things take more than one attempt." He patted his son on the shoulder. "You'll get it in time, son."

Aris shook his head. "No. I did it. It's just that it was very painful. I felt my body burning and freezing; my mind was bursting from the overwhelming strain." Aris gave a little shudder as he thought about it.

Victus was startled but then comprehended that his son was capable in every duty assigned to him, feeling immense pride. "Well done! Best to keep it hidden and use it only when you absolutely have to. Many of the superstitious or envious will think killing you will give them the ability."

Aris twisted both hands to reveal his wrists. "Biddy thought of that and made the runic tattoos our sigils: Bear and Falcon."

Victus nodded his head. "Clever."

Father and son shared a few more bites of food, watching Serin and Jess play the mug game—which neither was winning. Victus turned to his son. "Come, let us take in the night air."

No one noticed the two slip out from the dinner table and break off into the woods. Making their way through the trees, they headed upstream away from the merriment, but they could still hear the festivities. Victus turned, believing they were far enough from the party. "So, show me, Aris."

With his eyes closed, the young squire summoned the image of his blades, feeling their presence in his hands as he held the gladius and dagger.

"Remarkable," his father exclaimed, watching as the blades evaporated into the boy's tattoos. "Well done indeed, my boy. Some things are difficult to achieve, even painful, but they are worth going through. You chose to do this. You chose pain and hardship for the reward of improving yourself as a warrior and leader. Followers or soldiers notwithstanding, self-leadership is a prerequisite to leading others. Your competence as a squire manifests in your willingness to endure hardship for a favorable outcome. And I am proud of you. You are making great strides toward becoming a renowned warrior and future leader. The easiest path is traveled by many. Never be afraid to take the harder path."

Aris used his father's pause as his chance to explain. "I did it because I believe it will make me better in the future. I want to be the best."

Affirming his son, Victus nodded. "Thinking of the future makes you wise beyond your years. Too many of our kin think only for the day, never seeing past the present. But we must be mindful of the present and plan the best we can for the future."

Aris moved past his father to sit by the stream; Victus followed to sit next to him. "Da… tomorrow…" The young squire paused, mulling over the words he was about to admit to his commander and father, "I am scared."
Victus wrapped an arm over his son and looked directly into his eyes. He offered Aris a warm understanding that only an older, wiser soldier and father could express. "All of us are scared, including me. But fear heightens our awareness of death. It helps us remain cautious and thoughtful. If someone ever says they are not afraid, they are either lying or too stupid to understand their own mortality."

Relieved by his father's words, Aris asked, "What will we do when we arrive?"

Victus interlocked his legs, removing his arm from his son as he looked out into the slow-moving river. "When we arrive, one of two things will happen. They will attack us on sight, or they will try to arrest and hold me for some mock trial of betrayal. Though killing us as soon as they see us would be a wiser course of action, I do not believe they will. Nibarn likes to display his power and wield it for all to see. The dark elves, too, like to humiliate and torture their prey." Aris's heart was racing as he listened. He was worried about his father. He was worried about Serin. He was worried about it all, but he did not interrupt his father. "I will forgo the trial and go straight to judgment, where I will ask for a trial by combat to clear my name and for the right to claim the city under House Andreas. Though I do not actually need to clear my name, nor do I want control of the city, it will be a challenge to House Neske and Nibarn himself. His own ego will not allow him to refuse."

At this, Aris did interrupt, "Nibarn won't fight you. He is a coward like his son. And the elves won't honor the fight—or at least they won't fight fair."

Victus nodded. "Yes, you are right. Nibarn won't fight me. And the elves will go along until they begin to lose. This is why you, Jess, and Janus will be there near me when they do show their true colors. I will have Titus, Marcella, and the rest of the legionnaires sneak into the town separately from us. They will find any allies we still have and start ushering civilians from the city through the boat gate. It's the fastest way out of the city and straight down the river."

Aris could not argue with his father's plan. Under the circumstances, this was a pretty solid plan, especially considering the objective was to save as many innocents as possible. But Aris was uneasy; he did not like the idea of him and his father being bait.

Victus glanced at his son, almost able to hear his thoughts based on his expression. "We have to draw the attention away from the others. They will be transfixed on the spectacle and duel. We are the bait; we are the sacrifice for all the others, but that is our duty as knights. We willingly go into the places or situations others will not. We stand when others falter."

Aris's thoughts and worries calmed as he listened. His father's words filled him with a chill—in awe of his father's words and his courage. All he could say was, "I stand with you, Father. I stand with you as a soldier and as your son."
His father acknowledged, "I know you will."

Victus looked back out to the stream and then up to the stars. "Something is beyond this world and these gods. We, as humans, have been pushed aside, bullied, and cast down. Someday we will rise and rewrite the pantheon of tyranny. It will be a representation of all that is good in us. Someday enough will see and turn to fight against the tide. The gods, the archs, the mortals—all of them that crave power and gain power; they fear losing it. You can have all the power in the world, Aris, and it will mean nothing if you lose who you are in the process of gaining it. Never forget that. Never forget compassion; never forget to aid those who are of a lesser station than you. The ideals we hold dear are greater and superior to any god's edict. No matter what peaks your interest, remain humble. And do not fall prey to losing who you are. I am proud of the man you are and the man I see you growing into."

Aris smirked. "I am an extension of you. I am all that you taught and raised me to be."

His father, his teacher, his commander, looked him over and embraced him. "I have built a foundation in your heart that you must build on. Only you can build it. I have done what I can for you. But you are your own man."

Aris hugged his father back. “Never could I have wished for a better father. You have been and mean more to me than anything in this world. Thank you for everything you have given me. I owe my life to you, and I will never forget all that you taught me, no matter how much time passes.”

Victus thought about his own father and their relationship. His father, Tiberius, was a black-and-white thinker, with no room for gray. Some saw the man as a shrewd businessman and tactician. He cared only for the rise of his House. How Victus had wished he could have had this relationship with his own father. But after Victus enlisted, his father never spoke to him again. Tiberius died alone, surrounded by servants. Alone because he missed out and forgot what it meant to be humble; he forgot life was more than station and forgot how to be human. Victus inherited the titles and wealth, but it was not what he had desired. Victus had found his way to his station and rank by being generous, loyal, and smart—never seeing himself as better than those around him.

Aris saw that his father was deep in thought as they separated from the hug. He did not wish to interrupt his thoughts, so he gazed out toward the stream, allowing his father the time he needed. Victus broke the sounds of the night with, "Let us return to the feast. Our absences will be noted."

Victus and Aris walked back together, eager to rejoin everyone. But both knew that the words expressed here by the stream were words many sons never had with their fathers. Aris was thankful and hopeful that someday he could be a father like his. The thoughts morphed into a vision of marrying Serin and having children with her. He imagined his father sparring with his own children and teaching them lessons. He was warmed at the thought. Then Victus snapped him out of his fantasies. "Race me back." With that jolt, he pushed Aris a little to give himself a playful advantage.

"Oh! You cheat!" Aris yelled as his father outpaced him. It was not much of a race; they only had about twenty feet to go. Aris ended the race two steps behind his father. The others looked confused, thinking that they were being chased. Victus raised his arms, "No, no, we are fine. Just a race." Some of the soldiers decided that sounded like a good idea and began discussing a race among themselves. Everyone was well past being sober, and most teetered on tipsy glee. The enchanted alcohol kept them from getting drunk but allowed the feeling of nearly being there.

The celebration continued for a few more hours, but around midnight, everyone was settling in for sleep. Aris and Serin sat outside the tents, wishing to sleep underneath the stars. The guard rotations continued throughout the night as Serin and Aris fought to keep from falling asleep. They felt the waves of sleep crashing into them minute after minute. Serin grabbed his hand and whispered, "I love you, my knight." Aris was already fast asleep, his body embracing the rest after such a long day.

20

Aris arose when he heard his father whispering a few feet away. He rolled over and saw Serin sound asleep. Throughout the evening, she had gone from just holding his hand to encapsulating his entire right arm. Her body was snuggling, gripping his arm with her legs and arms. He grinned, trying to figure out how he was going to get up without waking her. Flexing his hand, he could feel the tingles pumping blood into his sleeping arm. Slowly, he slithered his way out of her grasp, but then she groaned, and he froze. Once he was certain she was still sound asleep, he began again. The only thing remaining was his hand. With a swift yet gentle tug, he freed himself from her and stood.

Despite the approaching dawn on the horizon, many legionnaires were still slumbering. Aris's attention was drawn to the soldiers sleeping near him and Serin. The legionnaire nearest him differed from the one who had been lying there when they went to bed. It was probable that the sentries were alternating throughout the night, he thought. He turned his attention to the muffled sounds of his father and Biddy. Their demeanor was strictly professional, and their discussion, though muffled, seemed intentional and determined compared to the ease and jest of the previous evening.

As he approached, his father’s words were the first to slip past his ears. “Success on your part is not in question. If you do not get to Arch Skylighter, we will be overrun.”

Biddy’s goggled face was stoic and unmoving as his head nodded slightly. His squeaky whisper was solemn and determined. “I will get to him. Hold fast; help will come from above. I swear I will not fail you, Victus." Victus and Biddy embraced as brothers. Victus rose from his crouch, saluted the gnome, and the gnome returned a bow, noticing Aris as he raised his head. "Good morning, young Aris," the gnome smiled wide at the young man. "Feeling refreshed and whole?"

Aris nodded and walked right up to the gnome, leaning down to give him a hug as well. He whispered, "Thank you for all that you have done. I wish you the best in all your endeavors. Will you be returning with Commander Skylighter?"

The gnome holding the young man tightly patted his back. "Regrettably, no. I am afraid neither Skylighter nor your father can protect me from the wrath of elves. So, upon reaching him, I will need to contingency myself out of the city. Discreetly, of course." Aris could hear the sorrow in his voice. He knew the gnome would come to aid if given the chance. But his life was at stake just by returning to Asmadine. And from what Biddy had mentioned privately to Aris, the elves truly despised the "devilishly devious gnome," as quoted from the wanted posters. Parting, Aris too saluted the gnome, and Biddy bowed. "Food is ready in the hut for you all. Nothing as fancy as last night. But the drinks and food are enchanted. Not that you will need it to be. Last night, I made certain that everything would have you all feeling at the peak of your abilities." He smiled nervously, rubbing his hands, worrying for his friends and the danger they were walking towards. "Keep yourself safe. And I will find you after it all."

Victus looked him over once more, patting him on the shoulder. "You are going to attempt to penetrate the paladin's magical dweomers and enter the sanctum?"

Biddy giggled as he responded, "Even if I cannot get directly to Skylighter right away, I will get close enough that I can at least sneak in and find him. Don't worry, Victus; I have many contingencies, and the elves will not catch me. Hehehe."

Victus smirked at the gnome's cockiness. "Then you should be on your way, dear friend."

Biddy spun one hundred and eighty degrees, clasping his hands in a small ball. The gnome's chant caused the surroundings and even the atmosphere to darken, while his hands emanated a glow. The luminescence was maroon with highlights of gold as his chanting trailed off. In his hands, he held his transportation, a self-made portal. He had attuned his spell to summon himself directly into Skylighter's temple. He knew the precise location where the paladins and clerics under Skylighter would be offering prayers and meditating. That is where he intended to land.

Biddy slowly separated his hands. Aris marveled at the sight of what looked like a miniature sea ebbing and flowing between his hands. The gnome completed the spell, turning his head back to see Aris and Victus. "Help will come from above," he promised with a wink. He spread his hands far out from his chest. The goldish maroon ocean enveloped the gnome, and he was gone.

Victus placed his arm around the young squire. "In all my life, I have never known a better gnome. He will not fail us, and we will have this day," he said, reassuring himself and his son. He believed the gnome would deliver the news to Skylighter. He also knew that Skylighter would come to their aid—but whether Biddy could actually escape the high elves? He chuckled softly, his thoughts turning to words. "Of course he will. Contingency."

Aris looked up at his father and asked, "What?"

Victus smiled. "Nothing. I was just thinking about Biddy and his escape. Perhaps, though, he won't even be noticed by the elves if he is able to get directly into the paladin's sanctum. Never mind. It's time we prepared ourselves. Start waking those still sleeping. We have work to do."

Aris saluted and spun, choosing to start with Serin first.

~~~
~~~

Biddy was flying in a slipstream of arcane magic, like a funnel pulling him to his destination. His spell was perfect. Though he felt no air pass his body to signify the speed at which he was traveling, he knew he would be there in seconds. It was a dangerous way to travel for mages, but it provided one of the fastest modes of transportation in the known universe. The problem with it was that the spell could easily be mispronounced, or the magic could be released too early or late. If so, one of two things would happen: first, the traveler would dissolve into the arcane, becoming a part of the hidden stream; or—the traveler would perpetually flow in the stream until they died of starvation, but usually of thirst.

The gnome could see through the bluish-white flow and saw the colossal city of Asmadine approaching. It glowed from this distance in a halo of white gold, which Biddy knew to be a ward against teleportation. He saw the multitude of granite-diamond towers and walls. Still, to this day, it marveled him every time he saw it. What an achievement to build such a monstrous city with such beauty! He continued his flight through the slipstream, passing the outer barrier with ease. The arcane pulled him down into the city and buzzed past people without notice. He was in the human quarter of the city, which itself was the size of Lindly. Upon breaching the barrier to the inner sanctum, which held not just the palace but the elven nobles' homes and all the paladins' temples as well, he felt pretty confident that he would get to Skylighter without even having to deal with the elves. He continued his speedy flight, zipping past the elven paladins' temples. Being whipped around, he saw the human temples. They stood out from the rest because they were crafted with Doric columns and were not as flashy and extravagant as the dwarves, gnomes, and elves. Simple and beautiful.

Seconds before he entered the temple, he was rebuffed, and the force of the arcane slipstream slammed him hard into the magically dweomered temple. Biddy was thrown out of the stream onto the ground. Forcing the air from his lungs, he hit the marbled streets outside the shrines. Catching his breath, he gasped, "Paladins have contingencies too? I have contingencies for those contingencies!" He spasmodically cursed out of frustration with Skylighter's always-prepared paladins. "Contingency! Contingency! Countenance! Whoopsie! CON-TIN-GENCY!" He sounded out the word one last time as he chuckled, his vexation passing.

Rising from the ground quickly after realizing he had been sitting there far too long to remain inconspicuous, he scanned the area and found nobody. The gnome hastened to take cover behind a line of stationary wagon carts. He thought he could hear chanting and singing echoing around him. "This is good. Perfect timing. They are all in their revelry with the gods." Snickering, he looked up at a signpost that had posted bounties and then looked back toward the human temple, thinking about just casually strolling up the stairs and entering. But then his head twisted back to the post. He saw many faces he knew posted there. His goblin friend, Puka, was one such warrant poster, he noted. It was magically enchanted to spin a full three hundred and sixty degrees so you could see the outlaw fully. Biddy giggled as Puka's picture on the warrant parchment spun. The goblin had burned off the backs of his pants, showing his backside fully. The gnome, clearly distracted as he looked at all the other warrants, stumbled upon his own warrant. "Hey! I may be an outlaw, but come on, my hair does not look like that." His hair was spiked and still burning in his spinning pictograph.

Biddy looked around and made certain no one had come out, and then flicked his fingers. He released a small torrent of fire, and his bounty burned off the warrant board. Smiling, he turned, speaking to himself, "Stupid elves."

As he began his stroll to the human temple, he heard flames flashing and began looking around. The entire length of the street had warrant boards and recruitment requests, and they all began lighting with golden flames. "Uh-oh. Clever elves." Every warrant board in the city flickered to life with flame, and Biddy saw on the one he set ablaze that it was back and burning. "Uh-oh, big contingency."

He began to run towards the temple, his short little legs pumping as fast as he could. He heard elven horns bellow, and he knew they were coming. Elven gryphon riders were circling the area and had spotted him. Within seconds, paladins from all races burst through their temples, some wearing full plate, others haphazardly dressing as they came out. An ornate and tall elf saw the gnome first and yelled, “Kill that gnome!” The elves charged towards the human temple. The humans, now outside their temple, saw the elves charging, and confused, they formed lines and braced for an attack. Biddy kept running towards the humans. He was now a mobile beacon as the warrant had placed a small light over his head, following him wherever he went. He knew the elves would kill him and then ask questions afterward.

He screamed, "I need to see SKYLIGHTER! VICTUS! I NEED SKYLIGHTER!"

The humans stood firm on the steps of their temple, watching the panicked gnome running and screaming. Three gryphons slammed into the ground in front of Biddy, halting his advance. Spears tipped down towards him; they led him from the humans towards the charging high elf paladins, who were still trying to scream past the gryphons to the humans.

“HELP ME! LINDLY IS UNDER ATTACK! HELP!"

Some of the paladins began charging down to stop the slaughter. Biddy, frustrated, tried to run around the gryphons, but they just kicked him back. Shaking his head, he said, "Contingency then." Shrugging, he put his hands up high, "I surrender." With his head downcast in defeat, he began to cast. In seconds, the giant lava creature formed behind him.

The lava giant blinked his eyes as he came into being once again and saw the gryphons and Biddy's hands up. "BIDDY TROUBLE!" He ran past his gnome creator and grabbed the gryphon closest and unfortunate enough not to fly up at the appearance of the monstrous golem. As soon as the bird was in his hand, he pulled it back down as it tried to fly away; he wrapped his large arms around the creature, melting both rider and mount together in a second. Many of the charging elves slowed their advance at the sight. Others began casting and summoning their own beasts to help. One clever elf summoned a water elemental that charged immediately and slammed into the lava giant, causing the fiery beast to groan, "BIDDY, DEY HURTED ME!"

Two other gryphons flew off to get a better vantage while Biddy yelled to his giant lava friend, "Hurt them back!" The fire golem was being slammed with water elementals, crashing into his legs and shrinking the beast. Biddy placed both hands out and began tossing fire streams right into the water elementals, which slowed and stopped many from reaching his lava giant. The lava giant began charging the elves; as it got closer, Biddy saw the damage done to his creation was not sustainable.

The lava giant smashed his left arm and then his right arm on the ground in a desperate attempt to stave off the magical attacks hitting him. Fire shot from the ground and enveloped one of the elven casters and his contingent of shield bearers. The elves had had enough, though; they all focused and blasted the lava giant hard with arcane magic, elemental magic, and death magic. The lava giant boomed in pain, "BIDDY RUN! TOO MANY!"

The humans reached Biddy and surrounded him in a square formation, shields overlapping and protecting him. They ushered him back towards the temple. The gnome kicked and then bit the hand of the paladin holding him in the square. "Let me go! I need to help him!" Wiggling himself roughly away from the human, he pushed himself to the front of the formation, seeing his magnificent creation crushing water elementals with his hands, screaming when he missed one or when the elves hit him with a myriad of magical attacks. The giant kept yelling for Biddy to run, and it sounded like the creature was crying. "RUN BIDDY!"

Biddy stuck his hands out towards his friend and yelled, "LOGI!" Through his hands, fire seared out into his lava giant, and the lava giant shrank into the stream of fire, becoming one with Biddy's fire and disappearing back to his plane to heal.

The elven commander moved from the back of his men and yelled towards the humans huddled in their protection of Biddy. "Where *is* Arch Skylighter? Does he know his men harbor one of the most dangerous criminals to our way of life?"

None of the humans said a word. They held their formation, and the paladin that had been holding Biddy grabbed him and pulled him back into the center. The elven gryphons returned with backup, and Biddy saw that the largest one of them all was an elven arch. He was at least seven feet tall, and his mount was twice the size of the other gryphons. He spoke to the human paladins with authority. "I am Arch Ashlenil, and you will release this gnome to my soldiers."

Behind the square formation, at the top of the human paladin temple steps, appeared another towering figure. His helmet was down, and he was clad in full plate, a giant longsword at his belt and his shield out in front. He had a non-hostile approach while remaining defensive because behind him stood at least twenty-five fully plated paladins, all of significant rank. Each paladin donned their own flair to their armor, save for the white cloaks they all wore. "We will do no such thing," he said.

The elven arch kicked into his gryphon and jumped over the formation of paladins, walking alone up the steps toward the human arch, known as Skylighter. As he approached, Skylighter walked down toward him, grabbing the reins of Ashlenil's gryphon as they met one another halfway.

"You dare stand against my word, the chosen of Asmolor, Commander of all Paladins, including you and your humans?" Ashlenil huffed.

Skylighter stared into the elf's burning white eyes. "This gnome comes with word of the city of Lindly, our city's sister city. If that city is under attack, then I would hear of it. If this fugitive could help us in defending Asmadine from another major invasion, then I think it is prudent to hear him out."

Ashlenil could not argue the point, so he turned away and faced the square formation. "Let us hear his words. Then we will execute him."

Biddy shook his head. "Even when I am trying to help these idiots, they still wanna kill me." One of the paladins around him laughed but quickly stifled it with a cough. The paladins relaxed their stance and spread out so Biddy could be seen by the two Arch Paladins. He walked up a few steps, giving a half bow to the two, though he only really meant respect for the human arch. "I have come to speak with you, Commander Skylighter."

Skylighter looked him over, his face unforgiving and stoic. "Then speak quickly. I am he."

Biddy shuffled around and pulled out a parchment, wrapped and sealed. He walked up the steps toward the two archs, speaking comfortably and confidently to them. "The half-pal...Oh...right. Umm...Sir Commander of Chevaliers, Victus Tiber Andreas, requests immediate aid to the city of Lindly. Dark-elves have overcome the city with subterfuge, and they are going to consume all the residents with dark magic, destroying mind, body, and soul."

Skylighter looked deep into the little gnome's eyes as he reached them. Ashlenil laughed. "That is impossible, gnome. The dark-elves have not made any major movements in years. Our spies would have seen such a massive invasion. Under the Pact of Brothers, both Asmolor and Eu'rok have had peace."

Biddy scrunched his face up defiantly. "You're too stupid to see. Hence why this letter is addressed to Arch Commander Johnathan Skylighter and not Arch Commander of the blind elves."

Ashlenil's face darkened red, and he reached down to slap the gnome off the temple steps. Biddy saw the swing, but

Skylighter had grabbed the elf's arm before he could think twice. "I would hear it all before you break his jaw."

Biddy watched the two exchange glares and waved the parchment up towards Skylighter. "In this parchment, Victus has detailed everything that has gone on and included some details of the investigation you are aware of. It also explains what we know of the device they are going to unleash on the city this very day."

Skylighter looked over the seal and saw that it was above reproach, not tampered with or magically enchanted. He broke the seal, read the detailed report, and then passed it over to Ashlenil. "Is this all you have for me?" Skylighter asked.

Biddy lifted off his goggles and looked up at the two archs. "If you don't send aid now, you will never make it in time. All in the city will perish. Victus needs your help immediately. Did you see the part about the 'high elven' disguises and no standing army in the city? You must help them."

Ashlenil reached down and picked Biddy off the ground by his shoulders so quickly that Skylighter reached for his sword. "Why would we take the word of a fugitive? A gnome? I know not what brought you back into this city, but today justice will be met against you." He tossed Biddy off and over the paladins at the base of the temple.

Biddy soared in the air and laughed loudly, yelling, "CONTINGENCY!" When he landed, his body split into duplicate versions of himself. There were Biddies everywhere in the marbled courtyard. In one voice, they all spoke, "Come and get me. Hehehe!"

At the same time Biddy was flying through the air, Skylighter swung his sword around backward, using the hilt of his sword to smash it hard into Ashlenil's face, crushing his helm and knocking him from his gryphon. "We are paladins. We help all in need."

Ashlenil ripped off his crushed helmet. "I will deal with you later, Skylighter." He hopped back on his mount and yelled to all below as he rose into the air, "That trick won't help you escape, mage." He brushed his hand in the air, and all the mirror images of Biddy dissipated. The only problem was that the real Biddy was no longer there; he had disappeared with his duplicate images. Cursing, he glided back down to Skylighter. "You have allowed this menace to escape!"

Skylighter's attention was on the parchment in his hands. Without even acknowledging Ashlenil, he turned to his battle-hardened paladins. "We leave this hour. All gryphon shock troopers take another paladin with you. We will double up to get more of us there to help. The rest wait here for the knights’ thresholds to be open in the city."

All the human knights and paladins saluted at Skylighter’s words and stormed about the area, shouting and preparing themselves. Skylighter looked over to Ashlenil. "Come with us or be known as the arch who could not rise past petty race issues to save Asmolor's kingdom."

The seething elf kicked his mount high into the air and flew off. Skylighter walked back into the temple to finish his prayers, whispering to his god Kalisdel and to himself, "We are going to war. We need you. If everything in this letter from Victus is true, Lestar is there, and we cannot fight her alone." He heard no response from his god, but he turned and looked in the direction of Lindly, whispering into the air, "Hold fast, Victus! We are coming!"

21

Aris woke Serin up as gently as he had left her. “Serin. Serin, we have to get going,” he said softly, patting her arm. She yawned and rolled away from the voice. Her mind resisted waking up due to the delightful dreams she was experiencing. Aris rubbed her arm gently. “I will be back to get you.” Not wishing to delay in getting the others, Aris jogged over to the different tents. Upon checking the first few, he noticed everyone was well on their way to being dressed and ready. Some of the tents were already vacant, or the legionnaires were walking out as he arrived. He left each tent with a brief word before heading to the next. “The commander wishes to speak with everyone before we go.” The legionnaires unfailingly offered a salute and a prompt verbal reply as acknowledgment. “We are heading there now.” Or, “Coming.”

Aris moved in and out of the tents quickly and arrived at the last tent. The canvas was the most worn out of all the tents, and he knew it was Janus’s. He stood outside for a moment before saying, “First spear, Janus—sir. My father wishes to speak with us.” Aris thought it odd that he had nothing to add to address Janus besides “Sir.” It was not because the man had not earned his place, far from it. He believed this man should be a commander, general, tribune, something other than just *sir*.

No response came, and Aris believed the soldier must have already moved out. But before he left, he peeked in and saw Janus on his knees, his armor polished and radiant. His spear, sword, and shield lay to his side, a small candle burned, and little humanoid figurines surrounded the candle. He was muttering prayers. Aris tilted his head so he could listen. Janus's voice was tranquil and soft. "Ancestors, may I honor you in combat. May my life be a testament to the greatness of our long-forgotten home and name. Guide me to be fast and true. If I die this day, may I be embraced in your light and love. Selah." Janus's hand pinched the soft candlelight flame, and he turned to acknowledge what Aris had said. "I am on my way." Saluting from his knees, he rose and placed all the figurines into a small leather pouch he tucked under his armor.

Aris had hastily turned his head away from the soldier's tent, attempting to appear as though he had not trespassed on the soldier's intimate moment. But as Aris left Janus's tent and headed back to his father, he stopped himself. He turned back to see Janus leaving his tent. Upon looking at the man, Aris was struck by the grit and beauty of such an imposing figure. The wear and tear of his armor were apparent, but it was glorious. Aris wondered if he would be able to fight against a foe like him. *Could I fight him and win? Likely no. Could my father?* Rubbing his forehead in thought, he pushed the thoughts away with, *well, at least he is on our side.*

The soldier looked over toward Aris, hearing him speak again. Janus asked, "What was that, squire?"

Aris straightened, pulling his arms down to his sides. "Nothing. I was just coming back to apologize for disrupting your prayer, sir."

Janus walked toward the young man and smiled. "Think nothing of it."

Aris returned his smile and they moved toward his father and the others. The others were already surrounding the table and Victus was speaking. "Jess, Janus, Serin, Aris, and I will be heading through the main city gate. We are to be the distraction for the rest of you." His gaze met the others and stopped specifically on Titus and Marcella. "You, Marcella, and the rest will sneak into the city from a separate gate. I would recommend the river gate as your chosen entrance.

However, as we approach, circumstances may arise where you will need to change that. I leave it in your capable hands. Now you will need to be disguised, so make sure all your armor is covered. No shield, no spears visible upon reaching the city. You will have concealed gladii only. Once you are in the city, secure the river gate. Scout out the guards you can see and take them down quietly. Marcella, you will be seeking to rally any soldiers dismissed that remain in the city. Start with the Stars Fall Tavern. It's nearest the gate and will have plenty looking for a fight."

She acknowledged his order with a nod. "I will see it done."

Titus looked from the table to his commander. Victus was moving rocks representing soldiers as Titus began speaking. "Sir, when we take the River Gate, how will we get people to leave the city? When do we deploy the defensive barrier constructed by the Hewer Clan?"

Victus held onto the rock he was about to move, lifting it up and staring at it as he answered. "When crystals begin their ascent, it will cause a panic, or at the very least, confusion. At that moment, you will need to slam the dwarven device into the ground and smash it with your boot—sooner rather than later to prevent more loss of life to the vile device of Lestar's minions. As far as getting people to come towards you—when Marcella is out gathering soldiers and people willing to fight, she can also have them spreading the word through the city. Tell all that will listen when they hear the River Gate horn blow three times to flee in that direction. I know it is clumsy, but you lot have the most important part. Adapt as you need, and as always, I trust your judgment."

He looked between Titus and Marcella. Titus nodded, saluted confidently, and said, "It will be done, Commander."

Victus placed the rock he was holding in the center of the city map. "We—" He looked between Serin, Janus, Jess, and Aris — "We now have a much better picture of how they plan to use the crystals. Last night, while we slept, Thorm-Hammer of Clan Hewer sent word to Biddy through scrying magic. It will be deployed from wherever Nibarn is. It is my understanding that he will speak to the city, and most of the citizens will be present, which means we will be in the middle here. Our job will be to keep Nibarn and his main contingent of dark elves enthralled. If he is going to hold a public trial to discredit me, then that will be to our benefit. Whatever deception he is using to get everyone bundled together, we will use it to our advantage, stalling them so that Titus and Marcella can get everything in motion." Aris's eyes bounced around the table, looking at everyone. They were all focused, attentive, and ready, he thought. His father continued, "Titus, a mile from the city, we will separate, and you will be given thirty minutes before we move through the main gate."

Aris's mind drifted from the discussion as he continued looking around the table. Jess was standing next to Serin across the table, and Aris realized he had forgotten to run back and get her. He looked at her beautiful green eyes as she stared into the map and clung to every word expressed by those speaking. He loved her, and he was worried about her. This was going to be a fierce clash. This had the potential to be as awful, if not worse, than any of the battles they were familiar with from their upbringing. *She is a capable fighter, he thought—clever and will surely catch any overconfident dark elf off-guard with her abilities. Still, though, I need to stay close and make sure she is okay.*

He paused his contemplations when she looked up at him and grinned. His face suddenly felt warm, and he knew that he had been caught staring. He focused again on the conversation between the knight legionnaires and his father. Marcella was speaking, "I will sing a blessing for us all, which will grant us speed in our travels, much like we did to get here. Biddy helped me perfect it. On top of the food and drink we shared last night, the song will help us to be better than what we already are. Meaning we will move faster, fight harder, resist poisons, and die slower." She winced at the word *die*. But everyone surrounding the table knew the risks, and no one shied away from the prospect of death. Marcella looked around the table, her eyes stopping on Victus. He nodded to her, and Titus helped her stand on the table. She lifted her hands high to the heavens, closed her eyes, and began mouthing words. She was sweating, nervous, but believed Biddy's words would help her tap into a deeper level of magic. A warmth was filling the area, and all could feel it, but none could hear what she was mouthing. Suddenly, like a dam bursting, everyone could hear her voice. It sounded as if she had split herself and was standing behind every soldier, singing just for them.

Aris attempted to comprehend the words emanating from her melody, yet it was a song from her spirit in an unfamiliar tongue. No one understood her words. The melodic sound of her voice had everyone in a state of confusion but enchantment. Each individual felt infused with light and power. A unique song was heard by each person, created to stir up inspiration within them specifically. Aris felt that it was what it must feel like to be a god. He felt strong, fast, and unbeatable. He saw the faces of the others, and they too, he knew, felt as he did. As the music slowly ended, Marcella was helped down from the table, and everyone stood waiting for Victus to issue the command to move out.

"Marcella, you truly are magnificent, and we are honored to have you with us," Victus said solemnly.

The others added, "Huzzah!" A compliment on the blessing she had bestowed upon them all; she blushed but remained silent.

Victus added, "I have two more things before we head out." He rested his arms on the table, looking over the map. "We need to be aware that after the battle, some of the more powerful elves may take on our form and try to hide among us as allies. Our core group will be hunted by the dark elves, especially when they determine who helped counteract their plans. They will seek us out. Thus, we will have a countersign. If you suspect anyone here afterward, including me, say the word 'Bear.' The correct response to this will be

'Falcon.'" As he said the code words, his eyes trailed to Aris, offering him a little wink.

The legionnaires nodded and repeated to themselves, "Bear - Falcon."

Victus added, "And lastly, I need you all to take the hand of the person next to you. I would like to try to mind-meld with you all. Though my psionics are not nearly powerful enough to communicate directly with you, I can, or rather, my hope is that it will help us work in unison even when we are apart." Aris could see his father was a little uneasy at the odd request but hid it well. No one uttered a word. They just did as he had requested. Victus held hands too and quieted his own mind. He let the minds of the others flow freely through him. He felt fear, hatred, courage, and love. A multitude of other things from his soldiers slammed into his soul and mind. He felt it all, the weight of the others' burdens, joys, and pain. His head slumped as his eyes remained closed, soaking it all in. Never in his life had he felt closer to any beings. The weight of his duty weighed heavily around his heart at this moment. From his own mind, he projected courage and bravery. He projected his love for the innocent and for his duty. He buried deep within himself his own fear, hiding it from their consciousness. The others felt this, and he could feel them unanimously supporting him. He knew that it had worked when they felt his impulse to let go. Everyone released their hands and looked at Victus with hesitant astonishment.

"I believe it was a success," Jess said with a laugh, "I say we are as prepared as we can be."

Victus smiled widely. "Indeed. Knight Legionnaires. We march to save the city of Lindly! We march to save our kinsmen! We march to show the pantheon of tyranny that we are capable and willing to stand against them. FOR DUTY! FOR HONOR! FOR US ALL!"

Titus and Marcella led the formation out of their camp on foot. Aris readied his father's horse, which he realized his father had already prepared, so he just stood there holding the reins. Janus was already atop Aris's horse, ready to be his father's shield-bearer. As Victus walked to his horse, he smiled and leaned down to hug his son. "We fight together again." Victus pulled back from the embrace and held his son's head in his hands. His voice was firm but warm. "No matter what happens, you do as I say. No questions, no hesitation. Our lives may depend on it."

Aris stared into his father's eyes, allowing the moment to sink in. He saw pain and worry beneath his father's confident demeanor. He could feel his father's feelings in his mind stronger than anyone else's—or at least he believed he did. His father was worried about him and Serin, but also about everyone's welfare. Aris also knew through his father's mind that without Asmadine's help, all their efforts would be in vain.

Aris closed his eyes, trying to speak to his father without uttering a word. Speaking to what he thought might just be himself, he said, "I will do as you say, Father. But—"

His father's voice interrupted him. "No buts. Either you do or you don't. And if you are not going to, then I cannot allow you to come with us. Swear to me that you will do all that I say."

Aris hesitated to promise, with his eyes closed and his father holding his head. His father's voice spoke into his mind this time. "Look at me."

Aris opened his eyes and saw his father's broad, confident smile. "I do swear to do all you say. No deviations. I just wanted to add that I feel your fear and love. I feel and understand it. But if anyone could make this a success, it is you and only you. And that, after all this, I would like to talk to you more about what you mentioned last night regarding the gods and the law of nature or the universe? I can't remember which it was—if that would be okay?"

His father, still smiling, replied, "Of course. When this is all settled, we will have plenty of time together on our way back to Delwan. We still have to make our yearly pilgrimage, just slightly later than we wanted."

Aris hugged his father again, stepped back, and saluted. He jogged away from his father to his place with Jess and Serin.

Janus rode up to Victus. "I am with you, Commander. Shall we catch up with the rest?"

Victus reached his arm over to shake Janus's hand. "And I am with you. Come." They lightly tapped the horses and trailed behind the already fast-moving quarry ahead.

22

Brandan woke from the disruptive sleep he'd had off the side of the main road from Lindly. His makeshift camp was nothing more than a small fire and his cloak as a bedroll. The cool evening air and the rough ground, topped off with an empty stomach and no alcohol, had made his night miserable. His eyes were puffy as he searched his unrecognizable face in the reflection of his only weapon, a small dagger. Dirt had found a home in every crevice of his face, and his body had even more. He had slept in a ditch off the road, and his guards had offered to go catch dinner. Delighted at the thought of eating a hare, or perhaps even venison, his mood had lifted for a time. But as time went by and the sun had set, he realized they would not be back—they had abandoned him. He had struggled to get a small fire going and had nothing to cook, so he had gone to bed miserable and had risen just as miserable, but with the added benefit of now being miserably tired.

He smacked his lips, rubbing his tongue against his teeth and onto the roof of his mouth. The dry metallic flavor was not deterred by his efforts, and the man sighed. Rising from his makeshift cloak-bed, he shook it out. The dirt and grime created a brief imprint of the cloak in the air. Fastening the cloak over his shoulders, he walked towards the main road. Irritated that he had no bath, no food, no water, and no wine, he let out a moan of frustration. He took a step onto the road, and as he looked back towards Lindly, he couldn't help but think of all the reasons he should turn back.

"It's possible that I completely misunderstood what I saw. I am pretty sure I was still intoxicated," he said aloud to himself, placing his hands on his head. "No." He attempted to pry the dreadful thoughts from his mind. Sighing, he took a moment to collect his thoughts before continuing. "No, they murdered those children. Even the Inquisition has some semblance of mercy. Besides, if I go back, they will probably kill me." He shook his head, deliberately turning his body away from Lindly and began walking. "How will Victus react when I tell him what I saw? What will he do to me?"

Rubbing his head in frustration, he continued his personal argument, his hands shaking from wine withdrawal. "Victus is noble. He will recognize that I am trying to help fix whatever the hell is going on there. Ah…damn it all! I will tell him when I find him and hope that he can fix it."

As he trudged along the road, the sun mocked his misery with its warm rays. Despite his head throbbing and his body protesting with every step, he persisted. Deep down, Brandan believed that for all his flaws, he was a good man. Victus had emphasized that becoming the man he always hoped to be was achievable through small, consistent, daily actions. A man venerated and esteemed by the people. However, Brandan was aware that implementing those small steps became more difficult when one's life was filled with extravagance and indulgence.

It was a struggle, but he kept his body moving forward on his march. He passed a small caravan of merchants, with whom he bartered, exchanging a ring and necklace for a wineskin and a small meal. Uncorking the wineskin, he gulped the liquid down in one large swig, the excess pouring over his dirt-covered face and clothing. To his surprise, it did not hold wine; it held water. He turned back to protest the trade, but the merchants had already moved too far. He chided himself, "Idiot! You overpaid for water and some dried meat and stale bread." The words were barely out of his mouth before he stuffed the food he had been criticizing into his mouth.

He began his walk again, chewing the unsatisfactory meal, but a glint of light in the distance caught his eye. His first glance revealed little, but upon reflection, he noted the pace and military demeanor. The gleam of armor that Brandan had spotted in the distance was now much closer, and he could see the reflection of the sun on the polished metal. His heart raced. He panicked and ran from the road to some nearby trees. Not seeing insignia or banners, all he could tell was that they were possibly humans. He suspected it was the elves from the city—his personal guards had gone back and told them of his plans to warn Victus!

However, the only flaw in his thought process was the fact that they were coming from the opposite direction of Lindly. They should be behind him, not in front. He wrapped his head around the left side of the tree to the right and then looked back towards the city, expecting to see another group approaching from Lindly. Nothing. He let out a sigh of relief and then immediately stiffened as the point of a blade pressed into his back.

~~~

Johnathan Skylighter was observing the preparation of his paladins, Inquisition clerics, and initiates. As a whole, the arch opted to bring his entire squadron of gryphon shock troopers in Asmadine to Lindly. They were fast and lightly armored paladins. The full-plated men and women would ride doubled up with the clerics and initiates on the backs of the gryphons, slowing their flight to Lindly. However, Skylighter knew every soldier was needed. He had grown up in the first war, achieved his rank of archdom after that war, and knew his enemy well. Lestar was deceptively clever, and for whatever reason, her eyes were upon Lindly. He had seen firsthand what she could do. Eu'rok's created demigods were all malevolent and wicked, but Lestar stood out for her particular inclination towards inflicting agony and chaos. It was the suffering of those caught in her webs that brought Lestar joy, and that was her purpose. Skylighter knew that her actions were guided by her maker and lover, Eu'rok, and this meant another war between the brothers was upon them.

Skylighter pulled himself atop his white gryphon as he watched his troops begin their ascent into the air. A stern
~~~

voice he recognized spoke just a moment before he jumped up into the air with the others. “Skylighter! A moment!”

Instinctively, Skylighter’s head bowed and his eyes closed in respect. “Yes, Lord.”

A small crackle of light sounded, and a fully plated, golden-white elven paladin materialized next to the human paladin. He towered over Skylighter and his large gryphon. The elven knight reached over and touched Skylighter’s shoulder, and the human’s gaze lifted towards the bright green elven eyes glowing through the Corinthian-style helmet. The voice echoed audibly when it spoke again, and Skylighter felt the words in his soul. “Johnathan, I am assembling the Inquisition. You will have no more than thirty minutes from the time you reach Lindly to save as many people as you can. There will be no warning. There will be no quarter given. The city will undergo a process of extermination and purification.”

Skylighter stared directly at his superior, unflinching. He attempted to hide the anger in his eyes, but the elven prime-arch could still sense it, causing a momentary pause in the conversation before he continued. “You will have to be fast. Ten of my most highly decorated paladins will ride with you. They are under your control and have been instructed to ignore all commands, save mine or yours. You have a difficult day ahead of you. Asmolor will be with us, but in his name, Lindly will be razed.”

“Lord Elivindel, keep Arch Ashlenil out of my way, please. And I do appreciate the warning and the aid, sir.” Skylighter spoke reverently but mistakenly made a demand instead of a request. His superior overlooked it, and the prime-arch watched Skylighter carefully before speaking again.

“I will keep him near me, on the outskirts of the city. Save as many as you can. But anyone left in the city, including you, your men, and civilians, will be exterminated if they remain.”

Skylighter nodded but was furious. “We will not have enough time to save them. I will need more time.”

Elivindel, the prime arch and archetype of all high elves, was deemed more genuine and faithful to the beliefs of the religion than its very originator, the god Asmolor. He was the firstborn of the demigods or prime archs. His appreciation for loyalty and bravery transcended race, and he had been instrumental in Skylighter's growth since the first war. He took a quick glance at Skylighter before turning his gaze to the gryphon riders who were already departing with their mounts. "Get on your way, Arch Commander Skylighter. You do not have much time." He did not look back; the cracking of the air around him caused static, and thunder roared as he disappeared from next to Skylighter.

Skylighter didn't waste time; he tapped his left foot into his gryphon and hopped up into the air. As his gryphon flew into the formation pattern of the others, their flight to Lindly officially began. All Skylighter could do to prepare was pray, and he started with his beseeching of Kalisdel. "I do not feel your presence and cannot hear your voice. We need you. A new war is to begin. Where are you?" He felt nothing, and his gut wrenched in defeat. He had never been unable to commune with his goddess before a battle. He closed his eyes and let the gryphon fly itself, beginning to pray harder, focusing all of his mental faculties on the task. He reached deep into his core and used his soul to pour into his goddess Kalisdel. Again he felt nothing. However, in his fingertips, a warmth began flowing into his arms and up through his body. His goddess had responded but was not willing or able to speak back. That was enough, though, for Skylighter, and he shouted out for all his gryphon riders to hear, "Our gods are with us! ASMOLOR VICTOR! ASMOLOR VICTOR! RIDE HARD! ASMOLOR VICTOR!"

In response, he heard the others shouting, "ASMOLOR VICTOR!" The chant and rallying call for all those of the faith and all warriors of the light. Skylighter closed his eyes and thought of Victus and Lindly. He was willing them courage in his mind. He began whispering to himself as if he knew Victus and the others could hear him. "Stand firm. Your salvation comes from above!"

~~~

Brandan raised his hands in the air as the blade tip prodded into his spine. He shook when he spoke, "I…I have nothing of value."

The voice that responded to the man was not what he expected; it sounded younger and more familiar. "Brandan? What are you doing out here?"

The blade tip dropped, and Brandan turned to smile broadly at young Aris Tin. "As a matter of fact, I came out here looking for you and your father."

Aris pointed his sword to the road where his father and the legionnaires were, only twenty feet away. "You found us."

Aris jogged to the road and waved for the others to slow. Brandan saw the young man move from his line of sight, but it was so fast he lost him. He heard Aris yell back to him, "Come on!" Aris laughed internally because he knew his magically enchanted movement had definitely confused the young noble.

Titus and his legionnaires surrounded Brandan within moments, and Victus slid down from his horse. Janus followed less than a pace behind Victus, and Aris slid into the opposite position with Jess and Serin on his right. Victus walked into the circle as the others were absorbed into it, save for Janus, who diligently stayed next to Victus at all times.

Brandan collapsed to his knees and flung his hands down to his belt. In seconds, the older legionnaire had the young man's hair held back from behind and a dagger poised to slice the noble's throat. Victus said, "Hold." He stepped closer to the young man and knelt to grab what Brandan had been reaching for—the Rod of Lindly.

Brandan's voice was strained as he spoke. "I…I came with a warning. I am doing as you asked, Victus. The Rod of Lindly
~~~

is yours again. I submit it back to you. The city needs you. My—"

Victus held up his hand as he took the Rod from the young noble's belt. Every atom, fiber, and part of his soul wanted nothing more than to take out his anger on this young noble. He clenched his free hand tight, leaning to grab him by the collar of his shirt. He lifted the noble up to his level and raised the Rod high in the air. His hands shook in rage, but he held it captive in his mind. "Brandan of House Neske." He released the noble and let him slump back to the ground as he stepped back from him. "I, under the command vested in me as Commander of Chevaliers and now the new steward of Lindly, hereby revoke your family's titles and all accompanying privileges. Furthermore, you will be returning to Lindly as a witness to your father's crimes."

Brandan nodded happily. "You're not going to kill me? Uh—thank you."

Victus responded sternly, "Have you committed a crime? Being complacent, indifferent, or just plain stupid does not justify a sentence of death. What is it you have come here to tell me?"

Brandan noticed his sister among the group. Distracted, he demanded, "How did you get here?"

Janus interrupted the man with a jolt from behind as he grabbed and shook him. "What brings you here? Answer the commander!"

Brandan glanced back at Janus and then to Victus. "Okay, okay… I saw my father and the elves sacrifice children in the council chambers. It was abhorrent. I felt something from within them all, and it scared me. I have never seen or felt—"

Victus finished the sentence for the noble. "Evil. What you felt was evil. And it is at the very heart of Lindly because of your father." Victus looked to Titus to issue the command to continue on. "Keep moving with your group and hit hard and fast. We will be behind you."

Titus saluted, and the group assembled into formation, beginning their fast-paced approach to Lindly. Marcella looked back, and Aris' eyes met hers. She smiled warmly at him, and then they were gone. Victus looked at Brandan and said, “Get up.” Brandan rose to his feet. “You are coming with us, and you will speak against your father.”

Brandan rocked in place. “No… I shouldn’t… my father…”

Victus slammed his fist into the young man’s stomach. “That was not a request. You will have your own trial with Arch Commander Skylighter to see if you will be able to retain the right to hold your family name. But until then, you will be helping me do whatever I can to save our city.”

Brandan gasped for air but took the punch with barely a groan. The punch caught him off guard, but it snapped him out of his shaky alcohol withdrawal state. The words ‘our city’ resonated in his heart as he stood back and looked into Victus's eyes. Coughing, he spoke as assuredly as possible. “I will do as you say. I will help you. I will help you save our city.”

Aris watched Serin’s response as this unfolded with her brother and saw the hope in her eyes. Aris saw the longing for her brother to be something other than a beloved noble, who was drunk and celebrating everything and anything with masquerades. Aris felt her appreciation for him being out here alone, trying to do the right thing. She had not given up on her brother, and Aris knew she loved him deeply even though he was, well—Brandan.

Janus moved back towards Victus. “Sir, we need to get moving again.”

Nodding, Victus strode back to his mount. “Let's get moving. And Brandan, stay next to your sister. If we get into trouble, she will be the one protecting you.” Everyone, including Brandan, chuckled at the quip, but Victus had not finished. He faced his horse halfway back to the young ex-noble. “Today you have begun your road to redemption, Brandan, a citizen of no house worth mentioning. This is the wetting of your sails; may it speed you to a new path for you and perhaps to the absolution of your discredited and disgraced house." The reference to wetting your sails was not lost on Brandan—it was something his ancestors did when they were seafaring people. Wetting the sails would increase speed on the ships, and sailors would often do this to make up time or to increase speed in combat.

Brandan acknowledged the gestured words with a nod and a quiet, "Thank you." He bowed his head to Victus and said, with his chin to his chest, "As ever, you are fair in your chastisement, and yet you encourage at the same time. I appreciate this."

Victus gave him a curt nod, turned, and began his ride to follow the others at their magically enhanced pace to the city. Victus felt a voice in the air, or what he thought was a voice —but in truth, it was within him. Skylighter was reaching out to him through his soul, whispering to his own. He could not make out audible words, but he knew that the arch had been given the word from Biddy. He was sending word through his soul to tell Victus that help was coming. Victus felt joy rise within and said to himself, "Well done, Biddy. Well done." His heart leaped in hope and joy, even with the knowledge that this day was going to be one of the hardest he would face. He rode hard straight toward the chaotic tyranny before him—without fear, without hesitation, and with the love of all his people in his soul. This was a day that would stand as a testament to the ages and become the beginning of the end of the pantheon of tyranny.

23

Titus, Marcella, and the rest of their contingent of legionnaires made it to Lindly and were approaching the River Gate, which they all noted was the only gate actively letting people in and out. They saw many people entering but none actually leaving the city from the other gates they had passed. Upon nearing the throng of people queued up to enter the city, Titus turned to the others.

“Spread out amongst the crowd. When we get in, Marcella will split from us. She will spread the word to anyone who will listen: Three blows from the horn, run to the River Gate.” He stole a quick look at Marcella, visibly reassuring her that she would be alright before moving on. “We need to position ourselves so that we can quickly take down the guards and secure the horn. We will direct as many of the citizens down to the river and to the ships. Defend and hold this position at all costs.” His voice lowered as the shuffling of the crowd coming up behind them guided them closer to the line. The soldiers nonchalantly commenced to scatter and blend in with the masses. Titus whispered quickly, before everyone was too far to hear, “May Asmolor protect us. May Kalisdel give us the courage. May we not be found wanting.”

Titus looked at the ramparts of the walls and the two towers attached to the River Gate. He saw tall high elves standing guard and little helmets poking slightly above the walls. Titus scowled and wondered, *What are those things standing next to the elves? Child soldiers? Gnomes? Dwarves?* He watched, stepping forward to keep himself moving in the line; he saw that the elves were not moving and that the small helmeted heads were bobbing up and down, moving along the walls. Sweat trickled down his neck, making him feel uneasy as he anticipated what was to come, thinking again to himself, *If they know our plans, we are already doomed.*

Marcella could feel Titus's uneasiness and reached her own hand down to his. Clasping it, she smiled at him as he inclined his head to hers. She muttered to him, "We are a happy couple returning to visit relatives. There is nothing to worry about."

Titus returned her smile. "Yes, and what a visit it shall be." He shifted his eyes up to the top of the walls and the gatehouse, whispering, "Do you see those little helmets? Next to the elves?"

She gave a slow nod and studied the wall intently. Leaning into him and rubbing his arm, she whispered back, "Looks like dwarven helmets."

Titus pursed his lips tightly. "Dark Dwarves?" he asked.

She looked up at the man quizzically, shrugging. "We are about to find out."

Slowly but surely, the line progressed forward. Titus and Marcella suddenly had the impression that the elven guards posted at the gate were barring individuals from entering. Titus shifted his head so that he could hear the words of citizens who were turned away—"Aye, they ain't letting no one else in. Inquisition always standing between a man and a good meal. Bastards."

Titus relayed what he had heard to Marcella and asked her, "Why would they refuse more sacrifices? Why turn away more people? It makes no sense."

Marcella shook her head in confusion but suggested, "Perhaps they have reached the capacity to which the magic will affect. Or maybe we still have allies in the city, and they have acted against the dark elves."

Titus shook his head. "Doubtful—the dark elves are clever and devious. Whatever reason they have for turning away these people, it is not good for us."

Titus continued to worry as he watched and found himself staring too long and too often at the guards on the walls. Reaching his hands down to his coin purse, he counted the coins and gave a few to his "wife." As they waited for the line to move, he told her, "This is your allotment for the trip, my dear. Please try to make it last. We are trying to save."

Marcella, not skipping a beat, giggled, smiled coyly, and said, "Of course, my sweet hunny. I am getting better. Perhaps one or... a few more silvers to help the family pay for the feast, at least for the evening?"

Titus handed her a few more silver coins, rolling his eyes. "Yes. But no more." A few of the others waiting in line with them chuckled and exchanged smiles at what everyone believed to be a young newlywed couple. Each small step in the line made Titus more anxious, but they continued to move up in the line, despite no one being allowed through the gate—at least not this gate. Many of those waiting in line began walking towards other gates, hoping to get in. No matter what might happen, he would remain steadfast in his belief in Victus and their duty. Nevertheless, that recognition did not hinder his inherent surge of adrenaline, nor the flapping of butterflies in his belly.

~~~

Nibarn walked out from his palace, down the hundreds of steps that led to the central district. The central district served as the hub for significant declarations, prominent court cases, and numerous celebratory events hosted by the city throughout the year. Nibarn walked down the fine white marble steps in his regal robes, displaying his Neske House colors and Lindly's colors cleverly embroidered upon and within them. His smile was broad as he made his way to his beautifully crafted throne at the bottom, which sat on a platform made for him and his counselors. On the side nearest to the palace, his throne was positioned, with empty stools rather than chairs flanking his grandiose kingly seat.
~~~

As he sat down, his crown slipped a little, and he adjusted it back into place. Casually, he waved his right hand, twirling his fingers in a circular motion. From a concealed location beneath the platform, his advisors emerged and took their assigned positions. The crowd had been muttering among themselves as they waited but quickly hushed when Nibarn walked towards the podium. His hands were lifted high over his head, clenched tightly in a display of dominance and power. The gesture was informally adopted by the commoners to convey that the person performing the gesture was the ultimate authority or judge of the city, without any official endorsement from the Inquisition. He stood at the white and black marble podium, hands descending. Upon his palms touching the corners of the dais, his magically enchanted voice echoed through the crowd. "CITIZENS!" He lifted his right hand, balled up, and continued, "COUNTRYMEN!"

All the citizens who were present, and even some on the outskirts of the town, heard his words. The closest in the crowd, surrounding the large platform, shouted in roars of cheers. Nibarn allowed the crowd to scream on for a few moments before raising his hands domineeringly, opening them so they were flat and waving them slowly as if to push little waves over them to drown them in silence. "First, I bring to you news. The city of Lindy has been chosen to be a city of the Inquisition. With this honor, our own soldiers have been dismissed. We have turned in our weapons for a trade of skill. Our protectors, the elves, are the purest creation and the most stalwart in defense of their vassal states."

Many in the crowd booed, but enough of them were jabbed with spears by the elven guards that they quickly changed their tune to joyous roars. Again he moved his hands to silence them before continuing. "This honor does not come without sacrifice. For many years, we have been plagued with a cult. A cult of the vilest kind." He leaned in toward the crowd. "The vilest, darkest kind—that of Lestar!" The crowd nodded at Nibarn. A cult had existed within the citizens' knowledge that committed multiple murders every year, but it never really affected anyone outside those directly murdered and their families. It had been noticed but accepted as just something that would happen. Nibarn stood back, straightening to his full height as he continued his speech. "With full cooperation from the council and myself, the Inquisitors have rooted out our blight. The leader of the cult was Commander of Chevaliers, Defender of our city, Patron of Righteousness—Victus Tiber Andreas."

The crowd audibly gasped in disbelief and slowly began to turn angry. The dark elves disguised as the high elves from the Inquisition prepared for a riot. They shuffled guardsmen into key positions to repel the mob if necessary.

Nibarn raised his hands into fists and shouted a roar into the crowd. "LET ME FINISH! LET ME FINISH!" The words were barely out of his mouth when the crowd began to quiet, seeing the high elven priestess step up from below the platform carrying a small box. Nibarn turned and saw the priestess of Lestar, beautifully dressed and deadly in her high elven Inquisitor form-fitting armor. The armor danced as she moved, reflecting the light and shadows that made her look aflame. Seizing the moment of distraction, he continued, "I have proof of Victus' betrayal."

The crowd watched the high elf priestess and scrunched their faces slightly in subdued disbelief. "I have this signed confessional from Citizen Calder, his second in command. In this document, it states how and when all the murders were committed. It states that Victus confessed it all when he was drunk with Calder." He pulled a large scroll from his robe and held it high for all to see. "This will be unrolled and displayed to all citizens so that they can read for themselves. We also have a box of evidence that is directly owned by the Andreas House, which was found under the floorboards of Victus' bedroom. It was also magically enchanted, tragically causing the deaths of a few of our precious Inquisitors."

Nibarn turned his head and bowed in deference to the priestess next to him, an attempt to show the crowd how sorry he was for the loss of life to the city's new patrons. Turning back to the crowd, he continued his charade of lies. "Within this box, we have handwritten notes by Victus. We have his ceremonial dagger and many more things you can study for yourselves. All of this will be on display but well guarded." His right hand rose and pointed to the crowd. "Only to disrupt anyone from destroying or stealing the evidence. Now the high elves have offered us protection, and we offer up our traitor. On this day, Victus Tiber Andreas is repudiated."

The crowd murmured and began talking amongst themselves. What Nibarn was really saying was that they did not have Victus, which meant that by disowning him he had no recourse but trial by combat or immediate death. With this repudiation, every citizen was to attempt to kill Victus on sight, thus preventing him from requesting a trial by combat, which the accused could defeat. The crowd talked until the high elf gently moved Nibarn aside and put her hands up to quiet them. Everyone noticed that she did not move her hands into fists, nor did she put them very high off the podium. In this, she indicated that she was there solely as a protector and Nibarn was the one truly in charge. Everyone inwardly acknowledged, appreciated, and accepted this as a good omen. The elf's enchanted voice soothed the ears and hearts of all who heard her speak. None actually understood what she had said at first; none realized she wasn't even speaking to them, but rather casting a spell.

The people in the crowd felt at ease, and a peace washed over them as they listened. As the elf continued her prayer to Lestar, the towers began to hum and glow. The purple and black colors in the towers were dark, springing from the towers and ascending upwards. As each of the crystals rose slowly, drifting towards the center of town, they began to project a barrier around the area they passed. They gradually pushed to their destination—the center of the town—and the barrier would then encompass the city completely. Most of those entranced by the priestess were not able to see the barrier trapping them. If one did see it, a blink later and it would be gone. The dark purple-black translucent, coagulating flame formed before their eyes and vanished.

The priestess saw her work was well on its way and began to actually speak to the crowd. "Today is a great day, not just a day to mourn the betrayal of your first citizen." The subtle wordplay was lost on the crowd; indicating Victus as the first citizen instead of Nibarn was clearly a slight. The priestess made certain Nibarn knew her disdain for him, and she also realized the evil in what she was construing—that Victus was actually innocent and that the stories of this man were actually somewhat admirable.

She continued to an eager audience, "Today we, the Inquisition, offer you a blessing of long years and better health. Today we will quite literally rain down the warmth of power, joy, and healing. It will open your eyes to another realm of possibilities. Nibarn failed to share with you the blessing your city will be given. You will be the most advanced, highest-ranking humans in Asmolor's kingdom. You will be given access to change your station and field of work. You will be respected as equals to us elves." She lifted her hands high but out wide as if embracing them as family. "We are UNITED!" The crowd erupted with glee and screams.

~~~

Titus and Marcella were the next to be waved over by what Titus saw was a dwarf and an elven guard. Titus looked the dwarf up and down, wondering if he would be able to recognize him even though he did not know many dwarves; the ones he knew he could easily identify. He asked Marcella, "You recognize him?"

She whispered back, "No, you?"

Titus shook his head. Before the conversation could continue, the citizens before them were turned away, and they were called forward. His words were so deep and long, yet somehow sounded so quick; his accent did not sound remotely like the common tongue. "Yooouuuuwwhhhhz!"
~~~

Marcella and Titus stepped forward, steady but not overly confident. Titus reached out his hand to the black-haired, black-braided, bearded dwarf and greeted him. "Well met, Master Dwarf." He began pulling his hand back when the dwarf crossed his arms indifferently. Titus nodded. "Straight to business. I need entrance for some, well, business." He leaned in and looked back towards Marcella; he whispered to the dwarf, "This woman is a mistress of Nibarn's son Brandan. I was sent to bring her back from her travels and would like her to have time to clean and ready herself before he knows she is back." Glancing back at her again, he added, "I promise to make sure you are rewarded handsomely." His gaze turned to watch the unmoving, forward-staring elven guards around him. He waited for a reply, but the dwarf before him just stared.

Titus finally asked, "What is with these elves? They are just staring straight forward?"

The dwarf shook his head slowly and grunted, "Not yer business. Off with ya! Gate closseeedd!"

Titus began to protest, but another voice from the side spoke from beside the guard's hut. "Titus Oxenilis, legionnaire under Victus Andreas. I have one word for you."

Titus turned to face the voice approaching—a sturdy, tall dwarf wearing wolf pelts and owl feathers over chain mail was smiling. Two war hammers sat at his sides, swaying slightly as he moved towards Marcella and Titus. Both of the legionnaires closed the small distance between each other and pulled out their weapons, allowing their cloaks to fall to the ground. The dwarf laughed and continued to close the distance, his hands positioned non-threateningly. "One word and ye can come at me if ya want—*Bear*."

Titus looked quizzically at him and then at Marcella. "What?"

Thormhammer shook his head. "Nah, that ain't the right response."

It dawned on Marcella that "Bear" was the code to verify the identity of those loyal to Victus. She blurted the correct response, "Falcon!"

Thorm smiled broadly again. "Aye, lass, that be it. Come on in. Me and me boys have secured the River Gate."

Titus chuckled softly, dumbfounded. His mind whirled with the possibilities and how these dwarves had known to aid in this way. He smiled and said, "There are more of our side spread out behind us."

The tall dwarf who stood nearly as tall as Titus nodded, "Not gonna be a problem." He looked down at a black-haired dwarf. "Ye been following them a long time? Be the bear and gather up the rest of the little falcons."

The younger dwarf nodded with a yelp of "Yep!" And with that, he ran off down the line, finding and gathering the rest of the legionnaires. Thorm motioned for another of his kin to come over and guard the entrance while he beckoned Titus and Marcella through the gate into the city. He led them into a makeshift animal-skinned tent, attempting to catch them up to speed on the way. "We ain't got a lot of time to be talkin'. So here be the short of it. Me and the boys got wind through Biddy that your boys be needin' some help. We showed up knowin' the plan and helping with the same plan as you all. Questions?"

Titus and Marcella both had questions but believed every word the powerful dwarf had said, starting with their lack of time. Titus did have one question that needed an answer, "What of the elves here guarding the gate entrance and gate towers? How long will...whatever you've done last?"

Thorm roared with laughter, "Aye, good! Yer on board. They ain't doing nothin' till we need 'em." He paused, looking directly into Titus' eyes, grinning. "Needin' these dark elves to be dyin'." Thorm's confidence in his display of power and the assuredness that he knew who they were dealing with filled Titus and Marcella both with the certitude, self-confidence, and conviction for this valiant quest to save the city of Lindly. Thorm had paid a terrible price to be here in the city of Lindly, but he paid that price without a flinch.

24

Victus sat atop his majestically muscled warhorse, halted at the back of the caravan lines into the city of Lindly. Janus slowed his horse too, with Jess, Aris, and Serin moving to the front of the two mounted men. Brandon slunk in the back behind the horses. Victus smiled at the three standing before him and turned back to look upon Brandon. "Be brave, young noble. Your actions today will be remembered. Do what is right and stand firm with me."

The young noble, stripped of his house, was nothing more than a citizen of Lindly. However, Victus offered him the opportunity to redeem House Neske and restore himself to a position of influence. He walked towards Victus and stuck his hand up to help him off his horse. "I will." His eyes were low to the ground as he kept his hand up to Victus.

Victus, the patron of House Andreas, took his hand and slid down the horse easily. "Look at me, Brandon. I have known you for a long time. You are ashamed." Brandon looked down, and Victus continued, "You are ashamed. But look at me, because what I am going to tell you will be good for your heart." Brandon looked up and met his gaze, remaining silent. Victus gave him a warm, fatherly smile, making him feel comforted. "You are ashamed," he repeated. "And this is good. It means you still understand what is right and wrong. It shows a willingness to repent and alter your life." He clasped the hands of the young noble in his own. "Seize this opportunity! Seize your new life! Be the noble I believe you can be! Stand against your father!"

Brandon nodded, offering a quiet response, “I will.” He paused, forcing himself to stare into Victus's piercing blue eyes. “And thank you, Victus, for believing in me all these years.”

Victus nodded. “A poor teacher I would be if I did not correct an error and did not continue to believe in your growth as a student.” With that, he turned to Janus and nodded. Janus hopped down from his mount and gave hand commands to the horses to follow behind them. Victus turned away and began walking away from Brandon. As he passed Aris and Serin, he patted them both on the head. “Family, Duty.” The young ones both nodded up to him as he passed them.

Jess reached to touch his shoulder, and he paused. Turning to her, he pulled her close. “I love you and always will.” He kissed her forehead and then her lips softly.

Jess spoke softly, a quiver in her voice. “And I love you, Victus. Move fast and hit hard.”

He said nothing else and continued to make his way up through the crowd. Janus kept pace to his right, and the others trailed close behind. As the citizens and caravan people turned to scold the line-cutters, they soon realized who it was. Victus was with Nibarn’s son, and none dared speak to either disrespectfully, so they moved aside without complaint. Janus employed his spear to remove from the line the few who did not move. He steered them out of the way gently and respectfully, making certain they knew he meant them no harm. Soon the word that Victus and Nibarn’s son were moving down the line spread, so the crowd split, clearing an even path for them to approach the gate.

Upon reaching the gate, the guards took little notice of them as they were ushering people in with no recourse. However, as they passed through the gates, one guard recognized Brandan and then, in a moment, noticed Victus as well. He yelled at them, but the noise of the crowd was roaring and cheering so loudly in all the chaos that the effort was in vain. The elven guard shrugged and concluded it did not matter as the city was doomed anyway. The crowd had heard that Victus was a traitor, an evil cultist who worshiped the dark goddess Lestar. But when those in the back realized he was making his way with a few others through the crowd, they too let him through. Though he was a wanted man, and it was each of their citizens’ duty to kill him, none touched him. Too many still did not believe he was corrupted, as if the bearing of Victus pushed aside the lies, showing him to be above reproach.

Aris and Serin were talking amongst themselves as they trailed Victus, Janus, and Jess. “Do you see that?” asked Aris.

Serin, with her mouth wide as she stared up at the dome barrier around the city, replied, “Yes, I do. This is evil. I can feel it. Do they not see?”

Brandan, who was eavesdropping, answered, “They have been magically blinded to it. And those beyond these walls obviously cannot see it. If these are dark elves…” He corrected himself after a brief pause. “Because they are dark elves, everything is cloaked in a web of lies. Illusion and deception are their forte.”

Aris reached over and squeezed Serin’s hand. “We are here to stop it all. Right?” Serin nodded and squeezed back.

They made it halfway to the platform in the center of Lindly when someone in the crowd not only recognized Victus but also began yelling that he was there. Others began yelling too, and eventually, it grew loud enough for the priestess and Nibarn to take notice. Nibarn yelled into the crowd, “Where is he? He is here? Kill him!”

The priestess waved her hand at him in a not-so-subtle, quiet-down motion. She looked into the crowd and saw where the citizens were parting. “He is there. Bring him to me.”

Her elven captains started issuing commands, and soon, a path lined with elven warriors led from the platform to Victus and his quarry. One elven captain marched straight for Victus and, upon reaching him, spoke coldly, “Lay down your arms.”

Victus shook his head. “I will not. I claim my right to defend my name and this city.”

The arrogant elf laughed. “Can you not see that you and your people are defeated?”

Victus asked the elf a question in turn, “Would you see yourself as defeated, dark elf? That’s the difference between you and us. We will never willingly be pawns to our own destruction, while you accept defeat daily in the way you live and the gods you serve.”

The elven captain blushed in rancor and reached to unsheathe his sword. The crowd awed and let out a collective, “Woooh!” But before the elf could get his sword out, he saw the city upside down, spinning, and then the dirt on the ground before losing consciousness. Janus had let go of his spear and ripped his sword from his belt, cleanly chopping underneath the elf’s armored chest and helmet, removing his head. It happened so fast that the spear he had let go barely began to drop before his sword was back in its scabbard and the spear was back in his hand.

All the elves lining a path from the platform to Victus stared in disbelief from their dead captain to the priestess, waiting for the command to kill. The priestess took a moment before she responded. “Let them forward. I would hear his words.” The elves listened to their priestess and stayed in their positions as Victus and his quarry made their way to the platform, the two warhorses making up the rear.

Serin, Jess, and Aris stood at the bottom of the platform and watched Victus ascend the few marble steps towards the priestess and Nibarn. His sandy blonde hair had accumulated many gray hairs since his youth, but his age had never affected his charisma nor his vigor. Victus stepped towards the podium. The priestess feigned politeness as she stepped back and to the side. Through her wicked grin, she said sardonically, “Your last words before we execute you for your crimes?”

Victus turned his back to her and pulled out the Rod of Lindly, placing it on the podium. "I have the symbolic power of this city." Janus slid himself in between Victus's back and that of Nibarn and the priestess. Victus spoke loudly, and the magic surrounding the podium enhanced his voice. "We are deceived. This is not the Inquisition. They are dark elves disguised as high elves. Above you, in the sky, is the creation of a new weapon that will harvest your very souls." The crowd did not react; they just looked confused. However, a few started to see the dome forming, snapping out of the enthralling enchantment of the priestess. "Citizens of Lindly, we are under siege. The River Gate is your escape. Stand, fight, and get you and your loved ones out of the city."

A few from the crowd listened and moved to leave, but the elves kept them from leaving the center of town, blocking them quickly.

Nibarn laughed. "They don't believe you, Victus. You are a traitor, a liar, and a cultist. We will have your death this day."

Victus spun around, his hand reaching back, grabbing and tossing the Rod of Lindly at Nibarn's feet. "I demand trial and vindication by combat. Not just for myself, but for all present. Your darkness will come to light this day, Nibarn." Victus turned back to the crowd. "I have claimed my right to a duel. Heed my words when the moment comes—River Gate!"

Nibarn looked pale as the blood drained from his face. "You have no citizen of note to second your claim to the city, and I decline your right to vindication through combat. Your death sentence stands." He looked to the priestess, whose eyes watched Nibarn's son stepping up to the platform. "I said he does not get a chance. Kill him." Nibarn's eyes narrowed as he saw his son, almost unrecognizable from his night outside.

His mouth opened in a gasp, but before he could scold his son, the priestess spoke to him sharply, "I do not take orders from you, Nibarn."

Brandan walked up to Victus, patted his shoulder, and turned to the crowd. “I am Brandan of House Neske. My father has sold our fair city to the dark elves. They are before you, even now, disguised as high elves. I saw him murder helpless children with all the council members sitting behind him.” The councilors shook their heads and yelled slurs toward the young noble. Brandan was determined and ignored them. “I beg your forgiveness, citizens of Lindly. I have failed to protect you, as was my duty. But I am here to help fix what I have done.”

The priestess watched, astounded at the tenacity these humans were showing for their city, for their countrymen—she hadn’t expected pushback, much if at all. She hid her admiration under a smug grin, but she was impressed.

Brandan continued facing sidelong towards his father and the crowd. “I defy you!” He pointed at his father. His flamboyant gestures and tone of voice drew the crowd in. No magic, no tricks. The young man had a talent and flair for public speaking, and he was winning the crowd over. He brought weight to what Victus was saying. Two of the city’s highest-ranking nobles were standing against all the changes, all the promises. Brandan sighed as he continued, “For whatever honor our House still has, I defy you. I deject you! You have lied and betrayed us all. I second Victus and will share his fate in the vindication trial and for the right to claim this city under his House’s protection.”

Nibarn swore under his breath, “You wretched whelp! We have the confession of Victus's second, Calder! We have proof!”

Brandan waved his hand firmly down, cutting his father’s words off. “More than likely he was forced to sign the confession. It does not matter. I have seconded Victus. Choose your champion, Father.”

Serin and Aris watched in amazement at the events unfolding. They had never seen Brandan like this. It was truly marvelous, and they shared a grin. Jess was facing the crowd, watching for any attempts by the elves to attack. Nibarn spun and marched angrily to his throne. Seated on the throne and readjusting his crown, he spoke with a strained composure. “I choose the Inquisition’s priestess as my champion. The duel will be to the death.”

The crowd roared, cheering. Some booed Victus and others booed Nibarn; it seemed to be divided on who they wished to see win.

Victus walked over to where Nibarn had been standing and leaned down to pick up the Rod of Lindly. Holding it high in the air, he walked over to Brandan. Victus gave a small nod, placed it into Brandan’s hand, and lifted it together with his. “A TRUE SON TO HIS HOUSE!” The crowd went wild, cheering for Brandan. The young noble looked into Victus's eyes. Quickly, he wiped the swelling of tears and thanked him in a hoarse whisper. “I will never forget this, Victus. Thank you!”

Nibarn fumed in his seat and watched the priestess as she removed her cloak, preparing for the fight. She put her hand out, and one of her soldiers tossed her a spear. She left her longsword in its sheath as she knelt down, closing her eyes as she prayed to Lestar.

Victus took off his kite shield and placed it at the edge of the platform on the ground. Janus was around the horses as he pulled out Victus' gryphon shock trooper helmet. It was trimmed in dark azure and had a plum signifying his current rank. The feathers that stuck out from the top formed a mohawk of dark blue. The faceguard was a metallic face imprint, much like a death mask—formed in plaster and iron to fit firmly onto its owner’s face. Aris had only seen this helmet once before and knew his father only wore it when he was going to war. It was magically enchanted and offered many advantages that Aris did not know. But he did know that when it was worn, it gave the wearer vision from all directions—above, below, side to side. This particular helmet had been given to him by his old commander, Arch Skylighter.

Janus marched up the steps of the platform, and Victus took the helmet, placed it upon his head, and nodded in thanks to Janus. Victus then pulled his gladius and twisted the Bear pommel left and then pulled it down. The sword elongated into a bastard sword and glowed in House Andreas' colors. Victus, looking at the silver-blue glow of his sword, placed the tip down onto the platform. Kneeling, he began collecting his thoughts and praying to the unknown god he believed in and to Kalisdel.

Aris watched his father with pride. His skin prickled with goosebumps, and a static charge seemed to fill the surrounding air, but he realized the electric charge he felt was because of the magic of the crystals ascending. He looked above and saw that the crystals were nearly formed and that in the distance it looked like black rain was pouring down on the outskirts of the city. The rain was heavy, and in the midst of it all, he saw translucent humanoids making their way up toward the crystals. He nudged Serin and asked, "You see this?"

She squinted in horror, then gasped, "By the gods! Is it souls?" She could not be certain, and neither could Aris, but it seemed to be hundreds of souls in the distance being wrenched up towards the crystals. Aris and Serin, horrified, huddled closer together.

Aris kept his voice low, thinking that if he was quiet, their souls would remain safe in their bodies. He looked at the young girl now clinging to his waist. "Serin, whatever happens, don't let the black rain touch you or whatever that is."

She nodded, her mouth still gaping in fear. "What has my father done?" Her voice was broken as she tried to hold back tears.

The young squire wrapped an arm around her. "He has never been your father. And this will not be the end. We are standing firm together against this, and help is on the way." He pulled back his arm, reaching his hand underneath her chin, gently pulling it to look into her eyes. "I fight for family, duty…" he paused, "and you, Serin." Leaning in, he kissed her rosy lips.

Serin kissed him back passionately, and as she pulled away with tears streaming down her face, she whispered, "Family, duty, Aris."

25

Thormhammer of Clan Hewer leaned his hands on the handles of his war hammers. Next to him stood Titus, eyes fixed on the center platform, as they both watched Victus step up. Marcella was heading down the street towards the taverns, hoping to enlist more help for their cause. Titus listened carefully to every word spoken from the magically enchanted stage. His blood pumped faster as he listened to his revered commander speak. The anticipation of what was about to unfold built a righteous fervor within him. It was bubbling just underneath the surface, and Thorm could feel the man's excitement and respect—partly because of the magical dweomers placed upon himself and his equipment. Thorm never left the sanctity of Malakas's lands without significant magical enhancements, adjustments, and defenses. Some of these that overlapped with magic intensified his ability to understand the body language of others and even feel their emotions. But Thorm did not need magic to see the pride on the man's face. When the young noble Brandan spoke, Titus let out a small cry, "YES! GOOD MAN!" Thorm chuckled with a pat on Titus's shoulder.

"Victus inspires the best in all of us."

Titus glanced over, nodding. "Yes, he does." The legionnaire reached into his cloak and pulled out the disk-shaped device that Thorm had given Victus. "Time to use this, I think." He threw it down to his feet but waited. He crouched low, squinted his eyes, and strained to see the height of the dark dome rising above him. He spoke more to himself than to Thorm, "Oh yes, definitely. It's nearly peaked." He raised his leg high and slammed down hard with the heel of his boot.

Nothing happened. He smashed his leg down again and again. Still, nothing happened. He looked puzzled towards the tall dwarf, Thorm. “It’s supposed to… do something that will protect against the dark elven magic?”

Thorm, who was being sucked into the events unfolding on the platform, turned his gaze down to the device and then back up to Titus. “Aye, it’s gonna do something.” Taking his leg, he slammed it down onto the disk. With just one crash of his heel into the disk, it cracked open. “Just needin’ a bit of help, is all. Tricky things to get workin’.” As the words fell on the human’s ears, a warm blue wavelike fog pulsated out and around the River Gate and some of the nearby buildings. It did not cover nearly as much as Thorm had told Victus it would. He grunted to himself, “Shoulda been bigger.” He looked around the ramparts and the gate, waiting to make eye contact with each dwarf next to an elf, and once all the dwarves above were looking down at him, his countenance traced all the dwarves on the ground. Each, in turn, looked directly at Thorm, and the dwarven arch began his prayer. “We shed blood for what is right. Not on orders from our god. We honor those fighting here today. Both sides will suffer, but we stand with Victus. We praise Malakas for her love for us. We stand with Kalisdel’s people. We stand as one with our kin and not just our blood. Let our aim be true and our hammers be pulverizing. Raise the flag! Let ‘em know we’re here.”

The dwarves guarding the dark elves disguised as high elves moved in unison after Thorm had finished. Each took their hammer and, in a fluid motion, struck the back of the knees of the frozen dark elves, buckling them. As they succinctly crumpled, a second hammer found its way into the skull, caving it in before they hit the ground.

Titus watched, somewhat repulsed by the brutality, and then nodded approvingly. “They are dark elves,” he said to himself. He then saw that when the elves’ lives were extinguished, so was their veil. Or at least, Titus thought it was in death that the skin returned to its natural dark pigment. But to him, it did not matter. Whether it was by death or by Thorm's magic, it did not matter; it was proof of Victus's words. Not that Titus needed convincing, but it validated it all. Titus looked over at Throm and saw his finger go up towards the River Gate's towers. He saw dwarves pulling down the Inquisition's flag. After a few moments, the barely visible dwarves began raising the city of Lindly banner, and as it rose to its peak, two smaller banners were underneath.

The first flag underneath was black with House Andreas's blue lettering large enough to read, "Broktas ven Blouda" or in the common tongue, "Brothers in Arms." Underneath this clear salute to Victus was what Titus believed was Clan Hewer's banner.

~~~

Marcella was moving quickly but not running as she made her way to the closest and largest tavern in town, "Ye Olde Forte." She knew this would have the most ruthless, toughest men in town. As she kept out of the center road, skirting the buildings, a blue wave splashed over her. A wall quickly formed as she kept pace. Her instinct to recoil from the new obstruction was too late, but to her amazement, she was outside this translucent barrier. Marcella kept moving forward but glanced back, turning her head down as she heard shouting in elven. From what she could guess, some alarm had sounded, and she knew where they would be heading—the River Gate.

As she reached the outside of Ye Olde Forte, she glanced back towards the River Gate. Approximately thirty Inquisition elves were marching briskly towards the gate, vanishing and reappearing as they passed behind buildings. She smiled. "Fight well, Titus!"

Marcella unfastened her cloak, let her hair down, and used the shadows to approach the stage once she was inside the tavern. A drunk man with no teeth reached from his table and grabbed her belt. Pulling her near, he burped, "Here, lil…
~~~

little lady! I got a present for ya!" As he pulled the female legionnaire closer, he didn't notice he was also pulling her fist to his throat faster. The impact knocked the man down from his chair, where he lay coughing. His friends at the table laughed and cheered for the young woman.

Without a word, she spun away and continued toward the stage. Once she had gotten near enough to sneak on, she pushed herself between those already on the stage and out in front. The band and the delectably dressed female singer stopped, and with that, the entire tavern quieted. Everyone began staring at the stage. The music never stopped but instead played on, having been abandoned by their singer.

A few in the crowd booed, while others began catcalling Marcella. She raised her hand to speak. "Citizens!" The crowd grew angry and shouted at her interruption. Some even rose from their chairs, making their way toward the front. Marcella put both hands up in a plea. "Wait! LISTEN!" she yelled.

The crowd was having none of it. They approached, and some began throwing bread and fruit toward her. Marcella closed her eyes and belted out a long, melodious melody, stringing the highest note to shock and the lowest to calm. Everyone stopped as she trilled soothingly to them all. When she stopped, they were all sitting and watching, deciding whether they had been too quick to judge. After a moment, where the last of her notes hovered in the air, Marcella tried again. "Citizens! We have been infiltrated by dark elves!" The crowd muttered among themselves in confusion as Marcella continued. "Commander Victus has returned to confront them, and he needs you. Lindly is about to be consumed! We must rally and make a stand."

A small group of about ten men sitting far to the right of the stage stood at the mention of Victus. Marcella nodded at them as the eldest of the group spoke, "Looks like we are reenlisted!" The man flipped over the table, and the group began pulling up the floorboards. She watched as the gruff-looking man moved down the steps and began passing out weapons and chain mail from beneath the floorboards.

Marcella looked back at the crowd. "If you cannot fight or are unwilling, get yourself and any loved ones to the River Gate and out of the city!"

In the opposite corner from the ex-legionnaires arming themselves were a few cloaked, humanoid figures. They sat at a table, surrounded by the gentle flicker of candlelight, enjoying the cool respite of the shaded area. A man from the hidden group stood up and moved into the more revealing light to speak. "We, the magi of the blades, will offer any aid we can."

The accent was so thick that it was difficult for Marcella to understand. They moved from their table as a group of one mind towards Marcella—they disappeared and reappeared directly in front of her. She understood who they were now—mage-blades, trained in forbidden magic, masters of blades, and deeply rooted in dragon lore. The short, cloaked man in red and black, the one who had spoken, removed his hood, revealing his shaved head and short, well-trimmed goatee, black as his cloak. He looked over the crowd, speaking deeply, "If you're going to help in the fight, get up here. If you're not, you best get out of here now."

At this display and encouragement, a few stout, surly-looking men moved to the front. Some others still sat confused, but the rest moved towards the exit. As they did, two elven guards walked in. The herd leaving the tavern pushed past them and ran in the direction of the River Gate, heeding Marcella's and the mage-blade's words.

The tallest elven guard spoke to the crowd in the tavern, but he was cut short. "Everyone outside now! We—" Two of the mage-blades shadow-stepped, or rather, teleported from the front of the stage to standing on the opposite sides of each of the guards. In no more than a split second, their dragon-hilt daggers sliced in unison cleanly under both elven helmets. The elves grabbed their throats in panic. One stumbled, slipping on the blood now pooling underneath his feet. He pushed himself out the door, ripped off his helmet, and tried to yell. His mouth made the motions, but his vocal cords were severed. The loss of blood pulsing from his clenched hands around his throat was too much, and he collapsed in the street. The mage-blades quickly grabbed the fallen elf and dragged him back inside.

Everyone watching gasped as they saw the skin of the elves turn dark gray, nearly black. One man yelled, “Dark elves! It’s true!” Others began to murmur and rise from their seats, moving closer to the so-called high elves lying on the ground dead, and indeed they saw they were dark elves. The small group looked from one another to the dead bodies and eventually all turned to face the leader of the mage-blades and Marcella. Their eyes implored Marcella to tell them what to do.

She smiled warmly at them, reassuring them. “We need to get as many people out of the city—including yourselves when the time comes. The weapon they are unleashing enslaves your soul, leaving your body a mindless drone. I wish this fate on no man or woman. Go out and spread the word, and if you are stopped by an elf, fight them! They are our enemy. Arm yourselves! Fight for your freedom! Fight for your families! Fight for your city!”

The men and women responded in agreement and began breaking chairs for makeshift clubs. Their blood was already raging from the booze, and now they were getting into a fight. Marcella stepped down from the stage and made for the exit. She turned to the mage-blade leader and said, “We should bring them out and place them for all to see.”

The mage-blade rotated his wrist, his hand flipping topside, and the bodies levitated from the floor. He followed Marcella out of the tavern with the bodies. Everyone from the tavern began splitting up into small groups. Some went off toward the River Gate, while others began making their way to the large crowd around the platform. Each person they passed was warned quickly.

The mage-blade leader lifted the dark elf bodies so they stood upright in the middle of the street. Two of his accomplices walked over, each holding a small cylinder in their hands. When they reached the dead dark elves, they seemingly pushed a button, and the cylinders burst out into spear-tipped staves. They positioned them at angles that lifted them into a propped-up position. The opposite ends were placed securely into the cobblestone. Marcella was intrigued by the staves; they seemed to be made from an ancient material that she couldn't identify.

The mage-blade spoke in his accented common and deep voice. "We are here at your service. What would you have us do?"

Marcella took her eyes from the bodies strung up by the spears, gazing off toward the platform where Victus had begun his duel with the priestess. She turned back and looked at the mage-blade leader. "Follow the others who are headed to the River Gate. You will come in behind the dark elves I saw marching earlier, and you will run into my commander Titus and a dwarf named Thorm." The mage-blade grinned at the name Thorm but continued listening. "Help them hold the gate for as long as possible. We are indebted to you. Your ways are not our ways, but I understand your potency. Fare thee well. Stand firm."

The mage-blade gave a small bow, and the others followed. Giving the command to his people in a language that Marcella had never heard, he turned to her again. "Live on, to the health of your enemies' enemies." He winked, spinning, phasing in and out of Marcella's vision. A trick, she thought as the man got farther and farther away. A question screamed in her mind, *Who is this man?* Prompting her to yell the question out towards the mage-blade leader, "Wait– What is your name?" She paused as she saw the men hesitate and then stop, listening to her. "I would have your name, sir. Please? I will give a full accounting of this to Victus later."

The man did not turn, but she heard him clearly, “Odyful is my name.”

Marcella lifted her hands up in confusion and mouthed, “What?” She snorted inwardly as she thought of the name, *named after a dragon*. Then, as she turned to move into the next tavern, she began having a practice conversation with Victus. “You see, sir... I found these dragon cultists. Not like the cultists who brought this doom upon us. No... No. No. They are special cultists that worship and name themselves after dragons. Oh... and they are really good at fighting.” Shaking her head, she chuckled, thinking about Victus's response. “So... they are the good kind of cultists? Didn’t know they existed.” Smiling as her thoughts concluded, she moved into the Dragon’s Puff tavern to speak to its patrons.

~~~

Thorm and Titus stared up at the flags, and then they heard the hoots and howls from the dwarven sentries. Thorm growled, “The elves are coming, lad.”

Titus reached into the bag he carried, signaling to the rest of his quarry standing by the gate entrance. “Ready up! They come!”

Every legionnaire was in their packs, pulling out helmets and weapons. Individually, they started running over to Titus and forming up. Thorm looked them all over briefly, then pulled out one of his war hammers and waved it over his head in a circle. “Rally to me, boyos!”

The last of Titus's men had formed up, holding swords and wearing mostly chain shirts. Titus, with his horizontally plumed helmet, issued his commands. “Two-man walls. One shield, one blade,” he said, employing a common battle tactic when fully armored legionnaires were in want; they would pair off into teams—one playing the role of defense and the other attacking. Keeping a loose box formation, they would be able to counter all attacks from all angles. Titus continued, “We hold here! No retreat! WE HOLD!”
~~~

His men and women stamped their feet into the dirt. “Wuh-huh! Wuh-huh!”

Thorm smiled, watching the human soldiers. Fifteen or so dwarves huddled near their leader. He spoke to them in Dwarven, and Titus could not understand it; however, when Thorm finished, all the dwarves moved in front of the legionnaires. The first row of dwarves held giant war hammers, and their spacing was gapped appropriately for the weapons’ radius. The second row of dwarves were melee berserkers. They carried two weapons, and at least one of them was a hammer. The armor they wore was pointed like thorns. Titus understood the reason for this special armor: it was so that every part of the dwarves could be used as a weapon—knees, feet, elbows, helmet—each piece represented the thorns upon a rose bush: beautiful, sturdy, deadly.

Thorm turned and answered the question Titus was thinking. "We will be the tip of the spear here, lad. Better armored than ye lot. Let us suck 'em in, and you spread out to their flanks."

Titus pursed his lips, then slowly nodded. "As you say, master dwarf."

The dwarf spat into his hand. "Bah." Grumbling, he stuck it out to Titus. "Ain't no master. Ye be calling me brother or Thorm."

Titus reached his hand out, then quickly pulled it back, spitting into it and reaching again for the dwarf's extended hand. "Then I wish you the best of luck, brother Thorm."

Shaking hands, the two warriors shared a brief moment before Thorm spoke again. "Keep your feet! And hit 'em hard."

Titus moved to the front of his men and behind Thorm's. The dwarven leader moved directly to the front of his soldiers, his hands holding his wonderfully crafted warhammers. He yelled out towards the approaching elves, "A’ight ya gray-skinned bastards, come on in!" By saying "gray-skinned," he equated the dark elves to dark dwarves, thus degrading their stature to a lower species. They hated it, just as their cousins hated being compared to lesser races. Most of the dark elves were the color of night; however, a few were grayer, and when any of them was killed, they would turn ashy gray. The dark dwarves had the same color pigments as the dark elves, only lighter; most were known as graybacks or gray skins. The insult worked, as the main group of dark elven soldiers marched straight toward the human and dwarven army, and Titus saw that they were no longer concealing themselves—or maybe the barrier was somehow revealing them. The dark elves' spears were tipped down, only one line thick. The rest behind this formation began throwing their spears toward Thorm and his dwarves, the first line of defense. As the spears flew toward Thorm, he lifted his hammer up toward the sky, and they dropped to the ground. More elves were spreading from the sides of the streets.

"Hundreds," Titus said as he looked to his sides and then back to the front. Titus yelled up to Thorm, "They are surrounding our flanks!"

Thorm nodded and bellowed back, "Aye! Me berserkers will herd them back like cattle. Be ready, lad! You'll know when to strike."

Titus yelled back to his legionnaires, "On my command, we break down the middle to the left and right flanks, pushing the sides as Thorm's men hit the front!"

The legionnaires' response was stomping into the ground with "Wuh-Huh! Wuh-Huh!"

The first row of elves, the phalanx, quickened their pace toward the dwarves. With that, Thorm's first row stepped up in sync with their commander. Thorm's berserkers bolted from in front and began to run toward the pockets of dark elves approaching the legionnaires' flanks.

The battle for the River Gate had begun.

26

Aris took in the magical dome and then turned his attention to the souls already being harvested on the outskirts of the city. The young squire did not understand why people were not noticing the dome, nor the souls being ripped from their bodies and soaring up to the crystals. Musing to himself about the myriad possibilities of why, he concluded that some type of magic had transfixed most of the city. It seemed Victus had interrupted the process, as some people were leaving toward the River gate, but it was not the majority and was not enough. In the wake of Victus' speech and Brandan's defiance of his father's leadership, some people were set free from the enchantment, but not all.

Aris understood his father had wished to delay the formation of the crystals. However, that was not happening. But at least his father could keep the leaders of this darkness close to himself, perhaps thwarting their full success. Nibarn and all of his counselors were there. The dark elf leaders were there, though veiled as high elves. Victus' duel would hopefully keep them in place for when help arrived, allowing justice to be done and removing the roots of darkness from the city.

Aris' eyes then turned back to his father, who was rising from his prayers to face his opponent. Serin tugged on Aris' arm. "Aris, do you see that?" She was pointing to the River gate tower. The Inquisition flag was gone, and underneath were two new flags.

Aris shrugged, looking quickly, then back to his father. He did not want to miss the fight. "Wait," he said as he looked again. Reading the words painted in House Andreas blue on a black flag, he said, “Dwarven for brothers in arms?” The young man shouted a yell to get his father’s attention, pointing when his father turned. “Father... Commander Victus! Dwarven friends?” he asked. Victus followed the invisible line Aris pointed from to the River gate.

Victus nodded, smirking in disbelief. “Allies!” The commander turned back to his upcoming fight. Tears welled in his eyes as a knot grew in his throat. He steadied himself and inhaled deeply, directing all his energy toward the current task, whispering to himself, “Thank you, Thorm. Brotaks ven blouda!”

Aris looked at Jess and Janus curiously. “Do you know who they are?”

Jess answered, “Dwarven, friends of your father. The leader is Thormhammer, and his people are the Hewer clan.”

Aris smiled, feeling hopeful as he knew the name. “Thorm helped create the armor I wear.”

Jess clenched her jaw, her voice hinting at anger. “Thorm is duplicitous. Your father is wrong to trust him. If we survive, ask him how many masters he has served. Ask him how many of our people he has killed. Your father has a soft spot for the dwarf and sees him as noble. But he is a traitor to his kin and to us.”

Aris squinted in confusion. “Is he not here now to help us? Did he not raise a flag that says, ‘Brotaks ven blouda?’ That is not an expression used lightly. It is used by dwarven clans to unite them under one banner. What Thorm is saying is that he fights with us. Yes?”

Jess turned back to watch Victus, who was moving to the center of the platform. “Perhaps. But be vigilant. And how do you know so much about the dwarves?”

Aris smiled broadly. “Da has made sure that I studied the histories and languages of all the mortal races before I could train to be a warrior.”

Jess chuckled. "Work before play." Her own laughter calmed her as she continued speaking to the young squire. "If he is truly here to help us, then I will stand corrected and make my apologies." She smiled at Aris, reassuring him with a tight grip on his shoulder. "Just because I don't trust Thorm doesn't mean I don't trust your father. He is my commander, the true leader of this city. And my lover."

Aris's face blushed as he turned to look towards his father. He was aware of their relationship and understood why it was not flaunted publicly, but hearing her speak about it to him, of all people, made him uncomfortable.

"Aris, when this is all finished, I would like to be a part of your life. That's to say I wasn't there for your birth, but I intend to be there for you in the future. And perhaps, in time, you will see me as your mother..." She paused, embarrassed.

Aris picked up on her tone and quickly added, "I already see you as a part of our family, Jess."

Jess nodded. "Yes... thank you." The woman was uneasy. She knew that if Victus died, she would be the one looking after him. But if everything went to plan, Victus and Jess would marry, and she would be Aris's mother. The difficulty came in explaining that to the young man. However, his maturity and understanding had relieved her tense timidity. Jess and Aris twisted their heads and then shifted tensely at the sound of Nibarn speaking.

Aris quickly added, "Don't worry about being my mother or any of that. We have our duty now to focus on. Besides, you will be an exceptional mother." It was Jess's turn to blush, feeling the heat rise to her cheeks as she kept her thoughts to herself while listening.

"Citizens! As we bask in the glory being bestowed upon us, let us enjoy watching justice meted out against the deceiver, Victus." Standing in front of his throne, Nibarn had to pause his speech as the crowd erupted in a deafening roar. To him, it seemed that the audience was divided, with half booing and the other half cheering. Nibarn thought, *decent enough odds.*

If I were a betting man, this would be worth betting on. Nevertheless, the fools are doomed anyway. He raised his hands to silence the crowd. “Are both combatants ready?”

The priestess twirled the spear around in her wrists so quickly that the motion was a blur. She tossed it high, spinning in the air, and caught it, wrapping it around her body, the point forward in a display of mastery. She ended her flair with both hands holding the spear out in front of her, pointed directly at Victus. “The Inquisition stands ready to meet this challenge,” she said sardonically, placing the spear down into a relaxed but ready stance with both hands gripping it.

Nibarn turned to look at Victus and waited for the man’s counter-response. Victus pulled his glowing silverish-blue bastard sword up into his ready position called *The Fool*. His right leg was extended back as an anchor, and his left foot was lined up with the crossguard of his sword. The sword was low by his inner thigh, pointed down. The name *The Fool* stemmed from the fact that it hindered the defense of the upper body. Most trained warriors considered it too slow in countering and a very dangerous defensive position. The sword appeared so heavy that certain members of the crowd thought it couldn’t be lifted.

For Victus, this was an advantage. The dark elves, especially spear-wielding ones, loved to sweep the legs out from heavy-armored opponents. Victus was lighter than most knights because he preferred half-plate armor. Victus adopted the fool position with aggressive intent instead of defensive. Releasing his grip on his sword, he repositioned his hands slightly, exhaling and taking a deep breath. “Family, Duty, Lindly!” Victus waited for a response from Nibarn.

“Then let it begin!” The steward of Lindly cackled, coughed, and sat down on his throne, watching in delight. The dome was nearly formed, and the souls floating to his mistress’s bosom gave him the undeniable sense that all they had planned would succeed.

Victus heard the word "begin" and sprinted from his side of the platform. The priestess, taken aback by the knight's aggressive move, had no choice but to respond with a sprint toward the center. She wanted to be the first to engage and to keep him off balance. Victus kept his sword low and pressed forward. The two covered nearly the same ground, with the priestess just barely beating him. While still sprinting, the priestess swiftly side-shifted and aimed her spear toward the man's feet, ready to strike. This attack was fast, and she had executed it to perfection, and like many knights who had fallen before, she knew it had caught Victus off guard.

However, Victus did not get swept off his feet, nor did he get clipped by the spear. With his sword held low, he ignored the opening the dark elf had left him and deftly parried her spear. The force with which he knocked the spear up was enough to push the elf back a few steps. But Victus did not stop there. He spun, lifting the sword in a fluid motion with his momentum, deflecting upwards as he repositioned on the elf's right flank. She barely got the spear back to block the downward blow, and even that pushed her knees to buckle. She was forced to roll in retreat, and Victus was on top of her in less than a second. The priestess flipped and cartwheeled with her spear a few times from the ground, backing away from the wrath of this knight. Once she was far enough, she began to spin her spear in acknowledgment that he had won the first bout, but she was also stalling as she cast a spell. Weaving a curse into her spear, she reengaged. She pressed Victus now, who lifted his sword to parry and deflect the attacks. Victus watched the thrusts and swings carefully, learning her strategy. When she went to thrust towards his left side, he released his two-handed grip and wrapped his arm around the spear. The elf pulled the spear back hard. As she did, one of the barbs sliced into his side. Victus held on through the pain and swung hard down, snapping the spear.

The dark elf hissed and rolled away in anger, and the veil in which she held her appearance concealed faltered for a moment, and the crowd was aghast. Some yelled, “She’s a dark elf!” Others yelled, “Traitor!”

Victus heard the shouts, but his vision was blurring. Immediately he understood—*poison or magic?* he wondered, and then he knew. His eyes burned from within his helmet, melting down his cheeks, and he dropped to his knees. He screamed in pain, which morphed into words: “FAMILY! DUTY! HONOR!”

Aris tried to jump up to the platform to go to his father’s aid, but Janus held him back. “Your father is not done.”

Aris tried to unclasp the man’s grip but couldn’t. He pleaded, “We have to help him!”

Janus shook his head. “This is a sanctioned duel. We will not interfere.”

Aris yelled, “She cheated! Let me go!”

Janus nodded. “She has, but your father is not finished. We hold our honor higher in value than the dark elves. Understood, squire?”

Aris straightened, ending his outburst with a submissive, “Yes, sir.”

Victus could hear the crowd yelling, “Dark elf treachery!” and all the “Boo’s” from the crowd. Some even tried to get on the platform, but the guards kept them at bay, spears piercing the few who charged in. Victus quickly pushed himself up from the ground and placed his sword in front of him. His helmet hummed with magic of its own and tuned itself to his mind. He regained his ability to see, but it was an unnatural vision. He could perceive in his mind the positions of the priestess and even his son. His vision was enhanced by his helmet and his psionics. Victus, recuperating, maintained composure, but he appeared vulnerable.

The priestess was walking toward him, unaware that he could see her. She held a dirk and a whip in her hands now. As she approached, Victus turned to face her, waiting until she was just a few paces away. Her mouth sneered as her face recoiled in disgust and disbelief. Victus' sword went out and blocked the dirk's first strike. He reversed his sword's position so that the crossguard caught her hand, smacking the dagger out wide. He swung down low to cut through the whip that was attempting to wrap itself around his legs. Since Victus had his right leg back too far, the whip missed its mark and wrapped around his left leg, which the dark elf tugged taut, but he quickly severed the coil.

The priestess backed away, tossing the useless whip handle to the ground. She turned and waved her free hand to one of her captains, who quickly tossed her a shortsword. Victus was trailing behind her, methodically marching toward her. The sound of his voice echoed underneath his magically enchanted face mask helmet—"Family, Duty, Lindly!"

Aris and Serin were cheering as they watched his father recover and press his attacks. Brandan leaned over to Janus. "When we inevitably fight the elves surrounding us, I am going to need a weapon."

Janus grinned. "Don't worry, I will make sure there are plenty on the ground for you to choose from."

Brandan insisted, "Yes, but I may need one before then."

Janus pulled out his dagger and handed it over. "This will have to do for now."

Brandan thanked him and gripped it tightly at his side. "I appreciate it."

Janus nodded, his eyes fixed on the fight.

The priestess closed in again, matching Victus's attack with her own. Both swords rang, echoing through the crowd. Victus was forced back defensively as she began attacking with the dirk, plus two quick jabs and one strong strike from the sword. She was pressing the attack, and her speed was increasing, making it more difficult for Victus to keep up. Again, he understood she was using magic to hasten her attacks and make herself more powerful. He also understood that if he could continue to parry, the use of magic would weaken her, and he would be able to strike back and overwhelm her. He backed away and allowed her to close in again. The clashing of swords and dirk echoed as Victus fought hard to sustain his defense. The priestess was putting all her effort into breaking through Victus's defenses, but her martial skills fell short.

The spells she wove were taking their toll, but she began casting another. This one she would not hide in a weapon. She was going to cast it directly into the stupid knight's chest. Dropping her dirk, she lifted her arm to cast a bolt of lightning. Victus slid his left hand down the sword, reversing his grip so that he held the hilt high and the sword tip down like a staff. He turned into her sword arm, which she struck with and blocked. He then jabbed up with the hilt towards the elf's jaw. The bear pommel struck into her jaw, and the crunch made everyone groan as it echoed. Unable to complete the spell, her head snapped back hard, her arms spreading wide. Victus used his left hand to push his sword upright. As it rose above his head, both hands gripped it and swiped down hard. The elf's failed, fizzling spell arm dropped to the ground as Victus' sword passed easily through. With the priestess' jaw broken, she tried to scream a curse, but it sounded more like a painful howl from a banshee than anything else. As she stumbled backward and fled from the knight, she could feel the blood rushing out of her arm, like melting snow flooding a river. It poured all over. She dropped her sword and grabbed the wound.

Her hand released a magical white substance that Victus could feel was as cold as ice. It cauterized the wound, and she crouched down to pick up her dropped sword. She held it in front of herself as Victus moved to engage again. "Family, Duty, Lindly!"

His mantra was now sounding more like a spell in the priestess' head, annoying her already aching head further. *What human daemon is this?* she thought. For the first time, she felt uneasy, uncertain, and unworthy of her opponent. All of these emotions weighed within her soul, culminating in what she realized was fear. Genuine fear—fear of death, fear of failure. For the first time in her two thousand years of life, she was terrified by this human knight.

Victus did not relent and could feel the slow release of magical anesthetic from his helmet working. It did nothing to heal his melted eyes or the cut on his side, but it numbed his pain, allowing him to focus on his target. He stepped forward, completely offensive, showing no mercy as he swung from high, cutting back and thrusting towards her. He knew she would move her sword from her chief defense to meet his quick reversal, and when she did, Victus stepped back, pulling away his sword, not allowing the blades to touch. Immediately, he swung his sword from the outside of her sword arm, which she held to the side to rebuff. Her sword was tipped to the ground, which was Victus's goal. She tried to correct the mistake as she realized she should have just disengaged a few steps back, but it was too late. Victus had allowed his sword to be pushed back and up, bringing the hilt near his face.

This overpressure from the elf caused her to lose balance in her defensive posture. Victus capitalized as she teetered and brought his sword down into her chest. Her parry was too weak to stop the strength of the man's thrust. The priestess's eyes widened as the sword penetrated her magically enchanted armor and pierced her heart.

Excitement coursed through the crowd, causing them to scream and cheer. As the priestess gasped for breath, her true dark form began to reveal itself, and the veil that had concealed her identity was lifted. She could not speak but sent an imprint to Victus's mind—what he heard, he would never forget: "I am afraid to die." To Victus, the sound within his mind was reminiscent of a helpless child who had been ruthlessly beaten and was now cowering in fear of an endless punishment. He pitied the lifeless priestess as he slid his sword from her body, allowing her to collapse dead on the platform.

27

Victus knelt down, his hands touching the priestess's face as he brushed her eyes closed. Nibarn hopped from his throne in shock, staring in disbelief as his mouth gaped. Stuttering, he yelled, "This is not possible!"

Victus, his voice booming beneath his helmet, said, "It is done. And you will be brought to justice."

Nibarn glanced over to his counselors, giving them a knowing nod, and turned back to address Victus. "I think it is time I take my leave, Commander Victus." Pulling out a small stone, he held it out towards the crowd, as did his sycophants. In unison, they all spoke the command word to activate their safety-net spell, "Pigeon Flight," which teleported them to a secret, safe location.

Victus began moving towards Nibarn to apprehend the corrupt man, but he and the others dissolved. The crowd, after the priestess's death, had been released from the enchantment. Cheers and booing ceased, and people began to scream in horrified realization. A dome had surrounded the city, and only a small gap at the top remained open. The crystals were forming the completion of the dark elves' magic, as signified by the funnel of souls being sucked up from bodies in the distance. Panic-stricken, people ran in all directions. Victus yelled into the crowd, his voice projected through the platform's magic. "Flee to the RIVER GATE! Get to the River Gate!"

In the distance, the River Gate horn blew. Victus yelled, "RIVER GATE!" Some in the crowd heard, but it was not enough. The dark elves were revealed, displaying their natural obsidian-like skin and a proclivity for murder. They massacred everyone in their vicinity. At least one hundred dark elves guarded the pathway to the River Gate, and though the attempts of the people to break through were valiant, they were in vain.

Aris, stunned by the carnage and death being unleashed upon the city, stared. Janus tugged on the young man's armor, snapping him back. "Time to go."

Jess was behind, pushing Aris. "Get on the platform," she said. When Aris turned to run up the platform, dark black-purple fire burst forth and outlined the platform, preventing Victus from getting down and halting the others from coming to his aid. Laughter bellowed through the city, causing uneasiness in everyone. Some citizens began vomiting at the sound; others just held their heads frozen in despair.

Janus saw that Victus's shield, which he had placed on the edge of the platform, was not touched by the flames. "That way, go!" Aris, Jess, Serin, and Brandan ran up the platform into the narrow gap made by the shield. Janus followed behind, securing their backs. A few dark elves were coming, but Janus did not wait for them; he ran toward his commander. "Victus, I do not believe the flames will hurt the elves. We will be attacked from all sides at once."

The commander, his voice calm, said, "Back-to-back!" Victus and Janus, Jess and Aris, Brandan and Serin all turned outward, determined to fight as one and die as one. Victus could see through the flames with his helmet and saw the elves coming. "Be ready! We have seconds before they are here! Family! Duty! Lindly!"

~~~

Victus noted in the distance, beyond the elves charging, dark circular portals opening with what appeared to be orcs and goblins pouring through them. He also watched dark anti-paladins marching in behind the hosts of orcs. Suddenly, he saw about five of these fallen knights surrounding a ragged-looking skeleton—tall with elegant red and blue robes, with
~~~

fleshless hands gripping tightly to an onyx staff tipped with a stormy jade crystal. The whisper of disappointment fell from Victus's lips, "Dread Reavers and Liches."

Backs to one another, sides close to one another, Janus noticed the ground beneath them was moist. It was collecting, pooling blood. A bubbling, oozing pit was forming underneath their feet. Janus yelled, "Move back!"

They stumbled back as a magnificently tall female dark elf rose from the blood. She was much like the priestess that Victus had fought, but this female was far larger—standing nearly ten feet in height. The armor she wore was plum, with a texture of glass. She came into being with her cackle falling down toward them all. Her beauty was undeniable, and the aura of power surrounding her was like a noxious gas in the air. It flew forth from her like a low fog early in the morning. She stepped toward Victus and the others, her voice haughty, "Kneel before your new goddess! Kneel and become one of my knights, Victus."

Aris looked from his father to the dark elven goddess, who he concluded was Lestar. Victus held his sword firm and pointed it in a threat to the elven goddess. Janus had his spear over his shield pointed directly toward her as well. Lestar looked down at them, her hands open and inviting. "No need for this, Victus. You have earned a place with me. Come, your destiny beckons you. Join me. You can even keep your pet." She pointed toward Janus.

Aris looked from his left and his right and saw dark elves standing at the edges of the platform, waiting for word from Lestar. Brandan also saw the elves surrounding the platform and yelled at them, "Come on! You have us, end it!" Serin was holding her dagger, which she now realized was not going to be much help against a god.

Lestar looked up to her crystal formation above Lindly and then back toward Victus. "You are running out of time, human."

Aris interrupted the goddess as he yelled to his father, “Up there!” He pointed, and everyone, including Lestar, looked up. High above the city were Skylighter’s gryphon shock troopers. They were flying in formation, seemingly looking for a way to enter through the dome.

Lestar laughed, “Ah, sadly, they have arrived a bit late. And who is this charming specimen, Victus?”

Aris didn’t give his father a chance to answer and responded for him. “I am Squire Aris Tin of House Andreas.”

She roared in laughter, “Victus, you brought your son to die with you? Foolish. Join me and save your son!”

Victus took a deep breath before responding, his heart pounding, sweat dripping down his face underneath the mask. “I will never bow to you. I openly resist everything you are! We stand against you! FAMILY, DUTY, LINDLY!”

Skylighter watched from above, upon his gryphon, frustrated. He could not get his men and women through the barrier. Outside the main city gate, portals began opening with Elivendel’s high elven mages marching. Skylighter watched as the mages began opening more portals and throwing out small trinkets, sprinkling the ground with powder. He knew that every single one of the elven mages sent here carried with them siege engines in miniature form. They would place them where they wished to begin an assault against the city and then re-enchant them to normal size. Skylighter began praying as he watched the formations of elven soldiers pouring through the high elven portals. “I am running out of time. Kalisdel! Help us! Help me!” he pleaded. His gryphon troopers continued circling the enclosed city, and he saw Lestar standing before Victus. It took everything he had to hold himself in the air. The desire to aid Victus in battle burned within him, and he longed to be able to fight at his side.

Skylighter was angry, and his prayer reflected his anger. “KALISDEL! Your children are dying! We are stuck and unable to intervene. Where are you? Come to our aid. Lestar is here–" He paused as he continued watching below. He saw a disgusting behemoth that looked like an orc, but somehow twisted. "Oh... damnation. Tagar is here too!"

The sounds from the city were truly horrifying. The flying troopers all saw, heard, and could feel in their very souls the death. Souls were screaming as they were being pulled by the vortex to the crystals. Citizens were being trampled by one another and slaughtered by the orcs and elves. Skylighter felt helpless as he cried yet again out to Kalisdel, "Please! Where are you?"

After a moment, he felt her. He felt the surge of his goddess' power coursing through his body before hearing her voice. "I am here, noble paladin." Then he saw a pillar of white and gold smoky fire falling from the heavens straight down past the flying troopers. It slammed into the crystal formation, shattering them into millions of tiny pieces.

Skylighter watched in awe as the dome barrier surrounding the city collapsed, turning his head to the sounds of, "Whooah!" His troopers cheered and looked at him for their orders. Some were already flicking their magically enchanted boots—boots which provided the wearer a more controlled, stable descent, allowing for in-flight directional changes. Skylighter lifted his hand out to them, pointing his hand like an arrowhead and dipping it down towards the ground. The gryphons cawed and then rolled to the side; troopers disembarked, dropping like rain from the clouds. Upon releasing their riders, the gryphons tucked their wings in and dove down, passing the falling troopers on the way down to the city's surface. Skylighter stayed atop his mount, riding his gryphon down in the center of the wedge formation. He was leading their flight path straight into the chaotic lines of orcs and goblins forming. The gryphons would sweep through the first wave of enemies and allow a clear landing zone for their paladins.

Skylighter realized this was not just cult activity they were defending against. This was not just Lestar toying with mortal lives; this was an all-out invasion. The armistice between the brother gods, Eu'rok and Asmolor, was clearly broken.

~~~

The goddess' gaze shifted to see her crystal formation destroyed by a ball of fire. She screamed in rage and was then blown back off the platform a hundred feet in the air by a figure who matched her in size and beauty. The tallest woman Aris had ever seen rose from her assault through the barrier. She wore white-gold and silver plate armor and held a massive sword and kite shield, with an aura that glowed white. Her red hair flickered with flame tips as she tucked in her twelve-foot angelic wings.

She smiled at Victus and his son as she spoke in a melodic voice. "Family, Duty, Lindly!" Though Aris heard her speak the words, he could have sworn she said, "Family, Duty, Serin!" Victus bowed before her, and everyone followed suit. Kalisdel returned the bow, and her voice resonated with every one of her children in Lindly. "FIGHT ON! Fight for your families. Fight for your city! Fight against the darkness! Stand as one. I am with you!" Every human in the city felt her, every human knew her, and every person was invigorated by her presence and power. Kalisdel pointed her sword upwards, and the city was blanketed by a dome of her own. Instantaneous and white in color, the city was protected from the barrage that would surely come from her brother Elivendel. She turned to Victus and waved her sword hand around the platform, extinguishing Lestar's magic. "Get as many as you can out. I will deal with Tagar and Lestar!" With that, her wings sprouted out, and she flew off towards Lestar, who was stumbling to her feet, dazed with blood trickling from her nose.

Lestar wiped the blood, huffed in anger, and rose to levitate above the ground as wings sprouted from her back. Unlike her cousin Kalisdel's brilliant white wings, hers were more bat-like in form, and when she spread them, her body transformed from the body of a dark elf into a two-foot cloven monstrosity. Her head was adorned with massive
~~~

horns, while her tail, with barbed tendrils, waved in the air and threatened to spread poison. She cracked a large whip made of black flame, whipping an unsuspecting human in her demonstration. With her other elongated clawed hand, she began casting. The man she had wrapped up with her whip squirmed to get away, but she easily pulled him to her. His flesh was melting from the flames. She bared her teeth as they molded themselves into sharp, tiny razors. As she opened her mouth, the disembodied smile she gave the man chilled those who saw it. What used to be a soft and soothing voice now came off as bastardized due to her own corruption and transformation. Sounding less sensual and more demonic, she said, "Welcome home, cousin."

Her jaw was unhinged, and her mouth hung open like a python's. She devoured the man's torso in one swift motion, clamping her jaw tight and swallowing it whole. "Mmm," Lestar moaned in pleasure, savoring the flavor. Her whip released the lower half of the human, letting it drop to the ground. Her free hand reached forth and pulled his soul from the air, harnessing it. With a careful gaze, she observed the spirit and relished the man's soul's shrieks of fright before devouring it entirely. She released a shriek that made all present in the city wince with a sharp pain in their heads. The banshee scream transmuted into an audible yell, "KALISDEL!" She croaked in a horrible hissing laughter as she continued, "Failing your people again!"

~~~

The gryphons continued their crescent descent, swerving only millimeters, avoiding incoming archer fire. Skylighter kept his head low to the left of his gryphon's neck. "Hold!" He yelled to the faithful beasts. "HOLD!" With his gaze fixed on his targets below, he listened to the cries of some of his gryphons to the left and right of him as they plummeted from the sky. He looked back behind the line of orcs and elves and saw a skeleton-like figure hurling greenish-black ballista bolts from his staff. He yelled again, "HOLD THE LINE!" as the next barrage of ballista bolts was released.
~~~

Skylighter called upon his archdom abilities, altering the course of the bolts, causing them to pass through the gryphons safely. When they were twenty feet from the ground, Skylighter shouted, “NOW!” The gryphons’ wings untucked, spreading out, their innate magical abilities helping as they prepared to engage. They changed directions, using the momentum to carry them horizontally, passing over the citizens attempting to flee. Skylighter jumped off his gryphon into the narrow gap between innocents and the enemy. The gryphons continued on through into the wave of orcs and elves. Talons ripped bodies apart, splitting them in half and tossing them back into their allies. The complete forefront surge came to a stop and was thrust into disorder. Dark elves maintained their position, unleashing a barrage of magically enchanted arrows. The orc brutes’ battle lines were shattered, leaving them vulnerable.

The chaos being caused by the gryphons gave Skylighter the time he needed to prepare his next move. He stepped forward, tapping his left bracer, allowing his transparent tower shield to appear. Its magic immediately began its work. White beams reached out towards the retreating and disorganized orcs and elves. Like a whirlpool, it swirled the air around him and sucked twenty enemies in towards him. Each ray of light it touched held tightly the orcs and elves fleeing the gryphons’ wrath and pulled them harshly. Some were even dragged, clawing into the ground. Right on time, as enemies surrounded Skylighter, his paladins’ descent slowed, and they landed next to him. Each paladin activated their own bracers as they touched down, allowing for their own shields to be activated. They formed two lines as they landed, one line facing in towards Skylighter and his trapped enemies and the other facing outwards towards the enemy.

The sharp, righteous wrath of the paladins systematically executed the enemies within the first line. The second line of paladins, each individual held a small cylinder tube in their dominant hand, which they activated. The device transformed itself into a spear, which they placed atop their tower shields.

As the interior ring of paladins finished up, they all let out a communal, "Hoo-hah! Hoo-hah!" The sound of fifty paladins reverberated into the ranks, who were still being waylaid by the gryphons, demoralizing the enemy. Skylighter and his interior warriors moved into positions behind the speared ones. He centered himself amongst his men and women, ordering the interior group to switch their shields to kite style, which would offer them more maneuverability into the flanks of the speared phalanx that now marched towards the chaotic lines.

With a slow and measured approach, the warriors advanced while simultaneously and masterfully reflecting and absorbing any magical attacks that came their way. Over half of the gryphons lay dead on the ground, and Skylighter waved the rest off. A lich was picking them off, like a horse's tail swatting flies. Skylighter gave another sharp command, "Tighten up! We march straight through the Dread Reavers. That lich is our priority!"

A familiar voice rang in Skylighter's ears off in the distance. "Friendlies coming in!" he shouted. The large arch turned toward the voice and saw Victus and his compatriots jumping off the platform, heading through the crowd. Immediately upon seeing them, Skylighter moved from his paladins, sprinting toward his allies, who were heavily under fire. He threw up a temporary wall of ice, preventing the arrows from finding their targets. "Hurry," he yelled to them. Victus, Janus, Jess, and Serin were the first to reach the paladins.

Brandan, who had picked up a crossbow, was bent over, cranking and trying to reload. Aris, who had stayed to wait for him, found himself fighting two orcs. The blows from the two would have been impossible to absorb, so he was dodging the attacks rather than deflecting them. The young squire got behind one and stabbed him through the knee, dropping him howling. More orcs were coming, and Brandan was not ready.

"We have to go!" Aris yelled as he kicked the back of the next orc, ducked an axe blow, and stabbed the confused, wounded orc now lying on the ground. Brandan's hands were shaking, and he finally threw the crossbow down in frustration and fear, starting to run toward the safety of the paladins. However, upon taking his initial strides, he realized that Aris had remained behind to ensure his safe escape. He slid to a stop and turned back, grabbing the crossbow from the ground. He charged it, placed the bolt, and pointed. He fired wildly but effectively into the orc still fighting Aris. Its head snapped back, and the body dropped dead before Aris. The young squire threw his father's dagger hard and struck an approaching goblin in the neck. Spinning, he yelled, waving his sword in the direction of safety, "GO BRANDAN!"

Brandan smiled at Aris, his kill awakening his inner warrior. "Let's hurry, Aris!" Brandan began sprinting toward the paladin line, and Aris trailed closely behind, focusing as he ran, absorbing his dagger back into his body and then into his hand.

28

Marcella continued down the streets of Lindly, poking her head in and out of every tavern and shop quickly to warn anyone she saw, and kept moving when she saw no one inside. She moved farther and farther away from the River Gate and the center platform in the city's main square. Covering as much ground as possible, she searched for and warned anyone she came across. She could still hear the crowd's roar of boos and cheers, but the sound had become muffled and distant. She was nearing the outer ring of the inner part of the city when her eyes looked up to see souls in agonized torment being pulled to the crystals.

She closed her eyes in despair, wishing not to see, but her mind could not escape the cries and screams. Hundreds upon hundreds of souls were rising, all collectively writhing in elevated floating torment. Marcella had gotten close. "Too close," she thought as she looked at the black rain pouring just outside the ring of the inner city. Quickly, she turned and began heading back toward the River Gate, deciding that she had done her part and it was now time to stand and fight. She kept her pace away from the doomed citizens in the outer ring of Lindly, glancing back every few steps. The sound of a whoosh and pop sounded behind her, and black circular pits opened in the air. She knew they were portals, and she was not interested in seeing what came through. She darted down a narrow street, hoping to backtrack and get back to the gate using the narrow corridors between the major streets.

Marcella's heart was beating loudly in her chest, and she held her breath as she heard more swooshes and pops. She halted, looking for the best way to escape undetected. She hid behind some barrels near a tanner shop, keeping her eyes on the black rain. From what she could gather, she had about a few minutes to get out of the area before the rain reached her. Collecting herself and peeking out to see which way would be best to go, she heard a man yell. The sound came from the rain, from the outer rim of the city, where she had just come from. Instinctively, she grabbed her sword and ran out toward the sound.

"HELP ME!" She heard the voice, but it sounded like it was moving away from her. Chasing the phantom sound, she came upon a man lying in the dirt. He was dragging himself, sliding his torso slowly. "Please help me...!" His voice lost strength as he sobbed, looking up at the woman who had come to his cries, "Puu... please. They took my legs."

Marcella ran over, sliding down to crouch and look, rolling the man onto his back. She knew without inspection that the man was lost. He was in shock and shaking uncontrollably as she held him. "Shh... it's okay, I am here. You're not alone."

The man's right hand rose, shaking. He reached up and touched her face. His voice was trembling, "Save my family..."

Marcella asked, "Where are they? Are they close?"

The man in his death throes lifted his other hand, pointing back from where he had come. His eyes looked up into Marcella's, and he whispered, "Audrey." The man stopped shaking, and Marcella looked to where he had pointed. Her eyes widened as she stumbled to her feet, her mouth gaping. Slowly moving toward her were the lifeless husks of the citizens of Lindly, soulless and controlled by the darkness of Lestar's minions. They lumbered slowly, almost aimlessly, but they were moving toward those still living. She started running but realized she knew where to go. The portals that were opening had deposited orcs, goblins, and Dread Reavers. She ran into the tanner's building and watched as the orcs and goblins sprinted off toward the crowd at the center of the city. Thinking she was unnoticed, she headed out the back of the tanner shop and continued running the back way up to the River Gate.

As she stepped out, though, a humanoid figure stood hovering in the alleyway. Its tattered black robes fluttered, and she could smell the decay. It was facing away from her, but as she sprinted out and started running, it turned, sensing her lifeforce. When it set its dead eyes upon her, she froze, unable to move. It floated toward her. She looked up at the lich, and her eyes began to ice over and freeze. She felt the cold, icy burns and closed them rapidly, trying to stop the ice burn. Through her blurry eyes, she saw its onyx staff tipped with a vermilion-colored stone. Every muscle in her body flexed and tensed as she tried to break free. She tried to scream, and yet nothing came forth from her lungs. Her mind raced in a panic. She quivered with fear as the lich stared at her with its bony, fleshless skull, grinning wickedly. She recoiled at the sound of its snake-like hissing voice. "I will have you both."

Marcella scrunched up her face, or at least in her mind. Confused, her eyes darted around, looking for another poor soul trapped with her. She saw nothing. She tried again to break free from the lich's hold but felt sharp, icy pangs throughout her muscles and mind, followed by a burning sensation. The warmth from the heat at first felt welcome to her frostbitten body until she could feel her body on fire. Though she saw no sign of actual fire or ice, she could feel it. The lich spoke in amusement, "Ha... ha... ha... You don't know?"

Marcella screamed in her mind, "KNOW WHAT, FILTH?" Her jaw began to clench so tightly from the pain that she started breaking her teeth as the lich hissed in laughter, "I will have you and the welp forming in your belly." Its laughter sounded ragged and hoarse. "Just a few days old, but the soul is strong."

The revelation left Marcella shocked; though her face could not convey it, the lich felt her anguish. A few days back, she and her crush, Titus, had shared an intimate moment, but surely she could not be with child. Desperate, she tried to sing in her mind, but the pain caused by the rotation of ice and fire kept her from focusing.

The lich tapped his staff, and she felt her body freed. She didn't look back; she just ran. The voice of the lich's laughter echoed as she put distance between herself and him. Marcella groaned in pain as she pushed through the ache in her eyes and body. She screamed in terror, "TITUS!" but the dark rain poured down all around her as she kept running. Soon her legs stopped, and she slid to a stop. She saw as she became disjoined from her body, a translucent copy of herself. She saw the small life force of her days-old child being pulled from both her body and then soul, like a small ball of light barely formed. It floated up past her eyes toward the crystals. She screamed, "TITUS!" reaching for her baby. Despite attempting to grasp her body and drag herself to it, the vortex was already drawing her in. She joined the multitude of others, crying in fear and pain as they were dragged to their eternal torment.

~~~

Thorm stood in front of his dwarven and human brothers and sisters. He kept the barrage of arrows and spears from hitting any of them. As the dark elves reached striking range, the earth beneath them collapsed. The cobblestone bent down into a trench, causing the elves to fall into a makeshift moat created by Thorm's earthen magic. As the elves tried to recover, the two-handed war hammer-wielding dwarves smashed down like hammers to anvil, crushing and obliterating the first rank of dark elves attacking.

Titus heard the sounds of metal crunching and bones breaking, but he was watching the thorn-armored berserkers corralling the elves from the flanks. They were beating and attacking the elves with a ferocity that Titus had never seen before. It looked chaotic but was deliberate. The berserkers were forcefully driving the elves toward the trench Thorm had magically excavated. The hammers collided with the spears, daggers, and swords, creating a chaotic symphony of
~~~

metal. Thorm yelled back toward Titus, but he was not directing his words to the man, "Get a blowin' on the horn, boyos!" The River Gate tower bellowed three times. Thorm and his two-handed war hammer executioners continued their slaughter as more and more elves were funneled into the trench. One elf tried to use the bodies of the dead to hop across and attack Thorm. The dwarf grunted and swatted him in the chest, caving him into a crumbled mess. Thorm looked down at the dead elf and spat, "Mediocre."

Titus saw now what Thorm had meant when he said, "You will know when." More dark elves had come to the gate, and the spiky berserkers were facing away from them. They were continuing their push into the kill zone made by Thorm. Titus looked over to his fellow legionnaires, "For Victus, FOR LINDLY!" He charged out to the next wave of elves approaching. He knew that his few men and women would not be able to stop that many, but they would protect Thorm's dwarves' backs. Five paces ahead of his men, the others followed, fury and duty leading them to protect their city. Titus knocked away the first spear he encountered, allowing his fellows to pierce the dark elf's side. Titus then shifted to the left, drawing the elves away from Thorm's dwarves. The melee was a frenzied blur of swinging weapons and flying debris as the two sides clashed in disarray. The humans huddled close, as they were soon surrounded. One legionnaire had his sword disarmed, and he charged right into an elf, knocking him to the ground, punching the elf's face over and over until he was ended with a spear.

Above the chaos, a light bright from the heavens broke through the dome and smashed the crystals. The elves, dwarves, and humans collectively paused to look briefly and then began fighting again. Titus felt cold steel superficially pierce into his shoulder from behind. He turned and swung his sword toward the elf attacking him and then spun it back to the front to deflect a spear. Only three of the legionnaires remained, and they were being pushed farther away from Thorm and his men. Titus was standing in front of his two legionnaires as they held each other up in retreat.

Thorm's hammer swung through the air with a thunderous crack, hurtling toward the elf nearest to Titus. It took the elf from her feet and tossed her like a rag doll as the hammer spun around, back into Thorm's hand, who was standing behind the predatory elves. "I am here to be evening out the odds, pointy ears."

The elves turned to face him and his horned berserkers. The berserkers, covered in blood as if they had been swimming in a lake of it, charged straight into the elves, giving no heed or concern for their own lives. They smashed in kneecaps and offered the dark elves a quick coup de grâce.

One particular berserker had already placed two elven heads upon the high thorn points of his pauldrons. He yelled something unintelligible toward Titus as he barreled through to the three remaining legionnaires. The dwarf nodded to Titus as he reached him and turned to face any dark elf that would dare challenge him. Sticking out his tongue, he roared toward those that remained, but they were too busy being decimated by Thorm and the other warriors.

The dwarf turned back to Titus while keeping his eye on their surroundings, "Name is Nordor. Fancy a drink?"

The dwarf was bald and tattooed with smoky painted eyes. A long braided gray beard framed his mouth, and the recently killed dark elf heads impaled upon his pauldrons intimidated Titus. However, at the word drink, Titus grabbed the wineskin that Nordor offered and gulped deeply. "Well met, Nordor."

Titus attempted to pass the wineskin back, and the dwarf laughed. "Bah! Keep it! Got me more!"

An approaching elf gave Nordor a strange look, triggering him to start shouting and run after the dark elf.

The sheer ferocity and pitiless slaughter of the dark elves resulted in the dark elven newcomers cresting the path to the River Gate only to turn around and head back in retreat—or so Titus assumed. In reality, Lestar had recalled her elves to make way for the waves of Tagar's forces being unleashed in the city.

Only two of the dwarves lay dead, and only three humans, including Titus, lived and were left to fight. Thorm, stepping over the dead elves, went to look over the three wounded human legionnaires. "Get ye patched up, but ya need not be fightin' no more today."

Titus shook his head. "No, I will stay and we hold this gate."

Thorm dipped his head in a nod towards the two severely wounded soldiers, holding one another up. "They ain't doin' nothin' but dyin' now. We patch 'em up and get 'em out with the others."

Titus sighed, knowing that his two soldiers left were not capable of fighting and could barely stand. He could easily persist despite his injuries, but he wouldn't force that fate on the two men beside him. "You are right, of course. You two—go back to Thorm's tent and get medical assistance. When people flee the city, I will expect you to help guide them down and out to the riverboats. Understood?"

Remarkably, both soldiers stood straight, though swaying without the support from one another, and saluted. As they were about to fall, Thorm smiled and caught them both, holding them upright. "Use each other and get to me tent. Ya did good, lads." Thorm watched as they stumbled their way off and spoke to Titus. "Need to reform and get ready for the next wave. Gunna be a long day."

Titus was looking off into the distance as he felt a shiver flow from his neck down his spine. He thought for just a moment he had heard Marcella's voice. Shaking his head, he nodded to the dwarf. "Right again, brother Thorm."

The tall dwarf patted the man's shoulder. "We hold! This is our gate!" Thorm howled out to his dwarves, who were collecting souvenirs from the dead elves. "A'ight, boyos. Let's clean this mess up. I want all the bodies placed like a wall on both sides of the main road. Let 'em see their dead before they too become gray-skinned corpses."

29

Elivendel, the demi-god of the high elves, stepped through one of his mage's portals outside the city of Lindly. He surveyed his soldiers as they hurriedly prepared to demolish the city. The transformation of catapults progressed from toy-like models to full-scale functional siege weapons. Elivendel began walking along his lines and inspecting the work of his elves. The few elves that looked in his direction bowed their heads in deference and redoubled their work. He inspired all high elves, as they believed him to be the closest embodiment of Asmolor. He was fearless and willing to make hard decisions, a perfect example being the present circumstances in the city of Lindly. Lestar had tainted it, and once she got her tendrils embedded amongst humans, the choice became simple in his mind: "Purge the corruption." There was no hope of redemption in his eyes. Humans, being feeble and vulnerable to her deceitful words and pledges, had time and again proved their tendency to succumb to her evil. His decision had been made a long time ago; the corruption and blemish of Eu'rok and his offspring had to be removed violently, just like a disease in the body.

Elivendel did not relish these purges and was not looking forward to the extermination of Lindly. In his mind, it was the only way. His sister, Kalisdel, believed that humanity was not doomed to perpetual corruption. She believed the innocent should not suffer the consequences of those who delved into darkness. Kalisdel believed she was to be the god that showed humanity the light in the darkness.

Elivendel watched the gryphon shock troopers circling above the city, and he knew they could not get in. A flash of light and a pillar of flame slammed down past the flying troopers, and the elven god smiled. *My sister knows how to make an entrance,* he thought. He turned to his arch generals, who served as an extension of his will. “Are all the quadrants around the city prepared?”

Each responded in turn. “The East is ready.” “North is ready.” “West is nearly there.” “South is ready, Lord.” Elivendel observed the dark dome shrouding the city shatter as his sister intervened, creating a new translucent white dome.

He smirked. “It seems Kali doesn’t want me to interfere.”

His archs chuckled, knowing that she could not stop them. Lvenower, one of the younger archs, laughed and added a quip that he believed would impress his peers and his lord. “She is too weak to save this city. She could not even stop me.”

Elivendel turned so quickly that the other archs jumped back in alarm. His clenched fist yielded to an open backhand to the young arch’s face. The blow struck so forcefully that Lvenower was knocked into his fellow brother’s arms. “That is too far, even for you. We may be the firstborn of Asmolor, but we are to be stewards to our weaker siblings. And as for you, standing in her way—” his voice tilted toward amusement, “she would swat you away from her without a second glance. Your power is nothing to that of an actual god, elf whelpling. Do not confuse my sister as being a human, even though she is the mother of the race. She is a goddess, and you will respect her. If you ever speak ill or mock her again, I will remove all your power and make you a servant to the lowliest of humans. Is that understood?”

Lvenower’s head was down as his brother pushed him back up to stand by himself. He nodded to his god. “I do, Lord. Forgive my arrogance.”

Elivendel turned his gaze back toward the city. “Go to your quadrants. We begin the cleansing momentarily. At my signal, unleash Asmolor’s wrath on them all.”

His arch generals saluted and departed. Elivendel closed his eyes, remembering when Asmolor created his younger sister. They had been inseparable, and he devoted much of his time to her. He loved her deeply, and training together only strengthened their bond. His hope this day was that she could rescue as many children as possible, despite knowing that she would be furious with him. He acknowledged internally that Asmolor's will and hers were occasionally at odds, but Asmolor was both of their father. Elivendel would not disobey his father, unlike his willful sister, Kalisdel. Elivendel was going to hold out for as long as possible, delaying his assault to allow Kali more time. As a dutiful son, he understood that he would have to obey his father Asmolor's command, even if it meant unleashing unprecedented destruction.

~~~

Kalisdel charged toward her cousin, who was finishing devouring the human's soul. Her feathered angelic wings sprouted out wide, pushing her forward in a low-flying lunge toward Lestar. Behind the dark elf goddess were two large black armored knights, huge in size. They resembled her brother Elivendel's archs, save for the jagged noir armor. Instead of continuing her forward assault, she shot herself straight up. She hovered above and then descended on the Dread Reaver Knights. They were pushing past their mistress Lestar, advancing to attack while keeping their goddess protected. However, Kalisdel brought the fight to them before they could prepare. She flew over the two slower-moving knights, her wings vanishing as she dropped the twenty feet down behind them. The first Reaver swung in with his great battle-ax. Kalisdel rebuffed the blow with her shield. She moved slightly over and saw Lestar whipping her poisonous tail toward Kalisdel, whose wings formed without thought, and again she flew high above. With Kalisdel in the air, the tail's blow slammed into the ax-wielding Dread Reaver, knocking him to the ground. Lestar screamed in anger and slashed out with her demonic whip, missing Kalisdel again as
~~~

she flew out of range. This time, instead of dropping behind the knights, she dropped on the one still standing. She came down so hard and so fast that her sword swept down through the helmet and body of the Dread Reaver, splitting him in two. The second knight began a forward charge from his knees. He brandished his battle-ax with confidence, swinging it from behind and lifting it high above his head in an attempt to deliver a fatal blow to his prey.

Kalisdel used her shield again to absorb the blow and push the heavy weapon back in the direction it came. The Dread Reaver became off-balance and stumbled back down when she thrust her sword straight through the knight's heart. The blackish-white effervescent soul of the creature poured out. Lestar had a wicked grin on her face as she taunted Kalisdel. "You think killing two will save you from the hundreds more of my Dread Reavers or even from my Dread Reaver Liches? I find such beauty in you slaying them as you're killing your own children."

Kalisdel quickly surveyed the battles surrounding her. She imprinted thoughts to her paladin, her arch Skylighter. "Keep your focus on the liches. There is more than one. Defensive advance."

Kalisdel heard the paladin's response in her mind, "It will be done." Ignoring the words still spewing from Lestar, she focused on using her spells. Lifting her shield towards Lestar, she let out a burst of white firelight. The reinforcing line of dark elves and Dread Reavers behind Lestar froze. As they began to slowly burn, flickers of ash floated off their armor, and they shielded their eyes from the blinding light.

Some of the dark elves tried to flee, but it was too late. The righteous light burned within their souls, and they all burst into ash. Lestar's face was burning too, and she shielded her eyes with her clawed fingers. She cast her own defensive spell to shield against the burning that was crawling underneath her skin. Cognizant of her cousin's preoccupation with casting, Kalisdel threw herself into the air. She was determined, as her sword dipped to impale Lestar, that she would end it all here and now.

A loud thud shook the ground, and Kalisdel stumbled in her flight as the force of the air pushed her off course—it sounded like an elephant had landed next to her. Kalisdel slowed her advance and moved away from whatever had landed, understanding that she would not make it to Lestar if she stayed on her current trajectory. She glanced over to size up her new opponent. Peering through the rubble and unsettled dirt, she saw the giant muscular blob of the orc god. His arms were massive and looked like the trunks of a large oak tree. His stomach was not yet engorged with the dead or dying, which meant he was there for war, not his dark pleasure. He wore dragon-bone armor, his large tusks opened wide as he roared, landing from a nearby building, shaking the earth with his steps. He waved his giant bone sword high over his head.

Kalisdel gasped, "Tagar!" She quickly floated away from the orc god and turned to see Lestar flying toward her. She reversed her flight and embraced the attacks from whip and then tail. Though she deflected both, she moved directly into Tagar's range, and he snatched her leg from the air. She was jerked from the sky as Lestar began laughing. Tagar's forceful blow sent Kalisdel crashing to the ground, disorienting her and causing her to lose her grip on her shield. It only took seconds for her motor skills to recover, but as she lay there, it felt like an eternity. She felt her body being lifted like a doll, the weight of Tagar's grip crushing her leg. As he slammed her again, she sprouted her wings and pushed up toward the heavens. Kalisdel slashed back down as hard as she could with both hands, cutting halfway through Tagar's arm. He wailed in pain and anger, releasing her. His wounded arm slumped as he jabbed toward her with his bone sword.

~~~

Elivendel heard the pained voice of his sister in his mind. "Tagar is here with Lestar. I need your help, Eli." He
~~~

grimaced as she called him by the name she used as a child. "Support my cause and show our father that there is another way. Please, Eli. I know you're here." The elven god closed his eyes as he forced his body to stay put. He could hear her breath and feel her pain. The high elf god melded with her body and offered her peace and strength. He could feel the relief in her voice, "Thank you, Eli."

For a split second, the high elven god almost transmuted his body to stand with her and fight. He had even begun the spell in his mind and was, in fact, doing it when he heard Asmolor's voice. "Purge the city!"

The booming voice in his mind broke his connection with his sister. Elivendel nodded, raised his hand, and gave the command. "Unleash Asmolor's fury!"

Kalisdel reached out to him again, "Where are you?"

Elivendel curtly responded, "I am not coming. Get as many of your people out as possible."

Kalisdel, enraged, yelled back into his mind. "If any of you," referring to her indifferent siblings, "would stand up with me and show our father he is wrong, it would force him to listen. But because of your complacency, your cowardice, your unyielding blind devotion, you hurt all of our children."

Elivendel fought back his overwhelming rage and calmly replied, "I warned you that you would be alone in this. And you are. I will not defy our father. Get yourself out now." Hearing no response, he looked over the city, watching the fiery explosive payloads slam into his sister's shield. "Get out," he whispered and then thought to himself, *I wish I was with you, Kali. I am sorry.* He sniffed hard to gather up all the emotions he was feeling, swallowing hard, and then quickly wiping the tears from his eyes. "I am so sorry."

He turned back from the city and motioned to the nearest arch-general. "Raze it all! Nothing is to be left. My sister's barrier will not hold. I want each catapult firing double the normal capacity. Instead of eleven shots a minute from each, I want twenty-two."

The young arch stood, confused. "Lord, that will place a tremendous burden on our mages." Elivendel tilted his head. "Do as I command." The arch acknowledged Elivendel with a salute and then began issuing the commands.

While Kalisdel was flying and communing with her brother, Lestar was in pursuit. But Lestar was not as fast nor as skilled a flier as Kalisdel. She kept losing Kalisdel around some of the taller buildings. Lestar hovered for a moment, looking for a sign of her cousin. She saw her flying past some buildings on the outskirts of the city. Lestar guessed that if she moved behind a few of the buildings that Kalisdel had not passed yet, she could ambush her. But as she positioned herself to hide, she stopped mid-flight, looking down toward her brother Tagar, who was making a commotion.

Tagar yelled, "BEHIND YOU!" Lestar spun in the air, her tail whipping up defensively. Kalisdel had backtracked and come from behind the dark elven goddess. The human goddess's sword sliced cleanly through the tip of the poisonous tail. Lestar dove hard in fear and pain. She screamed as she raced to her brother Tagar. Kalisdel pursued closely behind her, blinded by fury and rage. She was going to kill Lestar and end her vile reign here and now. Kalisdel suddenly tumbled in the air as she felt a lich's warlock bolt hit her left wing, and it rotted away. She was completely out of control. She tried to steady herself by recalling the remaining wing as she maneuvered toward Lestar. This helped, and she grabbed hold of Lestar's wounded tail.

Lestar slowed her decline and tried to whip her tail to the ground to knock Kalisdel off and throw her towards the ground. However, she was too low for it to do any actual harm, and Kalisdel just let go and charged towards Tagar. Lestar stayed hovering above and began casting a summoning spell. Around Tagar and Kalisdel, four Dread Reaver Liches materialized, each holding a black chain. Kalisdel, deflecting Tagar's blow and retorting with her own, did not see the trap being laid. She was focused on stopping her two cousins and was blinded to everything around her.

Tagar did his job by goading her and keeping her occupied. Lestar's Dread Reaver Liches held out the chains as dark black and purple smoke surrounded the two gods fighting. The liches' incantations filled the air as Lestar descended, the once ordinary chains now pulsing with powerful magic.

On Lestar's command, the chains shot out towards Kalisdel and attached to each leg and arm, snapping her body taut, frozen just off the ground. Tagar roared in laughter. "We have her!"

Lestar floated down to her cousin as Kalisdel struggled to free herself. Lestar soothingly spoke behind Kalisdel's head. "I have you, and I will feast upon your soul for all of eternity. All that has been done today was for you. You have danced perfectly, right into our hands, and now you will be imprisoned and drained."

Kalisdel screamed in rage, but the black smoke swallowed up all the sounds. She tried to reach out to her brother and then Skylighter, but she could not feel or touch them. Lestar walked to the front of the imprisoned human goddess. "It seems this will be the last time you fail your people." Lestar turned to Tagar and said, "Time to go, dearest brother?"

Laughing in response, Tagar replied, "Yes, let us show our new pet her home."

Kalisdel's head slumped in defeat as Lestar used her magic to dissolve the three of them and the chain-wielding liches out of Lindly.

All in the city heard a mental message as the evil goddess departed. Elivendel heard Lestar's taunting laugh. "You listened to your daddy, and now I have your sister. I am going to destroy her over the millennia."

Elivendel clenched his hands in anger, his voice reflecting the frustration he felt. "Destroy it all! NOW!"

30

The legionnaires, paladins, and everyone standing against Lestar heard her wicked laughter. As she laughed, her voice took on a haunting quality, sounding like a dark choir of voices rather than a single person's taunt. "Innocents suffer in the joy of my chaos, and now you all will be destroyed. Not by me, but by those you call allies."

The voices jumbled together as Lestar spoke, and the choir of Dread Reavers responded, "Not by our mistress's hands, but by those you call allies."

The defenders of Lindly felt a wave of despair pump through their bodies—the feeling was so overwhelming that everyone stood frozen for a few moments, allowing the raging orcs and calculating dark elves to snag a few unearned kills.

Skylighter issued commands to his two senior officers. He towered in his Asmolorian golden-plated armor. Victus did not need to see the disappointment in Skylighter's eyes nor hear the heartbreak in his voice when he cried out, "Kalisdel!" Victus could see the tide turning from above—the city was surrounded by knights' threshold flares of the true Inquisition. The sight of the hundreds of flaming catapult payloads being launched at Kalisdel's shield barrier filled him with horror and dread.

Victus grabbed Skylighter's arm as the arch stared off into the distance where Kalisdel and Lestar had been fighting. Skylighter's voice was slightly broken, but he kept himself in control. "They have captured Kalisdel, and Elivendel commands me to halt my advance and retreat…to the River Gate."

Victus looked at the flowing banners of "Brotkas ven Blouda." He looked up at Skylighter and nodded. "Paladins don't retreat. The orcs are pressing toward the gate, and the dark elves seem to be disengaging and leaving. This leaves the Dread Reavers and the Liches. Take and hold the gate, Skylighter. My men and I will press in toward the Dread Reavers."

Skylighter shouted incredulously, "That's suicide! You cannot hold them back alone."

Victus raised his hand deliberately. "That is duty. That inn just behind the cloister of Dread Reavers?" Skylighter looked past the smoldering bodies and smoke and saw a small flag denoting citizen-soldiers hanging from an inn. Legionnaires who had been previously dismissed had placed the flag outside the window of the inn. From the opposite window, a soldier was holding a horn, blowing as hard as he could. "I have men in there. My men, Skylighter. That is one of the largest inns in this city, and if I were to wager a bet, I would say there are at least five hundred citizens holed up in there. I will not be leaving them. Secure the road to the River Gate, and we will distract and hold the Dread Reavers off so they can escape."

Skylighter shook his head. "I cannot authorize this. You need to pull back with us."

Victus looked down for a moment and then back into Skylighter's face. "I am not one of your paladins. I am Commander of the Chevaliers in the city of Lindly. I will not save these walls from crumbling, but I will do my damned duty to save the heart of Lindly. Its people."

Victus could feel the curse that had taken his eyesight moving through his body. It would continue to destroy him from the inside out, dissolving organs and forcing death. Eventually, it would hone in and begin consuming his soul. Skylighter glimpsed his friend's thoughts. "Victus... I am sorry."

The half-pal nodded. "I have time yet. Do as I ask. There are still people that need saving." Skylighter stepped back and saluted Victus. "Paladins! Defensive about-face! Secure the River Gate."

The paladins, in unison, switched their phalanx sides so rapidly it looked like a wave rolling over rocks. They cried out together, "Hooh-hah! Hooh-hah!" as they began their advance in the opposite direction.

Skylighter reached over and offered Victus his hand. Victus pushed his hand away and hugged the arch tightly. "If not for your courage and that of your paladins, we would have lost. Thank you, Sky!"

Skylighter smiled underneath his Corinth helmet. "I have loved you and will always love you as my brother, half-pal." Each let the other go. Skylighter turned to follow his paladins down and up the River Gate road.

Skylighter teetered and then spun back. One of his paladins was running toward them with Aris and Brandan, swinging at orcs and goblins as he ran. "Sempronius!" Skylighter yelled, surprise in his tone.

Sempronius had heard the command to fall back to the River Gate. But Sempronius had been, in another time, Victus's best friend and had decided he would disobey this order. Janus gave a quick look to Victus, and Victus nodded. Janus sprinted off to help the lone paladin. Sempronius used his helmet's magic ability to empath to Skylighter. "I am staying with the half-pal. Paladins don't retreat."

Skylighter groaned slightly to himself, "As you wish."

Victus and Skylighter shared a nod, and Victus smiled underneath his masked helmet. Skylighter hurriedly caught up with his soldiers, who had already engaged with orcs on the road to the River Gate. Dark elven shadow phantoms were poking in and out from the outskirts of his men, from rooftops, from inside buildings, and shooting their poisoned darts before slinking away. He knew that his own shock troopers needed him and that he could do nothing for Victus. His heart broke twice that day. Kalisdel had been killed or imprisoned, and he was going to lose one of his closest friends. No known magic could stop a god's curse upon a mortal. It was the perfection of death magic with the added dark elf touch of tormenting before death.

Skylighter placed a small, holy, magical shield over his warriors as he neared them, blocking the crossbow bolts, arrows, and javelins from penetrating. A few goblins thought they could jump from the buildings near the moving phalanx and slip through the barrier, but they quickly found out what a bad idea this was as they bounced off and were impaled by paladin spears. Skylighter magically empathed to his Caedes outside of the main phalanx. "I need you to draw some of them back toward Victus. And once you have drawn them in, kill them all. Fight alongside Victus; his commands are law. Defend this city. We will hold the River Gate."

The Caedes broke off into a double-step charge toward the ranged attackers, who pelted into their shields with bolts and arrows. Their armor absorbed the shots that were not stopped by the shields. They quickly overtook the buildings, with all opposition inside eliminated, and they withdrew in a defensive posture, marching with increased speed toward where Victus was located. They dispatched any orc or dark elf that came near with ease, using only two or three sword blows or thrusts. Among the paladins, this specific branch of the gryphon shock troopers known as Caedes Paladins possessed the highest level of experience, thus rendering them the most lethal. Their preferred method of defense was to attack. Ignorance alone would cause an orc or dark elf to charge them without concern. They were drawing attention as they moved, giving the rest of Skylighter's paladins a chance to advance freely.

Victus positioned the group with him into a wedge, with him and Janus at the tip, Aris and Jess behind. Serin and Brandan were at the bottom of the arrow formation, with Sempronius in the back middle of the gap, ready to run to whatever side needed reinforcing. Before them were the massive amounts of Dread Reavers, orcs, and goblins on the path to the inn. Victus shouted, "Advance!"

31

Thorm watched the bombardment from the catapults from his position at the River Gate and listened to the distorted explosions that sounded like muffled hailstones. The danger sounded much farther away than it was, and Thorm noted they had not once fired near the River Gate. It struck the old dwarf as odd that Elivendel would so brazenly destroy an allied city's residents. He continued his thoughts to himself as Titus watched the impending destruction with awe next to him. Thorm was bewildered by what he perceived as a violation of trust and fidelity among humans and elves. They were kindred spirits just like the dwarves and gnomes, all created by the same god, Asmolor. Though Thorm's tribe had left Asmolor's worship and followed Malakas in the year of harmony, a time long since passed, he could not comprehend the reasoning behind sacking the city when his own people were still fighting to hold it. "Damned shame. Coulda won this day."

Titus blinked, his mouth open as he continued to stare. "What?"

Thorm shook his head. "Not a thing, lad."

The dwarves were completing their makeshift body wall. Atop the towering mass of dead dark elves, Nordor let out a piercing screech. "WWWHOOOPPP!"

Other dwarves started yelping back to him in the same tone, "WWWHOOOPPP!" All around, Titus and Thorm, dwarves were 'whooping.'

Titus turned away from the spectacle above and asked, "What are they doing?"

Thorm chuckled. "Just Nordor lettin' everyone know that more enemies are a-comin'. The other boys are just lettin' him know they heard him."

Titus gazed intently down the road, poised and prepared to confront the approaching surge.

A few moments passed, and Nordor yelled again, "Orcs! Orcs!"

A whole mob of orcs sprinted up the road towards the gate, but they were in a panic. The scene was one of utter confusion as some orcs threw their weapons at an unseen enemy while others held fast. They were terrified, and they were running straight into a dwarven trap. Titus witnessed the orcs crushing each other in their frantic attempt to escape. The legionnaire detected a few shadowy silhouettes flickering in and out of sight. But the speed at which they moved made it impossible for him to identify their point of origin or destination. As the closest group of orcs made their way down the walled path, Titus readied his weapon. Nordor was the first dwarf to engage; he leapt down from his perch and ambushed four orcs at once. Nordor was yelling and smashing, smashing and whooping, "No runnin' orc. Git ov'r here! WHOOOOOP!"

Titus noticed that the three enigmatic figures were closer now, and he could see the intricate designs etched on their dragon blades as they danced through the air. The orcs were the audience to a deadly symphony, played flawlessly by these musicians of shadows. Their constant movement hindered his memory, preventing him from figuring out who they were. Whatever they were doing, they were helping. To Titus, it appeared as if storm clouds had taken the form of humanoids, small black puffs of smoke bouncing between the fleeing orcs. A chain reaction of black clouds resulted in the death of multiple orcs.

Thorm laughed. "That's Odyful! Bet ya hundred gold pieces!"

Titus shook his head in confusion. "Who?"

Thorm chuckled. "Aye, you wouldn't know. Mage-blades, the Moirai, good guys."

Titus made a shrugging motion before stepping forward to assist in fighting the orcs. However, with the combined efforts of the three mage blades and Nordor, there were no surviving orcs.

Seconds had passed in the brief exchange between Thorm and Titus, and that was enough. As Titus took those few steps, a figure materialized behind him, in the place he had just stood. Startled, he whipped around, sword swiping the air. Instinctively striking, he realized it was a friend and halted the swipe just in time for the dragon hilt blade of the Moirai to easily deflect it.

"Careful, friend. We are aiding your cause." The power in his words was softened by the deep, soothing tone of his voice.

Thorm smacked his thigh. "Bah ha ha, I knew it! Odyful!"

The mage blade leader bowed slightly as he turned from Titus. "Master dwarf, still alive, I see." The dwarf growled out his response, "Ain't gonna be no pointy-eared dark elf killing me. Nor is a damned greenskin."

Odyful grinned underneath his hooded cloak. "You deserve a far better death, my friend. A dragon perhaps? They could write a ballad of your mighty defeat," he said with a pause, grinning at Thorm. "Or victory?" His hands went up with the question hanging as he continued, "Who knows, though? You are the craftiest dwarf I have ever met."

Thorm roared in laughter. "A dragon! Aye, that would be one helluva way to go."

Titus made to interject, but Nordor shouted, "Get de bodies on our wall, boys!"

Titus twisted his neck back to see the insane dwarf grinning wildly. Nordor noticed Titus staring, reached down to his waterskin canteen, offering it a wiggle. “Needin’ more, lad?”

Titus shook his head quickly. “No thank you.”

Nordor shrugged. “More for me.”

Odyful’s other companions assisted the dwarves with clearing the bodies and then moved back towards their leader. Odyful looked up at the bombardment still raining upon the barrier placed by Kalisdel. “The city will not hold for long, Thorm. We are heading out of the River Gate and to the docks. From there, we will ensure that the ships and boats are filled to capacity and protected.”

Thorm nodded. “Good. We’ll be a little light on the defense of our refugees outside of the city.”

Odyful surveyed the road they had come from. “We took out this wave, but there is another that is being pushed up this way. A phalanx of Gryphon shock trooper paladins is progressing towards this location. Skylighter is leading them.”

Thorm nodded and asked excitedly, “What of Commander Victus?”

Odyful’s jaw clenched. He knew Thorm was fond of the human and understood that Thorm was risking a lot by being here, supporting a cause outside of his god’s concern. He wondered if Thorm had disobeyed Malakas to be here. Odyful’s clenching jaw gave Thorm the impression that Victus was dead as he responded to his own question. “He fell?” His voice was soft, straining to make the words audible.

Odyful shook his head once. “He is leading a charge back in to save civilians holed up in an alehouse inn.” The Moirai lifted his hand to stop Thorm’s next question. “He is not alone. The Caedes have splintered off from the main phalanx and charged back in to support Victus.”

Thorm nodded as his held breath released. "Oh, I like those paladins! Nasty boys and girls, they are. Paladins of Slaughter. Asmolor's righteous fury? More like my berserkers; I like 'em."

Odyful chuckled. "Righteous Berserkers, perhaps?" The mage blade leader twirled his finger in the air, and his companions moved past Titus, heading towards the River Gate docks. Odyful looked to Titus. "Farewell, legionnaire."

Titus, still thoroughly confused about who these people were, nodded. "Ah, and you too, sir."

"We are away. See you on the other side, Thorm."

Thorm smiled. "Aye! Knowing Victus, he will be wanting to thank you for your aid today. Where can I tell him he can find you?"

Odyful grinned. "Presently at the docks. After... well, after we will be about."

Thorm shook his head as he laughed. "I figured as much… I'll tell him to look in Asmadine."

As the leader of the mage blades walked away, he added, "That would be a fair place to start."

~~~

Sempronius was at the back of the makeshift wedge formation Victus had formed, which was moving towards his fellow Caedes paladins. When they crossed paths, he showed them to position themselves at the rear of the wedge and provide backup, supplementing Victus's team as the spearhead.

Victus and Janus were still advancing, spear, shield, and swords slashing and hacking into the careless charge of orcs. Serin and Brandan were tag-teaming one particularly large orc. With an orc sword in hand and a crossbow slung on his back, Brandan deflected the heavy blows while Serin rolled behind him and hopped to her feet, landing a solid kick on the orc's knees. She dodged the orc's wild swing and could
~~~

hear the whoosh of his weapon passing by. Her brother swung down with his short sword, the blade slicing through the creature's chest and sending a spray of blood into the air.

The orc growled menacingly, holding his spiked club with both hands as he swung it back from his missed attempt to hit Serin. He expected to annihilate the human who had harmed him. His effort to split Brandan in half with his club failed as Brandan jumped back. Evading another attack from behind, Brandan's younger sister cartwheeled away. She swung around to face the wildly aggressive attacks of the newly descended orc. She ran at full speed, shouting, "FAMILY!" With a cry of "DUTY!" she leapt into the air. The orc halted abruptly, attempting to shift its weight to either dodge the girl's attack or catch her in midair. Her swift kick to his chest sent him staggering backward, his balance completely thrown off. Using her momentum, she ensnared the beast's neck with her other leg like a lure. The force and weight of her body yanked the orc toward the ground. He landed firmly on his back; the impact knocked the wind out of him. Serin quickly untangled herself and hopped atop the orc's chest. Leaning down into his face, she screamed, "ARIS!" With a sudden movement, she pulled away from its face and plunged her small dagger into the creature's chest, causing it to gasp and choke. The sight of the dark, blackish blood pouring from its mouth made her stomach turn. She watched in horror as the orc's hands tightened around her before he threw her aside in his final breath.

Aris heard Serin yell his name as he withdrew his gladius from the belly of an orc that had been pierced in the side of its neck by Jess's sword. Giving the young man a nod of approval, she said, "Go help them! I can hold."

Aris spun from her and sprinted over toward Serin being tossed aside. Seeing the young squire sprint away, Sempronius stepped forward to fill the gap that Aris had left.

Aris saw Serin bounce off the ground as gracefully as she could. The movement did not seem to slow her a bit. Without hesitation, she rushed back to her brother's aid. Her fearless and fierce demeanor instilled vigor in Aris as he darted past her toward the orcs that had crept up unnoticed. He whispered in every movement of his sword and dagger, "Family, Duty, Serin."

Serin jumped onto the gargantuan orc her brother was struggling against and began stabbing into its neck with ferocity. "Family! Duty! Aris!"

Brandan drove his sword into the orc's leg, causing the beast to collapse and Serin with it. Aris's sword whirled from two fresh attacks to his left. While he reversed his grip on his dagger to stab the reaching sword hand of another, it bit hard into the orc and retracted. Aris kept backing up as he deflected the attacks, nipping with his dagger when they got too close. Brandan pulled Serin to her feet, and they both charged to Aris's flanks. Brandan could not decide where to help Aris, so he waited and chopped down hard at a thrust aimed toward Aris, cleanly removing the hand of an orc. Serin likewise waited, then ducked from a blow, keeping her head down as she struck into the calf of another. While she was down, though, her balance was off, and she slipped fully to the ground. Aris positioned himself defensively to deter any attacks directed toward her.

The orcs stopped attacking, though. Aris and Brandan pressed forward to attack, thinking they had turned the tide. But from behind the three, they heard pummels methodically being hit into shields. The voices of the Caedes rumbled like a thunderstorm as they chanted in their advance. "FAMILY! DUTY! LINDLY!"

Aris saw the magnificent Caedes paladins, blood intermixing with the rose gold and black of their armor. He could not help but gasp, letting out a "WOW." They were every bit of what Aris had read about. Towering knights of bloodshed, they knew no fear. They advanced past Brandan, Serin, and Aris, continuing their chant of "Family, Duty, Lindly." The Caedes formed a wedge, granting those in the center a much-needed break from the chaos. Aris glimpsed what seemed to be a wink from one of the Caedes beneath her helmet, but he wasn't positive.

He helped Serin up as the paladins passed him. "I have never seen you fight like that, Serin."

Serin grabbed Aris in a hug. "I didn't know I could either!" She quickly let him go. "Ya think we're winning?"

Aris looked around the carnage, saw his father and Janus waving them over, and responded, "Hard to tell. But we are giving them as much as they are giving us."

Aris ran to his father, motioning for Serin and Brandan to follow, his heart pounding with each step. He couldn't resist stealing a glance back at the Caedes. The paladins of vengeful carnage waded into the orcs as if giants into men. Aris came to a slow halt, utterly amazed and awestruck. He noted that any enemy who approached within a few meters was met with swift and deadly force. The enemy fell back in fear as they approached, like a tide receding before a storm. The orcs rallied to counterattack, but the Caedes were well-prepared and equipped for any battle, anywhere. They were shuffled and dispersed in their assault, but as the enemy started to push back, they promptly gathered into more condensed clusters. Aris watched as the paladins interchanged their shield arm with sword arm, transmuting their weapons to their alternate hands by magic. A select few made their sword and shield disappear completely, their weapon replaced with a halberd, catching the orcs off guard when they realized they had not backed up far enough. It was the bracers and armor the paladins wore that allowed them to interchange weapons with a thought. Watching their equipment materialize in a sudden flash was a mesmerizing sight for Aris, and he pondered if it was an intentional design choice.

Any enemy watching the beauty of their movements would soon be a dead enemy. They fought perfectly together, unlike any other legion or soldier he had seen before. Not once were they overcome by attacks to the flanks. Aris surmised it was the helmets providing mental visions of their sides and back. Soon, none dared stand before them but the Dread Reavers. The orcs pulled back as if waiting for a command to reengage. The Caedes shouted Victus' anthem, "Family, Duty, LINDLY!" Aris turned back towards his father and the others, a smile playing on his lips as he surveyed the group, but then realizing he had wasted time staring like a child in wonderment, he ran to catch up with the others.

Once Jess, Sempronius, Aris, Brandan, and Serin had huddled near Victus and Janus, the commander spoke. "Janus and I will press the attack and draw the attention of the Dread Reavers and Lich by the Inn. The rest of you need to get to the Inn and get everyone out and up to the River Gate." Victus' voice sounded strained, and Aris believed he sounded wounded. Victus pulled off his helmet, and they saw his eyes, which were closed and covered in blood. He unsnapped the face mask that was attached to the helmet. He held it out to Aris. "Take this. It is the death mask of our house, and the living heir of our house should always have it."

They all looked at him confused, and the weight of what he had just said slowly sank in. Jess interjected, "What do you mean? You still live."

Victus put his helmet back on, allowing him to see again. "I am sorry, my love, but I have been cursed in the duel. It is spreading, and I will succumb."

Aris' heart sank, then climbed up into his throat as he placed the mask away in his satchel. His eyes swelled, and tears trickled down his face. Serin instinctively grabbed Aris' hand, and he squeezed it, feeling the grief starting to ache. Serin remained silent as the weight of the news rendered Aris speechless and unable to think.

Jess, unwilling to accept what Victus said, tried to argue with him. "Nonsense, surely we can get you help. Of all the people you know, Skylighter is a master healer, is he not?"

Victus nodded. "He is, but in this, he can do nothing."

Tears streamed down Aris' face as he stood frozen, unable to comprehend what was happening.

His whole world crashed down around him; his legs began to wobble uncontrollably. He heard Victus and Jess speaking. He felt Serin's warm touch, her hand in his. Never had he felt so disconnected and broken.

The translucent barrier placed by Kalisdel was cracking, and with one final barrage from the Inquisition, it dissolved completely. All around, the fiery explosive payloads began to crash into the city. Aris, still frozen, did not even move as hundreds of projectiles began exploding and demolishing the city. He felt a tug from Serin, and then he saw nothing. A few moments passed, and then his ears were ringing as he lay upon the ground. Dirt and blood covered him, and from the ache in his head, he knew some of the blood was his own. Some of the debris had exploded on top of the Caedes' formation, and thus the fallout had impacted Victus and the others.

Aris attempted to pull himself up as he tried to look past the fires, unsettled dirt in the air, and smoke. He saw all of the Caedes lying dead or dying. One particular paladin, the woman he thought had winked at him, was lying crushed under the debris. All but her shoulders, head, and arms were underneath. Aris tried to get up, but his legs would not hold him; his head was spinning, and he fell back down. Instead, he tried crawling toward the paladin, but he could not move, so he sat up on all fours and watched her helplessly.

The woman's hands shook as she struggled; Aris could see her coughing through the smoke. She fumbled with her shield attached to her arm, sprawled out and trapped. He understood what she was doing when the bright flare shot straight up into the air. She had released a knight's flare designating "friendlies." He watched as she made sure the flare went to the position in the sky she wanted, and then her head slumped down in death.

Aris dropped down defeated, feeling the dirt on his face as he tried to make sense of all that was happening around him. What felt like an eternity passed by, but it was mere moments, and he felt his shoulder being pulled back as someone rolled him over. "Aris, are you okay? Aris!"

The concerned voice was that of his father. Aris croaked, "Da!"

Victus pulled him up and began quickly bandaging his son's head. "Can you walk?"

Aris nodded, and with the help of his father, pulled himself to his feet. When they were standing, Aris wrapped his father in a hug. "You can't die, Da. Not yet! Please!"

Victus understood the pain in his son's voice and wanted to give him what he desired, but he also knew the situation around them. All he could do was comfort his son. He hugged him back, lifting him off the ground. "I love you, my boy! I will always love you! And you will always have a part of me with you. Always!" He put Aris back down, stepped back, and looked down into his son's eyes. Aris looked and saw his father's eyes were not closed but were glowing white, with a viscous white smoke drifting from them. His father's tone was warm but firm. "You have to get to those people. Continue to carry on our proud name. You are the greatest achievement of my life, and I am forever grateful for what you have taught me."

Aris scrunched up in confusion, his eyes still streaming tears. "It was you that taught me my whole life."

Victus chuckled, "You'll understand when you have a child of your own."

Janus stepped over with a noticeable limp and a broken arm. "I could not find Jess or Brandan, sir."

Victus looked over to him. "Serin? Sempronius?"

Sempronius's voice sounded at the mention of his name with a cough in the smoke. "I am here."

Aris, now realizing Serin was still on the ground, ran over to her body. "Serin?" He brushed her hair from her face and kissed her cheek and forehead. "Serin!" he yelled.

Her eyes popped open, and she smiled at Aris. "That hurt."

Aris pulled her up to her feet. "We have to get going."

Victus' heart warmed watching his son and Serin. "Get to the Inn. I will draw their attention." Aris, still helping Serin stand, turned to face his father. "Janus and Sempronius can take Serin to the Inn. I will stay with you."

Victus began to scold Aris. "Get out of here now; that is an order. Janus, see to it."

Sempronius and Janus huddled around Serin and Aris, ushering them away. Victus pulled his sword into position and reignited the Andreas house-colored flames around it. He turned and faced away from his son, who was struggling against Sempronius's strong grip. "Da! I can help you! NOOOO!!!!"

Victus focused on the Dread Reavers still standing amidst the constant barrage of catapult payloads. He saw three Dread Reavers surrounding the Lich. Their swords were pointed straight at Victus, and their palms were placed out toward him. He whispered, "Family, Duty, Lindly!" A torrent of black beams came forth from the Dread Reavers. It surrounded and penetrated Victus, encasing him in a globe of black, sticky, tar-like substance. He was covered and trapped in the sphere.

Aris fought Sempronius's grasp. "DAAAA!!!!!!"

The paladin pulled on him. "We have to go, lad. Come on."

Victus felt the curse and the tar eating away at his flesh as the weight of the sword and armor he wore caused him to crumple within the sphere. His soul was fighting what his body could not. He believed and reached out for strength—he drew upon his love for his son, Serin, Jess, and his men. He felt everything fading as he collapsed into death. His consciousness was aware that his body was decaying and dying. He could see but was no longer feeling the pain. Deep within him, he began to draw on that love he had within him, and it fueled his soul. He began to stand; his body was no longer even there; he was a bluish-white light encased in his armor. Strength had returned to his body, but he had no body. Victus fueled his soul with the love he had for his family, for his city. He did not understand what was happening; perhaps his faith was being rewarded. Perhaps his telekinetic abilities had allowed him to harness his soul apart from his body. Whatever was happening to him, he was going to use it to help save as many as he could and defeat as much of this evil as he could, and he would start with the Lich.

Aris broke free of Sempronius’ hold and began running back to his father in the sphere. As he closed in, he heard his father's voice in his head. "Aris, my son. Go—so that I can know you are safe. I need you to leave so I can focus."

Aris slowed. "Da, I can't leave you."

Victus, still encased, said, "You will never leave me. Now go. I love you."

Sempronius had caught up with the young squire and pulled him away again. "We have to go!"

Aris allowed himself to be pulled away as he said in his mind to his father, "I love you."

He didn’t fight Sempronius this time and ran alongside him toward the inn, though he looked back and watched the sphere his father was trapped in. "Wait!" Aris yelled, and Sempronius stopped and looked back. They watched as bright white and blue light began to crack the black tar sphere.

Then, in a moment, it burst apart, and there stood Victus—his spirit, wearing his armor. The flesh on his body was gone; he was more ghost than human. His armor no longer looked of the material plane; he was an archon of his devotion and love.

Sempronius gasped. "It's an anomaly! How?"

Aris stood silent, having heard that word before and knowing it was rumored to be some forbidden unknown magic used by a few humans in the past, granting them temporary states of great power. So much power that when they happened, the gods would seek out who used it and have them killed.

Sempronius tugged on Aris. "Come—he has their attention, and we need to get these people out of Lindly."

Aris watched his father step forth, sword ready as he charged toward the Lich and Dread Reavers.

32

Aris, Serin, Janus, and Sempronius rushed into the inn. The legionnaires inside had unbarred the door when they saw who was approaching. Janus spoke first: "Everyone in here needs to leave now." Aris looked in the room, and it was packed; over three hundred civilians and just under twenty legionnaires were present. He also noted a somewhat flamboyantly dressed group wearing rose embroidery insignia on their tunics.

A gruff older woman legionnaire yelled, "Alright, you heard them. Soldiers up front. Everyone else, behind us."

Sempronius nodded in agreement. "The squire and I will watch the rear."

Serin smiled. "I can lead them out the back and get us to the River Gate."

Sempronius nodded. "Alright, let's go. Everyone out."

Everyone in the inn began to shuffle about and departed from the back entrance, following Serin’s lead. As they exited, Aris stood waiting in the front doorway as everyone was leaving, distracted by his father fighting in the distance against the Dread Reavers. Suddenly, two orcs appeared, throwing Aris backward. They were carrying a woman, and Sempronius stabbed one, successfully deflecting it. The woman being held screamed; when she saw Aris, she was shocked, calming briefly before screaming again. The orc carrying her tossed her to the ground and stepped to engage the boy before him. Aris did not think; after he jumped back, he had already begun his attack. He swept the orc’s blade away and countered with his dagger. The sword came from the orc again, but this time, Aris spun, deflecting with his gladius. As he completed the one hundred-and-eighty-degree spin, his sword came around to slash. The attack was rebuffed, and Aris knelt on one knee, placing his dagger straight into the orc's artery in his exposed leg. It dropped with a howl of pain, bleeding out in seconds. Sempronius smashed his head into the other orc's face when they locked swords. The orc, dazed, turned to flee upon hearing the squeal of his friend. When he tried to sprint through the door, the woman tripped him, and Aris was atop the orc. He began smashing the head of the beast into the floor. When the orc was unconscious, he began stabbing and stabbing. The dark, brownish-black blood pooled all over Aris's arms. He continued with another quick thirty or so stabs until he was gasping for air. He was covered in blood, and he was angry. He wanted more.

Sempronius spoke sternly, "Squire! That's enough! It's time to go."

Aris spat and rose from the dead orc. The woman next to him gave him a small, reassuring smile. "Thank you, young squire."

She was sincere, although Aris was certain that she was probably a little disturbed by him, especially with all the blood on him and what he had just done. He walked over to her, his hand outstretched to help her up. "My name is Aris Tin of House Andreas."

She nodded. "Yes, you are." She smiled warmly at him. "My name is Marie of Delwan. Well, now of Lindly."

Sempronius motioned for the two to come along. "We need to catch up with the others."

Aris looked one more time at his father battling and left the inn through the back door.

~~~

Victus felt the power of the anomaly, and it was overwhelming him; he could not contain nor control it. But
~~~

he focused all his might on taking down the Dread Reavers and the Lich. He attacked all of them at once. His spirit moved faster, hit harder, and was devastating when it struck. The Dread Reavers were falling back, and after a few clashes with Victus's sword, their own weapons began to degrade and were subsequently consumed by Victus's power. The light within Victus was eroding all before him. Each strike brought him closer to the Lich, and he could feel the Lich's anger. He drew within and let down his sword, placing his palm out as the Dread Reavers attempted to grab him. They stuttered in motion and then dissolved to ash. Raising his sword, he slammed it into the ground, and he charged right at the Lich. The Lich pelted him with warlock darts of magic that passed right through Victus, and he pressed forward, tackling the wretch to the ground.

The Lich let out a cry for help, but he was alone; most of Lestar's children had already recalled to safety. Victus grasped the Lich's neck and imbued all of his newfound power into the creature. It screamed in pain with its hoarse voice, "Nooooooo!"

Victus screamed back, "FAMILY, DUTY, LINDLY!" The Lich's body began to convulse as Victus drained it of its unholy power, killing it. Victus stood up, looked towards the inn, now vacant, and then felt the power grow briefly; he knew it was over. His ghostly body lost its shape, and his spirit, shapeless, hovered before disappearing. His thoughts lingered as he reached out to touch his son, Skylighter, Thorm, Janus, Sempronius, Jess, Serin, and Brandan. His last moments were spent trying to tap into their minds and assure them of his love and that he was well.

~~~

Thorm heard from Nordor that the Gryphon Shock Troopers were nearing the gate. "No orcs with 'em. Must have already killed ‘em all." The disappointment in Nordor's voice was noted with amusement by both Thorm and Titus.
~~~

Skylighter was leading his men and women when they reached the wall of dead orcs and dark elves. His paladins had replaced spears with swords but kept the shields in tower form, just in case they needed to switch back to their phalanx.

Thorm walked down to greet one of his oldest friends, but before he could say a word, the Paladin Arch yelled, "Thormhammer of Dewer! What are you doing here?"

Thorm turned his head to the dead orc and elven bodies piled up on either side of himself. "Looks like I have been helping Victus save the city."

Skylighter was curt. "Your assistance is no longer required. Remove yourself from this gate as it is in the protection of Asmolor's children." A clear slight to the dwarf, indicating that he was indeed a traitor, as most of Asmolor's creation would have viewed any who served Malakas.

"Ah, I see you, Johnathan Agricola, and I hear ya," he replied without skipping a beat, using Skylighter's given name before he had ascended to his current station. Skylighter had always disliked his name, even more after he ascended into archdom.

A light burst out from the city and ended the conversation abruptly. All turned to gaze at the spectacle behind them. They could not make out what was happening, but Thorm and Skylighter both looked at one another and understood. Someone was tapping into the forbidden soul magic, creating what the gods called an anomaly.

Thorm answered the question Skylighter had been thinking, "Victus. What have you done?"

Skylighter looked from Thorm to where the light was shining from. "Could it be?"

Thorm nodded, "It is. And he is gone, lad."

Skylighter moved towards the dwarf as if to attack him. Instead, he held himself a few inches from the dwarf's face, "He's not gone! He's a damned anomaly!"

Thorm raised his arm to Sky's shoulder, "He is gone, and I know because I can see underneath this emotion; I can see it in your eyes, lad."

Skylighter spun away from him, "We have more people that are being rescued. I suggest you leave before I inform Elivendel you are here." With that, Skylighter issued commands for his paladins to secure the River Gate and fortify the position.

Nordor hopped down and made his way over to Thorm, and as he passed Skylighter, he said, "Not needin' to be so rude der, Johnathan. We all losin' a friend today."

Skylighter nodded politely to the older dwarf but said nothing.

Thorm yelled out to his men, "A'ight boyyas, we done good work. Let's move out!" Thorm looked at Titus intently, "You coming with us?"

Titus nodded, "Ah sure, just once all this is settled, I will need to find Marcella… Is Victus truly lost?"

Thorm shook his head no, "Not lost– he is exactly where he needs to be."

Titus took by the tone that the dwarf did not wish to say that his friend was dead or dying. He left it at that and began to follow the dwarves out of the River Gate towards the docks down by the river.

~~~

Aris was moving down the corridors of the streets, and besides the bombardment from above, they did not face much resistance on the way to the River Gate. Something was shielding them from above too, like a lingering haze that followed the group. Aris realized it was part of his father's spirit, or perhaps he was imagining that intuition; he could not be certain. He could feel his father with each heavy step he took. Then he heard his father's voice in his head one last time. "I am proud of you, Aris Tin of our House Andreas.
~~~

Never forget, I am with you." Aris stopped as he listened and tried to empath back to his father how much he loved him. He tried to hold the tears back, but he could not.

Sempronius stayed beside Aris but did not interrupt, as he too was hearing Victus speak to him. "Sempronius, ever faithful. When your time comes, I will greet you in Asmolor's fields myself." Sempronius saluted, his balled-up fist over his heart, holding the moment for as long as he could.

They continued and reached the safety of the River Gate; the few hundred people of Lindly were thankful and happy—they celebrated as none of them were touched by debris or fireballs from the catapult payloads. Victus had saved them. He had saved thousands upon thousands, and yet the loss was still palpable to all.

Serin turned from the front of the group and began making her way back to the end of the flow of people so she could find Aris. As she did, a dwarf waved her over to the side, and she walked over. "Are ye being Serin of House Neske?"

She smiled, "Formerly yes. I am now Serin, ward of House Andreas." She looked at the rose embroidered on the dwarf's tunic and realized that behind the rose stitching was a crown. "Princes of the Rose? You have worked with my father!"

The dwarf laughed, "Nah, lass. Not worked with. We just made a deal with him regarding his daughter."

Serin turned to run, but she was surrounded and quickly ushered off to the side, into an alleyway.

Aris had been walking to find Serin at the front, not realizing she had gone back to find him. When he saw her talking with a dwarf wearing the same crown and rose-embroidered clothing as from the inn, he was horrified to see companions of the dwarf surrounding her aggressively. He could not make out what was happening but began jogging toward her.

Serin wiggled and squirmed as she fought against them, climbing so her head stuck out from them. She screamed out, "ARIS!"

The crowd was loud, but Aris knew she was in trouble. He went into a full sprint toward her, but people kept stepping in his way and slowing his advance. By the time he reached the spot where they had been standing, they were gone. All that remained was a dimensional portal with what appeared to be a bustling city on the other side. Aris sprinted straight for it, and when he saw Serin being carried off inside the portal to the unknown city, he jumped headlong into the closing portal after her.

Read on for a preview of the next in series, XIII Crows...

Enjoy an excerpt from the upcoming XIII Crows

Scribe Note

Tome Two

Some may be wondering why we, in the Order of Requirement, have paused in the tomes as Aris stepped through the portal. The Order and I have chosen to pause as a reflection of what has transpired. We have chosen to pause on the implications of what the Battle of Lindly brought to our world. If the events that happened in the previous tome had never occurred, none of us would be free now. For all of the darkness we have witnessed and will witness in the coming tomes, it is the light that overcomes. A few individuals standing up against accepted tyranny can and will be the spark that ignites a fire capable of changing the world, and this should not be overlooked.

The darkness is and was a tool that trained young Aris and others to eventually understand and overcome with the light of truth and justice for all. As we, in our present time, are invaded by horrors outside of our control, we will look back to the past and see the horrors that we as a people have already endured and what we have risen above. Stand firm in knowing our past and remember your duty to those whom you love in the present.

In the first tome, we saw the first Primarch of Asmolor, Elivendel, turn his aid away from helping the human goddess, Primarch Kalisdel. We witnessed the stalwart attempt of Thorm and his kin to help Lindly, though his goddess forbade him to interfere in any of the brothers' conflicts after the end of the Second War. We saw the heroic stand of Skylighter and his griffin shock troopers. The Battle of Lindly was the start of the change we call the 'Reformation.' Victus's death and Serin's capture began a long and dark road for the young squire Aris. The tale of Aris is fraught with excitement and darkness, which became our journey. It becomes our freedom. As you read and cast judgment on characters, even Aris, remember that this was before the world was illuminated. This was a time of barbarism and suffering. Tough decisions were made, and not all of those decisions are without regret.

We have been introduced to many players in Aris's life. Some we will see again very soon and some not for quite some time. The moment that the young squire stepped through that portal, his life forever changed. His father had passed, and his hometown was destroyed. Everything in his world had been razed, save for the foundation his father instilled within him. This foundation is the one thing that holds him back from the brink of chaos. It is that foundation that allows him to listen, adapt, and learn from his mistakes. We will see this together in the pages to come. Aris and the paths he chooses to walk down are both terrifying and exhilarating. Prepare your hearts and minds.

1

Sempronius had been helping usher others to safety, as had Janus. The bombardment was slowing significantly as most of the buildings were destroyed. The last vestiges of survivors were making their way through the River Gate. Both the legionnaire Janus and paladin Sempronius mingled in the crowd. Though they were apart, they both felt the air tingle with magic. Each was an experienced warrior and knew to look around, assuming the approach of more attackers or possibly a portal opening. Janus's arm was broken and his leg hurt, but he moved quickly toward the sound of a pop and crackle, telltale signs of a portal being opened. He saw the outline of a portal in the distance as he maneuvered himself through the crowds. Likewise, Sempronius made his way back through the crowd when he saw a portal set off the main road a fair distance away. As they both worked their way closer, both Sempronius and Janus noticed one another. Closing the distance between them, they merged, closing in on the portal, always prepared. As they continued together, the portal, a mere twenty or so paces away, revealed the form of young Aris inside the portal.

Janus yelled, "ARIS! No!" but cut himself off as the portal closed. Sempronius rushed forward, sprinting to try and catch the portal, knowing it was too late. He still tried running through the spot where it had been placed. Cursing, Sempronius spun around to the limping legionnaire Janus, who trailed slightly behind. He began to speak, but the sound of trumpets rang out from around the city. He could not hear the words he uttered. It was the call to halt the bombardment completely and send in elven soldiers to ensure nothing survived of Eu'rok's children.

After the horns finished, Sempronius spoke again, "Looked like Asmadine."

Janus grimaced, nodding, "It was."

Sempronius sighed, unsure of what to do, and walked up to Janus, reaching out for the legionnaire's arm. "Let me tend to that."

Janus shifted his shoulder to the side as Sempronius used his blessing of light to ease the pain and mend his tattered arm and leg. This was not Janus's first time being healed and would not be his last, he thought. As Sempronius checked him over, Janus spoke, "I will head to Asmadine. My loyalty and duty are to Victus, and now that he is gone, I will find his son and offer my services to him. Perhaps protect him if I can. But first, I am going to look for Jess and Brandan in the rubble. I need to know if they made it."

Sempronius winced at the thought of Victus; they had trained together since they were young men. They had become griffin shock troopers together, until Victus had stepped down to raise the boy from Delwan. Sempronius had argued with and scolded Victus. He thought back on the conversation. "Victus, you cannot be so foolish as to throw away the future we have together. We are a brotherhood, a sisterhood of warrior knights; we are your family. Leave the babe to a good family so that he can have a normal life. Our lives are devoted to Kalisdel and fighting the scourge of darkness."

Victus had taken Sempronius's tone and words very seriously, pausing to think over his words carefully. "I...or rather, our duty is not just to be used in war. Our lives are not set in stone. Nothing in this world is ever certain, and our wars are never-ending. If I have learned anything these past years, it is this: We don't need better-trained soldiers, we don't need better gear. We need better thinkers. We need men and women who will do right over wrong, even if that means damning themselves in the eyes of the gods."

Sempronius had cut Victus off, his anger swelling within him, "That is sacrilegious. The gods are GODS, and we obey! Have you lost faith? Should I report you? What then?"

Victus then recoiled from his friend, wounded by his anger, "I do not speak ill of the gods. I question certain things, and what faith cannot stand up to the scrutiny of honest criticism or thoughts?"

Sempronius eased his anger. "I... I am sorry, Victus. Of course, I support you and love you as my brother. But I believe you are in error in your judgments upon our faith. And if you cannot see that, then you are damned already."

Before his mind could continue to drift further into the conversation he had had with Victus long ago, Janus's voice drew him back to the present.

"I said, I think that you're done healing me," Janus said, placing his hand on his own shoulder where Sempronius had his hand.

Sempronius shook the thoughts of Victus from his head. "Yes, of course. Are you well enough?"

Janus nodded, "Yes, thank you. I will send letters to the temple in Asmadine as soon as I have word on Aris."

Sempronius stepped back, wishing the man good fortune in his endeavors. As he turned to find his way back to his commander and fellow paladins, he paused. "Janus, why do you have such loyalty toward Victus?"

The older legionnaire's face softened only a little as he stared back into Sempronius's eyes. "Because no other commander would accept me because of my age. Most laughed and told me that I was past my prime. Victus stood up for me when I came to offer my services here in Lindly. He treated me as every other soldier; he was a commander worth following. He is..." Pausing, he adjusted the mistake and continued, "He was a man worth following. And though I was unable to save him, I can still serve him by offering my help to his son."

Sempronius nodded to Janus and smiled, "He was a great man. I regret and will regret to my last day how I handled him leaving the Order of Paladins. For fifteen years, Victus wrote to me. He talked often of his life with his son. Perhaps I was jealous or angry that I did not have my closest friend fighting beside me. But I never once responded to him. And..." The paladin choked back the words, trying to prevent the tears in his eyes. "Now I have lost him. Do what you will, Janus, and I will be there if you ever need me. For Victus and for his son." He turned and headed toward his commander.

Janus watched the paladin, understanding his pain and appreciating the man's words. Taking a deep breath, he began the walk past the people leaving the city, towards where they had been fighting with Victus, Jess, and Brandan.

Aris slowed as he stepped through the portal from Lindly into the massive city of Asmadine, briefly looking for the fastest route through the bustling city. He could see Serin in the distance, bouncing as she was carried off. His arms were still covered in orc blood, his head bandaged and aching. He pressed forward through his exhaustion and pain. However, as he took his first steps, Aris buckled over as his breath was sucked from his lungs. He glanced over, trying to see who had hit him, but another blow connected into his back, hitting his kidney hard. He dropped to his knees and began crawling away as quickly as he could. Aris's eyes were blurring, and he was trying to recognize the man but couldn't.

Aris rose and faced this new adversary. The man was wearing a dark gray cloak and green tunic, which was all Aris could really see. Sidestepping in a circle, the man countered Aris's movements, spinning with him. Aris's eyes began to stabilize, and his lungs caught up with his gasps. The man paused, looking Aris over, his arms open and inviting, and said, "Come, boy." Aris shook his head as he looked back in the direction where he had last seen Serin. "Who are you?" Aris demanded, his voice audibly strained.

The man smirked. "I am the one who is going to stop you from getting to Serin."

That's all Aris needed to hear, and his body was in motion towards the man. Blinded by rage and the pain of his father's loss, Aris was going to unleash his wrath. No one would stand in his way. He could feel his blood pulsing with adrenaline throughout his body, mixing with his emotions, making him unstable but very dangerous. His hands pumped as he charged the man, his jaw clenched so tightly in rage that he could feel the pressure on his teeth.

The roguish character he charged simply smiled, his arms still wide, waiting. "That's it, boy," he whispered, his grin fueling the young man's rage. He could not believe the young man had charged him with no weapons in hand. The sword and dagger he wore were securely fastened as he charged. Aris was a few paces from the man when he lunged into the air, his left fist balled to punch the man in the face. His right hand stayed low as Aris felt his mind call his father's dagger into his hand. His jump was short and deliberate as he pulled back the punch and stabbed at the man's undefended belly. The rogue's eyes widened as he saw the dagger materialize, his hands quickly adjusting to stop the assault. Aris, in his rash determination, did not see the quick counter. It was not until his hand ached and his dagger fell to the ground that he understood his mistake.

Aris pressed his attack with his left arm, attempting to swat the man's ear, hoping to shock or stun him. The swing missed as the man ducked. Tightening his grip on Aris's wrist, the man started twisting, forcing Aris to try and unwind. As Aris tried to spin away, the man moved into his spin, and Aris flipped onto his back. The rogue's dagger in the man’s hand pricked a deep cut into Aris's neck as he lay stunned, the weight of the man's knee pressed into Aris's chest, making it difficult to catch his breath. The rogue grinned. "My name is Zephyial."

Aris's mouth clenched tight as he labored to take deep breaths through his nostrils. All Aris could think was how his rage had made him foolish. Stupid. Stupid. I am sorry, father, he thought. His lips let out the words, "Sorry, father."

Zephyial looked at him quizzically. "You're no son of mine." Laughing, he yielded the blade's tip a bit from Aris's neck. "I could kill you." He paused. "But what a waste it would be, though." The rogue brought the dagger away from Aris's throat completely, looked at it, contemplating, and without warning, stabbed it down hard into Aris's right hand. Aris shook uncontrollably with the pain but managed not to make much of a sound.

Zephyial leaned in towards Aris's face, contorted in pain. "I suggest you get that tended to and forget Serin, boy." Zephyial pushed himself up from Aris, pulling his knee from his chest. Adjusting his cloak, he walked away from Aris. "You've been given a second chance. Use it wisely."

Aris sat up and focused his mind on his father's dagger, magically pulling it out. The pain at its removal from his gashed hand nearly made him faint. His dagger fell to the dirt as he reached into his med pack, pulling out a pinkish powder. He smacked it into the wound on his hand, and the blood slowed significantly. Grabbing his dagger, he holstered it with his uninjured hand.

Aris stood slowly, staggering slightly as he yelled towards the rogue, "I am Aris Tin of House Andreas, son of Victus Andreas." His voice choked a bit at the utterance of his father's name before continuing, "I have not yielded!" He pulled his gladius from its scabbard. He stood up straight, his legs positioned one in front of the other, sword pointed directly at the rogue.

Zephyial could hear in the boy’s voice determination, fear, and anger. He traveled briefly back into his own past, remembering those harrowing early years on the streets. He understood the young man's feelings—never wishing to give up, fighting for something important, like his own sister all those years ago. This young man reminded him a little, and only a little, of himself, he thought.

The rogue sighed and spun back around to face the young man. "Well met, Aris Tin, spoiled son of a noble. You have lost, and best you learn now when you're defeated. Stand down." Aris kept himself in check at the slight, responding, "Would you?"

Zephyial grinned. "You were made for these streets, boy." He laughed and swiftly spun away from Aris, his hand reaching for a throwing dart.

Aris knew that he was not really turning from him but rotating himself to get a full swing or throw from a projectile. He hunched low, waiting, ready. Zephyial's arm arched as he spun his arm outward and directly toward Aris. Releasing not one, but three darts from his hand, each was released in different parts of his curved throw. They flew fast, speeding towards Aris. Aris rolled to his right, his right hand collapsing underneath the pain of his injured hand. He sprung back up, knowing the rogue was also sprinting towards him. Two more darts slammed into his enchanted leather chest piece, dropping helplessly to the ground.

The rogue smirked, noting the unique armor Aris wore. He pulled out his short sword and held another dart in his offhand. As Aris moved closer to him, the rogue smiled broadly, "You think your skill with a blade outmatches mine?"

Aris said nothing as he rushed forward, his eyes watching for the dart throw. He got himself into a range that would make the small dart ineffective at being thrown. Aris went to strike with his gladius from the side, his eyes watching the rogue's offhand flick the dart towards the ground. *No!* he thought as he tried to lift his tired leg up before the dart hit. He was too late, and the dart thumped into his foot, immobilizing him further. Aris pulled back his gladius defensively, just in time as the rogue's sword struck towards his chest.

Aris limped, deflecting again and again. The attacks continued, and Aris lost control of his sword arm as it was pushed aside. A boot firmly planted into the chest of Aris had him again on his back. His foot was throbbing in pain from the dart, but it was not just the physical pain; he was exhausted. He had lost everything. Now he was to lose his life. But he resolved within himself to die on his feet.

The rogue looked in disbelief as the boy rolled over to his hands and knees. Aris let out grunts of pain as he pushed himself up to his feet. His gladius still in hand, he lifted it towards the rogue. "Family, Duty, Serin!"

The rogue felt pity for the young man. "You foolish pretend knight. You have lost! Stand down, or I will kill you." Zephyial was not particularly merciful, but this interaction had thoroughly amused him, and as he watched this young noble, a part of him respected him.

Aris swayed, took the deepest breath he could, and forced himself through the pain to charge toward the rogue. The rogue casually stepped to meet the attack but put his short sword away.

As Aris got closer, he lifted his sword high, using all that was left of his strength, and tried to cut down through the man. But as his hand came from above his head, Aris could no longer see. The rogue had thrown dirt, Aris thought, but whatever it was, his eyes were clouded over. Unable to see, he panicked, pulling back from his attack and holding his sword close in front of himself. Seconds later, unable to tell where the rogue had gone, he felt fists pummel his stomach and then his face. Aris crumpled, dazed, unable to see, bleeding, his whole body accepting death over the pain.

Zephyial stood over him. Seeing that the boy was definitely done, he began to search through the boy's satchel. He found House Andreas's death mask and took it. Patting Aris on the shoulder, he said, "A fine trophy for myself, wouldn't you agree?"

Aris's eyes were still cloudy, but through the swelling, he saw that the man held his father's mask, now his mask. "No!" he groaned, blood spilling over his lips. In that moment, Aris felt a love for his father that he could never express in words. He forced his mind to focus and recalled his dagger to his injured hand. He yelled in pain as he coughed blood, punching the dagger into the air toward the kneeling man's face.

Zephyial caught sight of the dagger coming in the corner of his eye; he dipped his head back and turned to the side, but the dagger nicked his cheek superficially. The rogue grabbed Aris's wrist, twisting it and forcing Aris to drop the dagger. Grabbing hold of the young man's arms, he held him pinned. "Now you shouldn't have done that, boy!"

Aris whispered, "Kill me."

The rogue was tempted to end the boy's suffering. He considered his thoughts, weighing whether to kill him or to let him live. "I expect to see you again someday, Aris Tin. I will take good care of your family heirloom."

Aris's eyelids closed as he danced in and out of consciousness.

www.ingramcontent.com/pod-product-compliance
Lightning Source LLC
LaVergne TN
LVHW010637110826
845149LV00014B/2859

* 9 7 8 1 9 6 6 6 2 5 8 3 4 *